The Pit and the Passion: Murder at the Ghost Hotel

by

M. S. Spencer

The Pit and the Passion: Murder at the Ghost Hotel

COPYRIGHT © 2018 by Meredith Ellsworth

Cover Art by *RJ Morris*

The Wild Rose Press, Inc.
PO Box 708
Adams Basin, NY 14410-0708
Visit us at www.thewildrosepress.com

Publishing History
First Crimson Rose Edition, 2018
Print ISBN 978-1-5092-1841-7
Digital ISBN 978-1-5092-1842-4

Published in the United States of America

Dedication

To my friend, consultant, and dentist,
Michael O'Neil,
who guided me through the mysteries of teeth,
roots, and gums while I wrote this book.

Cast of Characters

Charity Snow, reporter, *Longboat Key Planet*
Rancor Bass, author
Rancor's family:
>Robert Bass Jr., great-grandfather
>—Robert Bass III, grandfather
>—Gertrude Bass (known as Trudy), grandmother
>——Rupert Bass, father
>——Gertrude Bass Culver, aunt (Rupert's sister)
>——Clara Bass, mother
>———Rebecca, Rothschild, Rory, Rupert Jr., and Rose, siblings

George Fletcher, publisher, *Longboat Key Planet*
Arlo Mickenbacker, owner, *Planet* newspapers
Jane, Charity's friend
Darryl, Jane's boyfriend
HHR Press:
>Edgar Finney, founder HHR Press
>Michael Finney, publisher (Edgar's grandson)
>Isabella Voleuse, editor-in-chief
>Atalanta l'Amour, author
>Bernard Guttersnipe, author
>Holdridge K. Wheelock, author
>Jemimah Heartsleeve, author

Tommy T, ghost
Police and investigators:
>Nick Kelly, chief, Longboat Key police
>Frank Ingersoll, sergeant, Longboat Key police
>Vernon Edwards, Sarasota County medical examiner
>Dr. Cornell Standish, forensic anthropologist
>Dr. Boynton Nash, forensic dentist

The police officer—a husky man

of about forty with the hard, brown skin of a fisherman—greeted her. "Oh, hi, Charity. Construction crew reported skeletal remains."

"Really? In the Chart House?"

"Nope." He gestured at a pile of broken asphalt. "Parking lot. Backhoe started breaking up the pavement in the southeast section, and a sinkhole opened up. The foreman found bones at the bottom. Called a halt and us."

"Mind if I tag along?"

"Nah."

Two medics were working on something in a deep pit. One of them looked up. "Hey, Pete, I think we're gonna need a specialist." His face was tinged an unattractive green.

"You okay, Carl? What kind of specialist?"

"Forensics." He turned away. They heard gagging.

The other EMT added, "And maybe one of those physical anthropologists. Or a dentist." He helped Carl up and they climbed out of the pit.

"How come?"

He laughed. "'Cause from the looks of this joker, he's been around a looonnnng time."

Charity ached to get a look at the thing but knew Pete wouldn't let her until they'd secured the scene.

Rancor apparently felt no such compunction. He marched past the policemen and peered into the hole. Turning to Charity, he yelled, "I think we've found our ghost."

Bill Jefferson, forensic biologist, Sarasota County
    crime lab
Beatrice da Lima e Silva Abernethy, haunted house
    resident
Lindsay and Sylvester Taylor, naughty boys
Deirdre Penney, Cà d'Zan docent

Chapter One
Ghost Stories

"It's a shame they're going to tear it down." The old man stared out the window. His companion followed his gaze. The New Pass Bridge was raised, and she could just make out the mast of a sailboat as it passed under. A line of traffic had backed up past the entrance to the Longboat Key Club. Drivers craned their necks out of their car windows, waiting for the gates to go up.

"What did you say, George? They want to tear the bridge down?" The young woman's gray eyes widened. "Who? The town? No, wait, it's owned by the state of Florida I think, but…" She paused when she realized that George had been paying more attention to his wine than to her. "Hello? Why are they going to knock the bridge down?"

He swiveled to face her. "What? What are you talking about? Raze the bridge? Why would they do that? I mean, sure, it's acquired a certain patina of age, but it fits the ambience. It's the only bridge I don't mind slowing down on. Did I tell you I saw an eagle sitting on the tender house roof once? He had a fish…a big fish…" George lapsed into reverie, a reminiscent smile on his lips.

She pinched his arm. "So what are they going to tear down?"

"The Chart House. Remember when they passed the referendum allowing Longboat Key Club to build five hundred more hotel rooms and a conference center?" He tapped the table. "This building is on Club property. Those rooms have to go somewhere, Charity."

She gazed at the people crowded into the dining room and spilling out onto the patio. "So do the patrons."

"Not a problem." He pointed. The glass-paneled room allowed an unobstructed view of the inlet separating St. Armand's Key from Longboat. Pencil-thin coconut palms nodded over the white sand beach and turquoise waters. As kayaks and bow riders glided under the bridge, men in T-shirts and ball caps stood on the breakwater, casting their fishing lines into the choppy sea. "It's only a hop, skip, and a jump to St. Armands Circle from here. Plenty of places to eat there."

"Still, it's a shame. I love this restaurant, even if it has gone a bit downhill in the last few years. It feels like it's been here forever."

"Downhill? You want downhill, Charity? You should have seen the Ghost Hotel." George closed his eyes. "That place was amazing."

"Thanks, Sarah." Charity accepted the sizzling plate from the waitress and waited for her to refill her glass. "Ghost Hotel? What are you talking about?"

"You never heard of the Ghost Hotel? You are *so* young."

"Come on, George, I'm twenty-eight. I've been on my own for five years now."

"Indeed you have. And you've grown into a stellar reporter."

"Thanks to you. If you hadn't taken me on when Dad and Mother died…"

"It's been worth a lot to me to have you on the *Planet* staff. You filled your father's shoes admirably." He chucked her under the chin. "Now, shut up and eat your steak."

Charity cut a small piece but left it on the plate. She had thought she was hungry when they drove down from the newspaper offices, but now…*Why did I have to remember that this is the anniversary of the crash?* She could still hear the voice of Officer Brown, speaking clearly and gently into the phone. "Miss Snow? I regret to inform you that your parents were killed in a boating accident last night. If you can come down to the station, we would like you to confirm their identities."

Not that there had been much to identify. They were riding in a Baja 23 fast boat when her father lost control and hit the concrete pier of the New Pass Bridge. The impact threw them onto the jagged riprap that lined the bank, where they were torn to pieces. The boat itself shot under the bridge, finally grinding to a halt on the beach at Quick Point. *Dad loved speed. If only Mother hadn't given him that preposterous boat for his birthday.*

George laid a brown-spotted hand over hers. "You're thinking about that night, aren't you?"

She pushed an errant auburn tendril back off her forehead and blinked twice to dispel the tears. "I'll be okay. Tell me…tell me about the Ghost Hotel."

He put his napkin down. "Ah, one of the last and most remarkable projects John Ringling undertook. You know he and his brother were the main promoters of the Sun Coast. At one point, they owned more than twenty-five percent of this part of Florida, including two thousand acres on Longboat Key."

"Didn't he design St. Armands Circle?"

"Uh huh—he even donated the statues." George sipped his wine. "It was supposed to be called Harding Circle because Ringling expected the then president to use Bird Key as his winter residence."

"And when that fell through?"

"It added to the downturn in Ringling's fortunes. His dream of Sarasota as a playground for the wealthy with palm-lined boulevards and pink sidewalks had to wait 'til the 1950s, long after his death."

"Still, the keys do look pretty much as he envisioned them." She gestured at the row of white-washed beach mansions swathed in bougainvillea and oleander that lined the far shore.

George nodded unwillingly, loath to give an inch. "Maybe so, but if he hadn't built the causeway connecting the mainland to the islands, they never would have been developed."

Charity leaned forward, her delicate features animated. "Maybe that dream didn't pan out, but he *did* build Cà d'Zan and the art gallery, and the circus museum and—"

He held up a restraining hand. "True, but the Ritz-Carlton was going to be his pièce de résistance—the grandest, most luxurious hotel on the Gulf Coast. He broke ground for it in 1926."

"Was? As far as I know, the Ritz-Carlton over on Bayfront is still there."

"Not that one. Ringling's hotel sat right here, right on this spot."

Charity put down her fork and pointed to the floor. "Here?"

George nodded. "In fact, it remained standing until 1964, when Arvida finally bulldozed it. They built the Longboat Key Club and the Chart House a few years later."

Charity's mouth dropped open. "I've never heard of it."

"There's nothing left of it now—although an archaeologist might be able to uncover its foundations. They had to stop work only a few months after they started."

"How come?"

"Money woes. First the bottom fell out of the Florida land boom, and then the Depression hit. After his wife Mable died in 1929, Ringling could never secure the funds to restart construction." He poured more wine into her glass. "Still, he refused to acknowledge that he might never finish it. Even after his death, his heir, John Ringling North, insisted the hotel would open."

Intrigued, Charity forgot entirely about eating. The steak lay forlornly on her plate next to the barely touched salad. "So how far along was it when Ringling suspended work?"

"The outer walls were complete but none of the interior. Staircases but no railings. From a distance, it looked like a magnificent castle, but once you got close you could see it was only a shell." George signaled for the check. He glanced at what was left of Charity's meal. "And a box for the lady, please." He rose. "We'd better get back to the paper."

They drove the five miles up Gulf of Mexico Drive

to the building that housed the *Longboat Key Planet*. Mark, the distributor, was filling the boxes in front of the building with the Wednesday edition. Charity grabbed one and riffled through it. "So you put Fred's photo of the sunset in? That's the second time this month. He'll be insufferable."

"Couldn't be helped. There weren't enough other entries this early in January." George glanced at the photo, a burst of orange and red cumulus clouds over the midnight blue Gulf. "It *is* a good one."

Charity turned a page. "I see the welcome-back parties filled the entire second section this week." She looked over her shoulder.

On the road behind them, cars crept along bumper to bumper, swerving like over-cautious slugs around the idling tractor trailers racked with the town cars and SUVs of returning snowbirds. Elderly drivers clutched their steering wheels with hands that trembled in fear whenever the speedometer registered more than twenty miles per hour. Which—happily for their hearts—occurred rarely, what with the minivans teeming with large Ohio families slowing down every few feet to crane their necks at the sabal palms and herds of grazing ibis. She sighed. The season on Longboat Key had become one long nightmare of traffic and crowds. She prayed that soon it would reach a tipping point, and all those armies of lily-white Teutons from Toronto and Chicago would decide to go elsewhere and she could have her beautiful barrier island back. "Did you cut my story?"

"No—it's there on page two."

She turned the page. "What's with the headline?"

He chuckled. "You mean, 'Vet to Bird: Stay Out of

the Gene Pool'? I couldn't help it. That pathetic osprey needed a tracheotomy to pry the sand shark out of his throat."

"Poor little thing. He was so proud of his catch."

They walked up the outside stairs to the second floor. Except for George's office, the rest was an open floor littered with desks and filing cabinets. A couple of young interns waved at them, then went back to their computer screens. At a long wooden table under the windows, an unfamiliar figure bent over a tray of back issues, reading intently. Charity nudged George. "Who's that?"

"Him?" George gave her a sidelong glance and said casually, "Fellow by the name of Rancor Bass."

"Rancor Bass? The famous writer?" Charity looked with renewed interest at the man who was one of her favorite authors. His thick, glossy, espresso-colored hair was pulled straight back in a ponytail that tumbled down over a broad back. He wore jeans and a blue suede jacket with patches on the elbows.

"Yeah. He's collecting ghost stories of the Gulf Coast for a book. We've been tasked with assisting him." He waved a hand. "Go say hello."

Suddenly shy, Charity edged nearer the man. She had come within a foot of him when he leapt up and spun around. "What are you, some kind of stalker?" He glared around Charity at George. "Didn't I ask to be left alone? I'm on a deadline here."

The publisher scratched his grizzled head. "Then I guess you don't want to meet the person I've assigned to help you with your research."

At this, Bass lowered his eyes to Charity's face, and his reading glasses fell off. He bent down to pick them up but dropped them twice before he got a good grip. Mixed emotions greeted this display. Charity, awestruck by luminous brown eyes and golden tan skin, couldn't help but be amused at his awkwardness. He must have heard her choke of laughter, for he snarled, "Sure, make fun of the disabled. Real friendly. Who the fuck are you?"

George interrupted. "Rancor Bass, I'd like you to meet Charity Snow. She's my best reporter."

He looked her up and down. She held her gaze steady, mainly so she could delve deep, deep into those chocolate eyes. Together with his sharp, angular nose and intense, almost predatory, expression, he reminded her of a peregrine falcon on the hunt. She caught herself just before she pitched into him. Bass gave a contemptuous snort. "Charity. Execrable name. Wouldn't use it for any of my heroines." And with that he flopped down at the table again.

She stared at his rigid shoulders for a second before stammering, "Enchanted to meet you too, *Mister* Bass." She swung on an unruffled George and whispered fiercely, "No way in hell. No way in hell."

The old man beckoned her into his office. He closed the door and said, "So he's a jerk. But he's here as a guest of the chairman, and we have to play nice."

"He's a friend of Arlo Mickenbacker's? I don't believe it. Arlo is way too decent a guy to cater to a creep like Bass." It galled her to insult the man whose novels kept her up most nights fantasizing about romance and unsolved mysteries, but it had to be done. "I'm not working with him."

"My dear Charity, Arlo Mickenbacker did not become the billionaire entrepreneur he is today by treating celebrities as they actually deserve. Bass just signed a contract for three books with Arlo's new acquisition, Kumquat House. If you want to be in the acknowledgements, you will help him." The specter of other, more financially objectionable, consequences should she resist hovered in the air.

Recognizing defeat, Charity grudgingly sat down. "What's the deal?"

"I told you—he's compiling Florida ghost stories. Book One covers the Gulf Coast from Tampa south to Fort Myers."

"That doesn't sound like his shtick."

"No, it's a new genre for him, and he'll need some guidance on finding anecdotes and interviewing people. That's where a journalist can be of assistance."

She looked through the glass wall at the newly minted bane of her life. "But will he *let* me guide him?"

George raised an eyebrow. "Oh, I think so. He finds you very attractive."

"Me?" Charity cast an eye over her trim figure dressed in a dove-gray linen sheath that matched her eyes and set off her slim legs. She'd always felt that, at five feet two, she was way too short to be beautiful. Her last boyfriend, a lanky basketball player, had to squat to kiss her. When his knees gave out, he dumped her and married the women's volleyball coach. Only her hair gave men pause. A deep ocher—the color of Georgia clay or maple leaves in autumn—it fell in a thick braid down to her waist. "He yelled at me."

"Ah, yes." The old man's eyes twinkled. "You be careful with him."

Charity shrugged. "So what's next?"

"The three of us will meet here tomorrow at ten.

Rancor wants to interview me first."

"You? Why?"

"Because, dear one, I happen to be familiar with at least ninety-five percent of the alleged paranormal sightings on the islands, as was my father before me."

"That makes sense." George's father had founded the *Planet* and was the sole reporter for its first thirty years. He had covered every event on Longboat Key and Anna Maria Island for the past half a century. "All right, at least you can run interference."

"Will do. Now shoo." He pushed her out the door. Charity checked her watch. Three o'clock. If she hurried, she could get her shopping done before the five o'clock rush of beachgoers. She drove down to Publix.

Rounding a corner a little too quickly, she rammed another shopping cart. "I am so sorry! I…Oh, it's you, Jane. Why aren't you at the shop?"

The woman she addressed—about sixty, slightly stooped, with a curly mop of white hair and a wry smile—pushed her cart to one side of the aisle. "Closed early. It's still pretty quiet." She pretended to scan the shelf of cereal boxes. "Um, Darryl is coming over tonight. I…um…thought I'd cook him dinner." Her cheeks turned a light pink.

Charity pretended not to notice her discomfort. "That's nice. So you two are back together?"

Jane had released the first few notes of a tortured wail when she noticed an older couple staring at her and lowered her voice. "I wish I knew. He's driving me nuts. We have a fabulous time, then he doesn't call for a month. I think he just waits 'til he's so horny he can't stand it."

"Well, he's sixty-eight after all. The man needs his

rest."

She cracked a smile. "He sure does after one of our dates." The couple picked up speed and trotted past the women, faces averted. "So, what's going on with you? Have you heard from that fellow you met at the online dating site?"

"All the time. So far I've successfully avoided giving him my phone number."

"Oh, for heaven's sake, Charity—you shouldn't start these things if you're not going to follow through. It's not fair to the guys."

"I know." She didn't want to admit she just didn't have the energy to date right now. She'd gone out a few times in the last few years, but she still waited in vain for the little words to ring in her head—*he's the one.* "Oh, by the way, I have a new assignment."

"Oh yeah?"

"I'll be working with Rancor Bass on a book."

"*What?* The hunk who wrote *Shades of Yellow* and *Murder Cuts Both Ways*?"

"The very one. Only he's not a hunk. Well, he *is* a hunk. But he's a bastard. Very rude and arrogant. This is not going to be fun."

Jane plucked a grape from the bag in her cart. "I'll be glad to take him off your hands, just give me the word. So…what's the book?"

"Ghost stories of the Gulf Coast. He's doing a series."

"*Hmm.* Different. Well, you should be talking to George."

"We start with him tomorrow."

"Have fun."

****

The renowned author showed up an hour late for their meeting the next day. From the rumpled condition of his clothes, Charity guessed he'd slept in them. *Or spent the night in a bar.* The white button-down shirt sported a red splotch—*pizza?*—and she noticed the cuffs of his suede jacket were frayed and grimy. He wore sneakers without socks.

"There you are, Bass. We've been waiting for you."

The man offered no excuse but poured himself a cup of coffee from the office urn. He sat down at the table, pulled out a tablet, and held a stylus poised above it. The publisher nodded at Charity. "Okay, hon. Let's get started."

For the next two hours, George told story after story of ghostly activities in the Tampa Bay area. "And last, but not least, tourists have claimed to see a woman in a long, red dress wandering through the Pullman car the Ringlings used on their trips between Sarasota and New York."

"A Pullman car! Is it still at the railroad station?"

"No, it's on exhibit at the Ringling Museum."

Bass rolled his eyes. "So, some family from Yonkers with sticky-fingered rug rats and sweaty necks claimed to see a ghost in a museum *exhibit?*"

George gave him an odd look. "As far as I know, ghosts are not restricted to areas marked 'Apparition Materialization Zone.' "

Bass opened his mouth, but Charity jumped in. "You didn't mention the Ghost Hotel. There must have been all sorts of incidents there."

George shook his head. "Strangely enough, no, although over the years eight people died falling either from the unfinished main staircase or the crumbling balconies. There have been reports of phantom shapes or sighs coming from under the New Pass Bridge and at several spots on Quick Point, but nary a peep from the hotel while it stood." He avoided Charity's gaze. She knew he feared his words would remind her of her parents' accident.

"Not true." Rancor's air of self-importance struck an unpleasant chord.

The other two gaped at him. "What did you say?"

"I said, you're wrong. There *has* been a sighting there."

"In the Ghost Hotel?"

"N…no. Not exactly." He seemed reluctant to admit it. "In the Chart House. It's built on the site of Ringling's Ritz-Carlton, isn't it?"

George put down his cup. "I can't believe it. I thought between me and my father we'd heard of every event here on the key."

Charity leaned forward. "What else do you know about it?"

Rancor looked past her to George. "Got the skinny from the bartender. It's a little boy, about seven years old. Kid shows up in the men's room fairly regularly. Plays with a toy or just sits there."

"But who is he?"

Bass heaved a sigh, as though her questions were too, too exhausting. "Should make you wait for the book."

"Oh, really?"

After a tense pause, he grunted, "Waiters call him Tommy T. Consensus is that he was the son of a carpenter working at the hotel. Fell down an elevator shaft."

"When?"

"How do I know? Isn't that your job? To research and authenticate these stories? I just happened to hear about it at happy hour."

Charity couldn't help herself. "And what exactly is *your* job then?"

"To put the crap you draft into proper English. I'm assuming you're incapable of decent prose, being a *reporter* and all."

She rose an inch, but George put a hand on her knee. "Easy now." He gave Bass a warning look. "Charity is here to help you, yes. However, you are perfectly free to contribute to the research, provided you have at least two sources for every item. The way a professional journalist would."

"Yeah, yeah. So, what's next?"

Charity reflected that she had never disliked a person quite so thoroughly—not even that first boss who loved to put her down in front of the staff—but she understood that George's reference to professionalism extended not just to Bass but to her. "I want to interview the Chart House staff."

"I'll go with you."

She kept her eyes on George. "That won't be necessary, Mr. Bass."

"Well, I want to." He rose and dusted something minuscule from his faded jeans. "I need a drink. And besides, I can worm more information out of the waitresses than you can."

Hateful. Absolutely, positively hateful.

Before she could come up with a crushing retort, George broke in. "Yes, take him along, Charity. We'd better get the story quickly—I don't know when they're planning to start demolition."

Charity retrieved her cell phone and purse and led the way to her car. Bass regarded it with dismay. "Are you nuts? I can't fit in a Mini Cooper."

She looked him up and down. "What are you, six one?"

"And a half."

Such a child. "You'll fit." She got in and started the engine. After a minute, his feet appeared, then his torso, and finally his head. He threw his jacket in the back and settled on the seat, his knees just grazing his nose.

"At least open the window so an extraneous appendage or two can stretch out."

"All right."

As they neared the entrance to the Longboat Key Club, a siren started up behind them. Charity pulled over to let two police cars and an ambulance go by. They turned into the club drive. She followed them.

"What are you doing?"

"I want to see where they're going."

"What are you—an ambulance chaser?"

"No…a *professional* journalist."

The ambulance made a left and headed toward the building that housed the restaurant, but instead of pulling up to the entrance, it stopped in a corner of the parking lot. Charity drove past and parked in another section. By the time Rancor had unfolded himself from the seat, she had reached the first squad car. "Hey, Pete. What's up?"

The police officer—a husky man of about forty with the hard, brown skin of a fisherman—greeted her.

"Oh, hi, Charity. Construction crew reported skeletal remains."

"Really? In the Chart House?"

"Nope." He gestured at a pile of broken asphalt. "Parking lot. Backhoe started breaking up the pavement in the southeast section and a sinkhole opened up. The foreman found bones at the bottom. Called a halt and us."

"Mind if I tag along?"

"Nah."

Two medics were working on something in a deep pit. One of them looked up. "Hey, Pete, I think we're gonna need a specialist." His face was tinged an unattractive green.

"You okay, Carl? What kind of specialist?"

"Forensics." He turned away. They heard gagging.

The other EMT added, "And maybe one of those physical anthropologists. Or a dentist." He helped Carl up and they climbed out of the pit.

"How come?"

He laughed. "'Cause from the looks of this joker, he's been around a looonnnng time."

Charity ached to get a look at the thing but knew Pete wouldn't let her until they'd secured the scene. Rancor apparently felt no such compunction. He marched past the policeman and peered into the hole. Turning to Charity, he yelled, "I think we've found our ghost."

Chapter Two
The Beach Bum

"Whoa, sir, I don't know who you think you are, but this is potentially a crime scene, and I'll thank you to back off."

Charity silently applauded Pete's words, at the same time admiring Rancor's ability to take over a set. *He's obviously used to being treated like a VIP. Prick.* She checked out the way his jeans clung to his butt and how his shoulders strained at the oxford cloth of his shirt. *Okay, sure, an extremely handsome prick, but a prick nonetheless.*

Rather than moving, Rancor beckoned Charity. "Come and see this."

Charity glanced at Pete, who rolled his eyes and said, "Just keep the asshole from contaminating the evidence."

She stepped toward the pit and, whipping out her phone, took a photograph before she even looked down. When she saw what the backhoe had uncovered, she gulped, desperately trying to hold back the vomit. "What…what is it, Matt?"

The EMT grinned. "Skeleton, ma'am."

She looked helplessly at Rancor, who growled, "We know that, buddy. What the lady wants to know is, what kind of skeleton. I mean, it's pretty grisly. What are those—maggot holes?"

The medic followed his pointing finger. "Could be. Nothing left to eat though. No flesh left." He called to Pete. "Can you get the medical examiner's office on the horn? We need the crime scene techs to take a look before we move it."

The policeman pulled out his radio, and Rancor helped Charity back to her car. She sat, panting, while he patted her hand awkwardly. "I'm...er...sorry, Snow. I figured you for a hard-boiled hack. Didn't think you'd react this way. Uh...you all right?"

When she'd recovered enough to avail herself of the anger, she hissed, "I don't usually do the crime beat, okay?"

He had the insensitivity to laugh. "I'm guessing the most serious infraction here is skinny-dipping after dark anyway. So what do you usually cover? Spelling bees? Middle-school field trips? Casino nights?"

Despite her irritation, she almost giggled. "More often pickleball matches and bridge tournaments. Longboaters aren't into betting—they can't take it with them, but they want to hang onto it while they're still around. And we don't hold spelling bees since it wouldn't be much of a contest."

"Why not?"

"Because we have a grand total of five residents under the age of twelve on the island."

"So it's true what they say—Sarasota is God's waiting room." He slumped on the seat. "No games of chance either. Too bad."

Curious, she asked, "Why too bad?" She took note of his nimble, manicured fingers and had a sudden intuition. "Are you a gambler, Mr. Bass?"

"Me?" He blinked twice. She could have sworn a

nictitating membrane flicked across the cornea. "You could say so. I can play any game—baccarat, backgammon, even Texas hold 'em. And win." He looked pensive for a minute. "I wonder…"

Charity lifted her chin. "I will not have you preying on my people, Mr. Bass."

He fastened his seat belt. She took the hint and started the car, but instead of returning to the office, she pulled in at the police station. Rancor trailed after her.

"Frank, what can you tell me about the skeleton they just found under the Chart House parking lot?"

The desk sergeant dropped his pen. "The *what*?"

"Hasn't Pete called it in?"

"Uh uh."

Rancor whispered loudly, "He's probably still trying to find the number."

Just then the phone buzzed, and Frank answered it. "Ingersoll here. Yeah, Pete. Yeah. I'll get right on it." He hung up and turned to Charity. "They want a forensics unit. Apparently the wrecking crew uncovered a skeleton under the restaurant."

Rancor interrupted impatiently. "We just told you that."

Frank did not take kindly to the stranger's tone. "Sir, I'm going to have to ask you to leave."

Charity appealed to the sergeant. "We'll go, but could you keep me posted on the investigation? I want to get an article in this week's edition."

"All right, all right. Check back with me in a couple of hours. And do me a favor." He cast a baleful look at Rancor. "Don't bring him with you."

"I promise you, I won't."

"Hey!"

She marched out.

"Hey!"

She swung around angrily and bumped into his chest. "Look, Mr. Bass. I'll help you when I can, but I have to cover this story. And your attitude isn't helping me in my job."

He slid onto the seat next to her. As his knees bent, they broke through the worn material of his jeans. Still angry, she snapped, "Is this the new fashion statement for famous writers? If so, it fails to impress."

"No." He sat quietly until they reached the newspaper offices. George's beat-up old Volvo sat alone in the parking lot.

"Where's your car?"

"I…uh…left it at my place."

She had by now calmed down and felt rather badly about her outburst. "Do you want me to drop you anywhere?"

He kept his eyes on the ground. "No, it's not far."

I refuse to feel guilty. "Tell you what—why don't I ring you when I have a break in the case?"

"I…er…don't have a phone." He pulled a shabby wallet out of his back pocket and handed her a card. "You can email me at that address." The card read,

Rancor Bass Author
RancorBassAuthor@RancorBass.com

There was no other information on it. "By the way"—his tone was a touch too easy—"where's the closest Starbucks?"

"Off the island. Why?"

"I…uh…let my Internet subscription lapse. While I'm traveling. Need a place that has Wi-Fi."

Her reporter's sense kicked in. *There's something*

fishy going on.

"So…any place I can try that's nearer?"

"We have it in the office. And about a mile up the road is a lunch place—they've been advertising free Wi-Fi."

"Great!" He jumped out. "Stay in touch." He loped out of the parking lot and turned right. On an impulse, she kept her eyes on him. A block farther on, he crossed Gulf of Mexico into a small beach resort and disappeared. Rubbing her temple, she climbed the building stairs and knocked on George's door.

He looked up. "Hey, I just heard about the discovery on police dispatch. Are you on it?"

"Yes—we were there when the cops came. Saw it. Talked to Frank. EMTs think a specialist should inspect the remains."

"You mean the skeleton. Matt said it's pretty old. You thinking what I'm thinking? That it might be Bass's ghost?"

"Ghost? Oh, you mean could it be the body of the little boy who died at the hotel? No idea. Frank said he'd let me know when they had anything new." She remained standing. "George, I thought the Sandlot— you know, the resort up across from Jungle Queen Way? Isn't it closed for renovation?"

"It is. Supposed to reopen in March. Why?"

"No reason." She went to her desk.

By six o'clock, she'd given up on hearing from the police. "I'm going up to Milton's for a drink. I may stop in at the police station on the way home—see if they'll give me an update."

Milton's stood at the end of Broadway in the Village, the oldest community on the island. The

21

restaurant looked south across the bay toward Sarasota, flanked on one side by Longboat Key and on the other by Jewfish Key. She walked through the dining room to the bar. "Hey, Wilma, gimme a gin and tonic please."

"Sure. Say, Charity, did you hear about the body in the sinkhole?"

"I was there." She peered at the bartender. "Who told you about it?"

The woman plopped her elbows on the bar. "You asking as a reporter?"

"Of course."

She looked around and leaned in. "Okay, but I want my name in the article. Carl came in an hour ago all in a tizzy."

"Oh right, he was at the pit. Isn't he substituting for Joe, the new paramedic?"

"Yeah. Joe broke a finger helping old Mrs. Goldberg catch her cat. Anyway, Carl's only been on the job a day, and this happens. Poor slob had to down a draft before he could spit out the news. He says it's only a partial skeleton. Rest eaten by rats or insects or somethin'. Said it was all yellow and rotten, but they know it was a woman. Beautiful, tall like a model…or maybe a movie star." She wiped the bar enthusiastically. "Murdered by her jilted lover in the Ghost Hotel. Say, isn't Susan Sarandon doing a movie over on Siesta Key? Or is it Diane Keaton?" She shrugged. "Could be her."

"Um." Charity, faced with such a formidable demonstration of deductive prowess, took a sip of her drink and considered how to be tactful. "I think…um…maybe Carl was exaggerating a teensy bit. You know how he gets." The town snitch had a well-deserved reputation for hyperbole.

Wilma shrugged. "We'll find out soon enough. Prolly that little punk Kevin Corcoran planted it—it'll turn out to be a fake, mark my words."

Charity marveled at her friend's ability to leap blindly from one theory to the next without even a net.

The woman continued to brood. "Unusual to find a person at the bottom of a sinkhole—wonder if it was an old graveyard. Or maybe"—her eyes lit up—"maybe it was one of those Indian sacrifices—you know, where they slit the victim's throat and drink his blood."

"Er, Wilma, I think those were the Incas or the Aztecs. Not our Seminoles."

"Ah well, then, it must've washed ashore in a storm." She picked up a glass and rinsed it out.

Charity finished her drink. "I think I'll take a walk on the beach before I head back."

"You be careful, Charity. There may be a murderer out there. Or a masher." Wilma winked.

"Yeah, right. You know this is the safest island on the Gulf Coast." *Too bad. I could use a masher.* Three years was way too long to go without romance. *Or sex.* At the thought, she felt her lower regions pulse. The last boyfriend—the basketball player—wasn't much of a lover. *Of course, it's hard when your parts are so far apart.* She drove across the Drive, parking in the lot by the beach, then walked down the boardwalk and through the dunes to the shore.

The Milky Way spread a swath of cream overhead. One small cloud trundled across the sky. Behind it peeped a gibbous moon. The beach was wide here, sweeping south in a twelve-mile-long arc but ending only a few yards north of her at a severely eroded cliff.

Not a soul stirred on the sand, except for a couple of willets picking their way along the edge of the water. She turned and headed toward the cliff.

Someone had left a beach chair out. She sat and watched the waves, listening to the chittering of the sandpipers and the *putt-putt* of a trawler far out. She assumed the rustle behind her was a ghost crab and kept quiet, hoping to catch a glimpse of it. She loved the way they would stop, half in and half out of their holes, their eyestalks waving. *They're so sure they're invisible.*

"Charity?"

She jumped straight up, knocking the chair backward.

"What th—?" Her heart pounding, she turned. At that moment, the cloud shrouded the moon, and in the sudden darkness she could only make out a form. "Who…who's there?"

"It's me. Rancor. Rancor Bass."

She held out a hand and encountered a broad chest, lightly furred. She pulled it back quickly. "Are you…are you…"

He snickered. "Naked? As a matter of fact, yes."

She backed up. A splash told her that her brand-new sandals were likely ruined. She vaulted out of the water and landed between two bare arms.

"Easy there, Charity. I hardly know you."

"Stop it, Mr. Bass. And let me go. If I were you I'd drop that conceited tone. I wouldn't be caught dead in your arms."

His voice came low, laughter licking at its edges. "You don't feel dead to me. In fact"—she tensed at the touch of a finger on the inside of her elbow—"you feel very much alive. And quite…fresh. Call me Rancor."

"Rancor Bass, you leave me alone." She tried to walk around the shadow, but an arm snaked out and caught her. She opened her mouth to scream and found two lips smothering hers. She stood quite still, fear and…something else…*oh my God, desire?*…taking over her senses.

He let her go. "Couldn't resist. Wanted to see if those defensive walls could be breached." He sat down in the chair. The moon came out from behind the cloud and cast a pale glow on his hair. "You're a tough cookie, Charity."

She wanted to deny it, to tell him how vulnerable she could be, but knew that would be very stupid. She wanted to kiss him again but knew that would be even more stupid. So she settled for a grunt and walked away.

He didn't follow, and as she reached the dunes, she felt an unexpected twinge of disappointment. *Could this man be the one? Nah.* Still, preoccupied by this novel notion, she decided to skip the police station and go straight home. As she turned into her condominium parking lot, the obvious question finally occurred to her. *What the hell is Rancor Bass doing naked on the beach in the middle of the night?*

****

"Is Captain Kelly busy, Frank?"

"Are you kidding, Charity?" The sergeant grinned. "Yeah, he slept in, went out for a leisurely brunch, and has a tee time at two. Of *course* he's busy."

Charity adopted her best kitten-in-distress manner. "It's just that George is on my case to come up with something on the body they found. I'm under a hard

25

deadline." *Just because it's next Monday doesn't make it any less hard.*

The chief of police, a tall man with a military bearing and very shiny shoes, came out of his office. "Frank, get me the Sarasota County ME on the double. I've got a physical anthropologist from the University of Florida on the line."

"Edwards is at the morgue, sir."

"Shit. That's all the way down on Siesta Drive. Okay, see if you can set up a conference call." He noticed Charity. "I don't have to ask what you're doing here." He hesitated, then crooked a finger at her. "You might as well come in and listen. I'd rather you reported facts than rumors."

She skipped after him. Kelly sat down and pressed a button on the speaker phone. "Professor Standish? Are you there?"

A nasal voice with an Ivy League accent lisped, "What?"

The captain raised his voice. "Can you hear me? This is Captain Kelly of the Longboat Key police."

The voice grumbled, "No need to shout, Kelly. I understand from Dean Brown that you need a forensic examination of a skeleton?"

"Yes—" Charity heard a loud click, and a second voice filled the office.

"Edwards here. I'm in the middle of an autopsy, Kelly. This had better be good."

The captain grimaced. "Keep a lid on it, Edwards. It's about the skeleton EMT brought in last night. Have you had a chance to look at it?"

"God damn it, who do you think I am? Quincy? We're short-staffed here, and I have my hands full with that five-car pileup on I-75 from yesterday. I'll get to it when I get to it."

The professor apparently thought this was directed at him. "I'll thank you to keep a civil tongue in your head, young man. I've been a physical anthropologist since before you were a pint-sized tot playing Operation."

"Who's that speaking? Professor Standish? Professor Cornell Standish? Is that you?"

The captain interjected, "Yes, it is, Vernon. I've called him in on this case because it appears to be a very old corpse. Construction workers found it under the parking lot of the Chart House restaurant."

Edwards' tone altered dramatically. "It would be my honor to assist you, Professor Standish. You won't remember me, but I took your class on forensic pathology eight years ago as a first-year graduate student."

There was a slight pause. "Edwards. Vernon Edwards?"

"Yes, sir."

"As I recall, I gave you a C minus."

An uncomfortable silence followed this announcement. "You...er...taught me a great deal, sir. I did go on to graduate top of my class."

The professor harrumphed. "I have written the dean on several occasions concerning the liberal granting of high grades for what I consider mediocre work. He has yet to respond."

Charity's smile matched the police chief's. The medical examiner's over-sized ego was notorious. *This is fun.*

"Professor Standish, while I am a great admirer of

your work, I must—"

Kelly apparently decided it was time to step in. He coughed loudly. "At any rate, Professor, when will you be able to come to Sarasota and take a look at the evidence?"

"Let me see. Just a minute." His voice faded. They heard him call, "Sheila, did we cancel the Saturday seminar? We did? Good." His voice suddenly rang out, making Charity jump. "I am free tomorrow. How do you propose to transport me?"

The chief's eyebrows shot up. Charity could tell he was thinking mean thoughts about academics. "I can send a squad car. What time is convenient for you?"

"I rise at six."

"We'll be there at ten. It's a three-hour drive."

A whiffling noise came through the speaker. "Um…I have a golf game at one."

Kelly and Standish spoke in unison. "No, you don't."

Edwards sighed. "I'll cancel it."

"Great." The policeman cut across both doctors. "We'll meet at the Chart House at one-thirty tomorrow before proceeding to the morgue." He hung up quickly.

"Can I come?" Charity almost batted her eyelashes but thought better of it.

Kelly looked about to refuse, then smiled. "Sure, I can use an intermediary. Maybe they'll hesitate to come to actual blows in the presence of a pretty woman."

"Or a reporter." They grinned at each other.

Charity made her way up the road to the *Planet*.

Rancor sat at the table, swiping at the screen of his tablet. He wore the same blue suede jacket but sported a new pair of jeans. "There you are. Waddya, keep

28

banker's hours?"

Charity ignored him and went into George's office. "Guess what?" She told him about Professor Standish and the meeting.

"Good work. Say, why don't you take Bass with you? He could make it a coda to his ghost stories—'Ghost Hotel Ghost Uncovered'—something like that." His eyes shifted, and he spoke to his coffee mug. "Er…Maybe he'd be willing to write the copy."

"*What?*"

George glanced over her shoulder at the man outside. "Listen, I think Bass may be hurting for money right now—between books and all. Otherwise, why take on this job? Don't know if you've noticed, but his clothes seem more…"

"Filene's Basement than Rodeo Drive? Yeah, but he's got a new pair of jeans on."

He nodded. "He told me the other ones literally fell apart. I happen to know Fred Nickel donated the pair he's wearing to the Lord's Warehouse last week." He added, "I'm sure it's only temporary—you know the publishing world. Royalties fluctuate with the seasons, or whatever."

She studied Bass. He tapped away on the tablet, pencil between his teeth. "More likely he's one of those profligate types who spend and spend until they're broke."

"Whatever. We can utilize his talents and do him a favor at the same time. What do you say?"

Just then Rancor looked up and caught Charity staring at him. His raptor eyes glittered, and a slight, self-deprecating smile lit up his face. Charity felt a tug somewhere in her chest. *Must be that cheese omelet I had for breakfast.* "I guess so." *And just maybe I can find out what he was doing on the beach last night.* She went out and stood behind him.

He paused, finger hovering over the screen. "So why were you ogling me?"

Sigh. "We're invited to the morgue tomorrow afternoon to meet the corpse."

"Wow. You must have some influence in these parts."

She checked for a sneer but found none. "It's a small island. The captain understands that factual reporting is a must to counteract the steady stream of creative embellishment."

"A lot of bored retirees?"

"You could say that."

He cast a glance at his watch. "It's almost three. You want to take a drive down to the Chart House now? Snoop around?"

She picked up her keys. "My thoughts exactly."

Bass stooped and wiggled into the Mini Cooper. His jeans crackled. "Had to dig into my portmanteau after you wrecked my only other pair of pants."

"Speaking of"—Charity kept her voice neutral—"I can give you a ride to Beall's if you need some clothes."

She felt him stiffen beside her. "What kind of crack is that? Who the hell do you think you are, my mother?"

Reminded painfully of why she disliked him, she said nothing. They followed the curving road into the Chart House parking lot. It was empty except for a skid loader with a jackhammer attachment and a backhoe, both idle. Crime-scene tape had been strung across the entire section of the parking lot.

He pointed. "Is the restaurant open?"

"I don't know. Why don't you go see? I'll park over by the pit."

He got out, climbed the stairs, and peered through the double doors. Turning, he called to Charity. "I don't see…wait. Someone's inside." He rapped on the glass. "It's Nathan, the assistant manager."

She followed him up. "Will he let us in?"

"Let's see. Nathan! It's me, Rancor Bass."

A chubby, balding young man pushed open the door. "Hey, Mr. Bass."

"Can we come in for a minute?"

"Sure. I'm just setting up for happy hour."

Charity gestured at the yellow tape. "The police are letting you stay open?"

"Yeah. It's only that bit of parking lot that's off limits." He led the way to the bar. "Can I get you something, Mr. B.?"

"How about a beer?"

"Stella okay?"

"Sure."

Nathan raised an eyebrow at Charity.

"Me too, thanks."

The manager filled two mugs and handed them over. "What can I do for you?"

"You know they found a skeleton in the sinkhole."

"Yeah, gave us all a bit of a shiver."

"I wanted to ask you a few more questions about your ghost."

"Little Tommy T? You think maybe it's him?"

"Possibly." Rancor sipped his beer. "You told me you've seen Tommy in the men's room. How many times?"

Nathan stared off into space, his brow wrinkled. "Me? Mebbe twice. Walter—he's the manager. Been here twenty, thirty years. He claims he's seen the boy ten or more times."

"How old would you say Tommy is?"

"Hard to tell—he's always kinda blurry. Maybe six or seven."

"And what's he doing?"

"Mostly he just sits on the floor. Sometimes he's playing with a shiny object."

"Shiny? Like what?"

"Dunno. It's small—maybe a matchbox car or a coin. Can't really make it out."

Charity spoke up. "Why do you call him Tommy T?"

The man chuckled. "Not sure. Walter took to calling him that—name stuck."

"Do you think he's the ghost of the little boy who died when they were building the hotel?"

"Couldn't be anyone else." His eyes widened. "Wow. If it's his skeleton they found in the sinkhole, that would be awesome."

"Well, I wouldn't get your knickers in a twist just yet. It's early days. Thanks for the drink." Rancor walked out, leaving Charity to pay for their beers. He strode toward the roped-off area.

She ran after him. "What are you doing? We're not supposed to cross the police line."

He looked back. "And your point?" He shrugged off his jacket and scrambled down into the pit. "I just want to take a quick look." He pulled a folding garden fork out of his pocket and opened it. Raking through the gravel and sand, he started at one end and methodically sifted from one side to the other and back. Charity watched him, unable to keep from staring at the sinews rippling along his biceps. With his eyes focused on the ground, she could roam over his physique without fear of reprisal. His lithe body moved with an animal grace. The thick, brown ponytail only made him more masculine. She shut her eyes.

"Found something."

She leaned over him. His scent wafted into her nostrils—a salty mixture of ginger and seaweed. She took a deep breath. "Show me."

He held up a shiny object. "Tommy T's toy?"

She took it from him and rubbed off the tarnish, revealing a large gold ring inset with a green stone. "It's heavy."

"Yes. Looks like a college ring. I wonder how it got here."

"I wonder whose it was."

"Good question. Couldn't have been Tommy T's." He pocketed it.

"Hey, that's evidence. Captain Kelly will have my head if he learns we took something from the crime scene."

"How do you know it's a crime scene? If the remains belong to Tommy, it's an accident scene." At her expression, he said patiently, "Look, it's not like there are any fingerprints left. I want to study this more closely. We'll return it later, okay?"

Charity marveled at the man's total lack of deference to the legal niceties. *Guess he's above that sort of thing.* She helped him out of the pit, and they walked to the car. The sun was setting over the Gulf in a splash of corals and tangerines that burnished the aquamarine water.

"Where can we go to check out our find?"

"How about your place?"

He didn't answer. "Pull into Durante Park." They found a bench by the artificial lake and sat down. He took the ring out of his pocket. After a minute, he said, "It's no use. Not enough light here."

"We can try Milton's."

"Okay."

They drove up to the Village and down the street to the restaurant. The host showed them to a well-lit table on the porch. They ordered oysters and beer and sat poring over the object. "It's definitely a man's. Can you make out any inscription?"

He turned the ring. "I think so. You have a flashlight or something?"

Charity called to Wilma, who brought over a lighter. "Will this do?"

"Thanks." He rolled the spark wheel until it ignited. In the flickering flame, he read, " '*To my beloved RB from G*'…and there's the date 1931." He speared an oyster and swallowed it. "RB must be his initials."

"And G hers, yes." She took the ring from him and slipped it on her thumb. "If it belongs to the remains in the pit, the skeleton must be an adult male." She cocked her head at the bartender. "Wilma will be so disappointed. She was sure it was some long-dead beauty queen."

Rancor pondered, chin in hand. "If it's an adult, then it's not Tommy."

Charity frowned. "That would be disappointing."

"How come?"

"I dunno. I guess I was hoping we could use him in the book."

"We can still use him as a ghost story." Rancor swallowed another oyster. "You know…even if the skeleton does turn out to belong to a little boy, it doesn't mean the ring isn't significant. Tommy may not have fallen down the shaft. He could have been pushed."

Charity clapped her hands. "And the ring belonged to the killer."

Rancor nodded. "In any case, it must be related to the body somehow, and we need to find its owner."

She pulled it off. "Look here on the top. On one side of the stone is a *U* and on the other an *M*."

"If it's a class ring, the letters could refer to his school."

"University of…whatever. Maryland? Miami? There must be hundreds of schools with those letters."

"You'd best get right on it then."

She glared at him. "There's no rush. I…no, *you,* can work on it tomorrow morning."

"When do you plan to return the evidence to the pit then?"

"Me! You're the one who lifted it. You figure something out."

He didn't argue. He let her pay the bill—"It's the least you can do"—and they drove out to Gulf of Mexico Drive. "Just drop me off here. I can walk."

"Okay." She watched as he ambled up the road, then again, after looking both ways, crossed to the beach under a street light. She pulled into a spot in Whitney Plaza and waited fifteen minutes, fingers tapping the steering wheel, then drove slowly across to Broadway. She parked in the public lot and tiptoed down the boardwalk to the dunes. Leaving her sandals on a rock, she headed toward the cliff. The sky was brighter tonight, the moon almost three-quarters full. Waves splashed quietly on sand still warm from the sun. She shuffled toward the beach chair.

"Are you following me?"

She jumped a foot. "Yes."

"Why?"

"What do you mean, why?"

He gave a low chuckle. "Do you want to cop a feel or call a cop?"

She said stiffly, "I want to know what you're doing on the beach at this hour."

"Waiting for you."

The realization hit that this was exactly what she wanted him to say. Heart pounding, she held out her hand, palm up. "Are you...are you...."

"Naked? Not yet."

"Oh."

"Charity, come here." She went. He sat her down in the chair and knelt before her. His eyes glimmered in the moonlight. The rest of him was in shadow. Taking her hands in his, he spoke earnestly. "Let me tell you what I saw in the last wavering beams of scarlet sun. Hair the color of cinnamon toast. Charcoal gray eyes that remind me of a London twilight. Those little flashes of silver in them are the stars just peeking through." He touched her face lightly. "A clear, ivory complexion and a tiny nose that could belong to a pixie." His hand shimmied down her thigh. "And damn fine legs. You, Charity, are in fact the most beautiful woman I've ever seen. And I've seen a few." The retort died on her lips, mainly because he brushed her breast lightly and her mind cantered off into hitherto undiscovered pathways, both electrifying and strange. He went on. "Women tend to throw themselves at the famous author…I dunno—there must be something sexy about a man who works with a thesaurus. I've never"—he stressed the word—"*never* wanted a woman as much as I want you."

No, no, no. But it was too late—the melting had begun. She held her breath while he unbuttoned her blouse and slipped his hand inside. One finger wormed its way under the bra and flicked at her nipple. She sighed. He pulled the breast out and took it in his mouth, swirling the tip with his tongue. She couldn't help it. She grabbed the back of his head and crushed his lips against her. He pulled her hands away and stood. "Over here."

She walked unsteadily to a towel laid on the sand in the shelter of the cliff. "Lie down."

He gently removed her skirt and panties, then rolled his jeans down and off. Spreading her legs wide, he slowly planted kisses up the inside of her thighs. She held a hand to her mouth to stop the scream. "Rancor, no."

He raised his head. "No?"

"I…uh."

"Do you want me to stop?"

"No. I mean…don't…"

"Don't stop? Make up your mind, woman. I can feel you tremble. Are you afraid of me?"

"No." *I'm afraid of me.* It had been so long. She wanted him inside her. She wanted sex. *But this has to be a mistake.* It had to be. She'd known Rancor—and hated him—for a mere two days. How could she want him so desperately so quickly? *Shut up, Charity.*

His finger started working its way inside.

She lifted her hips and pushed herself onto the finger. The orgasm snapped into place, and she lost control, bucking against him.

He pulled out of her. "Wait." Something hard slapped against her thigh. He rose over her. Leaning down to kiss her, he whispered, "This may hurt a little."

If the juices sloshing around in her loins were any indication, Charity didn't think so. But then she didn't know how big he was. He entered her slowly, moving an inch at a time. After a minute, she relaxed and let him in. He began to pump, his hands under her ass. As he pumped, he talked—a steady stream of images. "I'm going to take you where you've never been, Charity. I'm going to take you on tables, on the car seat, on a bar stool in a crowded restaurant. I'm going to make you come in the ocean and in the bathtub. On the bed. Under the bed. And right here."

She could feel the tip of his penis under her belly button. He rolled his hips so it filled the passage wall to wall and began to pump harder. She rose to meet him, and they fought for control back and forth until he made one last great thrust and his body went dead still. She held on, not wanting to let go, and let the second orgasm wash over her.

After a minute, he pulled out of her and stood. She kept her mind blank, knowing she'd feel the guilt and shame soon enough. But oh, how wonderful it had felt!

"And then…and then…"

What else could he do to me?

"And then I'm going to marry you."

She fell back on the towel. "Oh, shit."

He turned away. "Well, that was a rather disheartening response. Good thing I was only joking."

Confusion wrapped long tentacles around her brain. She rubbed her forehead. "Rancor, hand me my skirt, please."

As she dressed, he pulled his jeans on and held out a hand. "Walk with me."

She took it, and they strolled in silence under the moon. Peace stole over her. Instead of shame, she felt oddly content. *As though I've found my place at last. Maybe he* is *the one…maybe.*

"Charity? I have something to confess."

Chapter Three
Family Matters

Apparently, the contentment was not destined to last long. "Oh?"

Water flowed over their feet as they walked, depositing sand and tiny shells between their toes. Rancor stated flatly, "I'm broke."

"Excuse me?" *So much for traveling the globe, TV gigs, and book signings. Oh, and raking in the dough.* "I don't understand."

He faced her. "I don't want you to think I'm one of those high rollers who can't manage his finances. It's true—I did make a lot off the last four books. Not much before that, but who does? Once my name was made, I received advances and enough royalties to buy a big house outside of Camden and only had to churn out a book a year."

"Camden, as in Maine?"

He nodded. "That's where my family's from. The Basses go way back. The first Michael Bass settled in York in 1623, and several Basses fought in the French and Indian war. They were paid in pelts. One Ferdinand Bass opened a clothing store specializing in furs in 1746, and the family has lived there ever since."

"Are you still in furs?"

"Oh no. By the turn of the century—that's the eighteenth century—several ancestors had branched out into the hospitality industry. We kept taverns along the post road in Massachusetts, Connecticut, and Rhode Island. Then in the late 1870s, Old Robert—my great-great grandfather—bought his first hotel from some guy named Biltmore. Today, we have boutique inns here in Florida, Seattle, and San Francisco." He paused, his brow furrowed. "I think there's one in Chicago too. But we're still based in Maine."

"My family originally came from Maine too—a place called Penhallow. Do you know it?"

"Oh sure—it's not far from Camden. Nice, quiet little borough. That is, until recently, when I hear they had a series of murders."

"Oh dear! My mother's sister still lives there." She thought about the little town where she'd spent her summers as a child. She'd only been up to see Aunt Maude once in ten years. She had seemed pretty normal. Charity resolved to call her soon.

"Charity? Could we get back to my confession?"

"What? Oh, yes. You're broke and forced to camp out on the beach. Which is illegal, by the way. Not that petty ordinances would deter you."

"So you guessed. That's why you showed up tonight. And here I was sure you simply wanted to manhandle me in wildly wanton ways."

In the dark, she couldn't tell whether he was teasing or not. Even so, she needed time to ponder their recent coupling and her feelings about it. The memory still left her rather shaky, but in a cozy sort of way. *It felt…well…quite therapeutic, but who knows if it was anything more than stars and sand and dirty talk?* "I did follow you. It seemed suspicious, you sneaking through a resort that's closed. Not to mention

41

wandering around in the buff."

"I've been living here for four days. I lost my car, and they've begun foreclosure proceedings on my house, so when a friend told me about this ghost story proposal I contacted Arlo Mickenbacker. We go way back. He was happy to sign me up. I...need the money desperately, Charity."

"But why? What happened?"

He halted and dropped her hand. "It seems my editor needed my royalties—and those of several other authors—more than I did. She cleaned out the company accounts and skipped off to who knows where nine months ago."

"What about the police?"

"They're investigating, but by the time we'd figured out what she'd done, she was long gone."

"You said nine months? Don't you get royalties monthly?"

"Quarterly. When two quarters went by without remuneration, I contacted some of my colleagues. We discovered no one had been receiving their checks." He kicked at a shell. "Ow!" He bent down to rub his toe.

"But...nine months! You didn't suspect anything?"

"Not really. See, us writers are an introspective lot. We're not particularly social. Most of my correspondence is via email." Charity remembered her initial impression of Rancor—*not a man with many social graces*. "I just didn't think about it until it was too late...but that wasn't the worst of it."

"What could be worse than her stealing the money you earned fair and square?"

"Stealing my future income."

"What do you mean?"

"Isabella filled one suitcase with checks. She filled another with manuscripts that five of the firm's top authors had submitted."

"Oh, dear. Can't your agent do anything?"

"Pansy? Pansy's job is—how do I describe it?— akin to the last passenger pigeon. She ferries my manuscripts to Isabella by hand, or wing as it were. Period. I only keep her on to make my Aunt Gertrude happy. She's a third cousin. Once removed."

Charity thought it best not to ask what that meant. "What about your publisher?"

"He's been incommunicado since the events in question. Or in deep despair—we're not sure which."

"Could he be in cahoots with her?"

"*Cahoots*? If I didn't know you better—or want to—I'd suspect you've steeped yourself in graphic novels. Pity." He paused. "Michael doesn't seem the type. But then again, neither does Isabella. *Hmm*."

"So…" She plucked a sand bur off her thigh. "You had no money coming in and no prospects for more. Meanwhile, you were spending cash hand over fist."

"I most certainly was not. An occasional bottle of Veuve Cliquot when I'd finished a chapter. A spin in my Bugatti. Perhaps a quick trip to Aruba in my yacht. But that's it."

Now she knew he was kidding.

They had reached a pile of driftwood that blocked the way. "I have to go home."

"Yes."

He didn't ask, and she kept her mouth tightly closed on the return stroll. *Should I invite him to stay with me? No!* She contemplated his profile, cast in sharp relief by the moonlight. A Roman nose lorded it over a rather aggressive chin. Long, dark lashes matched the smooth hair now flowing freely down his back. With his bare chest and muscled arms, he could have stood in for Geronimo, or maybe Tarzan. *Can I trust him? No! Can I trust me? Not in a million years.* "Do you...do you want to stay at my place? Temporarily, of course?"

In an instant, she was in his arms, lost in a deep kiss. When they broke apart, he mumbled, "Probably not a good idea."

"But where will you stay? You're bound to be arrested if Pete finds you here."

"Really? I used to camp on the beach in Ogunquit all the time and nobody bothered me."

"Maybe because the police thought anyone who'd make whoopee on a cold, seaweed-covered pebble beach is harmless."

He was quiet. As they neared the boardwalk, he said diffidently, "I know it took a lot to offer to take me in. I promise not to molest you—and I'll find a place tomorrow. How's that?"

Charity smothered the elation that rose unbidden in her chest and replied softly, "Okay."

He went back for his gear, and she started the car. When he got in, she said, "Perhaps you should tell George about your predicament." *He won't let on that he's already guessed.* "They have a spare bedroom. I'm sure he and Norah won't mind putting you up."

"I'll think about it."

Charity turned right on Gulfside Road and drove a couple of blocks to her building. Her apartment was on the second floor at the far end. A covered walkway ran along the front, ending in an exterior stair that led to the beach. She opened her door onto the kind of mess normally left by Mafia enforcers delivering a "message" from the Capo. Newspapers, books, and magazines lay upside-down and open on the floor by the sofa. Junk mail flyers served as coasters for half-filled coffee cups and empty water bottles. Clogs and sandals littered the entryway, and towels hung on every doorknob. A plastic bag fluttered in the breeze coming from the balcony.

"Did I miss the weather report? Looks like a tornado touched down in your living room."

She kicked the shoes out of the way, gathered the empty cups, and took them to the kitchen. As she headed toward her bedroom, she picked up the plastic bag and grabbed the towels.

"Don't forget this."

She turned around. Rancor held up a gauzy demibra by the lace ribbon, his eyes sparkling. She snatched it away, cheeks flaming, and ran into the bedroom.

When she came out—having straightened the sheets, put the pillows back on the bed, and stuffed a pile of clothes into the closet—she found a tidy living room and a smiling Rancor. He handed her a drink. "I took the liberty."

She sniffed. "My Glenlivet? The bottle I save for special occasions?"

He tried to snatch the glass back. "And this isn't a special occasion? You're entertaining a distinguished author, lusted after by droves of women all over the world not just for his prurient prose but also his body—a body that's been compared to Adonis, to Michelangelo's David, even to Arnold Schwarzenegger in his prime. Why—"

She knocked back the whiskey. "I knew I didn't like you."

He poured her another tot. "Relax. When our book hits the *New York Times* bestseller list, I'll buy you a distillery."

"I'm not sure how popular ghost stories are."

"Oh, they're box office candy. It's like reality shows—people can't get enough of them."

"Let's hope you're right." She took her glass to the kitchen. "I'll get you some sheets and a blanket. You'll have to make up the couch."

He indicated the balcony. "I'm used to sleeping al fresco. How about if I use the chaise?"

"Be my guest." Charity moved the bistro table out of the way and brought bedclothes and a lamp. "Do you need a clock?"

"Nope. I can tell the time by the stars." He held up his wrist. "Besides, I haven't had to hock my watch yet." He looked out at the water. "Beautiful, isn't it?"

She joined him at the railing. The water was calm, gurgling and whispering under a swarm of stars. "Yes, it is. I never get tired of it."

"We have a different sky in Maine—it's a whole different blue."

"Really?" Charity tried to remember those summer days on Penobscot Bay.

He nodded. "And it's smaller—cut off by the mountains. Here you can see all the way to the horizon." He put an arm around her waist. "Although somehow it's not intimidating."

She leaned into his side. "No."

After a few minutes, she went to bed, carefully

closing the door to her room. She lay awake for several hours, musing on the man in her apartment. Was his story about losing everything true? *He writes fiction after all.* She felt again his lips on hers. They at least seemed sincere. Her hand cupped a breast. *I've got to get him out of here tomorrow.*

"Charity? Are you awake?"

"No."

"Me neither." He slipped under the sheet. "It was cold on the balcony." His arms encircled her. "Ah, that's better."

"I'm going to sleep now."

"No, you're not."

She pretended to snore. He pinched her nostrils together. She opened her mouth to breathe, and he stuck his tongue between her teeth. She pulled his hand away. "You're incorrigible."

"I agree. Now, while you're busy spelling 'incorrigible' in your head, I have things to do." He pulled the nightgown over her head and fastened his lips on one nipple. She squirmed away. He caught the other nipple and rolled it around with his tongue. Before she could move, he left it and crawled down her belly. She jerked when he began to suck her tender flesh, spearing his tongue inside. Aching for more, she spread her legs wide.

He took her shoulders and rolled her on top of him. Instead of entering her, he let his penis graze her lips, rubbing the moist tissue and sending slivers of heat from her vagina to her throat. She caught it and, guiding it in, began to rock. He took hold of her breasts and rotated them as she rocked faster and faster. His hips lifted off the bed, and she felt his cock stiffen and then release. She collapsed on his chest.

After a few moments, Rancor rose and padded to the bathroom.

"Are you going to take a shower?"

"Yes, and you might want to brush the sand off your sheets. It'll be more comfortable."

Charity reflected that his suggestion came a little too late.

He spoke as though he'd read her thoughts. "Not too late if—as is likely—that was only the first episode of the evening. I suspect you, my love, are a ravenous beast. I intend to let you sate your hunger on my quivering flesh."

"Second."

"What?"

"Episode. Second episode."

"Ah. My hypothesis is confirmed."

****

The little gathering watched the patrol car pull up. The sergeant opened the rear door. A tall, lean, bewhiskered old man slid out, shaking each stalk-like leg to unkink it. Chief Kelly spoke first. "Professor Standish? I'm so glad you could come." He turned to his companions. "May I present George Fletcher, publisher of the *Longboat Key Planet*?"

George stuck out his hand, then introduced the others. "This is Charity Snow, my ace reporter, and Rancor Bass, the writer. You've met Vernon Edwards, Sarasota medical examiner."

Standish appeared not to hear. His eyes went straight to the yellow tape. "Is that where you found the skeleton?"

"Yes." Kelly led the way. Two CSI evidence

technicians were sifting through the gravel and placing markers here and there. At a word from Kelly, they climbed out of the pit.

Standish shook hands with the two men, who introduced themselves as Douglas and Ken. "Tell me what you know."

Ken spoke first. "There wasn't much here. Obviously an old site—decades old, I'd say. We removed the bone fragments. They're at the morgue."

"Fragments? Were they articulated or just a jumbled heap?"

"More of a heap—the backhoe did a number on them. Doug here thinks there could be enough for a pretty complete skeleton, though."

The other investigator added, "We also found some smaller bones mixed in—maybe of an animal. A few chunks of rotted oak. Oh, and a couple of scraps of cloth. Sent 'em to the lab."

"What kind of cloth?"

"One felt like flannel—suit material."

Ken chimed in. "The other one's probably denim."

"That's odd." Standish rubbed his chin. "Why would someone wear both a business jacket and jeans?"

Rancor drawled, "Casual Friday?"

Standish, ignoring him, spoke to Douglas. "What do you think?"

"No idea. We'll have to wait for the chemical analysis. The most puzzling items were several metal objects—thin iron cylinders."

Kelly stepped closer. "Well, this was a construction site. Could they be those rods they use to stabilize concrete when it's poured?"

"Too short." Ken waved at the pit. "We found them

buried in each corner, as though demarcating the space."

Douglas pointed down. "The pit is a few feet deeper than a portion of old pavement we found in a corner. And the walls were clearly prepared for drywall."

"Plus, it's eight feet square. We're guessing this was originally an elevator shaft."

"Only *prepared* for drywall, you say? You don't think it was completed?"

"Uh uh." Ken pointed at a darker line in the soil. Bits of blackened wood protruded from it. "See that? It was boarded over, probably soon after they dug the hole."

"Any idea why?"

Douglas shook his head.

Charity nudged Rancor. "Tommy T."

"Who?" The police chief stared at her.

"Tommy T. The ghost child. What…you mean you haven't heard the stories? He's been seen several times in the Chart House. The restaurant staff thinks he was the son of a laborer who worked at the hotel construction site. The child supposedly fell down an elevator shaft and was killed."

Rancor added, "And now he haunts the men's room."

The professor scoffed, "Poppycock."

"Nonsense." Edwards pursed his lips.

Rancor sniffed. "Your skepticism does a disservice to your reputations as scientists. In fact, there have been numerous documented instances of paranormal phenomena for millennia. Do not assume the science is settled."

This speech was met with amused condescension by the two doctors. Without bothering to respond, they turned back to the pit.

Standish asked Douglas, "So, nothing else unusual?"

"We took some scrapings of the dirt, but no, nothing else."

Charity glanced at Rancor. His face showed no emotion. *Am I doing the right thing by keeping mum?*

The two agents tidied up and returned their equipment to their cases. "We'll meet you back at the morgue."

George, trailed by Charity and Rancor, headed back to his car. Kelly stopped them. "Uh, sorry, you can't go to the morgue."

"What? Why not?"

He nodded at Standish. "Turns out he refuses to allow lay people in the operating room."

Rancor snickered. "So I suppose he'll bar the ME."

Kelly gave a half-hearted laugh. "I'm afraid we'll all have to wait for the great man to finish his work."

After grousing a minute, George shot Charity a meaningful glance. "You know what to do." He got into his Volvo.

The two police cars and forensics van left the parking lot. Rancor watched them go, frowning. "Well, that sucks."

Charity climbed into the Mini. "I'm going back to the office to write up what we have. At least we can get a preliminary article into the next edition."

Rancor joined her. "I wonder when the television people will get wind of this."

Charity pointed at a News Channel Six truck

turning into the lot. "I guess they already have. Come on. Let's get out of here."

"You don't want to share your information with the rest of the press? Where's your *esprit de corps*?"

"You never heard of a scoop? I got me one, and I aim to keep a step ahead of those bozos the whole way. George expects no less."

When they reached the office, Charity loped to her desk. Rancor stood uncertainly in the center of the room. "So what do you want me to do?"

"You have some research to do, pal. Remember the evidence?"

"Evidence? Oh." His hand clenched in his pocket.

"Go find out what *U* and *M* refer to."

He saluted. "Yes, ma'am." He kissed the top of her head. "Regroup for dinner?"

"You buying?"

"When my ship comes in. Or we solve the case."

****

"I'll have a mai tai."

"Make that two—but don't make mine very sweet. And make it a double."

Charity gave Rancor a dirty look. "I'm not made of money."

"Funny, you look as enchanting as a five-dollar bill."

"Don't you mean a three-dollar bill?"

"No." He reached across the table and took her hand. "Allow me to amend my assessment. I'd say you were a 1933 double eagle."

"Huh?"

"Last of the double-eagle gold coins from the US Mint. Creepy old FDR signed an executive order in

1933 forcing people to turn them in to the Treasury so the government could melt them down to spend on the thousands of ill-conceived federal programs that prolonged the Depression. Folks received worthless paper money in return."

"I thought FDR brought us out of the Depression?"

"Urban myth. By the beginning of his second term, America had fallen into an even worse recession, due, according to significant research, to policies that concentrated the money at the national level where it could do the least good. And those average Joes who used to own actual gold coins—coins that could have bought them clothing and shelter—ended up burning the paper notes to heat up their hobo stew."

"So, you're comparing me to a gold coin that no longer exists?"

"There are a few left. The last one sold at Sotheby's for over seven million dollars."

"Oh." To hide her embarrassment—*or pleasure?*— she picked up the menu. "I'm not getting the mullet sandwich again."

"Why?"

"Tasted like mud." The waiter brought their drinks. She pulled the paper umbrella out and sucked on the handle. "All right, did you find anything out about the ring?"

He sipped from his glass and grimaced. "Too sweet and not enough alcohol."

"Shut up and tell me."

"I can't do both."

She half rose from her chair, and he put the drink down. "The quick answer is no."

Her shoulders sagged.

"But I did narrow the choice down. Let's say for the purpose of discussion, the *U* and *M* refer to a university. In the lower forty-eight, it turns out there are nine universities of M."

"Okay, Minnesota, Michigan, Maryland—"

"Whose report is this?"

"Go on."

"*Hmmph.*" He pulled out a little spiral notebook. "Where was I? Oh yes." He read, "Universities of Minnesota, Michigan, Maryland, Mississippi, Maine, Missouri, Massachusetts, Montana, and Miami."

"Miami?"

"Miami, Florida. It's the only private school in the lot."

"Interesting."

"Not really. So…oh there you are, Donna." He winked at the generously endowed waitress, who tripped on a loose board. "We'll have the steak and grilled shrimp combination. And salad with vinaigrette on the side. You want a baked potato?"

This last was directed at Charity. She debated with herself whether to order something she didn't want or get the steak and shrimp as she had planned. *Like Mother always said, "Pick your battles."* She compromised by deflection. "Yes—with the works."

"Sour cream and chives and butter?"

"Please." She waited for the snotty remark.

"Perfect. Love all that cholesterol. Doctor says I need to hike mine a few ticks." He handed the menus back. "Do you want to choose the wine?"

She almost laughed but restrained herself. "Why, yes, how gracious of you. We'll have the Rex Goliath merlot."

He cocked an eyebrow. "The house wine?"

"Er...yes."

Donna left, dragging one foot in a blatant attempt to elicit sympathy from the dreamboat at the table. Rancor leaned over. "So, besides the school, we have a man's initials, plus that of his wife or girlfriend, and a date."

"Date?"

"1931. His graduation year."

"Of course. That does narrow it down, doesn't it?" Charity stopped, water glass halfway to her lips. "Rancor, you said your family went back a long way in Maine. Did any of them go to the University of Maine?"

He looked chagrined. "That I do not know yet. However, a more pressing question is, when was the university established? Has to be at least four years before 1931."

Charity polished off her mai tai. "Did you do *any* research this afternoon?"

He relented. "Yes, I did. The University of Maine is a land-grant college, established 1868. I have a call in to my Aunt Gertrude, repository of all family matters. She will undoubtedly generate a list of University of Maine alumni, along with their majors, their spouses, and running commentary on their faults."

For a second, she marveled at the way their minds worked together, then dismissed it as just a schoolgirl infatuation. Donna rushed up with their plates, setting Rancor's down gently and slapping Charity's before her without a second glance. Her eyes bright, she chirped, "Do you need anything else, sir?" Charity was reminded of an overwrought chickadee.

Rancor inspected the meal. "Sweetheart, I think you forgot something."

Hand on heart, she cried, "The sour cream? The ketchup? What? *What?*"

He gave her what he obviously considered his Messiah look—kindly and forgiving. "The wine?"

Charity held out an arm to catch the poor thing as she fainted. Thankfully, Donna rallied before she hit the ground and raced off to the kitchen, flying back with a bottle in one hand and a corkscrew in the other. She forgot to fill Charity's glass, so Rancor did the honors.

"Okay, how about the initials. RB—Rancor Bass."

"Ha ha."

Charity continued to muse. "Of course, Rancor has to be a pen name. It's much too outlandish to be real."

He poured more wine. "*Au contraire, ma petite.* It *is* my real name."

"Really? Rancor? Someone in the family detested you on sight? I guess that's not so surprising."

"Not exactly."

She took the bottle from him and peered into his face. His eyes were clouded. *Have I pinked an old wound?* "Tell me."

He glanced at her serious face and assumed a lighthearted air. "My father named me. You see, I was the sixth child in what was supposed to be a childless marriage."

"On purpose?"

"Oh yes. My father had renounced offspring. His father had abandoned his wife and children when Dad was two. Ran off with a lady of the night, according to family lore. Never heard from him again. My grandmother died soon after he left, and my great-grandparents took my father and his sister, my Aunt Gertrude, in. As a result, Dad swore he'd never reproduce."

"And then he met your mother."

"Clara Pendleton was the mayor's daughter. She had auburn hair"—he reached out to touch Charity's braid—"much like yours. Smart as a whip. She intended to go to New York to teach or, failing that, become a star of the stage."

"So…er…flexible."

"Indeed. And lovely. He once wrote that her breasts were like moons, her eyes like stars, and her vagina like a lotus."

"He didn't."

"He did. Where do you think I get my way with words?" He grinned.

"So, he…wait, what was his name?"

"Rupert."

"*Really?*"

"Yup. Another gift from his splenetic dad. According to Auntie, Grandpa refused to pass on the family name of Robert."

"So, Rupert fell in love with Clara. I take it she changed his mind about having progeny?"

"No, never. She just kept having them. Gave them all names beginning with *R*. Rupert Jr., then Rebecca, Rothschild—Mother thought the banking family exceedingly romantic—Rose, and Rory."

"And Rancor."

"That came later. Rory was five years my senior. My father thought himself well out of it. Then along came this squawling boy child with a shock of luxuriant hair the color of freshly turned Delta soil and a penis the size of Long Island."

The unfortunate Donna appeared at the table as he pronounced these last words and dropped the water pitcher. She knelt to mop up the spill and managed to rise just as Rancor stood up, thus finding herself nose to nose with the aforementioned organ. Charity felt sorry for her. *That blush must really hurt.*

"Will there, will there be anything else...sir?"

"Thanks. She'll take the check." He waved at Charity. "I need to pee."

The two women watched the tight jeans walk away, gulping in unison.

Charity didn't have a chance to resume her interrogation until they returned to her apartment. When she dropped her sweater on the back of the couch, Rancor picked it up and took it to the closet before heading into the kitchen.

"You hadn't finished about your birth...I mean childhood." *Moving on for now, if only for Donna's sake.*

He returned with two glasses. Handing one to her, he observed, "The last of the Glenlivet. You might want to pop into the liquor store tomorrow."

Mind-boggling. "Your childhood?"

"Yes, well, Father was not amused by the arrival of said infant. He claimed it was Clara's revenge for his negative attitude. Or was it for the fireworks he set off when Clara told him Rory would be the last?" His upper lip twisted. "According to Mother, he picked me up by the scruff of my neck, shook me, and declared me to be the spawn of her rancor. Hence the name. I am eternally grateful he didn't name me 'Spite.' "

Charity found herself at a loss for words. Rancor

interpreted her silence as an invitation to take her in his arms, spilling both their drinks. "Rancor!"

"Damn. Now you'll have to go out immediately for more whiskey. Do you want me to accompany you?"

"No." *The man is utterly oblivious.*

"All right. I'll wait for you here." He poured what was left of the whiskey into one of the glasses and knocked it off. When she made no move toward the door, he sighed. "I guess it can wait." An unproductive pause later, he sighed again. "But enough about me. What about you? Did you finish the article?"

"I have a single column drafted on the discovery, with more to follow. I sure hope we hear from Captain Kelly tonight."

He checked his watch. "It's almost eight o'clock. Don't expect anything today. Also, tomorrow is Sunday, and somehow I doubt the good professor works on the Sabbath."

She said uncharitably, "Well, it's a sure bet he doesn't go to church."

"However, I do. I noticed the Longboat Chapel has a service at ten. Care to join me?"

Her jaw dropped.

"I'll consider that a yes." He stretched. "I'm going to take a shower." His fingers grazed her breast. "Early to bed, you know."

After a suitable interval, she followed him. The rest of the night went pretty much like the night before had. Only upside down and backward.

Chapter Four
The Graduates

"Wake up, sleepyhead, we've only got twenty minutes."

"Wha'?" Charity rubbed her eyes. She sat up, only to realize she was naked.

Rancor stood at the foot of the bed, his admiring glance focused on her chest. He was fully dressed and carried a mug of coffee. "Up and at it."

Even in a crisp oxford shirt and chinos, he was a sight for hungry eyes. "Why do we only have twenty minutes?" She held out her arms.

"No way, you animal. You used me up like an old dish towel last night. I'm not sure I'll be able to stay awake through the whole service."

She had to smile. "You'd better make it through the confession at least."

He tossed her a dress that matched the silvery streaks in her eyes. "Thought this would be appropriate."

I can't believe it. My favorite dress. How did he know? "I guess it'll do. Is that my coffee?"

He held up the mug. "This? No, it's mine. Did you want some?"

"Yes. And you have time to make it while I shower." She ran into the bathroom before he could demur.

****

To reward themselves for remaining upright and attentive through a very long sermon by a very old man who wheezed more than he spoke, they went to the Island Crêperie on Bridge Street for brunch.

"I'll have a *croque-monsieur*. The lady will have a *croque-madame*." He peered at the waitress's name tag. "Or should it be the other way around? I don't want to be kinky, Amber."

Charity raised her voice. "I'll have the buckwheat breakfast special, thank you. And coffee." She glared at Rancor. "Since you refused to make me any this morning."

"We didn't have time. You were in the shower for at least an hour. We barely made it to church. Didn't you see all those biddies staring at us—shock etched into their wrinkles—as we edged into the back pew?"

Charity thought it more likely that the arrival of a ravishing man in a ponytail caused the stir among the mostly female congregation. She said mildly, "We weren't that late."

"*Hmmph*." Rancor accepted a Stella from Amber.

Charity watched him take a long swallow and gazed doubtfully at her coffee. "You know, I think I'll have one of those." When the waitress brought their meals, she ordered a beer. "So, tell me more about your family."

His eyebrows rose. "Why the sudden interest in the Basses?"

Charity scrabbled around in her brain for a reason less hazardous than admitting she wanted to know everything about the man who made her heart go pitty pat. "Journalistic curiosity?"

He hesitated, then, a suspicious light in his eye, said, "It isn't anything to write home about. Or even a best-selling autobiography. My father worked in the family business—"

"Furs or hotels?"

"You remembered." He bestowed a proud smile upon her. "We do still retain a few pelts for the distaff side, but they're only allowed to wear them to the grocery store. No, we're strictly hotels now—high-end jewels of the hospitality trade though they are. My grandfather Robert had just joined our company as a salesman when he disappeared. So my great-grandfather looked to my father. He started him in the mail room at sixteen, and Dad worked his way up to president and chairman of the board by the time he was forty-five. At which time he had me." He stopped and the woeful look came back into his eyes. "Only in his final years did he learn to dote on me. The others were settled in their own careers, and he wanted me to take over the Camden operation. Mother says he spoiled me rotten."

"She was right."

He gazed out the window. "I'll never forget the day I announced I was moving to Boston and wanted to write novels. Broke his heart."

"He forgave you when you became famous, didn't he?"

Rancor shook his head. "I fear not. Went to his grave muttering curses under his breath." He laid his napkin down. "You going to finish your beer?"

Charity handed him the bottle and took a last bite of pancake. *Better change the subject before he orders another.* "Want to take a walk down to the pier? It's a beautiful day."

"Nah. Aunt Gertrude said she'd call when she had something. We'd better go home."

"Home? You mean my home?"

"Er…yes. Mine only temporarily of course. As we agreed."

"She's going to call my house?"

"You don't mind? I—I'm also…uh, temporarily between phones."

Charity gave him a speculative look. "I've been thinking, Rancor. They're always hiring at Publix. Let's stop there, and you can apply for a job."

To her surprise, he nodded. "Is that the local grocery store? Good idea. It'll have to be part-time though. We have a case to solve."

And a book to write, my easily distractible friend.

Application submitted, Charity dropped Rancor at the *Planet* office. "There are nine U of M schools. You need to check out the classes of 1931 at all of them to see if there was an RB."

"Assuming the schools existed then."

"Yes."

As he started up the steps, he whirled around. "Wait a minute! Tell me again why I am spending precious drinking time on this?"

"How easily you forget, dear boy. You said—and I quote—it could give us a clue as to what happened to Tommy T."

"I said that? How clever of me."

"Plus, it's the only evidence there is except the scraps of cloth. And"—she couldn't help but gloat—"we're the only ones who have it."

He came back down to the car and leaned in the

window. "You and your scoops."

Charity tapped a finger on the dashboard. "I'd start with Miami University."

"Why?"

"Stands to reason. It's in Florida."

"Oh, right. How astute. My genius must be rubbing off on you like cheap lipstick. Me, I was going to start with Montana. Just to get it out of the way."

"I've learned not to waste a lot of time on unsure things."

He shot her a look. "Meaning?"

"Meaning, how much likelihood is there that a man who comes from Montana would be near an elevator shaft on Longboat Key in the 1930s?"

"An engineer?"

"Engineer?"

"Yes. Remember, the hotel was under construction."

"I think they'd quit work on it by then."

"Yes, in 1926. Nevertheless, Ringling always maintained he would complete it. He died in 1936, but his nephew continued to insist it would eventually open. They'd have employed engineers, if not construction crews."

She patted his cheek. "You *have* done some research, haven't you? Okay, start with Montana if you like. Don't come home until you have something."

"Yes, ma'am."

She left him to it and went off to spend the rest of the day at the beach.

Rancor didn't show up for dinner. Charity watched the eleven o'clock news, then went to bed.

A light scratching woke her. She went to the front

door. "Rancor?"

The only answer was a low sniffle. She opened to find her roommate leaning precariously on the railing. She took his arm and helped him over the threshold.

"You never gave me a key."

"Why would I do that?"

"So I don't have to disturb you when I'm coming home from a date."

For some reason, the quip did not make her laugh. "What took you so long?"

"Aww, you missed me. I've been working. Mostly. I took a mere three hours off for a well-deserved break at a local watering hole—"

"You found a pigeon?"

He drew back. "A pigeon? No, but there were a lot of peacocks around. Boy, do they make a racket. I—"

Charity put a gentle hand over his mouth. "A pigeon is a person you touch to pay for your drinks. Don't you know any idioms?"

"*Mmph.*"

"What?"

He pushed her hand aside. "I don't do idioms. Great writers eschew hackneyed phrases and common metaphors."

"Oh."

"However, I shall file away the term 'pigeon' for future insertion, possibly in some gangland repartee. Now, do you want to know what I discovered?"

Charity checked the mantel clock. "It's midnight. Can't it wait until morning?"

His eyes lit up. "Why, do you have a suggestion for alternate recreation?"

She started to unbutton his shirt. "Possibly…"

****

"A cheese omelet, I think, Tilda. With hash browns and sausage. No—bacon."

"Rye, whole wheat, or white?"

Rancor patted his stomach. "Whole wheat. I need to lose a few pounds."

Charity rolled her eyes. "Fat chance with a breakfast like that."

Rancor leaned across the table and kissed her. "Fortunately, I am in a position to beef up my exercise routine to offset the bacon."

Ignoring the butterfly fluttering near her heart, she snapped, "All right, out with it. What did you learn about the schools…or were you too blotto to read?"

"That came later." He pulled his notebook out. "George was kind enough to let me stay in the office after hours." He opened at a dog-eared page. "Okay, there were nine universities beginning with *M*— Montana, Missouri, Mississippi, Miami, Maryland, Michigan, Minnesota, Massachusetts, and Maine. I've checked them all except Maine."

"Why not Maine?"

"I don't need to. I'm counting on Aunt Gertrude to come through. Her research abilities far outshine Google."

"Oh, that reminds me. She called while you were out."

"Aunt Gertrude? Great. What did she say?"

"I don't know. I was down on the beach and missed it. She left a message that she would try again this morning. And something about making it collect." Her questioning gaze did not elicit a response.

The waitress brought two plates piled high with

eggs and toast. Rancor dug in. After a few bites, he resumed. "Okay, University of Montana. Established 1893, just four years after Montana became a state. Class of 1931 had 201 graduates, none of whom bore the initials RB."

"One down."

"*Shh.* University of Missouri—known affectionately as Mizzou—"

"*Muzzooo?*"

"Yes. Perhaps the first students struggled with three-syllable words."

"Sure, start off by insulting the great state of Missouri, home to many friends of mine, including one who moved there from the Galapagos."

He dropped his fork. "On *purpose*?"

"Yes. Now go on."

"Okay, Mizzou was founded in 1839." He read, " 'It was the first public institution of higher education west of the Mississippi River and the first state university in Thomas Jefferson's Louisiana Purchase territory.' Graduates of the class of 1931: five hundred and thirty-two. Nary a one with an RB monogram."

"Five hundred thirty-two people and no one with the initials RB? Rather a dismal showing for the Show Me state."

"It will eventually get better, but not yet. University of Mississippi, same deal. University of Minnesota, one member of the class fit the description, but, as luck would have it, her name was Rachel Bliven." He took a sip of orange juice. "Had a little more luck with the University of Michigan. There were four potential candidates, Raphael Buck, Rochester Bonnet, Roland Blaufontaine—"

"Bit of a mouthful."

"I'm guessing foreign exchange student. And Raymond Burton. Buck died in 1968, Blaufontaine lives in a nursing home outside of Paris, Raymond Burton became a woman in 1959, and Bonnet retired in 1975 from his happy duties as gadfly to the Ann Arbor city council."

"Any of them spend any time in Florida?"

"Not that I could find, although some of them must have gone to Disney World."

"Why do you say that?"

"I thought it was mandatory for American citizens."

She tapped her lip. "No, we're looking for someone here on business. Otherwise, why go to a closed construction site on a Florida key?"

"True." He took another bite of egg. "It can't be someone who merely dropped in for the teacup ride."

"So, Michigan is a no go."

"Correct. Now"—he turned a page—"what have I got left?"

"Maryland, Massachusetts, and Miami."

He signaled for more coffee. "Okay, you'd expect that U Mass would have an abundance of potential winners...or should I say losers? Except for one tiny inconvenient fact. It wasn't the University of Massachusetts until 1947."

"Ack. I would have thought that had the best chance."

"You'da thought wrong. So I moved on to Maryland, which had its ups and downs too. The first students entered Maryland Agricultural College in 1859, but it closed during the Civil War."

"That would make it MAC anyway."

"Picky, picky. Anyway, it became the University of Maryland in 1920, well in time for our boy to attend and get his ring."

"And did he?"

"Some twenty people with the initials RB graduated in 1931, but most of them were women or in the field of medicine. I doubt whether a veterinarian would be tootling around in an elevator shaft in Sarasota."

"Good point." Charity let the waitress remove her plate. "Thanks, Tilda." She leaned across the table and tapped the notebook. "Any more likely prospects?"

"Two. Both went to Florida seeking their fortunes. Richard Bundy opened a short-order restaurant in Ybor City. It came to be known for its Cuban sandwiches, and cigar rollers flocked to his premises. By 1959, he had changed his name to Sanchez and his story to one of fleeing Cuba with nothing but the clothes on his back and a sheaf of dried tobacco leaves."

"What happened to him?"

"In an excess of irony, he was mistaken for an escaped political prisoner and kidnapped by Castro's goons. Spent ten years in a prison in Havana. When the authorities discovered their mistake—"

"They sure took their time, didn't they?"

"It can be dangerous to move too quickly in a socialist utopia. Anyway, he went back to Bundy and Maryland."

"I see. And the other one?"

"The other one—Rodney Biddlesworth—sounds like Ruggles of Red Gap, doesn't it?…Where was I?"

"Biddlesworth."

"Ah yes." He grabbed the last piece of toast before Tilda could take it. "Biddlesworth did in fact go missing under mysterious circumstances."

"Aha. When? Where? How?"

"In 1933. He set out for a two-hour sail around Sarasota Bay and never came back." He hummed a familiar tune. "I stand corrected. Not Ruggles—Gilligan."

"Funny."

"No, really. They found the boat drifting up near Cà d'Zan. Here, give me your phone." She reluctantly handed it over, hoping it wouldn't go the way of her whiskey. He turned it on and made a few swipes. "See, here's the article." He pointed to the screen.

She read, " 'Investigators discovered the boat's engine had been tampered with. Since Mr. Biddlesworth had recently had a falling out with his business partner, police suspect foul play, but the body has not surfaced, and it is presumed that prevailing currents will have taken him out to sea.' " She brightened. "He could be our man. Was he married to a G.?"

"As a matter of fact, yes. Or more accurately, to an Edna Gwendolyn. But I figure with a first name like Edna she'd go with Gwen. They were married in 1933."

"Aha! We need to follow that one up."

"Agreed. However, we don't know when the ring found its way into the shaft—it could be any time after 1931."

Charity frowned. "After construction of the hotel ceased?"

"Yes. The murderer—"

"Murderer?"

"Remember? The article said the police suspected foul play…Say, I just had an idea. Our skeleton may not in fact be Tommy T, but Mr. Biddlesworth!" Rancor rose and did a little tap dance. "And his killer could have used the abandoned hotel as a convenient dumping ground."

Charity pulled him down. "What happened to Tommy then?"

"The luckless RB landed on top of him, thus evicting the little feller and sending him off to seek shelter in the Chart House loo."

"Talk about your crackpot ideas. That's the most outlandish scenario I've ever heard."

"Do you have a better explanation?"

"Not 'til after my nap."

"Ha. So my theory stands, at least for now. Tommy's remains are resting comfortably, bothering no one, when a large object decides to use him to break its fall."

"Biddlesworth."

"The one, the only."

"*Hmm.* Perhaps I've been hasty. There's something in what you say."

"There's *always* something in what I say. They're called words. However, it had to be fairly soon after construction halted—otherwise, well, otherwise…"

Charity snapped her fingers. "Otherwise, they would have found it when they paved the parking lot. So the shaft must have been covered or filled in or something early on."

"Covered. Just as Douglas—or was it Ken?—surmised. And that had to have been done after 1926 and before 1931."

"Why after 1926?"

"They started construction on the hotel in 1926. They wouldn't have dug an elevator shaft before that."

"Okay…"

Tilda filled their mugs but with a less generous hand than before. She glanced meaningfully at the crowd waiting hungrily for an empty table.

"So why would it have to have been covered before 1931?"

"Because the murderer wouldn't have thrown the body down an open pit—it would have been discovered too soon." Rancor puffed out his chest. "I *am* good at this, aren't I?"

Charity rummaged in her purse for a safety pin. She held it up. "I can prick that ego balloon if you like."

"No need. If Professor Standish can establish the date of the skeleton, we'll know when he died." He cupped his chin. "I wish I knew more about forensics."

"You didn't do any research for *Murder Cuts Both Ways*?"

"Oh, yeah. I read every Patricia Cornwell novel I could lay my hands on."

Charity stared at him. "And all this time I thought you were an expert!"

"So you did read my books. You lied."

"I skimmed a few. Most of them. Be that as it may, where are we now? We haven't finished with the schools."

"Now we come to your favorite, University of Miami, which does exist now."

"Did it in 1931?"

"No. Wait." He held a hand up to thwart the blow. "It was chartered in 1925 as a private institution, but the next year the Florida land boom collapsed and a hurricane hit. The school continued to meet but filed for bankruptcy in 1932."

"So, even if they existed they would hardly have the resources to provide class rings."

"Precisely." He closed the notebook and finished his coffee. "That's it for now. I think the lovely Tilda wants us to leave. Will you hurry it up?"

Charity refused to budge. "So all we have is Biddlesworth and whatever we find at the University of Maine."

"Let's hope Auntie comes through." He signaled to Tilda and pointed at Charity.

As she signed her name to the check, she inquired, without much hope, "So, have you heard from Publix yet?" When no answer came, she looked up to see the front door swinging closed behind a really sexy pair of jeans.

As they unlocked the door to Charity's apartment, the telephone began to ring. Rancor answered it. Charity could hear a high, scratchy voice shouting. *Gertrude must be one of those old ladies who think they have to yell to be heard through a telephone line.* She didn't mind—it meant she would have no trouble eavesdropping. Just in case, though, she picked up the extension.

"Is that you, my boy? Where are you? I can't hear you."

"I'm here in Florida, Auntie."

"Florida? I don't want you staying in that godforsaken place, Rancor. That's where your grandfather met that hussy and abandoned his wife and family. Come back here to Camden where you belong.

73

You hear me?"

"Yes, Auntie. I will soon, Auntie. Now, were you able to answer my question?"

"Question? Oh, yes. Now where did I put that note…" A loud clunk sounded, then a lot of rattling. "Hello? Hello? Rancor? Are you still there?"

"Yes, Auntie. I asked you if any men with the initials RB went to the University of Maine."

"Yes, yes. You don't have to ask me twice. I'm not deaf. Or feeble-minded."

"I know that, Auntie."

"Well, all right then," she huffed. "I checked with the chancellor, who is an old friend of the family's, although considering the circumstances, I don't know how we remained on cordial terms."

Charity squinted at Rancor.

"Excuse me?"

Gertrude went on with her monologue as though there'd been no interruption. "He was most gracious and looked up the student rolls from the 1930s. He found Basses, which doesn't come as a surprise to me. I mean—"

"So Basses went to the University of Maine?"

"Of course. In fact, your great-great-grandfather Robert graduated in the very first class of the Maine College of Agriculture and the Mechanic Arts in 1873. He was a handsome man. I have a picture of him here— he's standing next to his sister, and—"

"Auntie? Any others?"

"Of course. Basses were among the most celebrated graduates of the university—possibly because we donated masses of money to the endowment fund. Until your grandfather, that is…"

"What happened?"

"Well, Robert's son, Robert Junior, finished in 1903 and his son, Robert the Third, three decades later. They both managed to avoid serving in the Great War, which was a real comfort to the women of the family, I can tell you. The Bass men have been singularly lucky—why, the last Bass to carry a gun was Robert T. back in the French and Indian War. Of course, he shot himself in the foot. Come to think of it, most of the Basses were not accepted into the armed forces for one reason or another. Gerald Bass—my cousin—had flat feet, and Elmer…well, let's just say he was rather a dim bulb. Then there was—"

"Aunt Gertrude? What happened to my grandfather?"

"Robert the Third? You know what happened to him. He ran off with that tramp. It's not something we're proud of, but I don't hold with keeping secrets in a family, so I made sure you children all heard the story, if only as a cautionary tale. At the time, my grandfather, Robert Junior, blamed it on the intemperate social life at the university, and he cut the school out of his will. That's why Rupert didn't go."

"So the last Bass to attend the University of Maine was my grandfather Robert?"

"Yes. Now, I've got a list here of Bass women—we all proudly attended Vassar of course…that is, until that awful man forced us to go co-ed. I can't tell you—"

"Oh, but you have, Aunt Gertrude. Many times." Rancor paused. "Do you know the year of Robert Three's graduation? Would it be 1931?" He looked through the door at Charity.

"*Mmm*, let me see…1931? No, it was 1932."

His eyes widened, and so did Charity's. "Thank you very much, Aunt Gertrude. You're a doll. Give my love to Uncle Orville." He hung up over her loud protests. "Well."

"Well." Charity considered. "There go all our hopes. If he graduated in 1932, then he couldn't be the victim."

" 'Hopes'? How ghoulish of you. No. So we're left with...what was the guy's name? Biddlesworth?"

"I think so."

"Damn!" He slapped his forehead.

She gave him an amused kiss. "It's not going to knock any humility into your head, if that's what you're after."

"No, thank God. I forgot to ask about G."

"Call her back."

He checked his watch. "Her canasta game starts in ten minutes. She'll kill me if I interrupt her. I'll have to call tomorrow."

She sat down next to him on the couch. "So what do we do now?"

He checked the balcony. Black clouds roiled the horizon. "Storm coming. I say we snuggle."

"I say we do more than that."

****

"Auntie? Did I catch you at a bad time?"

"Little Rancor? Is that you again?" The blaring voice filled the living room.

"Yes, Auntie. How was your canasta match?"

"I don't want to talk about it. Thank you for asking." A noise like an irritated muskrat came through the receiver. "You remember Lucinda Alcott, of course. She...I can hardly say it...she did it again."

"What did she do?"

"Held her cards instead of laying them down. We'd all stopped the play, and there she was at the show, this Cheshire cat smile on her face, laying cards down right and left. And then…and then…"

"What?"

"She shouted Muggins, even though you're supposed to announce it at the beginning of play, but did she care? No. She pegged all my points before I had a chance to claim them. Dirty *mmph*."

"What was that, Auntie?"

"Never you mind, young Rancor." She paused, probably to pull herself together. "Is that why you called?"

"Uh no. Actually, I forgot to ask you one question about my grandfather. I…uh…was going through some papers and found something about his wedding. Do you know if…if…I mean, was it a grand affair or what?"

"Wedding? He didn't have a wedding. He eloped."

"He did!"

"Yes. The family should have seen the pattern. Always ducking his obligations…"

"Auntie?"

"Oh yes. He got married in his junior year at University of Maine. Of course, Mother was pregnant. So shocking for my grandparents. On the other hand, it was with my brother, so I guess it turned out all right, but still."

"Wait—you're telling me my grandfather was married in 1931?"

"Yes, and you can be certain there was a hullaballoo. It was all his parents could do to keep him in school one more year. Grandpapa promised him a job in the company sales department if he finished his degree. By the time he graduated, Rupert was a little over one, and I was on the way. Papa left us just before I was born." She paused. "It must have been too much for him to handle—children, a new job, an ailing wife. You know she died soon after he disappeared. A broken heart, I imagine. Very common."

"My grandmother—what was her name?"

"Name? Don't you know your own grandmother's name? My gosh, child. I can see Clara has certainly shirked her duties. I shall speak to her. I mean—"

"Aunt Gertrude. Her *name.*"

She continued to ruminate. "Considering…well…I suppose there's no reason for him to *know.*"

"Auntie?"

"What? Oh. Gertrude, of course. Who did you think I was named after? Gertrude Quimby. Everyone called her Trudy. Good family. From Penhallow. Father was a shipbuilder. Oh, she was a pretty thing but flighty…and, by all accounts, not very bright. I know I shouldn't say such things about my own mother, but after all, I didn't know her very well."

Rancor thanked his aunt, promising to come home soon. Before he could return the phone to its cradle, Gertrude's penetrating voice boomed. "By the way, did you get the check, Rancor? I have yet to receive a thank-you note and—"

"Yes, yes, will do. Thanks, Auntie." He hastily hung up.

"Check?"

Instead of answering, he rapped his knuckles loudly on the coffee table. "What a waste of time! I could have spent it drinking…"

"Thanks a lot." Charity stood and paced. "Wait a minute. The date is inscribed inside the ring, right?"

He pulled it out. "Yes. It says 'To my beloved RB from G 1931.' "

"Robert married Gertrude in 1931."

"What are you getting at?"

"Well, wouldn't the class year be on the ring itself? Not in an engraving?"

"Not necessarily…oh, I see. You're postulating that the date does not refer to the graduation year?"

"Yes. Looks like you're going to have to check all the classes from 1926 to at least 1932. Maybe even beyond."

"How come?"

"Cover all the bases. He could have graduated before or after the inscription was made. Oh, and cross-check those with marriage licenses between an RB and a G. dated 1931." Charity stepped just out of reach of his fists. "Then match those to people who disappeared after 1931."

"Why don't you just shoot me?"

She rubbed her chin. "On second thought, maybe you should start later and work backward. Any earlier and the corpse would likely be found…or smelled…in an area where people would still be milling around."

"You're too kind."

"How about this? You've already done 1931. Go back to the nine schools, find all the RBs in the class of 1932, then see who got married in 1931, and who died or disappeared soon after. Easy peasy."

"It'll take me days!"

"Better get started then."

Rancor gave the clock a meaningful look. "Aren't

we supposed to be at the morgue?"

Before she could answer, the phone rang. "Hello? Oh, hi, George…Okay, we'll be right down." She hung up. "Standish finished his autopsy. George wants us to come down to the *Planet* office."

"We can't go to the morgue?"

"Standish refused admittance to anyone, remember? George wants to reconnoiter—figure out how to squeeze the information out of Captain Kelly."

****

The publisher rose from his desk, a mug of coffee in his hand. "There you are. Where's your article?"

"I filed it Sunday, George. Didn't Violet tell you? It's already laid out."

"Then how the hell have you been occupying yourself since then?"

Charity and Rancor exchanged glances. Neither of their activities would be suitable to confess in mixed company, so Charity changed the subject. "Have you talked to the captain?"

A commotion at the door drew their attention. The medical examiner pushed past an intern and slammed into George's office. "Fletcher, you've got to help!" He plopped in a chair, holding a flabby white hand to his heart.

George let him catch his breath before asking, "What's up, Vernon?"

"It's…it's…that martinet, that…that…officious ferret…that—"

"Who?"

"Standish. You know what he wants to do? He wants to take his findings and publish them."

"Well, that's okay. Doesn't he have the right—"

"Before he lets the police see them?"

"What!"

"Yes. He's packing his bags now. Hired a limo to take him back to Gainesville tomorrow. He's all excited. Says he has to study the bones more before he'll release them. It's…it's criminal!"

"Can't Kelly stop him?"

"Kelly? That pantywaist? He has the gumption of a gerbil."

Rancor murmured, "*Tch, tch. Another* animal metaphor?"

Edwards had begun to shout. "Standish bullied him into it—threatened to call his cousin, the state police commissioner."

"What do you want me to do?"

"Stop them!"

George poured himself more coffee and waited a minute before asking calmly, "How?"

"The power of the press, man! Start a campaign—those bones could be Native American. Get the Seminoles involved. Don't let those skeletons out of my jurisdiction."

Charity opened her mouth. "Skeletons? As in more than one?"

"Yes, he found parts of two different bodies."

"Male? Female?"

"I don't know—he wouldn't tell me."

Fletcher rubbed his hands together. "I don't want to lose this scoop. Ted Garrish up in Ocala has been lording it over me since they cracked that serial murder case. Let's see…We could spread it around that there are reports yet to be substantiated."

Rancor jumped in. "Edwards may have something.

It could be a prehistoric cemetery. The pit has two skeletons. How do we know it doesn't contain more? We don't want to desecrate a sacred site, now do we?"

Heads nodded enthusiastically.

Charity spoke up. "How about I punch it over to the *Patch* papers? It will show up on every major neighborhood link in the Tampa Bay area."

"Go for it. And include the Sarasota to Fort Myers editions." He turned to his desk. "I'll put out an extra tonight." He picked up the phone. "Violet? Get me Larry Miller over at KWAZ. He owes me a favor." He tapped his foot. "Larry? George Fletcher here. Can I come on your five o'clock show? I've got something juicy for you."

He waved at the others, dismissing them. Charity sat down to tap out a paragraph for the online paper. Edwards paced while Rancor played with the television remote. After a minute, he put it down and, stepping into the other's path, cried jovially, "Say, Edwards, why don't you and I go hit a bar while we wait?"

The medical examiner glowered at him but appeared to reconsider. "Yeah, I guess so. A beer wouldn't hurt after the day I've had."

Rancor slapped him on the shoulder. "Great. I'll be happy to join you. Your treat."

Charity watched them go, a smile on her lips, then bent to her task.

Chapter Five
Body Parts

"This is outrageous, Kelly. I won't stand for it."

"I'm sorry, Professor Standish, but the commissioner was adamant. The evidence stays here." Charity knew the captain kept his snarky smile under wraps with great difficulty.

The old man slammed his briefcase down on the desk. "I want to hear it from Quentin's mouth."

"The commissioner said he would call you this evening. The commissioner feels that in light of the gossip swirling around the discovery of the skeletons, it behooves us to retain the evidence to ensure its safety while the investigation is ongoing. The potential entry of the Seminole Tribe into the debate is one we want to avoid."

Standish snorted. "Who came up with the ludicrous idea that the bones are Native American? They're clearly Caucasian."

George and Charity both gazed innocently at the man, while Rancor barely stifled a snigger.

Luckily, the police chief could honestly say that he had no idea where the rumor originated. "What's important is that we secure the site and hopefully determine the origin of the bones as soon as possible. Now, what can you tell us?"

The professor looked warily from one face to

another. It was obvious to all that he wanted more than anything to keep his findings to himself. "If I give you my report, will you promise to keep it sealed until such time as I can publish?"

"I'm afraid not."

"At least keep it from the press?"

George stared at him. "I think it's a little late for that."

Standish sighed and extracted a file from his briefcase. He skimmed several pages. "All right. Bone fragments came from two separate skeletons. The first—which includes only the tibia, the talus bone, and a section of the fibula—belong to a small child."

Charity quietly flipped the switch on the tape recorder in her pocket. "Pardon me," she asked meekly. "Could you perhaps put that in layman's terms for us?"

A martyred sigh came from the great scientist. "Leg and ankle bones. The fibula was severed below the knee cap, and partially crushed, leading me to surmise a heavy object dropped on the child's leg."

Rancor's eyes flickered. Charity knew what he was thinking. *Biddlesworth. Oh God, he's going to prance around for days like some cheeky rooster. Sigh.* "Could you date the bones?"

"Not without proper equipment, which I have in my *laboratory.*" In the face of his listeners' continued silence, he grudgingly admitted, "If you're asking how long since the child died, I would say less than a hundred years."

"That old?"

"I said *less* than a hundred. Late 1920s to early 1930s, I'd guess. But old, yes. The discoloration and the state of degeneration indicates—"

Rancor twitched impatiently. "Yes, yes. We can read all that in your report. What about the other skeleton?"

"Ah, that one is nearly complete."

Kelly rubbed his jaw. "Could they have died at the same time?"

"Unlikely. The disposition of the bones, as well as their condition, suggest he died several years after the first. A full-grown man, Caucasian as I said, probably of Anglo-Saxon ancestry, no scoliosis—"

"Indicating a middle- or upper-class background," interjected Edwards helpfully.

Standish glared at the doctor. "May I *continue*? Some breakage near the pelvis, almost as though he had been folded in half and shoved into the pit."

"So he may have been unconscious—"

"Or even dead—"

"Before he fell into the hole?"

"Oh, he was dead all right."

"How do you know?"

"Because he'd been stabbed to death."

"*What?*"

"There is evidence of multiple wounds inflicted by a sharp object—several ribs are chipped and the sternum pierced. A crack in the hyoid bone may also be due to a severe blow."

"Hyoid?"

Standish patted his neck. "A bone in the throat."

Kelly sat down heavily on the corner of the desk. "Murder?"

Standish said drily, "It would seem so."

Rancor elbowed Charity. "Told you."

She turned to Standish. "You say several cuts—

could it have been a crime of passion?"

"Possibly. You'd have to have more information to determine motive."

Rancor, his face showing only mild interest, asked, "Was there anything—the bit of flannel, say—that we could use to trace him?"

Standish took another sheet from the file. "The lab found the material to be very high-quality suit material—"

Edwards squeaked excitedly. "Again, evidence that the deceased belonged to the upper middle class or higher."

Standish took a minute to fix his colleague with a vitriolic gaze. Once the latter had been reduced to a more compliant smoking pile of rubble, he pointed at Kelly. "Interpretation of the evidence is the job of the police."

His tone projecting expert knowledge Charity knew he didn't have, Rancor asked, "Can't you match his teeth to dental records?"

"Ah, that would be difficult. He had no teeth."

"No teeth?"

"It appears from the empty sockets that they were knocked out deliberately."

Edwards said breathlessly, "In preparation for dentures?"

Standish looked down his aquiline nose at his colleague. "If a professional had extracted all the teeth, he wouldn't have left any root tips behind. He'd remove all traces of tooth and root. In this case, the roots were partially resorbed, a process that likely shut down at a certain point after death."

"You're right, of course." The medical examiner

blushed. "So…the murderer must have done it."

George looked at him curiously. "What makes you think that?"

Standish waved Edwards off before he could answer. "The murderer was clearly aware that dental records can in fact be used to identify a body—probably from reading too many police thrillers." His disparaging glance had no effect on Rancor. "He didn't, however, know how to do it properly." The others had the distinct impression that Standish would not have been so inept.

He handed the folder to Kelly. "And therefore the killer didn't expect the victim to be found for a long time."

"What do you mean?"

"He assumed the soft tissue would have dissolved by the time it was discovered, making the teeth the only method of identification."

Charity had a thought. "What about the bits of root you said were left? Would it be possible to identify him by whatever is left in the jaw?"

Standish picked up his briefcase. "Not by me. You need a forensic dentist." He headed to the door. "My car is waiting. I expect to receive the materials as soon as you're finished with them." He leveled an eloquent look at Kelly. "I know Quentin—my *cousin*—will agree." He strode out.

Rancor ambled to the window and watched the long black limousine leave the parking lot. "That went well."

George and Charity gave each other a high five. George chortled, "The power of the press!"

The police chief scratched his head. "What are you

all talking about?"

Charity gulped. "Er…nothing. Aren't you glad you didn't have to let the skeletons go, Captain?"

"I'm not so sure. Now I have two accidental deaths…or two murders…to solve. I don't have the resources for this."

"Can we help?"

"Sorry. Like the man said, this is police work." He stopped. "Wait…'Power of the press'…*Hmm*. Maybe you *can* help. We're looking for missing persons reports for, say, between fifty and a hundred years ago. Children and white male adults. Can you do that for me?"

Rancor kept a straight face. "Absolutely."

"Okay." He picked up the file and headed to the door. "I'm going back to the station to read the report— see if there are any other details that we can use."

He left.

Rancor grabbed Charity's hand. "I want lunch."

When she began to protest he gave her a tug. *"Lunch. Now."*

"I…oh. Okay." She turned to the publisher. "I'll be back later."

George didn't look up. "Sure…sure. I have to get going on this editorial."

Rancor didn't speak until Charity turned left into the Centre Shops. "The Blue Dolphin's too crowded. We can't talk in there. Let's go up to Olaf's deli and get take out."

They ordered *bánh mih* sandwiches, picked out a cold bottle of wine, and drove back up the island. Charity retrieved two folding chairs from her storage locker, and they took their food out to the beach.

Before she could take a bite, Rancor grabbed her wrist. "I can't believe Kelly played right into our hands."

"What do you mean?"

"I mean, we have carte blanche to search the police records. Standish's conclusion—grudgingly provided though it was—that the adult died a few years after Tommy T places him in the 1930s. Therefore, I can probably dispense with 1926 through 1930 of the university classes. Once I finish 1932, we can cross-check the missing persons' files before I start on the outlying years."

Charity shook off his hand and picked up her sandwich. "When are you going to turn over the ring?"

"Not until I've wrung every ounce of information from it. Besides"—he took a gulp of wine—"it might be a family heirloom."

"You wouldn't."

"I would. You should know by now what I'm capable of." He blew her a kiss. "And not just in the bedroom."

She decided to leave that remark unaddressed and ate her lunch. The noon sun beat down on their heads, but a breeze off the gulf cooled them. Low whitecaps trimmed the blue water, and far out two dolphins breached. A flock of pelicans soared past them in a perfect vee formation. One flew up high, folded his wings, and dove head first into the water. When he rose to the surface, he pointed his bill to the sky. A big lump made its way from the bill into the pouch, and he swallowed noisily.

"Not a bad spot. I might stay here longer than I planned."

Rancor's words gave her an unpleasant jolt. "And how long was that?"

"Oh, only until I finished the research on the ghost book. I was going to write it up at home."

"You mean in Maine?"

He nodded absently, gazing out at the clouds blowing bubbles in the azure sky.

So much for his proposal. Oh right, he was joking. She checked out his profile. *I say good riddance.* She poured more wine into her Dixie cup and drained it.

"You finished?" He took her paper plate and cup and shoveled them into a plastic bag. "Then to work, minion."

Charity left Rancor at a computer in the *Planet* office and drove to the police station. Captain Kelly set her up with the missing persons reports from 1920 on. "Good thing we hired young Crocker to digitize all our records last year. Otherwise, you'd be going through dusty ledgers wearing plastic gloves."

By dinnertime, she had had it. "I'm done here, Captain."

"How far did you get?"

"Up to 1950. I found ten reports of either a twenty-something-year-old white male and forty of a child under ten. None of them seemed to fit." She wished she could tell him about the ring and how that might narrow the dates down. "I think that's late enough—Standish said the bones were likely nearly a hundred years old, after all. Besides, we may already know who the child is."

"You mean the little boy you mentioned? The ghost?"

"You may laugh, but Rancor and I—Mr. Bass—

have been collecting local ghost stories. The little boy known as Tommy T was killed at the Ghost Hotel."

Kelly sobered. "You did mention him. Do you have a last name?"

"No. I don't even know if his real name was Tommy. That's what the Chart House staff calls him."

"And why do they call him anything?"

"Because he haunts the men's room."

"I…uh…see." He stood. "I'll check out the death records. If it really happened, it'll be there."

"I'm going home."

"See you tomorrow?"

"I'll try to check in."

Rancor still sat before the monitor when she arrived at the office. He looked up. "Anything?"

"Nothing. I'm taking a break until tomorrow."

"Wuss."

"Guilty as charged." She touched a finger to the back of his neck. "And you?"

"A light frisson. A rise in certain nether regions. Other than that, nothing."

"I meant with the schools."

"I know. I've been perusing the mug shots of the female students."

She cuffed him. "What have you accomplished?"

"I've slogged through most of 1932. As far as I'm concerned, way too many unqualified Americans went to college despite a crippling shortage of carpenters and plumbers. Hence the glut of poets and professors living off the backs of hardworking taxpayers. Not to mention a shocking lack of advancement in plumbing technology."

Charity wasn't in the mood to defend the New

Deal, even were she so inclined. "Have you had a chance to cross-check the RBs in the class of 1932 with marriage registrations?"

"I've done all but Maine. As before, no RBs in Montana, Missouri, or Mississippi. U Mass and Miami were already eliminated. Maryland—home to the absent Biddlesworth—"

"The one who disappeared in Florida in 1933?"

"The very one. In what is becoming a pattern at that border state university, yet three more men took themselves off to Florida after graduating. Roscoe Barnard, Randall Bartlesby, and a Rex Burnham, all graduated with honors and disappeared into the Florida swamps. The Florida land boom had collapsed by then if I recall correctly."

"Yes, by the end of the twenties. It started around 1920, but what with two hurricanes, the Great Depression, and the unmasking of thousands of flim-flam artists, it fizzled in less than a decade."

"At any rate, before our boys headed south. So tell me, if not filthy lucre, what would make them want to come to sunny Florida?"

She shrugged. "Work? Wives?"

"Come on, Charity, think. This is Sarasota, after all. Winter quarters for Ringling Brothers Barnum and Bailey circus—"

"Actually, I believe they're in Venice."

"Will you stop interrupting? That's neither here nor there, but if you insist on being pedantic, I must inform you that the circus didn't move to Venice until the 1950s." Before she could respond, he barked, "The point *is*, the Clown College is here."

"Ah."

"Which is why Barnard aimed his pointy head south. According to the Ringling Brothers website, he lived a long, fulfilling life as a circus clown."

"How about Burnham—was he a clown as well?"

"No. The hapless Burnham was last seen running like a dog through the Everglades." When she didn't laugh, he continued. "Apparently, he didn't know that flim-flam artists no longer constituted the majority of the population, and he stood out like a sore thumb."

Charity was beginning to feel restless. "And the third one?"

"Bartlesby was married to a Gretchen. And he did go missing."

"When?"

"In 1935."

"Might work. Put him on the list. What about any of the other schools?"

"I thought I'd hit another jackpot there. Two more young gallants with the initials RB graduated in 1932 from the University of Missouri and, as young men do, went west."

"I hope you mean west Florida."

"Well, duh. You just can't let me be cute, can you?"

She patted his shoulder. "Go on."

"They both married. One—a Russ Benson—married Georgia Hamilton in 1934."

"1934! That's too late."

"Not necessarily. They could have been engaged in college, and she inscribed the ring then."

"That doesn't make any sense."

"Doesn't have to. Young love and all that."

Charity feared the discussion was meandering off

toward pulp fiction and decided to take a firm hand. "What about the other one?"

"Reuben Brooke married Buffy Smith—daughter of a local businessman."

"Okay. And the University of Maine?"

"I haven't gotten to that yet, but we know of at least one graduate there who fits the profile perfectly."

"Robert Bass III."

"Yes. However, as with all my work, I intend to be extremely thorough. I have to be sure Biddlesworth and Bartlesby aren't our man—wait a minute, that's not right. Is it 'our man'? 'Our men'? *Hmm*."

"Whatever. Come on. I need sustenance."

"You ate that entire sandwich and half of mine just a few hours ago."

She held her watch to his face. "That would be six hours ago."

He clicked the computer off. "If I weren't quite so chivalrous, I wouldn't let you take me away from all this and buy me dinner."

"Speaking of buying, when do you start at Publix?"

He drew back, a look of horror on his face. "Why do you ask?"

"You *are* going to work there, aren't you?"

"Of course, but first they have to schedule my training session. It's purported to be quite rigorous. There's bagging, and cart retrieval, and stacking…customer relations—oh, ever so many things I must learn before they release me into the wilds of the service sector."

"You've got one week. That's it. Then you start buying meals. And maybe find your own place."

"Or pay rent?"

Her heart bounced twice. She couldn't look at him. If he saw the joy in her face, he'd know what his suggestion did to her. *Remember what he said—he's going home soon. To Maine.* "You couldn't afford it."

"Don't I get a discount for good behavior?" He patted her bottom.

Let's nip this in the bud. "Why don't we eat on it?"

"Great, I'm starved."

****

George ushered them into his office. "So have you finished checking the missing persons file?"

"Yes—I stopped at 1950. Followed up on some fifty leads. No winners. But Rancor has information on at least three men who disappeared in the thirties."

"Oh?" George turned to Rancor, who quickly put his coffee cup to his lips. "Are you helping Charity?"

Too late, she remembered that George didn't know about the ring, and therefore didn't know that Rancor was searching the universities. "He...uh...he is, yes. Aren't you, Rancor? But," she added hurriedly, "I still have to confirm his findings. Captain Kelly is going to look at death records from the period."

"Oh, right, I forgot to tell you. He found a match. Tommy T was in fact Theodore Dobbin, seven years old at the time of his death in 1926."

The phone rang. Charity picked it up. "Yes?" She put a hand over the receiver. "Captain Kelly wants to know if we can come over." George picked up his keys. "We'll be right there."

They piled into the publisher's Volvo and drove the half mile to the station. The police chief was in his office checking boxes on a form. He looked up. "There you are. We've identified the child."

George said, "I told them."

Charity asked, "What happened to him?"

"His father worked as a foreman on the Ritz-Carlton job site. One day, the boy's mother dropped him off with her husband while she went to a doctor's appointment. When she returned, Theodore was nowhere to be found."

Rancor feigned shock. "The father hadn't kept him on a leash?"

"That's frowned upon here in Florida. Anyway, they searched for five days. They'd about given up, assuming he'd tumbled into the water and drowned, when a carpenter reported a smell."

A cry of delight issued from Rancor's throat. "Putrefaction! A body exposed to the elements will begin to decompose after twelve to twenty-four hours, but it can take five or six days if the corpse is in a protected location. After four weeks, the tissue becomes a fluid—it actually *melts*—but to be entirely skeletonized can sometimes take several years. At that point—"

"My, you did learn a lot from Patricia Cornwell, didn't you?"

George turned away and coughed into his handkerchief. "I'm taking that picture to my grave."

Rancor, undeterred, persisted. "So, where did they find little Tommy?"

Kelly took a rattling breath. "At the bottom of an elevator shaft. Crushed under a wooden beam."

Charity's hand flew to her mouth. "Oh my God!"

"He probably died from the fall."

Rancor touched her elbow. "Instantly, I'm sure."

"At any rate, they didn't have the equipment to lift

the beam off him, so they cut off his leg at the knee and hauled the rest of the body up. He's buried in Manasota Memorial Park in Bradenton."

"Wait a minute. So they left his leg in the pit?"

"Yup."

"Don't tell me they planned to actually put an elevator in!"

"No, no. They boarded up the hole and posted a sign warning people about the pit. Construction on the hotel ceased soon after."

"When was that?"

"Theodore Dobbin was pronounced dead on September 15, 1926." Kelly paused, his eyes distant. "It must have been so hard to bury a child."

"Yes. It must be equally hard not to ever know what happened to your husband."

Everyone looked at Rancor. "Or…er…brother. Or whoever the adult was. Did you find any record of the man?"

Kelly deftly countered the move. "Well, I wouldn't find anything in the death notices, since he wasn't discovered until last week, now, would I?"

"Good point."

George wandered to the window. "You say the boy died only a couple of months before the site closed. Since Ringling expected to resume construction someday, they probably left the shaft alone for years."

Charity and Rancor exchanged glances. "So the murderer must have believed his victim wouldn't be discovered any time soon."

"Ah."

Rancor made a great show of rising. "So, that's it, huh? Charity, are you coming?"

Charity didn't want to come. She wanted to ask more questions. Right now, she didn't have enough new details to warrant a full article, and the journalist in her was frustrated. "Rancor, I—"

"Come *now*, Charity." He beetled his eyebrows at her.

"All right." She followed him out. "What is it? Why are you in such a hurry?"

He walked rapidly up the sidewalk. "I have to go home and make some phone calls. We now know who the boy is. We have to narrow down the possibilities for the man. I haven't done the University of Maine yet."

"What about Biddlesworth and the other one?"

"Bartlesby. You take them, and I'll concentrate on Maine."

She dragged him to a halt. "I don't think so."

"Why not? We're so close!"

"Because I have to write the next installment for the *Planet*."

"Doesn't it come out on Wednesday?"

"Yeesss. But I want to draft a column for next week. I missed this week, what with all this…"

"Sex?"

"That too." She smiled at him. He leaned toward her. Their mouths opened and closed, an inch too far apart.

"Am I boring you?"

"No. Why?"

"You seem to be yawning."

She drew back. "I keep forgetting what a romantic you are."

He turned away. "Wish I could."

"What did you say?"

"Um…it's all good?"

"Go away and come back later."

"Yes, ma'am." He pried her purse from her fingers and took her keys. "I'll pick you up." As he unlocked her car door, he said casually, "By the way, I'm off to Brazil tonight."

"What? Why?"

"To catch a thief."

Chapter Six
Tommy T's Ticked Off

"Are you ready to go?"

Charity jumped. "Rancor! I didn't hear you come in."

"You were concentrating on your column. I didn't want to disturb you, so I waited until you'd hit a snag."

"How did you know I had?"

"You were shaking your foot." Rancor raised his eyes to the ceiling. "I must say I had hoped you weren't one of those foot jigglers—the ones who make the table wobble when they're nervous or thinking deep thoughts. So disappointing."

"Yes. Okay. Now, why are you going to Brazil?"

"I'll get to that. Here's your purse. We're going to the Chart House."

"To eat?"

"What else?"

She peered at him. "You have something up your sleeve. Are you going to plant the ring back at the crime scene?"

"Not on your life. I told you, it may be a family heirloom. If I give it to the police, I'll never get it back. No, I want to visit the little boys' room."

Charity waved toward the hall. "There's one here."

"Does this one have a ghost?"

"Possibly. Past reporters who didn't make their

deadlines."

"George doesn't seem the homicidal type."

"No, but his predecessor and father, the notorious Eli Fletcher, was highly intolerant of goldbrickers. Stories abound of him kicking dilatory reporters down the stairs or shooting a revolver in the air over their heads."

"Longboat Key has a more colorful history than I imagined."

"Don't forget it had a ghost hotel."

"Not to mention superannuated babes in bikinis even their granddaughters wouldn't be caught dead in."

"You were on the beach."

He grinned. "Yes. Come on."

Once on the road, Charity asked, "Did you get any more research done?"

"Nah. Too busy ogling the flesh." He was silent a minute. "Actually, I had my training session at Publix. I'm sorry to say I had to postpone the first-day celebrations. Thankfully, Mr. Twittle—he's the manager—was most understanding."

"Brazil?"

"Brazil."

I'm going to wait until we get to the restaurant, then ply him with liquor.

Nathan greeted Rancor as an old friend and found them seats at the bar. "Martini?"

"Just one, thanks. And the lady will have a glass of wine."

"Hey! I worked hard today. I deserve a nice, relaxing drink."

"Sorry. Have to be at the airport by nine. I'm flying out tonight, and I want you awake enough to drive."

"Tonight!" She hoped he didn't hear the dismay in her voice.

"Why, little fawn, you'll miss me. How delightful." His lips showed a smirk, but his eyes glistened. "Here's where you ask me in a faltering tone how long I'll be gone."

Charity was determined not to give him that pleasure. "I don't care. If you don't want to hold up your end of the investigation, I'll carry on by myself."

He continued as though she hadn't spoken. "I don't really know how long it will take."

"To catch the thief...Oh! It's your editor, isn't it?"

"*Shh.*" He looked around and lowered his voice. "I heard from one of the other authors. Isabella may be publishing our manuscripts under a different name."

"What? How can she get away with it?"

"They were only submissions—we had no signed contracts yet. I have no proof that the work is mine."

"But it's your property. By law it's automatically copyrighted."

"Hence the moniker 'thief.' Unfortunately, without a contract, or a copyright registration, there's not much I can do to prove it's mine."

"You must have drafts."

He contrived to look affronted. "Me? Write more than one draft? I'm much too good a writer to have to do that."

"Baloney. Of course you do. Everyone does."

He nodded. "Yes, I admit it. And when I bring the scoundrels to court I'll use them. It's worth a try." He stood. "Now I have to visit the john and, with any luck, Tommy T."

"You mean, Theodore Dobbin."

"Whatever."

Charity nursed her drink. She didn't have to wait long. An agitated Rancor, his face as white as cotton wool, tottered to the table. "What is it?"

"Oh my God. I saw him. I saw Tommy, Charity!"

He slumped down on the chair, then leaned forward and snatched her wine from her hand, downing it in one swallow. "He was...he was sitting there, calm as you please. When he saw me—" He gulped for air.

"What do you mean, he saw you? Don't ghosts just have eye sockets?"

"Not this one. He had coal black eyes and...and they flashed. He was angry, Charity. Angry at me."

"Did he talk?"

"Of course not. He's a ghost. Honestly, haven't you read anything about ghosts?"

Charity took a deep breath. "Okay, tell me what happened."

"Well, he saw me and pulled himself up. He wore torn overalls and a cotton shirt."

"The scrap of denim."

Rancor nodded. "He opened his mouth as though he were yelling, but no sound came out. He took a step toward me and fell over. That's when I saw he only had one leg."

"That's right—they had to cut it off to get him out of the pit."

"Yes. He lay there, his hand outstretched toward me, his mouth gaping like a dying mackerel. Charity, he wanted something from me."

"His toy. The ring."

"Wow. How did he know I have it?"

Charity gave him a disgusted look. "Hello?"

"Oh." Rancor held up two fingers. The bartender nodded and began to mix another martini. "Do you suppose Tommy took the ring from the dead man?"

"He must have." Charity mused. "But the other body arrived later, after Tommy—I mean Theodore— after they took his body away."

"But his ghost still haunted the pit."

"And when Biddlesworth decided to sublet, he came out."

"Spotted the restaurant and decided the men's room would be preferable to being buried alive."

"A ghost can't be buried alive."

"True." Rancor scratched his chin. "So, first order of business is to find out when the other one died."

"What did Standish say? Early thirties. It had to have been after 1931 because of the ring inscription. How long ago was that?"

"Math's not your strong point I see. Eighty-five years."

"When did the Chart House open?"

"Not sure." He accepted the martini from the assistant manager. "Nathan, any idea when this place was built?"

"Before my time. I'll go ask Walter." He returned a minute later. "Walter says 1988. He knows 'cause he was one of the first people they hired. Started as a dishwasher, and now"—his face suffused with pride— "he's the executive manager."

Charity sipped her water. "So the man was killed sometime between 1931 and 1988."

"Now you're being ridiculous. What did you get on your SATs? Twelve? Professor Standish said the skeleton was around eighty years old. So he must have died at the latest in the 1940s."

She giggled.

"What's so funny?"

"I wonder why he doesn't haunt the men's room as well?"

"Apparition rules. The nether world is just as over-regulated as this one. Only one ghost per hundred square feet. He probably haunted the parking lot."

"Wait. If Tommy T left the pit in the thirties, what did he do before the restaurant was built?"

"How the hell would I know?" He checked his watch and tossed off his drink. "We've got to go."

"What? No food?"

"No time."

Charity's heart flip-flopped. "How…long will you be gone?"

He paused, then touched her cheek lightly. "I don't know, but I'll call you. Every night."

It wasn't much, but it would have to do.

An hour later, she waved him off at the terminal and slogged home. As she fell on the couch, the phone rang.

"Hey."

"Hey you."

"I…uh…just wanted to check in. Flight's about to take off. Thought I'd better tell you I'm not going to Brazil. I'm going to Paris."

"Paris?"

"Er…yes."

"Why the lie?"

"Oh, I figured you'd be jealous if you knew I was going to such a romantic spot."

"Why should I be?"

"Because I'm going to see a beautiful woman."
****

Charity wasn't sure how she made it through the night. Rancor, true to form, would give her no details, preferring, apparently, to make her suffer— *unnecessarily? Or not?* He merely said he'd call when he arrived.

She fired up the computer when she got to the office and attempted to work on the column, but questions kept intruding. *What about the Maryland graduates? And the University of Maine?* Rancor hadn't gotten to Maine before he left. *I'd better do it myself—he can't be trusted to finish anything...* Fingers hovering over the keyboard, she stopped. *Where in hell did he get the money to go to France anyway? He hasn't even started at Publix yet. Wait—Aunt Gertrude said something about a check.* She pounded a fist on the desk. *That little bastard had enough cash for a plane ticket but not enough to spring for my drink?* She got up and paced, then sat back down. *And then why did he leave so hurriedly? Was it something I did? Doesn't he like me anymore? Will I ever see him again?* As the questions receded further and further from the murder, she became more and more anxious.

The publisher came in. "What's the matter? You're bouncing up and down like a rock band groupie."

"Uh...nothing. Nothing. Working on the next column." She shielded the monitor screen, on which appeared a Google map of Paris.

"Good. I'm going to finish my editorial." He went into his office and closed the door. Charity minimized the Paris site and typed in University of Maine, class of 1932. Up popped a list, and on the top was Roger P.

Brewster. "*Mmm*...married Ginger Carpenter, class of 1933. We may be getting somewhere." She read on. "He received a BA, no honors. What did our Ginger do?" She clicked on the name. "Graduated in Anthropology. Went on for a master's degree...let's see." She typed in the name. "Ooh, goody. A Wikipedia article." According to the article, Ginger went off to do her field work in the Aleutian Islands and never came back. Survivors included a husband—Roger Brewster—and a three-year-old child. Brewster was believed to have gone in pursuit of his wife. She clicked to turn the page, but that was the end of the article. No amount of searching would unearth any more references to Roger P. Brewster. *Maybe he never got to Alaska. Maybe his trip ended unexpectedly in Sarasota.* That idea lasted a full ten seconds. *He'd hardly go through Florida to get to the northern Pacific.*

Okay—Rancor's grandfather. She plugged in Robert Bass III. The entry only repeated what Aunt Gertrude had told them. He graduated—barely—and went to work in his father's business. She checked for alumni class notes, but they were only available online from 1972 on. *He seems to have been pretty much of a cipher.* She chuckled. *I guess the gene for personality only emerges every third generation.*

On to the University of Maryland. Bundy and Biddlesworth. Oh, no, they were 1931. *Try 1932.* Bartlesby, Barnard, and Burnham. Who was the fellow who disappeared in 1935? Bartlesby. She searched for five minutes before coming up with a short article in the *Sarasota Examiner* that mentioned him.

" 'Sarasota police ended their search today for Randall Bartlesby, Esq., of Baltimore. No trace has been found of the businessman, although his ex-wife, Gretchen Bartlesby, feels strongly that he skipped out to avoid alimony and claims she found a brochure for Costa Rica among his effects. With nothing further to go on, Police Chief Stewart has closed the books on the case.' "

A possibility. She sat, chin in hand, musing. *On the other hand, 1931 could refer to the class year just as well as the marriage date. Just because Robert Three graduated in 1932 doesn't mean the dead man did.* "Let's see, where's that list?" She shuffled through her drawer and came up with the notebook Rancor had been using. "Ah, Biddlesworth, Rodney." She set the pad down and keyed in the name. Nothing. "Wait, what about his wife? What was her name?" She checked the list again. "That's right, Edna Gwendolyn…but her last name? Well, let's try Edna Gwendolyn Biddlesworth…"

Aha. Edna Gwendolyn Biddlesworth had had her husband declared legally dead in 1940. At the end of the article was a short obituary, stating he was in Sarasota on business at the time of his disappearance. It gave the story Rancor had found—a dispute with his business partner led police to speculate that a crime had been committed, but without the body they couldn't bring charges. The business partner—one Calvin Hagen—was believed to have left Sarasota once the police abandoned their investigation.

On a whim, she typed in Calvin Hagen. Third down was a link to a biography website. She skimmed the article. Calvin Hagen, originally from New York, had moved to Florida when his sister, Hedda Collingsworth Hagen, married John Ringling in 1930.

Billing himself as an entrepreneur, he struck several real estate deals with companies interested in relocating to the Sarasota area. Rumors of questionable transactions dogged him, however, finally culminating in his being declared a person of interest in the case of the missing Biddlesworth. When the police dropped the case for lack of evidence, he left town. He was last heard from in California. A footnote linked to an article on Hedda Hagen Ringling. Out of curiosity, Charity clicked on it.

Mable Ringling, first wife of John Ringling, died in 1929. John Ringling met Hedda Hagen, a wealthy socialite, in New York and married her the following year. By all accounts, the marriage was a rocky one, and Ringling served her with divorce papers in 1933 and again in 1934. They were divorced in 1936.

The article did not mention Hedda's brother. *Poor lady, to have a brother under suspicion of murder probably didn't enhance her relations with her husband.* Hagen. *Hmm.* Could he have murdered Biddlesworth and dumped him in the pit?

The office manager tapped her on the shoulder. "It's six o'clock, Charity. Aren't you going home?"

"Oh my, I didn't notice the time. Thanks, Violet." Charity turned off the computer and gathered her things. Waving at her boss, she ran down the stairs to her car.

Her cell phone went off as she unlocked the door to her apartment. She clicked it on. "Hello?"

"Hello. Charity? Can you hear me? I'm on one of those pre-paid phones."

"You're floating in and out. Let me go out on the balcony. The reception's usually better there." She stepped outside. A gull landed on the railing and eyed her suggestively. She shooed it away. "Can you hear me better now?"

"Yes…Um, I just wanted to let you know I arrived safely."

"In Paris?"

"Yes—I told you I was coming here."

"Well, I'm not sure what to believe anymore."

"A bit testy this evening, aren't we?"

She could hardly tell him she was jealous, so she settled for, "Sorry, I'm tired. What do you want?"

"Besides you?"

"Ha ha."

"That's all—just checking in. I meet with the local *polizei* tomorrow. I have located Isabella."

"Isabella?"

"Isabella Voleuse—my editor."

"Ah yes. I suppose that's her stage name."

"As a matter of fact, she did do a stint on Broadway as an understudy."

"Tell me it was for Ethel Merman."

"No, actually, it was for Daryl Hannah."

"So…she's beautiful?" *Remember Mother's dictum—don't ask questions you don't want the answer to.*

"I can't help it, Charity. She is in fact quite good-looking. It's what misled me in the first place. She's also exceedingly intelligent and a very smooth talker."

It popped out of Charity's mouth before she could stop it. "And good in bed."

Rancor paused. "Yes."

"Oh. Well, I have to go. It's—"

"Charity. It's no use pretending you're not jealous.

I can hear it in your voice. There's no need to be. Remember, Isabella is a crook. I'm here to stop her from publishing my book. I'll be back as soon as I get my hands on her…I mean, it."

"O…kay." She breathed deeply, willing herself to let the hurt feelings go. When she felt calm enough, she went on. "I have a bit of news. I did some more research on the graduates."

"And?"

"I think we may be zeroing in on the identity of the body." She told him about Bartlesby, as well as Biddlesworth and Hagen.

"I'd pursue Bartlesby first. Did you try Costa Rica's mortuary records?"

"Excuse me?"

"Didn't you say his wife claimed he had decamped to that delightful country to avoid his financial obligations?" He paused. "Spent a month there once…ah, the cloud forest, the beaches, the girls…"

"You might be better…*equipped*…to deal with the Costa Rican authorities. Why don't I leave that one for you?"

He responded in what could have been—under less remote circumstances—a fatally enthusiastic tone. "Sure!"

To head off further salivation, Charity decided to share her discovery. "Noteworthy fact—Hagen was Hedda Ringling's brother."

"Hedda Ringling?"

"John Ringling's second wife. He married her after Mable died, but divorced her six years later."

"*Hmm*. I wonder if there's a connection to Ringling in all this? Wouldn't that be something?"

"I don't see how. Calvin Hagen strikes me as the typical bad boy brother who gets in constant trouble and is a trial to his relatives."

"You said Ringling divorced Hedda—could it have been because he'd had it with her sibling?"

"What would that have to do with Biddlesworth's murder? No, the way I see it, Hagen's deal with Biddlesworth went south, so he killed Biddlesworth and chucked his body in the shaft. That's why he was never found. Case closed."

"Why didn't he just roll him overboard?"

"Because, silly, he was never on the boat. Hagen arranged for the sail, and he went on it claiming to be Biddlesworth. He'd already killed the real Biddlesworth."

"You have this all figured out, don't you?"

She couldn't help but preen. "I do. Biddlesworth graduated from University of Maryland in 1931. He married Edna Gwendolyn—there's your G. He went to Florida after college and disappeared in 1933. Ta da."

"What kind of deal were Biddlesworth and Hagen working on?"

"Some kind of real estate thing."

"Find out more about it. And check into the nature of Hedda's relationship with her brother. After all, Ringling was heavily into real estate at the time. You know he built St. Armands Circle and the Gulf of Mexico Drive?"

"No. Really?" She hoped the sarcasm would ooze through cyberspace and flick his ear lobe.

"Yup. You should know this stuff, Charity. He started buying up land and promoting the area in 1911, including parts of all the keys. If your grandparents had played their cards right, they could have purchased a bungalow in the Ringling Isles Estates."

"If they'd been built. They suffered the same fate as the Ghost Hotel."

"Well, there is that." Rancor was quiet for a minute. "I read somewhere that he used his circus elephants to build the causeway."

"Wow—where was PETA when we needed them?"

"Hey—it was good work for good pay. A bushel of carrots every morning, plus a shower massage administered by your own personal mahout, and all the peanuts you can eat. By the way, did you check 1932 University of Maine graduates?"

"Yes. Roger P. Brewster disappeared into the wilds of Alaska, and your grandfather apparently did nothing significant whatsoever."

"Really? That would be a first for our family. "

"Every family has a bit of dead wood. In the case of the Basses…"

"You were going to say?"

"It goes without saying."

"Well, after that remark I won't tell you how much I adore you. In fact, I'm rethinking this whole marriage thing."

"What marriage thing?"

"My God, woman, don't you ever listen?"

Charity gulped. "Tell me again."

"I can't. I'm out of francs—or is it euros? Anyway, call you tomorrow." She heard a click, and the line went dead.

Chapter Seven
The Jailbird

The next day being Saturday, Charity slept in. Once a week, she would indulge herself by doing nothing—not walking, not writing, not mooning. Over the years, she'd spent a lot of time mooning. There was Kip, her first boyfriend. They went steady in sixth grade, and he taught her sign language. That, and the time her mother caught her with her hair down while he ran his fingers through it, was the sum total of Kip's legacy. Then came Axel, the high school football star. As a total geek, Charity couldn't believe her luck. A tight end! She could still feel the scar in her heart when he sat her down and earnestly explained that she was too smart for him and they had to break up. She had never been sure if he meant it as an insult or a compliment. After that, she gave up on finding a man who didn't think she was either too intelligent or too weird.

Then came George. He scooped her up after her parents died and put her to work at his paper. He recognized the talent in her—and more importantly, her insatiable curiosity. "That's what I need in a reporter, Charity. I want a terrier, a bloodhound, a nose-to-the-ground badger."

"So…you want a vicious, bloodthirsty animal?"

"Not *blood*thirsty—news-thirsty. You're a natural,

Charity. You won't let a story go. And you don't care where it leads."

That had been five years ago. She'd had several offers since then—from the *Tampa Bay Times* and the *Miami Herald*, among others. She'd kept the email from the *Chicago Tribune* asking for her resume and reread it now and then when she needed encouragement, but something kept her here on Longboat Key. *Not my parents, surely.* If pressed, however, she had to admit that whenever some big-city paper made noises about luring her away, she'd find herself on the path to Quick Point Preserve, staring into the water at New Pass, reliving the nightmare dawn when the police called her with the news.

They're still here, I know it. Watching over me. Missing me. Her lips turned up. *Maybe they could watch over little Tommy T too, poor kid.*

Charity rose from the bed and padded toward the shower. Out the window, black billowy clouds raced across the sky. *West to east. They'll pass over.* She knew the sky well—a useful skill, since Longboat Key experienced weather significantly different from the mainland, or even Tampa Bay. The meteorologist would predict heavy downpours and residents would scramble indoors, only to have the storms skip over the island entirely.

As she was toweling off, the phone rang.

"Charity? It's George. Are you up?"

"Yes."

"Kelly let Standish have the skeletons, and the great man has deigned to send a final report, which I hold in my formerly ink-stained hands. He may be a jackass, Charity, but he's very thorough. We know quite a bit about the adult skeleton—even without his teeth. Can you come in?"

"It's Saturday!"

"And your point?"

Sigh. "I'll be there in twenty."

After dressing and stopping at Olaf's for a sandwich and a bottle of seltzer, she trudged up the stairs to the *Planet* office.

George was poring over a file. "You certainly took your time. Never mind, *I've* got all day." When she spun around and headed out the door he yelled, "Wait! Come have a look."

Charity set down her seltzer and took a big bite out of the sandwich. Egg salad dribbling from the corner of her mouth, she said, "Just tell me."

"Okay. The subject was indeed an adult male in his twenties, Caucasian, probably highly active sexually."

"How on earth do they know that?"

"The pubic bones are super thick, indicating an unusually large penis, and there's some wear on them, indicating heavy use." He grinned wickedly. "Who said forensics couldn't be titillating?"

Charity thought of her well-endowed lover. *Maybe we should take another look at Robert Bass...*"That's not really going to help in identification, is it? I mean, we'll hardly find corroboration of his...measurements in any news source."

George seemed disappointed. "I guess not."

"What else?"

"There's no sign of disease, but discoloration on the inside of the ribs may mean he had a lot of fluid in his lungs when he died. And he stayed wet for a long time. Standish says if he were immersed in water, it likely took longer than usual for him to decompose."

Biddlesworth and the boat ride.

"According to him, it could have been weeks. The stench must have been awful."

Charity put down her sandwich. "*Urk.*"

George didn't seem to notice her reaction. "But if he were interred in the thirties, it wouldn't have mattered, since the hotel was abandoned at that point—and stayed that way until 1963. Let's see…what else?" He flipped some pages. "Over six feet tall, he'd had a couple of concussions at some point and was probably married."

"Married! How did Standish figure that out?"

"Indentation on the third finger of the left hand. The doctor says it indicates pressure had been applied over a fairly significant period, causing a stress fracture at the joint. Ring was probably too tight." He looked up. "He asked if one had been found at the site."

Charity took a large swallow of seltzer. "Um…was there?"

"Not that I'm aware of. It's something to ask Kelly." He closed the file. "How's your column coming?"

She hadn't had time to recover from her anxiety attack, which included a vision of herself in a prison jumpsuit and leg chains, so she barely mouthed, "I'll do it today. Later." She skipped to the door.

"Where are you going?"

"Home."

"Oh, by the way, where's Bass? Haven't seen him for days. Not that I miss him—he ain't an easy person to work with. Plus, with this skeleton story to wrap up we don't need him underfoot making demands, now, do we?"

Charity reflected that she would most definitely like to have him under her but refrained from saying it out loud. "He's out of town for a few days." The words depressed her even more.

"Oh? I thought he was a little short in the funds department."

The old reporter still has a nose. For a minute, Charity toyed with the idea of not telling George, but it seemed pointless to keep the information from him. At least some of it. "You were right. He's writing this ghost book to make a quick buck." *While waiting for Sugar Mama to cough up?*

"What, running out of Dom Pérignon?"

"Something like that." She left quickly before he could inquire further.

She spent the rest of the day at the beach. Sunday dawned cloudy and chilly, so she did all the errands she'd been putting off. When she got home, she found Jane sitting on the umbrella stand by her door. "You forgot, didn't you?"

"Forgot?"

"Our lunch date. We were going to St. Armands today. I've been dying to try that new Greek place, Samos Nights. Don't tell me you can't make it?"

Lunch. Chat. Confession. "Of course I didn't forget. By the way, George called me down to read Standish's report."

"Report?"

"Ah, I can see you need updating. Let me change, and we'll head down."

"Hup to, I didn't get any breakfast."

They settled into a booth in the empty restaurant

and ordered retsina—"You'll like it, miss. Is Greek wine."

"Thank you, Costas." Jane unfolded her napkin. "So, the collaboration with the hunk is on hold?"

"For now. But he's...helping me with the skeleton story."

"He is? You two an item? Wow."

"No, no! He's not even in town now."

Her distress must have clanged through her words, for Jane gave her a sudden pat. "You like him, don't you?"

Charity took the glass from the waiter and sniffed. Her nose wrinkled—probably not charmingly. "What *is* this stuff?"

"Retsina. It's wine flavored with resin. It grows on you."

"Yes, like fungus...or mold. It smells like something left out in the hot sun too long." She put the glass down. "Could I have a glass of"—she ran her eye quickly over the list—"Roditis please?"

The young man shot her a look of mingled disappointment and admiration. "Right away, miss. Are you ready to order?"

Charity looked over the menu. "You know what you want, Jane?"

"I've memorized the online menu. I'm having the mezze plate and then shish kebab. How about you?"

"Oh look, they have *saganaki*. Isn't that the cheese flamed with brandy? That's yummy. I'll have that and...a Greek salad." Costas took their menus and trotted off to the kitchen.

Jane winked. "So where is lover boy?"

"Paris." Charity's shoulders sagged.

"Paris! *Hmm.* I suppose he's one of those F. Scott Fitzgerald types—very sophisticated, with a delicate palate and his own gondola."

"Actually, he's flat broke." *I think.*

"Surely you jest. I assumed he was raking in the royalties. He should've made enough off me alone to buy a private island."

"That would be true, except that his editor has absconded with the office petty cash. He's in France looking for her."

"Her?" Jane's eyes brightened.

Charity answered wearily. "Yes, her. Apparently, she's beautiful, articulate, and brilliant."

"And good in bed."

Sigh. "According to Rancor, yes."

"Oh dear. Well, not to worry—whoever she is, she can't hold a candle to you, my dear."

Basking in the glow of friendship, Charity didn't hear the waiter come up behind her, douse a plate with brandy, and light it. All she heard was a whoosh, followed by the aroma of singed hair. Costas gasped and dropped the plate on the tile floor, smashing it to bits. As he tried to smother the sparks still scintillating in her braid, he gabbled, "Oh, miss, I'm *so* sorry. Here—" He stuck a napkin in her water glass and dabbed at her head.

"Stop that!"

In response, his eyes filled with tears. He stepped back, whirled, and ran to the kitchen. In the sudden silence, Jane hiccupped. "Too funny."

Charity glared at her. "I begin to see why we're the only patrons."

Jane looked embarrassed. "It *has* gotten a few

reviews—mostly devastating—but I love Greek food, and it's the only one around. I'm sure they're just working out the kinks."

"They could start by training the staff."

Jane pointed an admonishing finger at Charity. "You're the one who made him cry."

At that moment, the waiter returned with another plate. This time he stood a full five feet away to light the cheese. He pushed it toward her and jumped back. All three people stared at the flames, Costas apparently mesmerized. Finally, Charity reached out and pinched him. He pitched forward and slammed the cover onto the plate, knocking a few chips off.

That did the trick, and the flames were out when he removed it. Everyone breathed a sigh of relief. Charity took a tentative bite. "After all that, it's pretty good."

"Here, try some *taramasalata*." Jane spooned a dollop of thick, granular, pinkish paste onto Charity's plate.

"What is it?"

"It's fish roe. From the gray mullet, I believe. They whip it with mayonnaise and lemon. It's wonderful."

Charity agreed and polished off her share and most of Jane's. As she mopped up the last of her salad with a chunk of bread, Jane fixed her friend with a gimlet eye. "So, our Lothario has traipsed off to France for a fling with his editor."

"No, it's not like that! He says she's been stealing the submissions of several authors and publishing them under a pseudonym."

"That's piracy."

"Duh."

Jane swirled the wine in her glass, her eyes

meditative. "Illegal enterprises that are lucrative tend to attract the wrong sort of people."

"You mean criminals."

"Uh huh. So…Rancor Bass went galloping off on his white horse to apprehend the wicked queen and bring her to justice."

"Well, when you put it like that…Look, she's usurped his reputation, not to mention future royalties."

"Why doesn't he just go to the police?"

"He is. He said he was meeting with the Paris police today."

"Today? You've talked to him recently?" She peered at Charity. "Is this relationship by any chance serious?"

Charity took a big swig of wine. "*Mmmph.*"

Jane gave her a long, hard look but said merely, "Okay, tell me what's going on with our skeletons."

"You heard about that?"

Her tone was dry. "It was in the paper. A column penned by…wait a minute. By you."

"I forgot. Yes, I'm working on a second installment." She told Jane about Standish's findings.

"Married, huh. It's amazing what they can glean from a pile of bones. Did they find the ring? That might provide a clue."

How does she get so disturbingly close so quickly? "Um…no…but…I did."

Jane's jaw dropped. "You found the ring? You went snooping around the crime scene and stole *evidence?*"

"Well…not exactly." Her voice dropped to a whisper. "Rancor did."

"Why?"

Charity signaled the waiter. "Another glass of wine, please." She didn't look at Jane. "Because…actually, I'm not sure. He just picked it up and pocketed it."

"You did point out that in some circles such a stunt is considered a felony?"

"I did. He was—we were—caught up in the adventure, I guess." She gulped. "He thinks the dead man may be his grandfather."

"His *grandfather*?"

"Yes. See, the ring has an inscription, 'To RB from G,' and the year 1931. It's a class ring."

"How do you know?"

"It looks like one—you know? Heavy gold, stone in the middle. On the sides are the letters *U* and *M*."

"So you think the dead man graduated in 1931 from a school with those letters, had a girlfriend whose name begins with G, and his initials are RB?"

"That pretty much sums it up. Except that he could have graduated in 1932."

"1932? Why? No, wait." She shook her head as though to clear it. "Let's set that aside for now. Any luck finding such a needle?"

"As in, in a haystack? Yes, as a matter of fact. Rancor found nine schools, but we've narrowed it down to two. University of Maine and University of Maryland."

"Not bad. Tell me about them."

Charity told her about Bartlesby, Biddlesworth, and Hagen, and about Robert Bass III. "We haven't done much research on the University of Maine yet, except for calls to Rancor's Aunt Gertrude."

Jane signaled for the check. "Gotta be

Biddlesworth. Everything fits. Even to the watery grave."

"But if the ring inscription doesn't refer to the class year…"

"You'll find it's Biddlesworth—mark my words." She took out her wallet. "Still, I'm a bit concerned about Light-Fingered Louie."

"You mean Rancor?"

"Yes. Why did he steal the ring? Was it the reflex action of a seasoned thief? Is he writing a new book? Or is there some as yet undiscovered motive…" She trailed off, chin in hand.

Charity's cell phone went off. "Hello?"

"Charity, are you alone?"

"No, Rancor." She stood up. Jane cocked her head.

"Well, get rid of whatever current suitor is mauling you and listen to me."

She trotted out of the restaurant. "Okay. I'm—" All she heard was a click and a buzz. "Hello? Hello?"

Jane arrived on the sidewalk. "You didn't have to run out on me. I told you lunch was on me. *Sheesh.*" She caught sight of Charity's face. "What's the matter? The great man hang up on you?"

"He did. I wonder why?"

"Hot date?"

"No. It sounded as though he had something important to tell me, but by the time I got out here, he'd hung up." She turned to Jane with worried eyes. "I hope he's all right."

"He strikes me as the type who always floats to the surface alive."

"Maybe." She clicked the phone on, then off. "I forgot. I have no number for him."

"Doesn't it show on your phone?"

"No, he has one of those disposable phones."

Jane whistled. "Oh, sister, he's a sly one. I suggest you back off as quick as you can before you get burned." She tittered. "Leave that to the professionals like our Costas."

Charity was quiet on the return journey. Jane seemed to be thoughtful as well. They parted at Charity's complex. "Keep me in the loop, will you?"

"Sure." Charity went in and lay down to review the day but found herself focused solely on Rancor. *Why did he call? Or rather, what was so important that he called in the middle of the day? How did he sound? Worried? Frightened?* She sighed in frustration. The call had been so short—almost as though it were cut off. *Is he in trouble?* She rose and went to her desk.

Outside, dark clouds streamed over the gulf, bearing the usual late afternoon storms. A group of painfully white adults in crisp new surfer shorts sprayed sunscreen on each other while their pack of small children played at the water's edge. They would break off now and then to point at the lightning that splintered the sky like shattered glass. Charity was on the verge of leaning out to advise them to get their crap and their butts inside, when she reconsidered. *Now there's a headline—Lightning Incinerates Iowa Family on Beach—Spooked Tourists Deserting Longboat.* This could be a godsend.

She went through the disorderly pile of paper scraps on her night table, hoping to find Rancor's note pad in case he'd scribbled the name of his hotel on it. No luck. *I'm just going to have to wait to hear from him.* She consoled herself that her imagination was running amok. *Probably the champagne had arrived, that's all.*

Three hours later, she was back on the bed staring at the ceiling. A beam of red light shot through her window. *Sunset already?* She got up, fixed herself a drink, and took it to the balcony. She watched as the sun sank unwillingly—long, needle-like pincers of light stretching out as though they wanted to hook the horizon and hang on for dear life. Whatever was pulling from below won the battle and the sun dipped, leaving its signature green flash as a token of affection for the world.

Restless, Charity paced from the balcony to the living room. *Why doesn't he call? What did he want? Is he ill?* Wait—he was going to meet with the police today. Did they believe his story? He'd said other authors were involved. Why hadn't they gone in a body to confront the thief? Why did he go alone? A horrible thought intruded. *Has he reconciled with Isabella? Does he want to break up with me?*

The questions flew around getting in each other's way until she felt dizzy. *Maybe a walk on the beach.* She took off her sandals and walked out to the water. The sanderlings and plovers ran back and forth at the low tide mark stuffing their bills with mole crabs. As the water rushed away from the shore, the tiny coquinas gasped in panic, rattling like castanets as they frantically dug into the sand. A puff of air cooled her face. She went north as far as a strip of beach bordered by several large mansions. Inhabited for only a month or so in high season, their darkened, hulking shapes loomed over the dunes. *They look like zombies marching to the sea.* She hunched her shoulders and turned around.

The telephone rang as she walked up the outside steps. She ran in and grabbed the receiver as it went to the dial tone. "Damn!" She sat by the phone waiting. A minute later, it rang again. "Hello! Hello!"

"Charity?"

She dropped onto the sofa. "Oh, Rancor, are you all right?"

His voice tentative, he mumbled, "Um, not really. Do you think you could round up five hundred dollars—in francs—to post bond? ASAP?"

"Bond! What for?"

"I'm...um...in jail."

Chapter Eight
Paris Follies

Charity dropped the phone. After picking it up and waiting for the panicky breaths to slow, she said as calmly as she could, "Before I shell out any more money, you need to answer a few questions, mister."

"Fire away. It's funny—here in France I'm allowed not one but two phone calls."

"I presume your first one was to the American embassy."

"That's next on my list. This may come as a surprise to you, but I so longed to hear your voice that I decided to check in with you first. Get the money ball rolling, as it were."

"It's always about money, isn't it?"

"Well, in this case, it's pretty crucial. The French police may be enlightened as to telephone communications, but not so much about accommodations. So what do you say?"

"I say, get on the horn to the embassy without ado."

He was silent for a minute. Finally, he said gently, "Don't you want to hear what happened?"

"Let me guess. You were caught *in flagrante delicto* with a beautiful fugitive from justice."

"Not at all. My heart is true. I've been faithful to you even if you don't deserve it."

Charity decided to let that pass—and maybe revisit it later at her leisure. "Tell me then."

"Well, said beautiful fugitive managed to turn the tables on me. I found her, but instead of consenting to come along quietly, she screamed bloody murder. In a performance worthy of Sarah Bernhardt—you know who she was, don't you? The greatest actress of her age. The Divine Sarah. Why, her Tosca was emulated by thousands of would-be swans. I—"

"What did she claim?"

"Who? Oh, Isabella? That I—Rancor Bass, author of eleven wildly acclaimed books—had stolen *her* manuscript! The gall of the woman." He subsided into incoherent rumblings.

"And?"

"And since this is France, the gendarmes refrained from asking any searing questions for fear of injuring the nymphette's fragile sensibilities. They swallowed her line without so much as a tittle of qualm and arrested me. It's appalling, really. These chaps are totally sexist. Chauvinist dinosaurs…"

"What do you want me to do?"

"Well, I'd love the money as soon as you can send it. How's that done nowadays? They used to say 'I'll wire it,' but I'm pretty sure technology has moved on. No matter, that was five hundred if you recall. I guess I can exchange it here—ooh, I just thought of something. It's euros, isn't it? Not francs. What a shame…this Eurozone crap has got to stop. It's ruining all the color and spice of Europe. Did you know French farmers can't sell cheese that isn't pasteurized? Criminal."

"Rancor? Have you by any chance not eaten in a while?"

"What? No, *la bonne femme*—that's 'wife' to you Yankees—of Monsieur le Brigadier Dumont provided me with a cheese omelet and a Picardie glass of a refreshing Sancerre. Her name is Antoinette. A very warmhearted woman."

I'll bet she is. "All right, then why are you babbling?"

"I think it's the cell walls—so close, so confining. They're beginning to get to me. Did I ever mention I have claustrophobia? I'm trying to fend it off with logorrhea."

"Logo...what?"

"Logorrhea. It's like diarrhea except with words rather than...well, you know."

Let's just skip on ahead. "All right, I'll see about the money. Who do I send it to?"

"My lawyer—a Monsieur Carotte. Hang on, let me find his email address...here it is. Carotte-at-AubergineCarotteAsperge-dot-com. That's all one word. Do you want me to spell it?"

"No, I've got it. Wait—you have a *lawyer?* Why do you need me?"

"He was assigned by the judge. He doesn't care about me the way you do, Charity. In fact, he actually hooted when I suggested he bail me out. Like a hyena, not like an owl. Most unsettling."

"How do you know he won't keep the money?"

"Oh dear, I hadn't thought of that. Just a minute." From a distance, she heard a dialogue in rapid French. Rancor came back on the line. "The officer has kindly offered to take custody of the funds. Send it to Brigadier Raoul Dumont, in care of the Commissariat de Police, eighth arrondissement, one Avenue du

General Eisenhower, Paris, 75008. Got it?"

"All right. I'll do it first thing tomorrow."

"Tomorrow! Can't you do it tonight? It's not exactly Shangri-La here."

"What time is it there?"

More French. "Dumont informs me it is three o'clock in the morning. So it's tomorrow."

"Well, it isn't tomorrow here. You'll get the money when you get it." When he didn't answer, she said sweetly, "Do call me when you get out."

"Will do," he whispered, his voice tight. "You're a saint. I'll be at l'Hôtel Paris, 13 rue des Beaux Arts, Paris 75006. Number is 33-1-44-41-99-55."

"Hôtel Paris? Where's that? By the train station?"

"No, dear. That's Hôtel de la Gare. It's *always* Hôtel de la Gare. L'Hôtel Paris is one of the most famous of all French hostelries. I'm shocked you don't know this."

"Rancor, I've never been to France. I've never even been to New York."

"Why, you sad, pathetic creature. While I still have you on the line, I shall tell you more. All kinds of famous people have rested their weary heads on the silken sheets of l'Hôtel, the most eminent being Oscar Wilde. I believe he breathed his last *bon mot* there. So naturally, it's the most suitable hotel for a wielder of clever phrases such as I, don't you think? Plus, it's a five-star and really rather special. Did you know its rooms are classified Mignon and Bijou? That tells you how precious it is."

Not having any response to this little speech, she said goodbye and hung up.

An hour later, money having been sent and receipt

confirmed, she went to bed, resolved to force the little reptile to confess just how he managed to bunk in a five-star hotel and yet still had to borrow bail money.

****

"Did I wake you?"

"No, Rancor. I've been waiting for your call. Are you free?"

"From the slammer? For the nonce. Um...thanks for the money. I'll pay you back, I promise."

"I'm not worried. I have Aunt Gertrude's number."

"You wouldn't."

Aha, a palpable hit. "I would. Now tell me what happened?"

"I will. Soon. Right now, I want you to do something for me."

"Something else? Rancor..."

"Hold on. I do need your help. If we can get this Isabella thing resolved, I'll get my royalties back, and I'll be flush. I shall take you to Michaels on East or Euphemia Haye. Or even Venice. Whatever you want. I'll shower you with candy and flowers and a diamond tiara. I'll—"

Charity cut through the torrent of promises. "What am I supposed to do?"

"Great. You won't regret it. Besides, it'll be fun."

I have my doubts.

When she didn't speak, he asked anxiously, "Charity? Are you still there?"

"Yes."

"Good. I have come to accept the fact that I must have backup if I'm going to make a credible case. That means enlisting my fellow sufferers."

"The other writers?"

"Yes. I told you that several have been treated as churlishly as I. I need them to come over here and testify. Or at least send depositions. Will you contact them for me?"

"Rancor, I do have a job, you know. And it's not as your personal assistant."

Dead silence reigned for a long minute. He finally said, "Okay," in a very subdued tone. Naturally, it worked like a charm.

"All right, what are their names?"

"You're a peach. First off is Atalanta L'Amour—she writes shapeshifter vampire erotica. You'll like her. Number is 212-555-6438." He waited for her to write it down. "Got that? Okay, next is Holdridge K. Wheelock, the essayist."

"Wheelock. Didn't he write that parody of *Zen and the Art of Motorcycle Maintenance*?"

"Yes and no. He didn't mean it to be tongue-in-cheek, and when it was roundly criticized as not zany enough, he took offense. He's at Dontugetsatireumoron-at-HoldridgeKWheelock-dot-com. I'd better spell that out." He did.

"Is that it?"

"No, two more. I want to descend on the French judicial system like an Ottoman horde. Besides, you may only pry one or two of them from their nests."

"Typical writers then?"

"Hey!"

"Names, please."

"All right, but you better promise to treat them with respect. And don't forget the kid gloves. Third is Jemimah Heartsleeve."

"Oh, I read one of hers. Not bad. What's that genre

of romance called? Something about steam."

"Steamy. Or did you mean steampunk? Yes, a reviewer back in the nineteen seventies told her she has a voice, and she's never let anyone forget it. However, when aroused, she's like a marmot with a bone, or whatever they gnaw. She lives in a hovel."

"A hovel?"

"Atalanta's assessment, not mine. That dyspeptic snob looks down her imperious nose at a house with a mere twenty rooms and only one indoor sunken garden. What's worse, it's in that bastion of rebel resistance, Charleston."

"A step up from a rusty beach chair, I'd say."

"Yes. Well. Her number is 843-555-2337…Ready? Last but not least is Bernard Guttersnipe (not his real name). Styles himself a modern progressive. In other words, he writes depressing novels with wholly unlikable characters and plots so vague you're not quite sure when the book is over. His email is nihilism-at-Guttersnipe-dot-com."

Charity whistled. "Bit of a motley crew, eh?"

"Hey, those are my friends you're maligning."

"So, what do I tell these friends?"

"That I tried to latch on to Isabella, and she is proving as slippery as expected. I need them to come stand by me or write a forceful letter to the judge."

"Did she steal their manuscripts as well as their royalties?"

"Yes, and has published two of them so far, although for the life of me I don't see why the review sites didn't smell a rat when they received a zombie ménage romance and a treatise on the role of carnivores in Buddhist theology by the same author."

Charity's stomach made its feelings known. "I'm hungry. I'll see what I can do with these names and get back to you, okay?"

"Great. You're a doll. Oh say, did you make any progress on the skeleton?"

"I haven't had time. It's still between Bartlesby and Biddlesworth. And maybe Bass."

"Biddlesworth's the one who drowned?"

"Yes. Standish said the victim had fluid in his lungs when he died."

"Standish did? When?"

"George got hold of his final report. There's evidence that the body lay in water for some time."

"So he may actually have been on the boat. So much for your hypothesis." He hummed tunelessly, then suddenly broke off. "Wait a minute! If he drowned, when or why was he stabbed?"

"Um." She tapped a pencil to help her think and finally decided to change the subject. "Interesting—his connection to the Ringlings."

"Yes. I believe I told you to look into it."

"Well, I'm sorry. I've been rather busy springing a man from the joint."

"And now you've got another assignment. Oh, here's room service. I'll let you go." He hung up.

Twit.

****

Four days later, Charity had reached only Holdridge K. Wheelock. He had graciously offered to write a letter, first asking if she set a limit on the word count. "I regret I cannot provide more personal support as I'm in the final edits of my latest treatise on exotic religions and the military." Apparently laboring under the assumption that she wished further clarification, he added, "It's the first-person account of a young man who converts to druidism during World War One and the somewhat mixed reactions from his platoon mates in the trenches of Chateau Thierry. Names changed to protect the innocent of course, but the message will undoubtedly resonate. Do give Rancor my best. To whom should I address the letter?"

She gave him the particulars. As she put down the receiver, she stared at her reflection in the hall mirror. *There's nothing for it but to go myself.* She pulled out her phone. "George? I need a few days off."

"Unless we're being evacuated, I don't think so."

"I want to go to Paris."

"Oh, that's okay then. *Not.*"

"To fetch Rancor Bass back."

"From Paris? What's he doing there?"

"*Um.*" She had a flash of inspiration. "I don't know, but he took the ghost story manuscript with him."

A pregnant pause followed this announcement, followed in turn by a period of heavy breathing. Finally, George growled, "Okay, but I'm only covering the airfare. And I want you back before next edition's deadline."

"Sure."

"You still have that passport you got when we thought we were going to Russia for the Olympics, right?"

"Of course I do." She booted up the computer and clicked on a travel website. One flight left from Tampa the following afternoon. She made the reservation and called the number Rancor had given her. The hotel concierge answered.

"Monsieur Bass is away from his room at present. He informed us that he would return tomorrow."

"Where did he go?"

"I'm unable to disclose that information."

"Was he with a woman?"

The man hesitated. "Yes."

"Who goes by the name of Isabella Voleuse?"

"I regret, mademoiselle, but I'm unable to provide you with that information either."

Damn. "All right. I'd like to make a reservation for Saturday night."

Again he hesitated but finally said, "Yes, of course. And how long will you be staying with us?"

"Indefinitely."

"I see." He took down her information. "Would you like me to apprise Mr. Bass of your impending arrival?"

"Yes. Tell him the flight comes in at seven a.m., and I expect him to meet me." *That should scare the daylights out of him.*

"Certainly, mademoiselle. We at L'Hôtel Paris look forward to your visit."

She hung up. *Now where did I put that passport?*

****

Rancor was not at the terminal when Charity arrived. She caught a taxi that took her to the Left Bank and St. Germain des Prés, then up the rue du Seine to the rue des Beaux Arts. The driver let her off in front of what would have been a rather nondescript building were it not for the very un-nondescript bronze ram's head guarding the entrance. Charity slipped under it quickly and entered an atrium that opened—six floors above—to the sky. A spiral staircase snaked around its walls.

The concierge greeted her with some trepidation. "I do apologize, Mademoiselle Snow. Monsieur Bass did not return last night. I sent a car to Charles de Gaulle to pick you up, but you had already left in a taxi."

"That is all right, Mister…er…uh…"

"Monsieur Atlas, at your service."

Oh God, how much of that eighth-grade French am I going to remember? Or need? "I'm sure you did your best."

He whistled to one of the bell hops and sent her luggage up with him. "We have put you in our Mistinguett room. I hope you will find it cozy." He crooked a finger at the other bell hop. "Jean-Pierre will show you the way."

The boy took her up in an old-fashioned iron elevator cage and down a narrow hall. He opened a door, revealing a room filled with sleek, mirrored furniture. In a charmingly accented voice, he said, "It is decorated in the art deco manner according to the tastes of Mademoiselle Mistinguett." A king-sized bed piled high with silk-covered pillows sat on a raised platform.

Charity could imagine a courtesan lounging on it, pink tongue peeping through rouged lips, inviting her current lover—a minor aristocrat—to a night of passion. "And who was Mistinguett?"

He shrugged, as only a boy of sixteen would to whom anything over twenty is old. "A singer, I believe."

When he had gone, Charity went through to a sumptuous marble bathroom. The sink held toiletries by Green and Spring. A thick, white robe hung from a hook. She ordered room service and sat by the window, watching the city awaken. The croissants were flaky, the butter richly yellow, and the cherry preserves thick and tart. She began to relax. *Maybe I'll just take a little nap before I go out and explore.*

She lay down on the bed, the satin sheets rustling under her hair.

The telephone woke her. "Mademoiselle Snow? I have Monsieur Bass on the line. Will you take the call?"

She rubbed her eyes and looked at the clock. Two? The sun was bright outside, but the city quiet. *Oh yes, the long lunch.* "Hello?"

"Charity! You're here! Why didn't you tell me you were coming?"

His mellow tenor filled her insides and spilled over. "I did. I left message after message. Where have you been?"

"The question is rather, where am I now?"

"Whatever."

"You're not going to like it."

"Try me."

"Um. Er. London."

She could barely hear him. "Did you say *London*?"

"Um. Yes. See, Isabella scarpered to London while I was distracted."

"Distracted? By what?"

"Never mind that. I'm about to meet her at the Victoria and Albert Museum—although she doesn't know it."

"Rancor, you *are* aware you skipped bail? I'm sure that's as much an offense here as it is in the States."

"Don't worry, it won't be a problem. As soon as I

get her signed confession, I'll be back. Then, whether or not my friends substantiate my claims, I'll win the day."

He sounded so pleased with himself she almost hadn't the heart to tell him what a nincompoop he was, but she girded her loins and bit the bullet. "You're a chump, Rancor Bass."

"I beg to differ. Say, did you bring any of the ragamuffins with you?"

"No. I couldn't get hold of anyone but Mr. Wheelock. He promised to fire off an irate letter to the Paris police."

"Well, it couldn't hurt...Look, I've got to go. Sit tight, and I'll be back before you can say 'jailbird.' "

Charity decided to take a walk along the quai de Conti. The city had begun to wake up on this dreary January afternoon. A damp wind blew old newspapers into little piles. The river was gray and choppy. She watched a Bateau Mouche chug along, tourists pointing and shouting as they passed under the Pont Neuf and caught sight of the Cathedral of Notre Dame in the distance. A small café near the Bibliothèque Mazarine provided a tiny cup of coffee and a cheese-filled crêpe for little more than it would have cost to buy a house in North Dakota. She mused on the vagaries of life. *I'm sitting on a sidewalk in Paris—number one on my bucket list for so many years.* The scene had usually included someone else though. Someone warm, generous, thoughtful. Someone wholly unlike Rancor Bass. *Who isn't here anyway.*

She paid the bill and returned to the hotel. With nothing else to do, she decided to explore the public areas. The bar, a pocket-sized room paneled in mahogany and reached through a colonnade of green marble columns, was deserted but for the bartender. "*Bonjour, mademoiselle.* I am Philippe. May I concoct a libation for you?"

Charity was still trying to translate his English words into ones she understood when he pushed a glass filled with a lavender-colored liquid across the highly polished surface to her.

She sipped. "Delicious. What is it?"

"My signature cocktail. I call it a Thirteen-S. I mix champagne with a dash of violet liqueur and a bit of lime zest." He smiled proudly as she finished it in two swallows. "Have you taken a swim in our *hammam* yet, mademoiselle?"

"*Hammam*? What's that?"

"Oh, it is Turkish for bath. We have a beautiful subterranean pool. If you like, I'll make a reservation for you with the concierge."

"I can't just go down and swim?"

"Oh, no, mademoiselle. We light candles around the coping, and you have it all to yourself. That is, unless you have a significant other person with which to share it?"

She tried to speak lightly, even though something gnawed at her heart. "Not yet, Philippe. Someday though."

He winked at her. "When you are ready, think of me!"

"Thank you." She wandered out toward the restaurant. Elegant velvet armchairs flanked side tables. Through French doors, she could see a fountain and a patio garden. *All very fin-de-siècle.* She sighed. *Maybe I'll just take another nap...*

The elevator clanked its way to the fourth floor. As she entered her room, the sun dropped behind the roofs of Paris and church bells began to peal all over the city. For a glorious instant, they were the only sound before the inevitable car horns started up again. She sighed. "On the other hand, a swim might be restorative."

She called down to the desk. "Is the *hammam* available?"

"Yes, indeed, mademoiselle. I will have it set up right away."

She checked her suitcase. "Oh dear, I didn't bring a bathing suit."

"*Ne vous inquiétez pas*, mademoiselle. I will have an assortment brought up for you."

A few minutes later, Charity faced a smiling bellhop and a bed covered with tiny bikinis. He held up a platinum-colored string with a triangular patch about two inches across. "This one is very nice, Mademoiselle Snow. It would go beautifully with your eyes." He winked at her. "They remind one of the silver fox, *n'est-ce pas? Sauvages, mais aussi beaux.*"

"My eyes? Savage but beautiful? You are too poetic, Jean-Pierre." Charity silently thanked her French teacher for all those vocabulary quizzes. She took the bikini from his outstretched hand. "Thank you. That will be all."

"I shall await you outside to escort you to our *piscine.*"

"Thank you." Charity put on the suit and covered it with the terry bathrobe. The boy took her down the elevator to a crypt-like alcove faced with old stone. Through a glass door, she glimpsed a steam room tiled in blue glass. Candles had been lit around the edge of the pool, and the sapphirine water beckoned. Charity slipped in and floated on her back, letting the warm water soothe her.

"They couldn't find a Victorian bathing costume for you?"

She raised her head. "Rancor?"

"The one, the only. Monsieur Atlas said I might find you here in the seraglio." Rancor undid the towel around his waist, revealing a tan, fit torso with a long white scar running down the right side. Keeping his eyes on Charity, he dropped his trunks and slid into the water.

A while later, she pulled herself onto the ladder and tried to catch her breath. "Wow. There's something to be said for your own private pool."

Rancor rose beside her. "Indeed. Do you suppose if I clap my hands, musicians will appear, followed by voluptuous maidens bearing grapes and wine?"

Charity ran her palm over the water's surface. "Are you telling me you're not satisfied by my recent efforts?"

He kissed her. "A little *lagniappe* is always in good taste. So are grapes."

She climbed out of the pool and slung a towel around her. "I'm going to my room."

"In a huff?"

"No, in a towel."

"Which is yours?"

"My what?"

"Your room. Each of the twenty rooms is devoted to a particular artist or celebrity. I'm—of course—in Oscar Wilde's room."

"Of course."

"It's decorated with dunning notices from the hotel. He said he'd die before he'd fork over his last *sou*, and he did."

"Die? Here?" She gave a little shudder.

"In the very room. Say—that could go in the ghost story book."

"Perhaps another one. May I remind you that you're supposed to be working on Florida ghosts only? No exceptions."

He climbed out. She couldn't help but touch his chest. "How did you get that scar?"

He held the towel over it, his eyes shifting over her head. "Never mind."

She had never heard him use that tone before—a blend of regret, shame, and fury. She let her hand fall.

After a minute, he asked, "So, which room did they give you? The Mata Hari? The Leopard room?"

"I believe Monsieur Atlas called it the Mistinguett room."

He goggled at her. "There's a Mistinguett room? How marvelous!"

She pressed the elevator button. "Why? Who or what is Mistinguett?"

"She was a music hall star—at one point the highest paid female entertainer in the world. By all accounts, worth more than even Gypsy Rose Lee. She played the Casino de Paris, the Folies Bergère, and the Moulin Rouge. I believe she even starred in some silent films."

"And she lived here in the Hôtel Paris?"

"It appears so. Say, do you mind if I come look at it?"

"Not at all." *What a dumb question.*

She unlocked the door, and he sidled in. "I forgot their rooms are either *mignon* or *bijou*—both of which mean painfully small."

She retorted, "I believe it's a category *chic. Much* larger than the *bijou* rooms." *And more expensive.*

Rancor picked up a small card. "It says here the bed and dresser belonged to Mistinguett herself."

Charity surveyed the bed with sudden doubt. "I wish I'd read that before taking my nap. I wonder how many 'gentlemen' left their spoor on it?"

"I'm sure they've changed the mattress at least once since then." He took her hand. "Come with me."

"Where to?"

"To Oscar's death chamber."

"A bit macabre."

"As I meant to be."

Rancor's room was bigger than Charity's and had a balcony. "It's partially decorated like Wilde's dining room in England. How do you like the peacock frieze? I think the decorator confused John Singer Sargent with Oscar Wilde. But then, they *were* friends. Now"—he sat her on the bed—"I shall order room service. We'll sit on my balcony, and I shall beguile you with tales of my exploits while we partake of a small repast."

Charity went to the door.

"Where are you going?"

"To change." She blew him a kiss. "I'll be back in half an hour."

When she returned, a small cart covered in a white tablecloth and gleaming silver took up most of the center of the room. Rancor was opening a bottle of champagne. "Let's go outside." He wheeled the cart out onto the balcony. Charity leaned over the parapet to watch the people and cars far below. A man on the sidewalk turned chestnuts over a hibachi. The comfy, Christmasy smell rose on wisps of smoke to her nostrils. Another man hawked cut halves of coconut from a tinkling fountain.

Rancor handed her a flute.

Now's my chance. "Rancor, how are you paying for all this?"

"Never ask the cost of things, my dear. It's not ladylike."

"But—"

He raised his voice, drowning her out. "I took the liberty of ordering because I know what you want."

"Whatever." Charity wasn't really in the mood to press, mainly because she was ravenous.

He whipped a silver dome off, revealing a platter of bright green asparagus napped with a cream sauce. He broke off a chunk of baguette and handed it to her. She dipped it in the sauce. Her eyes opened wide. "Why, it's fish!"

"Unusual combination of flavors, isn't it? It's made with haddock, garnished with garlic and razor clams. A specialty of the chef."

She polished it off and looked at the other covered dishes. "Next?"

"Ah—you'll love this one. I could have gone with something really mundane like steak *au poivre*—except that the chef refused to cook it, so I sprang for *pigeonneaux fermier.*"

On the plate were two tiny fowl, their legs sticking straight up, little paper frills serving as booties. "Really, Rancor—titmice?"

"They're nothing of the sort, you ignorant git.

146

They're squabs in a peppermint sauce with the earliest *petits pois*. If you're squeamish, I'll gladly eat your portion."

She gathered the plate to herself. "Not on your life."

He watched her eat, a Mona Lisa smile on his face. When she'd finished, he drew a plate of cheese with cherries and grapes from the lower shelf. "I stole the grapes from the pool maidens."

A few minutes later, Charity sat back, holding her stomach. "I can't believe I ate that much." During the meal, the sun had gone down and hundreds of windows in the beautiful medieval buildings began to glow. She remembered that Paris was called the City of Lights. *So true.* A band of young men sauntered down the street below singing "La Marseillaise" in drunken harmony. A Chopin prelude wafted from the restaurant across the way. Charity's eyes began to close.

The whisper came gently on little notes of mirth. "What? Don't you want to hear about my grand adventure?"

Her response was a slight snore. Rancor waved a hand under her nose. "Damn. Jet lag. I'll have to save the narrative for tomorrow." He lifted Charity out of the chair and carried her to the bed. She woke up from her doze long enough to put her arms around him.

"*Shh.* Sleep. You'll need your strength to hear my story."

Charity murmured sleepily, "Does it involve a beautiful woman?"

"Several. I've been a busy boy."

Chapter Nine
The Ghost and the Showgirl

"I am not ordering another room service meal. Get up."

Charity opened her eyes to find Rancor's face inches from hers. She leapt up, landing him a thump on the chin. "Ouch."

He rubbed it. "Where do *you* get off saying 'ouch'? I'm the one with the massive trauma. What's your head made of? Titanium?"

Charity looked around. "I'm in your room. Why aren't I in mine?"

"Because you fell asleep at the table, and in an stalwart act of gallantry, I carried you the five feet to the closest couch. You have been zonked out for twelve hours."

"Ah." She felt her teeth. "I need a wash and brush up. Where's my room key?"

"You left it at the pool last night, but Manolo the bellhop dropped it off earlier."

"Manolo? Oh, you mean Jean-Pierre. How did he know I was here?"

"I told him."

Charity blushed. "Oh dear."

He patted her head. "This is France, love. No one batted an eye." He handed her a key. "However, you really would improve with the vigorous application of both a toothbrush and a hairbrush. I'll wait for you in the restaurant."

When she arrived, he put down his newspaper and poured her a cup of coffee from a silver pot. She noticed the name of the paper—*Le Figaro*—and the headline: "*Americaine Trouvée Morte en Londres.*" She gulped. "Does that mean what I think it means?"

"That an American woman was found dead in London? Yes."

"It's not…it's not…"

"Isabella? No, more's the pity. She is, I'm afraid, still at large."

"You didn't meet her at the Victoria and Albert Museum?"

"I wasn't supposed to meet her. I was supposed to catch her. She slipped away."

"Perhaps you need to hire a professional."

"Perhaps. Meanwhile, I met another lady."

"Rancor!"

"I can't help it. They are drawn to me like mosquitoes to bare skin."

"Nice metaphor."

"I try to mix them up a bit."

Charity buttered a croissant and slathered it with currant jelly. "Tell me."

"Well, you'll find this amusing. I was standing like a little lost lamb in front of that great hideous portrait of Victoria when a woman in a wheelchair ran into me."

"Will you sue?"

"I might have, except she looked so apologetic…also rich."

"How did you know that?"

"She was encrusted with diamonds. And her purse

149

bulged."

"It could have been a gun."

"Luckily, I didn't think of that. I accepted her apology with extravagant grace and agreed to accompany her to lunch."

"You're always so amiable when you're sponging off people." She thrummed her fingers on the table. "You do seem to attract women in any position—sitting or standing."

"It's a gift." He sipped his coffee. The waiter nipped over with another pot and set it down along with a second basket of croissants. Charity smiled winningly at him. He returned the smile and backed away, bowing. Rancor glared at her. "Don't even try to compete with me." He eyed her. "Anyway, we went to this delightful Indian place. I do think the best curries in the world are found in England."

"Not India?"

"No—the Indians insist on cooking everything in slabs of ghee. Since you probably have no idea what ghee is, I'll elucidate. Imagine a yellow version of the stuff they might extract from the La Brea tar pits."

I am not going to admit that the only words I recognized in his speech were the verbs. Filing the questions away to Google at leisure, Charity nodded. "All right, go on."

"Well, her name was…hang on a sec"—he pulled out a notebook—"Beatrice da Lima e Silva Abernethy. She lives at number fifty, Berkeley Square. Alone."

"And you asked about a full-time job as a gigolo?"

"The subject didn't come up. She did tell me her family history, however. You'll never guess who she's descended from."

"Probably not."

"Then I'll tell you. Mistinguett. The very lady who lived in your room."

"The music hall star?"

"Yes. Beatrice told me all about her. Did you know that Fanny Brice stole her greatest hit—'Mon Homme'? You may remember it as 'My Man.' " He opened his mouth wide and warbled a few notes from the vaudeville song.

Charity leaned forward and gently pinched his lips together. "Coincidence?"

"There's more."

"Okay."

"Mistinguett—born Jeanne Bourgeois…now, isn't that a bit of irony? Where was I? Oh. She never married but had a son by this Argentine diplomat, a Señor da Silva. The diplomat took the child to America, and Mistinguett continued to live the life you would expect, with many admirers among the aristocracy and other celebrities."

"Oscar Wilde?"

He looked down his nose at her. "You are aware of how the great man came to die penniless in Paris instead of London?"

She held a hand to her mouth. "Oh! I'd forgotten. He was—"

"Considered a pervert for the crime of loving the comely Lord Alfred Douglas and run out of England, yes. Oscar was therefore emphatically *not* a paramour of the delectable Mistinguett, but the Prince of Wales, at least one of the myriad White Russian counts infesting Paris, and the Argentine diplomat were. In fact, there were rumors that John Ringling visited her on several occasions."

"Ringling!"

"Yes, you know he and Mable, and later his second wife Hedda—"

"The sister of Calvin Hagen?"

"Right. They traveled all over Europe picking up lesser known works of art. Naturally, they spent time in Paris and made the rounds of the theaters, low and high."

"Wait a minute." Charity put down her napkin. "You said Señor da Silva took his son to the US. So where does Beatrice fit in?"

"Ah. The son—name of Tomás I believe—bore two children...or rather his wife did. Leopold and my new bestie, Beatrice."

"This Beatrice confided quite a bit in you."

He drew a long face. "She's lonely, poor dear. I made the best of it by ordering champagne."

"Good call."

"Yes, indeed, but I had an ulterior motive. I shall reiterate in case you weren't listening—shocking as that would be, although you do seem prone to woolgathering—Beatrice happens to live at 50 Berkeley Square."

"As in, 'A nightingale sang' there?"

"The very place. Situated in the borough of Westminster, it has for centuries been one of the toniest parts of London."

"So you thought you'd wangle an invitation?"

"Yes, but not for the reason you think. Number fifty is also infamous. To be precise, it is haunted. Heavily."

Charity paused, croissant halfway to her mouth.

"Really? Cool!"

"Indeed. Built sometime before 1770, it's been the scene of several deaths and many ghostly sightings. Paranormal activity centers in the attic, whence apparently—"

"Ha ha."

"What? Oh. Anyway, several spectral forms have been seen there, including a child, a young woman, and a man foaming at the mouth."

"And this old lady lives there? Why?"

"Well, for one thing, the rent is cheap."

"I'll bet."

"And for another, she heard a rumor that Mistinguett had resided there for a short period around 1934 and may have left some belongings there."

"Did she?"

"Live there? Not exactly. It turns out that a friend of the singer had just bought the house, and one day Mistinguett paid her a call. According to the friend's diary—"

"And you know this how?"

"Honestly, keep up, will you? Beatrice found the diary when she moved in."

"I see. What did it say?"

The waiter dropped the bill in front of Rancor. He picked up the pen. "How do you spell Mistinguett?"

"O-S-C-A-R-W-I-L-D-E."

"Whatever. They'll figure it out." He wrote something and handed it back. "Mistinguett had heard the stories that eddied around the house, and she and her friend resolved to explore the attic room."

"Ooh. Did they see anything?"

"Just the police notice prohibiting entry 'Due to

Unexplained and Dangerous Phenomena.' "

"But they went in anyway."

"Naturally."

"What did they find?"

"Among other things, a trunk full of theatrical costumes. Mistinguett couldn't resist taking it."

"I see."

"Well, the guilt must have gotten to her—"

"Or one of the ghosts appeared to her, begging for the return of his property?"

"Possibly. Who's telling the story anyhow?"

"You are." Charity subsided.

"Okay. So, on her death bed, Mistinguett directed that the trunk be returned to Berkeley Square. Her wishes were carried out. When Beatrice married John Abernethy and moved to London from Boston, she went to see the house."

"Wait a minute. How did she know about the house?"

"How do I know? I only just met the lady. I'm merely relating what she told me."

"Oh."

"She spoke to the neighbors, who claimed it was still haunted and that they regularly heard screams and shouts coming from the top floor. When she couldn't get in—"

"Why not?"

"*Shh.* Because the door was locked, and a notice tacked on it said, 'Keep Out.' " He shot her a wary glance, and she closed her mouth. "But—*but*—she ran the owners to earth and offered to rent the place. She's been there ever since. I believe she eventually bought it."

"What happened to her husband?"

"Considering how warmly she welcomed me into her coterie, I imagine he's no longer an obstacle to her pursuit of pleasure."

Charity put down her cup. "Has she seen any ghosts?"

"Nary a one. I begin to wonder if it's all a bad joke."

"Still, it's worth a trip. I propose we go see this haunted house."

"That's my girl."

"We'll have to figure out a way to connect it to our American ghosts, though."

"Not a problem," he said happily. "The author has a lot of clout with the publisher. Arlo gave me carte blanche."

"And an expense account?"

"How else could I wine and dine you this way?"

"You aren't."

He made a show of checking his pockets and rose. "You'd better ask the concierge about London flights. I'll see you later."

"Where are you going?"

"I have to see a man about a dog."

"That's the best you can do?"

"Believe me, if I told you the truth you'd hold it against me."

Charity was inclined to agree.

****

"Why are we still circling Orly?"

"Dunno. Hey look, we're landing again."

A tinny voice came over the loudspeaker. "*Bonjour, mesdames et messieurs.* We will be returning to the ground momentarily. The captain has been informed that *someone* forgot to close a door." The stewardess blushed furiously.

Rancor laughed. "They don't call it 'Air Chance' for nothing."

Charity, hands gripping the armrests and eyes tightly closed, didn't respond.

Once safely landed at Heathrow, Rancor called Mrs. Abernethy and asked if they could drop by. "I'm bringing a friend—my collaborator in the ghost story anthology I told you about."

Beatrice would be delighted to see them.

They checked into the Cavendish in a downpour and arrived on the doorstep of 50 Berkeley Square at a very civilized four o'clock just as a pale sun peeped through the clouds. Charity reflected that Paris seemed much cheerier than London.

Rancor saw her look up at the sky. "London can be pretty bleak in January. Too bad we missed Christmas here—it's quite jolly."

A woman in a maid's uniform answered the door. "Mrs. Abernethy is expecting you." She led them into a bright parlor filled with chintz-covered armchairs and tables piled high with books.

An old lady raised herself slightly from her chair. "Welcome, Rancor. You're just in time for tea. Please forgive my manners—I regret that I am no longer able to stand for any length of time."

Rancor bowed. "You are most kind to let us come." He took Charity's arm. "May I present my friend, Charity Snow?"

Charity marveled at Rancor's sudden mastery of formalities. *Hidden depths.*

Beatrice gave her a searching look. "How do you do, my dear? Do sit down. No, over there, on the sofa, next to Rancor. There." Once they were settled, she said, "Shall I ring Irma for the tea?"

"Yes, please."

While they waited, Charity checked out the pictures—mostly prints of Mistinguett in various skimpy costumes, plus posters for her revues at Le Casino de Paris and the Moulin Rouge. One photograph on the grand piano showed her holding a baby, a man with brilliantined black hair and a flowing moustache standing beside her. Another had her surrounded by young men. Charity went over to it. "That one looks a lot like Maurice Chevalier."

"You have good eyes, my dear. It most certainly is the great crooner. He was my grandmother's lover for many years." She touched the frame. "Such a nice man. I remember him. He gave me candy once when my father brought us to visit."

The maid entered carrying a tray laden with a Dresden tea set and a three-tiered plate piled with sweets and cut sandwiches.

"Will you pour, my dear?"

Charity frantically went over past episodes of *Upstairs Downstairs* in her mind. *Ah yes.* With a hand that shook only slightly, she filled a cup from the teapot. The words came out of some forgotten recess of her mind. "One lump or two?" A snuffle sounded from Rancor's direction. She kept her eyes fixed on Mrs. Abernethy.

The old lady took it all in stride. "Two lumps, dear, and a bit of cream. Thank you. Now, if you'll pass the fairy cakes my way, I'll be happy as a clam at high water."

Charity poured two more cups. Rancor checked out the plate and cried eagerly, "Cucumber sandwiches! Weren't they Algernon's favorite in *The Importance of Being Ernest*?"

"Why, aren't you clever, Rancor. Yes, indeed. It's in the opening scene." Beatrice laughed, a light, tinkling sound. "Mr. Wilde wrote such cunning little plays, don't you agree? I often wonder if he knew my grandmother."

"I'm sure he did."

An impish smile flitted across her lips. "She perhaps felt it imprudent to bring his name up in gentle company." She sipped daintily. "You mentioned that you have taken the Oscar Wilde suite at the Hôtel Paris I believe."

"I did. He's been on my mind lately."

She turned to Charity. "And where, may I ask, are you staying?"

Charity gulped. "I...I..."

Rancor leaned in. "She means in Paris." He smiled at Beatrice. "That's one reason we're here. They've put her in the Mistinguett room."

"Ah yes. I spent a pleasant weekend there myself years ago." She ate the last fairy cake. "Now, you wanted to hear about the ghosts?"

"Yes, please."

She rang for Irma. "I think it would be best if we went up to the attic room. Then I can describe the various sightings."

"Wonderful!" Rancor leapt to his feet. "Oh...but how will you get up there?"

"I had a small elevator installed when I bought the

house. You two take the stairs. I'll meet you there."

When they arrived at the top floor—Charity a trifle out of breath since Rancor had dragged her up the last flight—Beatrice sat in her wheelchair by the garret door. She produced a key. "I haven't been up here since I first moved in. I confess my curiosity is piqued."

The small door opened into a rather dingy room. Its ceiling slanted at a severe angle, and Rancor had to stoop to enter. A small dresser took up one corner, an enameled water pitcher on it. In the other corner stood a single iron bed, its blanket and sheets full of holes. A large steamer trunk sat by the door.

Beatrice rolled to a small window in the dormer. "Here's where the young lady fell to her death trying to escape her cruel stepfather. Witnesses swear they have seen her dangling from the windowsill."

Charity pulled at the latch. "Doesn't it open?"

"No." She tapped the pane. "Over the years, several people tried to spend the night here on a dare, hoping to confront the wraiths. One young and foolish man ended up jumping out the window and impaling himself on the iron fence below. The previous owners had the window painted shut."

Rancor moved to the wall and stuck his finger in a hole. "What's this?"

"Ah, that's the bullet hole. Another muttonheaded bloke, as my husband would say. They found him dead of fright with a smoking gun in his hand."

"There seem to be more deaths attributed to encountering the ghosts than there are ghosts."

Charity giggled. "I guess it only takes one to scare a lot of people."

"Oh no, we have two, maybe three—the young

woman, a little girl...now who was the third?" She tapped her nose. "Ah, yes, the youth imprisoned here until he went insane and died."

"Righto. He's the one you told me about. Froths at the mouth."

"Yes, although it's rare to see the actual figures. Some have glimpsed the little girl crying, but otherwise the apparition usually consists of a formless white cloud or a kind of brownish mist that floats around." She moved toward the door. "A distinctive odor has also been reported."

"The smell of decay? Something rotten in the state of Denmark?"

"Pardon me?"

" 'I could a tale unfold whose lightest word would harrow up thy soul, freeze thy young blood.' Hark! Do I hear someone calling from the other side?" He held a hand to his ear.

"I think Rancor is making a little joke."

The old lady pursed her lips. "It was not a laughing matter to the victims driven mad by fear."

Charity pointed at the trunk. "Is that the one Mistinguett took?"

"Indeed it is. When I arrived, I found it in the front hall. I had the gardener bring it up here—but not before I sifted through it."

"Were the costumes still there?"

"A few. A feather boa or two, a peacock headdress, a pair of dancing shoes." A shadow passed behind her eyes. "Tiny little things. Amazing what small feet they had in those days."

"Did you save them?"

She roused herself. "Oh yes. Together with the

packet of letters."

Rancor froze. "Letters? What kind of letters?"

"Now they were the find of a lifetime." Beatrice smoothed her skirt. "My grandmother must have forgotten she'd put them in the trunk. They were mainly love letters. Some from Maurice Chevalier, others from a range of admirers."

"You know, they could be quite valuable."

Beatrice looked shocked. "I would never make such things public." Her eyes danced. "However, they do make stimulating reading. Would you like to see them?"

Charity, entranced, cried, "Oh yes, please."

"I keep them down in the library."

Rancor and Charity took the stairs to the main floor and followed Beatrice to a small room off the parlor. The furniture consisted of a delicate mahogany secretary, two leather chairs, and a sofa. The walls were lined with books. "My husband spent his time in here. It's too dark for me."

She went to the desk and picked up a small box lacquered in red. Taking a brass key from a mesh bag attached to her chatelaine, she unlocked it. The others could see a pile of envelopes. "Each is addressed to Mademoiselle Mistinguett, 30 rue des Saints-Pères, 6e, Paris."

"*Sixième*? What's that?"

Rancor explained. "Refers to the arrondissement. Paris is divided into twenty districts or arrondissements. The sixth covers St. Germain des Prés, the bohemian heart of 1920s Paris. L'Hôtel Paris is in the sixth."

Beatrice set the pile on a table. Rancor divided it between letters in English and those in French and handed the former to Charity. He grinned at her. "Go for it."

The top one on her pile was from the Prince of Wales, written on watermarked linen, the ink faded but in a clearly florid hand. "My, he's quite taken with her, isn't he? Such flowery language—'rosebud lips, a pert nose, and extraordinary stamina.' "

"Actually, he used precisely those phrases in letters to twenty other women." Beatrice clearly disapproved.

"Oh." Charity picked up another one. "This is from a Prince Michael Orlov. He says he's named a dish after her, and it has been a great hit in his restaurant."

Rancor laughed. "Let me guess. Sweetbreads? No…haunch of milk-fed calf? How about—"

"That's quite enough, Rancor."

"Fine, fine." He picked one from his pile. "Here's one from the master entertainer himself."

"Chevalier."

"*Mais oui.* The quintessential song-and-dance man. I'll translate. 'My dearest, most beloved, celestial daughter of the night. How I cherish my moments with you. Last night will always be precious to me. When you ran your soft fingers over my—' " He ceased abruptly. "They didn't mince words then, did they?"

Beatrice smiled serenely. "It was a much more honest age."

Charity had been skimming her pile when she came across a letter in very feminine handwriting. She opened it. "It's from Hedda." She looked at Rancor. "Do you suppose it's Hedda Ringling?"

Beatrice took the letter from her. "It is. They were quite close. My grandmother often spoke of the Ringlings. According to her, John was a bit of a cold fish, but she and Hedda—the second wife—hit it off. They corresponded for several years, although Hedda broke off communications after her divorce." She sighed. "It hurt my grandmother's feelings, but what could she do?"

"The Ringlings were divorced in 1936, I believe?"

"Yes. Hedda rather faded into obscurity after that. I remember Grandmama saying she wished she would hear from her, especially after her last letter."

"Really? What was in it?"

"It's rather unclear. Let me find it." Beatrice took a sheet of lavender paper out of another envelope. "Yes, here it is—it's dated 1934. Rancor? Will you do the honors? My eyes aren't what they used to be."

He took the paper from her.

Dearest Misty,

I hope you are well, and that your latest spectacle is a great success. I received a note from Emily Haag Buck who said you were garnering rave reviews. How I wish Mr. Ringling and I could be there! However, I fear I shall never have the pleasure of your company again. I have some bad news. John has served me with divorce papers. I am devastated. I thought we were so happy. I'm sure it can't be about the "incident." We took great care with the evidence, and there's been no news of it. That man—the one I told you about? He is long gone. So it must be that my dear husband is simply unhappy with me. At any rate, I will be out of touch for a while. I wish you all the best...and give my love to Maurice.

Your loving friend,

Hedda

After a minute, Rancor spoke. "I seem to recall that Ringling was virtually penniless when he died."

"Possibly due to Hedda's extravagances?"

"It's something to look into."

"After we finish the ghost book, okay?"

"Or I get a certain someone to give me back my property."

Beatrice looked from Rancor to Charity. By silent consent, neither clarified. The old lady stifled a genteel yawn. "Your visit has been delightful, but I must take some rest. Doctor's orders. Irma will show you out." She took Rancor's hand. "I do hope to see you again."

He stood. "Do you mind if I do one more thing while I'm here?"

"Not at all."

"I'd like to take a couple of photographs of the attic room. For my book."

For a second, it looked as though Beatrice would refuse. The wrinkles on her face deepened, and her faded eyes blinked. Then she rallied. "Certainly. Go ahead. If you don't mind, I shall stay here."

Charity patted her arm. "I'll keep you company." She looked at Rancor. "Do hurry. Mrs. Abernethy is very tired."

"Back in a flash." Rancor picked up his camera and skipped out the door.

The two women waited. "Would you like another cup of tea, my dear?"

"No, thanks. Perhaps I could have a look at a few more of the letters."

"Be my guest."

Charity laid aside the one from Ringling's wife and pulled out a note covered in doodled hearts from Maurice Chevalier. The florid French flowed, and she was soon lost in unfamiliar words of romance. As she reached for another they heard a yell. She dropped the paper. "Where did that come from?"

Beatrice pointed a finger. "Upstairs."

"I'll go." Charity ran out of the parlor and took the stairs three at a time. "Rancor! Was that you?"

For answer, she heard a crash. When she reached the attic room, the door stood open. She switched on the light to find Rancor face down on the dusty floor. A horrible smell pervaded the room. Gagging, she took her sweater off and held it to her nose. As she bent down to the prostrate man, Irma appeared in the doorway. "Is everything all right?" She hacked. "Oh my, what a stink!"

"See if you can pry open the window."

The maid started toward the window but stopped. "It's already open."

Charity didn't have time to wonder why. "He's unconscious. Help me turn him over, will you?"

Together, they rolled Rancor onto his back. Irma put a finger to his wrist.

"Pulse is fine. I wonder what happened?"

Charity checked for wounds or bruises. "Nothing visible." She held her breath. "You don't suppose..."

Irma stood up and backed toward the door. "I'm going to fetch the gardener. He can carry him downstairs."

Charity felt a rush of fear. "I...I don't want to stay here alone. Let's drag him out to the hall at least."

They did, and Irma ran down the stairs, shouting, "Frederick! Frederick!"

Charity sat on the floor beside Rancor. His breathing—which had been shallow and quick—had slowed. He seemed to have dropped off to sleep. As booted feet pounded up the stairs, he stirred.

"Wha—" He sat up, his eyes wide. "Oh my God."

A head with a shock of red hair rose up above the last step. "Here, here, what have we got?" Frederick, a beefy man in dungarees, asked no more questions but hoisted Rancor over his shoulder and carried him back down the stairs. To Charity's surprise, Rancor let him.

When they arrived in the parlor, Beatrice was clasping the box of letters to her breast. Frederick plumped his charge down in a chair and left without another word.

Irma shouldered past the gardener into the room. "Oh, Mr. Bass, are you all right?" She wiped his forehead with a napkin.

Charity sat down next to him, clutching his hand tightly.

He grimaced and touched his head. "Something hit me from behind. I must have blacked out."

"Was that you who called?"

"Yes. I'd forgotten the key, but when I got to the door I saw it was ajar."

"We didn't know if something had happened, so I ran after you. When I got halfway up, I heard a thump."

He winked. "Did it sound like this?" He rapped under the coffee table.

"No, and this is no time for frivolity. Someone hit you."

"True."

"And there was a sickening smell in the room."

"I did not, I repeat, did not, fart."

Irma spoke up. "Not that kind of smell. More like…rotten eggs."

"Sulfur." He gazed over their heads. "I believe

flatulence is produced by a buildup of methane gas in the bowels, which smells like sulfur."

Charity broke the uncomfortable silence. "Whatever. So what should we do now?"

Beatrice said firmly, "We call the police."

"And tell them what?"

"Tell them what happened. They can investigate."

"All right."

An hour later, Charity and Rancor walked out of the hospital. The rain had stopped, but vapor hung in the air, draping them with moisture. "I propose we get some food."

"But what about your head? The nurse told you to go home and rest."

"The doctor said it was only a slight contusion. Likely from something rather soft—maybe one of those bags thugs use...now, what are they called?"

"I don't know." Charity saw a pub on the corner. "Let's eat."

They ordered at the bar and took their plates to a small table. "Is Beatrice going to call us when the police finish their investigation?"

"Yes." He rubbed his chin. "Awfully bizarre occurrence right on the heels of our interview. Coincidence?"

"We'll see."

He stood up. "I think a stroll in the night air would do us good. Get my libido back in shape for tonight's exploits."

Charity said, "Exploits?" although she didn't really expect an answer. Nor did she expect to argue.

Later that evening, as they both lay panting from delicious exertion, the telephone rang. Rancor picked it up. "Yes? Oh, hello."

He listened, said "Thank you," and hung up. He turned to Charity and stroked a stray ringlet. "That was Beatrice. She says they found the ghosts."

Chapter Ten
The Lovely Isabella

"Who caught them? The police?"

"No, the London wing of the Ghostbusters. Of course the police."

"Well, they must have special equipment then."

"We'll find out tomorrow. She's invited us over for the unveiling, or whatever you'd call it."

"Exposé?"

He flicked her nipple. "It couldn't be any more fun than the present exposure."

She pushed his hand away. "I need some sleep. And I want a full English breakfast tomorrow before we head over."

"As you wish, my lady."

****

They reached Berkeley Square just as a patrol car left. Charity wasn't sure if its bright blue and yellow checkerboard markings were some sort of gag—*to foster good police-community relations?*—so she said nothing. Beatrice sat in her wheelchair on the top step. Irma held an umbrella over her head to ward off the steady drizzle.

Rancor paid off the taxi and handed Charity out. "Are we too late?"

"You just missed them. Come in and have some coffee."

They followed her into the parlor. Irma filled cups and handed them around, but instead of retiring, she stood by the door, a grin tilting her mouth.

Rancor put his cup down. "Well?"

"Our ghosts turned out to be quite warm and fleshy, if not friendly."

Irma burst out, "It was Lindsay and Sylvester Taylor, the little scalawags." She tittered.

Beatrice glared at her. "There was nothing humorous in their prank, Irma. Mr. Bass here could have been seriously hurt."

"It was only Lindsay's duffel. He didn't even have books in it."

Rancor looked from one to the other. "Excuse me?"

"I'll tell it, Irma." Beatrice composed her hands in her lap. "A young family has moved into the house next door. Mr. and Mrs. Taylor are quite nice, but unfortunately they have no control over their two boys. Lindsay is eleven, and his brother Sylvester is nine."

Irma interjected, "They come from Tunbridge Wells—my home town."

Beatrice raised her voice. "At any rate, the children at school must have told them about the attic inhabitants, and they determined to roust them out. So yesterday afternoon, while we were in the library, they scaled the outside of the house—"

"There's a thick vine that climbs up almost to the roof. Strong enough to hold a small boy." Irma seemed quite tickled.

"I told Frederick to cut that thing down a month ago. It's been nothing but trouble." Beatrice turned to the bemused couple before her. "Now, where was I?

Oh, yes. First Lindsay, then Sylvester climbed up to the attic and opened the window."

"Ah ha." Rancor nodded. "I noticed a breeze when I walked in."

"Yes, they broke one of the panes. I'll have to get Frederick on that right away. When I consider how much heat is escaping through the hole. Irma—"

"Beatrice? The boys?"

She took a breath. "Their plan was to set off a stink bomb, assuming that would draw the attention of the spirits."

"Stink bomb? Aha! That puts me in the clear, so to speak." Rancor looked pleased.

"*But…*" Beatrice held up a beringed hand. "When they heard Rancor coming up the stairs, they panicked. Sylvester tossed the bomb into the room and scampered down the vine. Lindsay was about to follow when he realized he'd left his backpack on the floor. He turned back just as Mr. Bass entered."

"I didn't see him."

"No, because the light was off, and it was pitch dark in there."

"That's right. I was looking for the switch when he hit me."

Irma clucked her tongue. "Poor little pet, he didn't mean to hurt you."

Beatrice sniffed. "Must you defend them? They're nothing but nasty little thugs."

Charity accepted more coffee. "How did the police catch them?"

"By following the smell. One of the bobbies recognized the…er…fragrance from his school days. They were canvassing the neighborhood, and when they came to the Taylors' house, it was pretty obvious. Mrs. Taylor went to fetch the boys. Sylvester was hiding under his bed. Lindsay was in the bath."

Irma couldn't stay still. "Then and there, Mrs. Taylor knew he'd done it. An eleven-year-old boy bathing without being forced to? She marched the boys over here and made them apologize. The constable let them go back to bed, and this morning the police took them down to the station."

"Surely they didn't arrest them!"

"No, of course not, but they will give them a good talking to." Beatrice allowed herself a spiteful smile. "If they are wise, they'll do the same to the parents."

Frederick stuck his head in. "Did you want me to cut down that vine now?"

"Yes, please. And burn it."

He scratched his beard. "Don't think that would be a good idea, ma'am."

"Why not?"

"Because it's poison ivy. Burn it, the smoke gets into your lungs. Very painful."

Rancor inquired, his face bland, "Poison ivy, eh? And little Sylvester and what's-his-name climbed it?"

Irma gasped, and Beatrice grinned. "Justice is served."

Charity put down her cup. "I thought poison ivy was an indigenous American plant. What is it doing growing on a house in London?"

"You didn't know?" Beatrice patted her hand. "It was imported from America in the seventeenth century. Europeans were fascinated by the exotic plants in the New World. Some people planted it instead of English ivy because it turns such a lovely shade of red in the fall."

Rancor put down his cup. "Mad dogs and Englishmen, eh?"

Beatrice raised her chin. "I beg your pardon?"

He stood up and took Charity's hand. "Well, at least we have one mystery solved. Mrs. Abernethy—Beatrice—I have so enjoyed making your acquaintance."

Charity added, "Please consider visiting me in Florida whenever you like."

They took their leave. When they reached the hotel, Rancor checked his watch. "We just have time to check out and catch the last plane to Paris."

Charity felt a rush of fatigue. "Can't we just go home?"

"Not just yet. First, I owe Monsieur le Brigadier Dumont a visit."

"Oh my God, I forgot all about your little problem with the gendarmes."

"Yes, indeedy. Fortunately, it so happens I only have to pay a small fine for disturbing the peace. *La petite* Isabella neglected to sign the papers charging me with assault before she took herself off to London, so I'm off the hook."

Charity brushed aside the thought that another night in a French dungeon might do him a world of good, and instead reiterated her request. "Then can we go home?"

"What, and miss our last night in France?" He kissed her cheek. "Don't you want one more swim—and perhaps a roll in Mistinguett's bed with me?"

"Well…a swim would be nice."

****

They reached the hotel just as the concierge was closing up. "Welcome back, monsieur, mademoiselle. Monsieur Bass, I have a message for you."

"Oh?" Rancor took the slip of paper and read it. "It's from Atalanta L'Amour. She says Isabella turned up on her doorstep—which is pretty remarkable considering she lives on the thirtieth floor of a Park Avenue high-rise."

"What did Isabella want?"

"According to Atalanta, she pretended *I'm* stalking *her*—"

"Just like she did with the Paris police."

"Yes. But now she's elaborating on her story. She claims that—rather than stealing our books, she's been on the trail of the real pirate. Atalanta says I'd better come home."

"To New York?"

"No, to Florida. Isabella went to Sarasota looking for me."

****

It was with a sinking feeling that Charity trod the jet bridge the next day and found her seat on the plane. Since they'd made their reservations at the last minute, they couldn't get seats together. It meant that, instead of being distracted by Rancor's clever discourse, she could stew for five hours over the ravishing Isabella invading her turf.

And that's how it went. The liquor helped. Rancor waited for her at the baggage claim. "You're wobbling."

"That's what five little bottles of bourbon will do to a gal."

"Well, we can't have you seen on a public bus

then. Too mortifying for me. Come on, let's find a taxi."

"I don't think I have that much cash."

"I'm sure he'll take your credit card."

Charity made a mental note to ask George if this expense account of Arlo Mickenbacker's covered her as well. The taxi dropped Charity off at her house, but Rancor made no move to get out. She leaned in the window. "Aren't you coming?"

"No. I have some things to do." He bent his head so she couldn't see his eyes. "I'm...um...staying with George." He tapped the driver's shoulder. "Eighty-five Pine Street on Anna Maria, please."

Charity happened to know that George lived in Buttonwood Harbor, so she was left to stew yet another few hours over where he was going. *Of course I know where he's going. Nothing I can do about it.* She resolved to get some work done after she caught up on her sleep.

The telephone woke her. "Charity? Where have you been?"

"Oh, Jane, hi. I forgot to let you know. I went to Paris."

"Of course, you did. Now, where did you really go? Atlantic City?"

"No. I went to Paris. Rancor needed me."

"Shouldn't you play a little harder to get?"

"Perhaps, but I figured his incarceration was serious enough to forgo games."

"*Hmm.* Methinks you have much to impart, little grasshopper. Meet me at Milton's for a drink?"

She checked the clock. "Oh, is it that late? Sure, I'll be there in ten."

She slid onto the stool next to Jane as the clock struck six.

Wilma plunked a coaster down in front of her. "Hey, Charity. The usual?"

"Not today. I think a vodka gimlet would hit the spot." The bartender poured vodka and a teaspoon of Rose's lime juice into a cocktail shaker with ice, capped it, and shook with a practiced hand. "No lime garnish, right?"

"Right. Thanks." She picked up the martini glass and clinked Jane's.

"Okay, cough up."

Charity told her about the Paris hotel, their lightning trip to London, and all about Beatrice and the boys. Jane whistled. "There are so many mysteries popping up like whack-a-moles, it's nice to discover a simple, mundane answer to one. Speaking of, the police may be zeroing in on who the Chart House skeleton belonged to."

"Really? How do you know?"

"It was on the radio. Remember, he had no teeth, and they speculated that the murderer had knocked them out to delay identification."

"Yes."

"Well, turns out if you only smash the teeth in, the roots are still embedded in the jaw."

"Yes, Dr. Standish mentioned that."

"So Edwards dug up this oral surgeon who says it's possible to tell if the victim had any teeth missing *before* he died."

"How?"

Jane shrugged. "I don't remember exactly. Something about how there wouldn't be any root in that case?"

"Because the dentist would remove it. Makes sense." Charity had a thought. "But what good would knowing he'd lost teeth before his death do?"

Her friend didn't miss a beat. "Say he had no front tooth. They could check dental records for white males of that age in the area without that particular tooth, then compare them to the missing persons file. And voilà."

Charity downed her drink. "Voilà? Since when do you speak French?"

"Since I lived in France when I was a little girl. You didn't know?"

Charity, wondering if she'd ever be lucky enough to go back, sighed. "No. What about the records?"

"Well, I was right all along—Biddlesworth's your man. The victim's wisdom teeth had been removed prior to death, and Biddlesworth's teeth were taken out in 1929. *And* he disappeared in 1933. Ta da."

"Do the police agree?"

"Police?" She hesitated. "They're working on it. Apparently, lots of people have their wisdom teeth extracted, so it's not as definitive as a front tooth."

The news that the victim was likely not Rancor's grandfather left Charity with a vague feeling of disappointment. "I guess I'd better get to the office first thing tomorrow and finish my column."

Jane tossed a bill on the bar. "Oh, shoot, I forgot. I'm having a half-off sale, and I haven't changed any of the price tags. I'd better run over to the shop."

"A sale? Oh goody. I want that glass platter—the one with the little ceramic turtle on it."

"I'll set it aside."

Although she wouldn't admit it to herself, Charity

was a bit relieved not to hear from Rancor that night. She slept soundly and only thought of him the next morning as she made breakfast. *Eighty-five Pine Street. Hmm.*

She spent the day getting updates on the investigation. George forgave her for nipping off to Paris once she told him about Mistinguett and the ghosts. "It could go in Bass's book, I suppose. Or the sequel. He did sign a contract for three…" He wandered off to his office.

Captain Kelly was not as sure as Jane that the dead man was Biddlesworth. "It's mainly circumstantial evidence so far. If we could get hold of any surviving relatives, it would help. We have a subpoena for Calvin Hagen's papers, but they've somehow been incorporated in Ringling's estate so we have to jump through a lot of hoops. Did you find any other likely prospects in your research?"

"There's Randall Bartlesby."

"Bartlesby? Who's he?"

Oh shit. The ring. He doesn't know about the ring. "Um, he was in the missing persons database. I…uh…forgot to tell you. Disappeared in 1935."

"I see. What else do you know?"

She related the news article about Bartlesby's wife and her claim. "I was going to check with the Costa Rican authorities."

Kelly shrugged. "A little far-fetched but worth pursuing." He called Frank into his office and filled him in. "See what you can dig up and get back to me quick. I want this thing wrapped up."

Charity hesitated to mention Robert Bass. *I probably shouldn't roil the waters until Rancor's ready.*

Column finished, she drove to the Centre Shops. Jane's sale was in full swing. "You saved me the platter, didn't you?"

"Of course. By the way, did I mention it wasn't on sale?"

"Oh no! I can't afford it at full price."

Jane grinned. "Just yanking your chain. It's wrapped and ready." She waved an expansive hand. "Anything else catch your fancy?"

Charity kept her eyes on the counter. "I'm not even looking."

She drove home with her prize. The sun had dipped halfway to the sea when she went down to the shore. She hadn't walked the beach in days and felt the need to reacquaint herself.

"Charity!"

She turned. Rancor waved to her from the pool. Beside him stood a statuesque, willowy blonde. Even from that distance, Charity could tell she had perfect legs, pert breasts, and a figure a supermodel would envy. Upon closer inspection, she noted with real alarm the face of a goddess—deep blue eyes, Aphrodite's nose, and a neck like a gazelle's. She wore a gauzy, flowing shift that matched her eyes. Rhinestone-covered gladiator sandals sparkled in the fading light. Charity's steps slowed as she neared them, finally coming to a halt just out of arm's reach. "Rancor."

He stepped forward as if to kiss her, but she stuck her hand out to the woman, effectively shunting him aside. "How do you do?"

"Hello. I'm Isabella Voleuse. I think Rancor's mentioned me?"

She hoped the hostility didn't show too much. "Oh,

yes, he did."

"Good. He thought you'd want to meet me. I'd love to take you to dinner if you're free. We can talk about this whole fiasco."

Now, Charity knew the last thing she would ever in her life want was to have dinner with a gorgeous creature like Isabella. That is, unless she looked *forward* to an evening spent wiping drool off Rancor's lips. Before she could say anything, however, Rancor jumped in. "Charity—it turns out this whole thing was a misunderstanding. Isabella's on our side. Please come, and let us explain." He took her hand.

She let herself be led back to her apartment. As he opened the door for her, he said a touch too loudly, "You'll want to get out of those dowdy clothes and maybe put on a little makeup. We'll meet you at Olaf's."

She toyed with the idea first of tripping him and standing on his head, and then, after they'd gone, of staying home, but her curiosity kept eating at her. *All right, I'll go for a drink and that's it. Leave Rancor alone with his latest conquest.*

She walked to Olaf's. Olaf himself, his giant frame encased in a white chef's coat, took her to the table. He whispered, "You know who that is? That's Rancor Bass, the famous author. And I think she's that top fashion model—what's her name? Erin something. Are you going to interview them?"

"No, Olaf. Rancor's with me. She isn't anybody you've heard of." *Take that, Isabella.*

Isabella sat a little too close to Rancor in the booth. She gave a flirty toss to her golden hair, cut in a deliberately tousled, gamine style—reminding Charity that she'd forgotten to redo her braid—and smiled graciously. "Won't you sit down?" She indicated the bench opposite. Rancor, his nose buried in the menu, appeared not to notice the proprietary way in which Isabella took over. "Rancor tells me you're a reporter. Would you like to do an article on us?" She gave the words just the right touch of archness.

"No."

This caught Rancor's attention. "No need to be rude, Charity. Isabella, will you have a drink?"

"Oh, yes, thank you. I'll have a cosmopolitan."

Why am I not surprised?

"Charity?"

"Bud Light."

Rancor signaled the waitress. He read her name tag and winked at her. "Elsa, is it? How are you today?"

The woman—a hulking Amazon who probably weighed in at two hundred pounds and wore her fifty years badly—simpered, "I'm great, Mr. Bass. What can I get for you?"

"Lessee…I've been dying for bourbon. It's so hard to find in Europe—"

"Europe!" Elsa's eyes grew wide with the thrill of it all. "Were you doing research for one of your books?"

Rancor rose to the occasion. He gave her a shot of his best profile, opened his mouth in a blinding smile, flashing row upon row of opalescent teeth, and replied, "Why yes, I was. Do you know my work?"

It took all of the woman's strength to stay upright. "I've read *all* your books, Mr. Bass."

"Well, if you've got one handy, I'll be glad to sign it. And when you come back, bring me a double Jack

Daniels on the rocks. There's a dear girl." Elsa skipped toward the bar, leaving Charity to wonder if she'd ever see her Bud Light.

Isabella apparently sensed there would only be a small window of opportunity for real dialogue before the entire staff came out of the kitchen to kiss the great man's feet and spoke quickly. "Charity, what Rancor says is true—I *am* on your side. I've been chasing Michael Finney, our publisher, all over Europe. He's the one who stole the manuscripts. He published them under a pseudonym to cover his tracks."

Charity asked the question second to uppermost in her mind, since the first would definitely be considered rude. "So why did you have the French police arrest Rancor?"

The beautiful woman's eyes flickered, but only for a moment. "I was so close to catching Michael, and then dear Rancor got in the way. I had to neutralize him." She rubbed Rancor's arm, sending a prickle of disgust up Charity's spine. "I'm so sorry, sweetie. Even so, I lost Michael in London." She threw a playful look his way. "My silly willy actually believed I was capable of stealing his work. Now he knows better, don't you?"

Charity wished she could tell whether this had the desired effect on Rancor or not. His face remained impassive. He accepted the brimming glass from Elsa. "And the other drinks?"

Hand to mouth, the waitress scuttled back to the bar, returning in a flash with Charity's beer and Isabella's cosmo. As she set them down, she bellowed, "Mr. Bass, my mother is on her way from Sarasota with my copy of *Murder Cuts Both Ways*. The bus is still on the off-season schedule, so it may be a while. I can take your orders if you like."

Rancor went first. "The shrimp-cargot sounds good. Lots of garlic, I hope?"

Elsa nodded mutely.

"And the veal Française."

Charity—improbably hungry—opted for the shrimp martini. "Is it doused in gin?" she asked with a perky grin. Elsa, eyes riveted on Rancor, nodded absently. "Er…and the steak."

Isabella smiled serenely, but Charity noted a slight hint of malice in her eyes. "I rarely eat dinner. I think, yes, a small dish of the warm edamame with sesame oil will suffice."

"That's it?" Charity couldn't tell if Rancor were irritated or amused.

"Oh, well…to keep you company, perhaps…um…" She pretended to peruse the menu. "The red lentil hummus. I presume the pita chips are gluten-free?" She gazed up at Elsa with liquid eyes.

"I'll check." She backed away.

Isabella called after her. "If not, I'll have a simple green salad, no dressing."

Charity, wallowing in a sea of animosity, said nothing.

Isabella leaned forward. "Where was I? Oh, yes. I had tracked Michael to Paris. We had a date at Willi's Wine Bar, but he never showed. I found out why when I heard you had arrived"—she blew a kiss at Rancor—"and were asking questions. Our quarry bolted."

"And you were so pissed at me you called the police." Rancor seemed to find this diverting. "I now know the French will do anything a beautiful woman tells them to."

She flicked his cheek. "You are too cute, Bunny." She turned to Charity. "That's my pet name for him. It fits perfectly, don't you think?"

Before Charity could comment, he picked up the story. "When I learned they'd both gone to London, I hightailed it after them. That was just about the time you reached Paris, Charity."

Isabella said, "I was supposed to meet Michael at the Victoria and Albert, but I saw Rancor enter the building and knew the game was up." In an impressive display of simulated ire, she drawled, "I don't think I'll ever forgive you, Bunny."

Charity, busy keeping the bile down, gurgled, "What did you plan to do with Mr. Finney when you caught him?"

This question seemed to floor Isabella. "I...uh...guess I hadn't thought that far." For once, she seemed unsure of herself. Then a crafty look washed over her face. She swiveled so her breast just brushed Rancor's arm and cast beseeching, ocean-colored eyes at her companion. "Rancor? Will you help me?"

Rancor tossed off his drink. "Let's order some wine." He opened a wine list the size of a small town's phone book. "Would a Bordeaux work for you, Charity?"

She nodded, not trusting her voice. *What is Isabella playing at?*

"I think the Moulis-en-Médoc, Chateau Malmaison 2008." He ordered it. "Isabella, I asked Charity to contact Atalanta, Holdridge, Bernie, and Jemimah. I've heard from Atalanta." He touched Charity's hand lightly. "Holdridge told you he would write a letter. What about the other two?"

"Jemimah Heartsleeve is on a book tour and unavailable. She returns in February. The other one—Guttersnipe? He left a voicemail saying he didn't believe in royalties—that they were all part of a cruel capitalist system that robbed the poor. He went on to say the government should provide free books to all."

"Number one, has he never heard of public libraries? And two, fine talk from a man who stands to inherit five million dollars from his capitalist-running-dog father."

Isabella frowned, but in a pretty way. "Oh, Rancor, you're too mean to poor Bernie. You know he's ashamed that his father owns all those parking lots. I do believe he has refused to accept a penny from him."

Rancor gaped at her. "Refused? Is that what he told you? Ha. His father cut off his allowance after that episode with his college thesis. Plagiarized whole chunks of it from his own brother's."

Isabella gave an indulgent shake of her head. "He was only a schoolboy, Rancor. He's a grown man now. And such a heavenly writer. I can forgive him anything."

No one—not even the hovering Elsa—responded. The waitress set down plates and displayed the bottle to Rancor before uncorking it with a practiced hand. They ate quietly for a while.

Isabella declined dessert—"I am *so* full." Charity had the peppermint stick ice cream with hot fudge and extra whipped cream. Rancor finished his wine.

As they walked out the door, he turned toward a fire-engine-red Lamborghini. Laying a hand on Charity's arm, he asked, "See you tomorrow?"

Charity, her key in the lock of her battered Mini

Cooper, hesitated. "I've…uh…got work to do."

He spoke low. "I have to find out if she's really on the up and up, Charity. Have some patience."

Well, it's not a great excuse, but it'll do. "Okay."

He got in the Lamborghini. Isabella honked her horn, startling several old ladies on the patio, and roared out of the parking lot.

Charity drew an X in the air, hoping the curse would land right on Isabella's head in the form of bird poop, and went home. Her answering machine was blinking. "Miss Snow? Captain Kelly here. I thought you'd like to know we've identified the skeleton."

Chapter Eleven
The Ubiquitous Biddlesworth

Charity checked the time. Nine o'clock. No use trying to call him back tonight, and tomorrow was Sunday. She spent a wakeful night, in which nightmares came and went, the worst involving Isabella nibbling on a corpse. She called the police department at eight Monday morning. "What do you have for me?"

"Oh, hi, Charity. I've got someone with me now. Can you come over in, say, fifteen minutes?"

"Sure."

She ate breakfast, then walked down to the station. The police chief was alone. "I hope you have time to get this into the next edition. We're ninety percent sure the dead man is Rodney Biddlesworth, Esquire."

"What about Bartlesby?"

"Bartlesby...Bartlesby..." He flipped through some papers. "Oh yeah. Randall Bartlesby. Frank found a death certificate for him. Died 1949."

"In Costa Rica?"

He checked the notes. "No, in Dallas, Texas. Killed by the irate husband of a woman he was diddling. I guess his wife was right—a real low-life."

One down. "So what did you learn about the other candidate...Biddlesworth?"

"Rodney Biddlesworth, originally from Maryland. Worked for a real estate company that wanted to buy several acres along the shore north of Sarasota. He was in negotiations with one Calvin Hagen, brother of John Ringling's second wife Hedda Hagen Ringling. According to papers filed in small claims court by a Philip Sousa, Hagen had represented himself as an agent with the authority to sell the plots. Court found against Hagen. Biddlesworth then filed his own lawsuit but disappeared before the trial date. If you add up all the judgments against him, Hagen would have had to declare bankruptcy…and that was *before* John Ringling called him out for pilfering from his sister's piggy bank."

Charity jotted it down for Rancor. When and if she saw him again. "So we have motive. How about a physical ID?"

"Examination of the skeleton's jaw revealed that four wisdom teeth were missing before the rest were knocked out. Dental records confirmed that Biddlesworth had had them removed a few years before he died. That, and evidence of water in his lungs, leads us to conclude that Hagen threw him overboard."

"After he stabbed him?"

"Yes."

"How did he end up in the hole then?"

The question seemed to fluster Kelly. He stood up and paced. "How about this? Hagen tossed Biddlesworth into the water, but then he began to worry the body would wash up on shore too quickly. So…he fished it out before it sank and dropped it in the abandoned elevator shaft."

"*Hmm.* Well, I'll write it up."

Frank came in and whispered in Kelly's ear. The captain turned to Charity. "Do me a favor? Wait a couple of days. I guess we're still trying to locate his relatives."

"Just give me the word." She rose. "I'll be at my office."

She arrived in time to see George slam his phone down, his face scrunched up and bright red. He saw her and crooked a finger.

"What is it?"

"Mickenbacker. He's demanding a draft or at least an update on the ghost book. He says Rancor hasn't returned his calls. The one to Bass's former publisher went unanswered as well. He's fit to be tied."

"What's the big rush?"

"This was going to be the first title published by Kumquat House since Arlo bought it, and they've already spent five thousand dollars promoting the release of a new book by a best-selling author. Arlo's going to have my ass if your friend doesn't come up with something in the next forty-eight hours."

"My friend?" Charity's fatigue—both physical and emotional—was beginning to take its toll. "Hardly. What do you expect me to do about it?"

"Find the bastard. Sit him down. Make him write."

"I can't do that. He's...he's with...Isabella."

"Isabella?"

"The editor. The one we thought had taken his manuscript. She claims the publisher, Michael Finney, is the real thief. Rancor has agreed"—she swallowed hard—"to help her catch him."

"Well, that would explain why Arlo couldn't get hold of the publisher, but Bass still owes Kumquat three books." He peered at her. "This Isabella...is she a rival by any chance?"

"A rival?"

"For his affections?"

Charity bit her lip. "I don't know what you're talking about." When he snorted, she said grudgingly, "But if you were…right, I'd have no chance against her. She's a—well, picture Bo Derek, only more perfect."

"A blonde bombshell, eh?" He patted her awkwardly. "He's had loads of them, I'll wager. I'm sure he'd prefer a more…um…" He petered out.

"Thanks for the endorsement, George."

"Look, Charity, you know I think you're the most accomplished, lovely, nice young lady on the planet. No one—not even Bo Derek—can hold a candle to you. So gird your loins, girl, and get to work."

"Yes, George." She went to her desk and pulled up the column she'd been drafting before the advent of Isabella. *I still can't believe they're going to knock down the Chart House for more tourist units at the Longboat Key Club.* Everyone knew it would only add to the already horrendous crowding in the season. *I'm lucky I'm within walking distance of the office.* From January to April, traffic on Gulf of Mexico Drive ground to a standstill—Cadillacs and Buicks stalled nose to tail, little old men sitting on pillows to see over the steering wheel, heading to the fourth errand of the day. *I'm sure it's just to get out of the house and away from their little old wives.* For the natives, it meant that for four months they sat inside from nine in the morning until seven at night, venturing out only during the snowbirds' nap times and after the early-bird dinner hour. When the new development opened, six hundred more people and three hundred more cars would pack the roads. The club made the pitch that guests would be satisfied to stay in the resort, and if they went anywhere else they would take public transportation. *Excuse me? If I'm paying $500 a night for a vacation, I don't sit in my hotel room. And I don't take the bus.* She began to type.

An hour later, she took a break. George knocked on the glass wall of his office. "Want to get a bite of lunch?"

"Sure." They walked down to the Blue Dolphin and ordered sandwiches. While they waited, George beat a tattoo on the place mat. "So, did you finish the Club article?"

"Yes—I'll format it and send it to you when we get back."

"How about the skeleton story?"

"I guess I'll just say that the police are nearing a resolution of the case. Kelly is ninety percent sure it's Biddlesworth, but he wants to notify next of kin before we announce it."

"It makes sense—all the pieces fit."

"I dunno. Something about it bothers me." *It couldn't be that I'm wishing the body were Robert Bass. That's just morbid.* On the other hand, a family scandal would be laid to rest. If Rancor's grandfather had been murdered, it was unlikely he ran off with another woman. *Unless...*

George finished his iced tea. "Well, get something down on paper. I need eight inches for A4."

"I thought Mike's Bikes bought a full-page ad?"

"They pulled it. I did get a half from Longboat Cardiac though." He chuckled. "Says something about the target audience on the island, doesn't it?"

Back at the office, Charity spent the rest of the afternoon pulling her notes together. She gave high points to Captain Kelly and to Vernon Edwards, but only made passing mention of Standish's contribution. "No flowery compliments, just name, rank, and serial number." *That'll fix him.*

At home, the answering machine did not blink. She fixed herself a drink and went to sit on the balcony. A flock of skimmers passed, bodies only inches from the water, red bills open to scoop up the silvery fish that jumped the waves. Below her, a yellow-crowned night heron danced a dance of death with a ghost crab. She watched, engrossed, as they squared off against each other, the crab jabbing his claws like a boxer and the bird aiming its beak at his prey's vulnerable belly. Beset by his nemesis, the little beast finally tired, and the heron snatched it into his jaws, crunching the shell with obvious relish. *If he had lips, he would have licked them.*

The breeze fanned her cheeks. She tried not to think about Rancor. *He must be busy with...her.* She went in, threw on a bathing suit, and went down to the beach. At low tide, she could walk out twenty yards before it was deep enough to swim. She sliced through the clear blue water with strong strokes, watching puffs of red kelp swirl around under her.

Feeling better, she heated up some leftover pizza and drank a beer while she watched the news. Nothing about the Chart House case. After a while, she shut it off, pulled a book at random from the bookshelf—noting with a sigh that it was by Jemimah Heartsleeve—and went to bed.

The next day was the same, except the skimmers

were gone and brown pelicans searched the gulf for slightly bigger fish. Two magnificent frigatebirds— their wings shaped like perfect chevrons—soared high overhead. Still no word from Rancor. George slammed around the office scowling. "I've had to put Mickenbacker off three times. I need something to show him by the end of the week or else."

When she returned from her walk the morning of the fourth day sans Rancor, there was a message on her answering machine. "Ready."

What the hell? Charity saw no reason to reply.

A few minutes later, a text popped up on her phone:—Hello?—

The question appeared rhetorical, so she ignored it. *It's not that I'm angry with him for ditching me. Not at all.* She crawled back under the covers and turned the TV on.

"Police have identified the remains of the skeleton found under the parking lot of the Chart House as one Rodney Biddlesworth, formerly of Upper Marlboro, Maryland. Using dental records, as well as missing persons reports and other evidence, they determined that he died sometime in the 1930s. Mortimer Peterson, Sheriff of Sarasota County, stated that the case will be closed as of today."

They're giving up! Charity jumped out of bed. She dialed the Longboat Key police number. "Captain Kelly? I just heard you're closing the books on the skeleton."

"Yes. I know there are a few loose ends, but it's really not worth the time and cost to continue. I mean, the man died decades ago."

"But he was murdered!"

"Be that as it may, his killer is likely just as dead."

"What about Biddlesworth's family?"

"The two distant cousins we managed to run to earth? They're happy it's over. Closure and all that." He paused. "By the way, loved your piece on the new club development. We can't handle the traffic now—imagine what it'll be like with all those new cars on the road."

"I know—FDOT says there were ten thousand more cars on Gulf of Mexico this month than during the same month last year."

"Ten *thousand*? I'm going to have to ask the town council for more officers."

The minute she put the receiver down the phone rang. "Charity? Why aren't you returning my calls and texts?"

"You mean the one call and the one text? I thought they were just informational." *I am* not *going to let him know how I feel.*

He clicked his teeth. "Charity, you're deliberately trying to provoke me. Haven't you missed me?"

Oh goody, an easy one. "No."

"Yes, you have. Can I come over? I want to tell you what I've been doing."

I can whap this baby out of the park. "No."

"I'll bring food."

"No."

"I won't bring Isabella." Merriment bubbled in his voice. "That's it, isn't it? You're jealous. Admit it. After all, she *is* stunning." When Charity didn't respond, he began to wheedle. "Charity, you know my heart belongs to you. That, and I'm extremely horny. It's been three whole days."

Before she could stop herself, she snapped, "Four. Four days."

"Aha!" His triumph galled her. "So, I'll bring dinner."

Grasping at the last life line, she stuttered, "I…uh…have work to do. Come over tomorrow evening."

"Another twenty-four hours? You wound me."

"You'll survive."

"I suppose I can find something to occupy me until then." Before she had a chance to form a sarcastic reply, he crooned, "Ooh, I'm thinking all sorts of lascivious thoughts right now, can you tell?"

She hung up, resolving not to spend the rest of her day imagining the lascivious thoughts running around in Rancor's id.

****

The doorbell buzzed at six. She didn't hear it because she was in the shower. As she stepped out, it buzzed again. "Coming." She threw on an old muumuu of her mother's and skipped to the door.

"Wow, I didn't think you could look any dowdier than you did the other day."

"Rancor!"

He held out the hand that wasn't carrying a white plastic bag and a dozen roses and touched her hair. "Stringy, wet hair, albeit a sizzling copper. Eyes unadorned, albeit the most lustrous of grays, teeth"—he pried her lips apart—"unbrushed after I'm guessing a steak and cheese for lunch…but," he added prudently, "still snowy." His eyes drifted down to her chest. "Breasts scandalously hidden under the sort of dress usually worn by women of a certain size. And yet"—he grabbed her as she turned to run—"the most alluring creature I've ever seen. Good evening, Charity." He brushed the tips of her fingers with his lips.

The object of his attention stood stock still, completely overwhelmed by the desire to kiss this wicked man. Finally, she pushed him off and went to her bedroom. There she drew the muumuu over her head. Scrabbling around in a drawer for a T-shirt, she felt warm breath on her shoulder. "That's better." A finger traced her spine down to the crack of her ass. His hand spread out over one buttock and squeezed. She slithered away from him. His other hand took hold of her left buttock and gave it a smack. She landed face forward on the bed.

Before she could move, he was on top of her. She could feel the hard rod pulsing against her thigh.

"Charity," he said huskily, "I'm going to take you now, from behind, and I'm going to scream in ecstasy. Up on your knees." She obeyed. "Spread your thighs." She did. "I'm coming in."

He held her hips and slowly, inch by inch, drove in. She began to sway from side to side, letting his penis scrape the inner walls of her vagina. He pistoned forward and back, occupying her body. One hand let go and gave her bottom a light slap, then moved up to roll her nipple between thumb and forefinger. Her orgasm flicked at her, beckoning her down the slippery slope to nirvana. She ran joyously, unrepentantly, toward it.

"I'm coming, Charity. I'm coming," he panted. He fell to one side, her breast still in his grip.

When she'd caught her breath, she said, "You didn't scream."

"Next time. Next time we'll both scream."

"What did you do with the food?"

Rancor, who was busy suckling one of her breasts, said, his voice muffled, "Left it on the kitchen table."

"Was it hot?"

"Not as hot as I was." She heaved him off and stood up. A wave of vertigo hit her, and she stumbled. He sniggered. "Blood must be concentrated elsewhere."

She started to pull the muumuu over her head but dropped it and instead got a long black lace negligee from her closet. As she tied it, he murmured, "Much better. Come here."

"Not now. I'm hungry." She went in search of the bag. It held three plastic cartons. In the first she found a large salad. The other two contained a brochette of grilled shrimp on a bed of wild rice and filet beans, and a bacon cheeseburger with fries. "Which one's mine?"

"The fattening one." He came out of the bedroom pulling on his pants to find her pinching a shrimp off the skewer. "Hey!"

"What?"

"Women." Grumbling, he stuck the roses in a glass and filled it with water. "You're welcome for the flowers."

"Thank you." She aimed for meek but only managed mild. *I'll try again after I've eaten.* She finished off the shrimp, sat back, and patted her stomach. "The roses are lovely. Now, where have you been?"

He blew out his cheeks. "It's been hell. I've spent the last four days with Isabella hanging onto one limb or another. She's like a limpet."

Charity liked what she heard. "Goddesses can be so cloying, can't they? Is that all you were doing?"

"As I assumed you knew, we were trying to track Finney down. No dice. Very vexing. Each time Isabella located him, he had just flown the coop—no, that's not right. He'd...uh...what does the fox do? Go to ground. He'd gone to ground. That's it."

"You're sure it's not 'going to the mattresses'?"

"Don't be absurd, only humans do that. Well, if you want to call mobsters human. Animals don't have mattresses...Where was I?"

"Hunting."

"Yes. You know, it's curious how often and quickly he managed to elude us. It was almost as though...no."

"What?"

He doused the French fries with ketchup. "Almost as though he were watching us or had some kind of GPS to keep him one step ahead of us. We got wind of him in New York at the Princeton Club, but by dinner time he was gone. Isabella picked up his trail on Amtrak—she knows the webmaster—but he disappeared from Union Station in Washington. He popped up at various spots in the District, then just as we homed in on him, he went off the screen."

She took a swig of beer. "Are you trying to do all this from here?"

"Well, yes. I don't have the money—and neither does Isabella—to go traipsing all over the mid-Atlantic."

Charity had a vision of a red Lamborghini and begged to differ. She tried a different tack. "Have you decided yet what you'll do with him when you nab him?"

Rancor stopped, a French fry dangling from his

lips. "Um. Er."

"Let me ask you this: can you prove he stole your manuscripts?"

"Um. Er."

Exasperation coloring her voice, she ground out, "Are you sure he was even *in* all those places?"

He swallowed the French fry. "Isabella—"

"Huh. It's just possible that Isabella is using you. Maybe she's in it with Finney."

"Are you nuts? Number one, she's out of a job because of his shenanigans. And number two, he's this little rabbity cat with all of three strands of bleached hair and a nose that could suck up the Indian Ocean."

"Women aren't as fixated on looks as men are."

"Oh yeah? Then what do you see in me?"

She started to laugh, then noticed the rather hopeless look in his eyes. *Rancor Bass with low self-esteem? Nah.* She opened another bottle. "Actually, you're a passable writer. I like that in a man." She knew—as all writers do—that such a compliment was more gratifying than anything else she could have said. *Besides, with a personality that needs so much work, it's the only good quality I can dredge up.*

His eyes crinkled with pleasure. "Bless you." He reached over and stole the last bean. "So what do we do now?"

"I propose we leave the lamentable Finney aside for now. You have another job."

"I already serviced you. You want more?"

"Maybe later. First, you must get back to the ghost book. According to George, Mr. Mickenbacker is about to explode. He had set a release date of March 1."

"Not gonna happen."

"Maybe not, but how do you plan to break the news to the boss?"

"I'll give Arlo a call. Fill him in on the spectral occurrences in London. Soothe the savage breast with visions of *Volume Two—Phantoms in London Town*."

Charity drained her glass and reflected that it really wasn't her problem. "Good luck with that. Say, did you hear the police have closed the case on our skeleton?"

Rancor stared at her. "God, I hope not."

"They are positive it's Biddlesworth, killed by Calvin Hagen."

"What sealed the deal?"

"He had had his wisdom teeth removed prior to death. That, and the missing person report. Oh, and the fluid in his lungs."

"All circumstantial. Lots of people have their wisdom teeth out."

"The yacht found empty, floating in the bay?"

"He could have fallen overboard and drowned. The idea that Hagen would drag him out and bury him elsewhere is daft."

"Nonetheless, the Sarasota sheriff has washed his hands of it."

"Nitwit." He stood. "Where's your phone?"

"Over there. Why?"

"I'm going to call Aunt Gertrude."

"It's a bit late."

"Doesn't matter. Auntie is one of those who eats supper at five, then stays up until midnight complaining about the younger generation. Although…" He checked his watch. "It *is* almost nine o'clock. Another one of those old-fashioned rules that sticks with you."

"No telephone calls after nine?"

"That's the one. I guess"—he dropped an arm on her shoulders—"we might as well wait until tomorrow morning. Ready for another round?"

She wiggled out from under him. "How about a nice walk on the beach?"

He sighed loudly. "All right."

She threw on a shift, and they took the stairs to the beach. They strolled south, listening to the waves slap on the sandbar and pointing out constellations to each other. Rancor pulled a protesting Charity down on the sand, and they sat in the surf, letting the water ripple over their feet. She asked idly, "So what is the delightful Isabella doing tonight, and how did you disencumber yourself from her clinging arms?"

He stiffened. "We…um…had a slight tiff."

Charity perked up. "Oh, *too bad.*"

"She heard the Finney man had spread his wings and flown to Albuquerque. I said, 'What rubbish,' and she said, 'Oh yeah? I'll just go down there and find him myself,' and I said, 'More power to you,' or some less idiomatic and more imaginative expression. She flounced out of her hotel room."

Charity, who had dozed off during the recital, woke up at the last words. "Rancor, were you *staying* with her?"

"Me?" He laid a virtuous hand on his breast. "Of course not. I've been enduring endless wet, empty, cold nights in Hernando's hideaway."

"Sleeping on the beach again?"

"I spent all I had on tonight's dinner, if you must know. The last of the bail money."

"*What?*"

"Oh," he remarked much too casually, "turns out

they returned the five hundred when the charges were dropped. I felt it necessary to retain the cash to cover my expenses. I will pay you back."

"Rancor, I'm not made of money, you know."

He took her ear between finger and thumb. "No, ma'am. You're made of warm, quivering, sucking flesh. Thank God."

"Why didn't you borrow some from Isabella?"

"I told you—she's as broke as I am. And if you're wondering about the Lamborghini, it's a rental."

Sure. And I'm Dorothy of Oz.

He stood. "Shall we hence?"

Not in the mood for a fight, she took his hand and they went home. The rest of the evening played out rather athletically.

The next morning Charity woke to hear Rancor talking. "Yes, Auntie, it is indeed me again. No, Auntie, I did not reverse the charges. Yes, Auntie, I am now gainfully employed. Aunt Gertrude? I had another question about my grandfather, if you can answer it...Yes, of course you know everything there is to know about your father...Yes, the Basses are indeed fortunate to have someone as dedicated to maintaining the family history as you are...Yes, I'll wait while you finish your toast..."

Charity pulled her robe on and stood by the door listening.

"Are you comfortable? Properly fed? Great. So, did Grandfather have all his teeth? No, I didn't mean it as an insult. Yes, I'm aware we were well enough off to afford good dental care...you do? I never would have guessed. They look so natural. You're welcome. About Grandfather...ah. Thank you. Yes, I'll be up at

Christmas. I love you too." He hung up and turned to Charity. "Robert Bass III had his wisdom teeth removed when he was a sophomore in college."

M. S. Spencer

Chapter Twelve
There's One in Every Family

"So what?"

"So, it's idiotic to halt the police investigation when there's at least one other possible victim out there."

"Your grandfather." She touched his cheek. "You'd love to have that cleared up, wouldn't you?"

"I admit it would be a consolation to my family to know that Robert Three was not a deadbeat."

"Would it be better to know he was murdered?"

His mouth twisted in a wry grin. "Well, I guess when you put it like that. After all, his wife is no longer alive. She's the only one it would really affect." He walked out to the balcony and leaned his elbows on the railing.

She followed him. The gulf lay calm and collected under the hot sun. A great blue heron stood at the tide's edge, staring intently, taut with hunger. In a lightning-quick move that made Charity jump, he stabbed into the water, coming up with a minnow that flashed in the sun. "It would wipe out the stain on your family's honor."

"Yes." He smacked his palms on the balustrade. "I'm going to Maine."

"Now?" *So soon?* "You just got home…I mean here."

"Aren't you coming with me?"

"Rancor, apparently unlike you, I have to show up at my job. I can't keep prancing around the globe whenever I feel like it. Isn't Publix expecting you to appear one of these days?" When he didn't answer, she added, "Come to think of it—you have another responsibility, and the big boss is getting antsy to see something."

"Arlo? I gave him a buzz before I called Aunt Gertrude. He's sanguine."

"What does that mean?"

"Check your dictionary. Oh, you're not asking about the word itself? Arlo's fine. I told him Atalanta was making noises about switching publishers for her military romance series, and he couldn't get off the phone fast enough." He went back inside. "*Hmm*...I'd better take that one good jacket. Aunt Gertrude is quite formal." His handsome brow furrowed. "Now, how to devise the best approach to get her to buy me some clothes?"

"What about your parents?"

"My parents? They couldn't talk her into anything...Oh, ask them? No good. As the sixth of six children with their hands perpetually out, my father has become immune to advances, and my mother would be devastated to discover my current financial difficulties. She'd only cry. On second thought, you'd better not come."

"I wasn't going to."

"Good, then we're agreed. I can schmooze Gertrude better alone."

"And what about the frabjous Isabella? Is she still in Albuquerque?"

"No. Evidently it was a false alarm. Finney must

have a doppelganger. So she hared off to New York to visit Guttersnipe."

"And that's how you came to have all this time with me?"

He looked at her gravely. "I sent her."

"Oh."

He picked up her cell phone and waved a hand at her. "Get us some breakfast, there's a dear." He started to dial.

Blessing him for making it easy to watch him go, she made eggs and toast for herself. When he entered the kitchen he looked around, puzzled. "Where's my food?"

She pointed mutely at the eggs, bread, and juice container sitting on the counter.

"Ah, I see. The silent treatment. Just because I'm going to abandon you for a day or two. I'll make it up to you when I return. Let's see..." He went down on one knee. "I could propose." He stood up again, grinning. "Nah. I'll save that for when you're *really* mad at me."

Charity, completely confounded, couldn't think of a suitable reply, so she concentrated on her eggs. After a while, he said, "Can you take me to the airport in an hour?"

"Sarasota-Bradenton?"

"No, St. Pete. I'm taking Allegiant to Bangor."

Sigh.

She saw him off and took the long way around so she didn't have to brave the Sunshine Skyway Bridge a second time. The bridge, soaring high over Tampa Bay, was indeed a remarkable piece of engineering but terrifying to drive over. Charity felt completely exposed to the wind, positive that at any moment a gust would push her little car right off the road and down, down, down the nearly two hundred feet to the cold depths below.

By the time she got home, it was late afternoon, so she picked up a grouper sandwich from Milton's and settled down to a movie.

She should have tossed and turned all night, but instead she awoke restored and reinvigorated at nine the next morning. She watched several news programs, went to the beach for two hours, and took a nap. No word from Rancor, but she didn't expect to hear from him until he needed another ride.

Sunday, she was up bright and early and walked to the *Planet* offices.

"Have a nice break?" George was in a good mood. "Mr. Mickenbacker called to say Bass was off doing research and not to bother him until he has enough to start writing." He ran a hand over his bald head. "That man is the biggest fool on the planet."

"Which one?"

"Take your pick. What are you working on?"

"Well, I thought I'd write up the conclusion of the police investigation on the skeleton."

George rubbed his chin. "I think they're being a bit hasty, but I guess it's no big deal since the crime is over eighty years old."

"He was still murdered."

"Good point. Do you want to start a campaign to have the case reopened?" His eyes shone with the fervor of a true crusading publisher.

"Not really." Charity went to work on the article, tossing it on George's desk three hours later.

"Excellent. Now this evening, I want you to cover Our Lady Queen of the Sea's Spring Ball."

"Okay. Any dress requirement?"

"I believe it's a Roaring Twenties theme."

"Great. I can finally pull my fringe dress out of mothballs."

"And you might want to cut off that braid and have your hair bobbed."

Charity went home and fixed herself a sandwich. According to the church's website, the dance didn't start until eight o'clock. At loose ends, she wandered the apartment. What to do? Rancor's shirt, neatly folded on the bureau, caught her eye. *That's it. I'll look up this Finney person. Get some background.* It would keep her occupied while she waited for word.

She booted up her computer. "Let's see…what was his first name? Can't remember." She typed "Finney publisher" in the search box. A list came up. Sprinkled among the ads, the coupons, and the death notices were three publishers—one in New York, one in Boston, and one in Seattle. She clicked on the New York link.

Xavier Finney, multimillionaire publisher of pornography. Assets include a television production studio (located on Fire Island, MA), and Alternate Routes, a magazine dedicated to LGBT and BDSM literature. A small book-publishing operation produces five titles a year, including such best sellers as Men Are Drones *and* Two Years Tied to a Mast. *He has published two novels by the well-known erotica writer Atalanta L'Amour under the pen name Vic Whippersnapper.*

It gave the address of the headquarters as 44 Lexington Avenue, New York, New York.

"*Hmm.* Could be him. There's at least one connection." She clicked on the next name.

Wagstaff Finney, 2 Copley Plaza, Boston. Publishes The Nose, *a magazine dedicated to fine wines and their owners. Known to his friends as Waggles, Finney is a ninth-generation Boston Brahmin and lives in the house on Beacon Hill his great-great-great-great-grandfather Artemis Crowninshield built. The surname of Finney still elicits some misgivings among the establishment, but the family claims they adopted it two generations earlier as a gesture of goodwill to Mayor Curley and to ensure diversity in the class of 1932 at Harvard. The Finney family continues to be a leading light in the Massachusetts Democrat Party.*

"Definitely not the Finney we're looking for. All right, number three."

Michael Finney. Grandson of Edgar Finney, who founded HHR press in Seattle in 1933. An independent publisher, he produces a broad range of genres, from romance to what has come to be called modern angst fiction.

She clicked on the website link.

Welcome to HHR Press. Established in 1933 by Edgar Finney, we release an average of ten fiction titles per year. Our writers include Jemimah Heartsleeve (for her historical romances) and Holdridge K. Wheelock, author of the controversial Christopher Robin's Later Years, *which spent six months on the* New York Times *bestseller list.*

She went to the tab marked "Our History."

Edgar Finney immigrated to Washington State from Florida, where he had served as librarian to the famous art collector and circus owner, John Ringling.

Another link to the Ringlings? She went back to the Google search page. An article in the *Seattle Dispatch* dated October 30, 1933, mentioned the new publisher in town. *Seed money for his business is rumored to have been provided by a member of the Ringling family of circus fame.*

Hmm. John? But why would he help the librarian? Wouldn't he have wanted to keep him at Cà d'Zan? His wife Mable? No, she was dead by then. How about his second wife?

She opened another tab and Googled Hedda Ringling. A short biography told her Hedda had been a well-heeled socialite, upon whose income John Ringling borrowed as his wealth dissipated. *So she could afford to set Finney up in business, and John couldn't. Why didn't she help her brother then?* If he had to resort to unscrupulous land deals, he must not have been too close to her. What was his name again? She opened her notebook. Calvin Hagen. So Hedda's maiden name was Hagen. *Wait a minute.* Hedda Hagen Ringling—HHR Press. *Ha.*

This was going to take some more digging, and she was getting further and further away from Rancor and Michael Finney. There had been no mention of Rancor in the list of highlighted writers. *Maybe he's published by several houses.* She set the notebook aside and typed in Rancor Bass. His website came up.

Eleven books, all with rave reviews. *Murder Cuts Both Ways* received the Poe prize, and *Shades of Yellow* garnered a Publishers' Weekly top pick. The last three had been published by HHR Press. A link took her to an interview conducted with Mr. Bass by Felicity St.

James for *People* Magazine.

In response to the question of why go with an independent publisher, Bass put down his cigar and leaned back in his chair. "Why, you ask? Well, an author of my stature has an obligation to help startups like HHR. I like to spread the wealth around a bit, encourage young sprouts to grow. Finney's firm is a good, solid business. Once I decided to publish with them, their sales increased tenfold."

When the interviewer pointed out that HHR also published big names like Jemimah Heartsleeve and Atalanta L'Amour, Bass scoffed.

"Limited audience for that kind of tripe. My books are read by millions of all ages and persuasions. Without me, Michael Finney would be nothing more than a niche publisher."

Charity had to stop before she gagged. *What did I see in this man? Pompous insolent, egotistical—no, egomaniacal.* The phone rang.

"Charity? It's me. I just wanted to let you know I arrived in Bangor safely, since I know you were waiting to hear from me. I'll be tied up with family business for a couple of days."

"Oh? I'd forgotten you were gone."

"Forgotten? You must miss me."

"Not really."

"Oh."

She waited. Her heart still vibrated with loathing, and she just wanted the call to be over.

"I…uh…miss you. A lot."

Shit. She couldn't help it. "I don't see how. You can't have enough room in that tiny brain of yours to fit anything besides your inflated ego."

"What are you talking about?"

"I've just been reading about how the world was merely a seething mass of jelly before you arrived in it."

"Huh?"

"An interview. With *People* Magazine."

A sound resembling a donkey who just got the joke about the priest, the minister, and the rabbi rattled in her ear. When Rancor finally spoke, it was breathlessly. "Oh, my dear, too funny. I remember that interview. The reporter was a total slut—she kept trying to grope me, and when that didn't work began to insinuate things—like I slept my way to the top…" Pause for more braying. "Or my family ties forced publishers to accept my books—and reviewers to give me five stars. What a toad she was. What could I do? I gave her the full force of my disagreeable personality." He stopped. After a minute, his voice came low over the line. "That's not me, Charity."

Charity stared at the phone. Bewildered, muddled, uncertain—she had nothing to say. Who was this man? How did he manage to maintain such a repulsive façade when he was…well…a bubbling cauldron of mush inside? *Or is that me?* "I…I don't know what to think, Rancor."

"Then don't. Wait 'til I get back, and I'll explain it all to you in one- to two-syllable words so you can understand." A hint of levity crept into his voice. "Or maybe I could follow the immortal words of that great editor, my high school English teacher, and 'show, don't tell.' "

Charity saw an out. "When are you coming back?"

"Tomorrow. I'll be in your bed by nine o'clock

tomorrow night if you'll let me."

Damn the man. "We'll see."

"Oh, and Charity. I have some news."

****

"*Pssst.* You awake?"

"Rancor, I can't do it again. I need some sleep."

"It's not that. Although"—a hand snaked out and fondled her breast—"I could be persuaded."

She rolled over and found herself teetering on the edge of the bed. To save herself, she grabbed the first thing within reach, eliciting a yowl from the man next to her. "Gently, my dear. That is not a handlebar, although it may be hard enough."

She let go and immediately tumbled off the bed. The lamp went on, and she looked up to see a face unmarred by concern. "I guess we can add gracelessness to your list of attributes."

"Give me a hand."

Rancor hauled her back onto the bed. "Now, will you stay still while I fondle you and tell you my news?"

"I can only lie still if you don't fondle me."

He let go of her breast. "Okay, for now."

She checked the clock. "It's only ten."

"Really?" He tapped her nose. "We got a lot accomplished in the hour since I arrived."

"Well, you needed the practice." She pulled on a robe and went to the living room.

" 'Nine-tenths of education is encouragement.' Anatole France. Can I trouble you for a drink?"

She obeyed and got herself one as well. Before allowing her to sit down, he retrieved a towel, two pairs of underwear, and a copy of *Atlas Shrugged* from her seat and piled them neatly on the coffee table. "My

God, woman, I'm gone a mere forty-eight hours and you revert to the habits of a particularly slovenly magpie."

She handed him his glass. "Your report, please."

He took a long sip. "Okay, I had a very pleasant visit with my family. Rebecca has welcomed her fifth child into the fold. You'll be happy to hear she named him Constantine."

"Anything, so long as it doesn't begin with *R*."

"Yes, indeed. Also, brother Rory has taken over management of our hotel in Camden."

"Hotel?"

"I told you our family business is real estate."

"Seems to be everyone's family business."

"Well, we've been in it for almost three hundred years. An ancestor of mine ran a tavern on the Boston Post Road that was frequented by both Paul Revere and Benedict Arnold."

"Your ancestor was a Tory?"

"No, of course not. We didn't know about Arnold's inclinations at the time. Old Nathaniel would have thrown him into the stable yard had he known."

"So, what other hotels does your family own?"

"Don't you listen to anything I say?" He relented when she didn't appear ready to apologize. "There's one in Kennebunk and one in Seattle. Oh, and that nice little place in San Francisco. Not to mention the three in Florida."

"Florida!"

"Let's see. We have the Pink Arms in South Beach, the Monkey Estate in Boca Raton, and a resort in Naples. Very exclusive."

Charity thought of something. "If you have all

these hotels, why do you have to sleep on the beach?"

"Oh God, I can't stand those places. Full of people whose very souls are artificial. The only thing keeping them upright is the jewelry—or in the case of the men, their golf clubs. Act as ballast."

"I see."

"That, and I have been banned from them by my brother Rothschild, the current CEO of Bass Hotels, Inc."

"What for?"

"He claims it's because I'm obnoxious, but I know it's because I kept beating the house at blackjack." He put his glass down. "Now, I was regaling you with stories of kith and kin. Don't you want to hear what Rose has been up to?"

"Not really." When Rancor stuck out his lower lip, she tried to recoup. "I mean, I'm sure it's fascinating, but weren't you going to talk to Aunt Gertrude about Robert the Third?"

"I'm getting to that. *Sheesh.* I can tell you were an only child."

"I wasn't anything of the sort. I have two wonderful brothers, which is how I'm able to handle you."

"I see. And what do they do? High wire act? Panhandling?"

"Never mind about my brothers. What did Gertrude say?"

"Oh, I see we're now on a first-name basis. Gertrude would not approve. No, she wouldn't approve at all. She's very old-fashioned—didn't I tell you? Strait-laced, straight-backed, straight shooter...but I digress."

"Yes, you do."

He chucked her under the chin. "You know, sometimes you're no fun at all. It must be the hard-nosed reporter in you." He finished his drink. "All right. Apparently, Robert number three did not follow in the footsteps of his ancestors. While they spent their youth learning the ropes of the business, shoulder to the wheel, nose to the grindstone, etc., our Robert was sowing some very undomesticated oats. The consensus of opinion in his high school yearbook was that Robert would, in the most optimistic of views, not amount to much. A plurality of votes went to 'Will be found face down in a Paris sewer stinking of gin,' followed closely by 'Dies in a barroom brawl at the hand of an enraged madam.' "

"I take it Robert was a ne'er-do-well?"

"What a lovely expression! Just the way Aunt Gertrude would have put it if she'd thought of it." He broke off to peer at Charity. "I take it all back. I think—yes, I'm sure—she'll take to you."

Charity refrained from smiling and prompted, "Go on."

"Then in his junior year at the University of Maine, he presented them with a wife, the adorable Trudy, at the same time announcing she was preggers. Suffice it to say, they were furious. His father, Robert Jr., proposed sending him to the Colombian salt mines. When advised that such a place didn't exist, he insisted that the lad be punished in some dreadful manner—perhaps transferring him to Harvard."

"The horror!"

"Yes, indeed. That's when RB Three's mother came up with a solution."

"Yes?"

"She proposed her husband give him a job, but only if he graduated."

"Running a hotel?"

"No, as a salesman in the real estate branch. At that point, we were still buying up properties to turn into hotels. In the late twenties and early thirties, Florida was the place to look."

"So they sent him to Florida?"

"No, they sent him to Nebraska. My great-grandfather was swayed only so far by his wife's arguments. He did not want to hamstring his thriving Florida business."

Charity poured more bourbon into her glass and pretended not to see Rancor's empty one placed strategically under her nose. "Forgive me, but why are you telling me this?"

"Because…" He grabbed the bottle and filled his glass, tossing her a withering look. "Because Robert did not go to Nebraska. He went to Florida."

"And we know that how?"

"His father received several large bills for entertainment expenses—all from Sarasota establishments."

"Did no one go after him? What did his wife do?"

"Trudy was a trifle busy giving birth to Aunt Gertrude. The rest of the family were too pissed—his father for disobeying his orders and his mother because she had invested so much marital capital in him, only to be let down. They waited a suitable period for him to show up, then moved on with their lives."

"They seem an awfully cold bunch."

"Well, to be fair, he'd never given them any reason

to care."

"What made them think he'd run off with a chorus girl?"

"Not a chorus girl. To save face, the family claimed she was a budding starlet."

"Regardless."

Rancor hesitated. "All I can say is, that was the story told to me by countless relatives."

"What did the long-suffering Trudy believe?"

"I have it on the best authority that she's the one who bruited the tale about that he'd deserted her for a trollop. Auntie maintains Trudy died of a broken heart, but every time she mentioned it to us children, my mother would roll her eyes. When I came of age, Mother told me that, by the time my grandfather disappeared, Mrs. Robert Bass III had had it and was seeking a divorce. She popped off before the papers went through."

Charity put her glass in the sink. "So, what you're saying is, no one ever really looked for him."

"They considered themselves well rid of the baggage. And presumed he was happy with Coco La Strumpet."

Charity turned around. "I'm going back to bed."

He took her hand. "Good idea."

She shook it off. "You can have the couch."

"What? Why?"

"Until I know that Isabella won't show up in her Lamborghini—"

"It's rented."

"Sure it is. Until then, you, my man, must hold it in."

"I shall have the affidavit in your dainty, if

somewhat work-hardened, hands tomorrow. Notarized."

"See that you do."

Chapter Thirteen
A Rap Sheet a Mile Long

"I haven't told you what I found out about Finney." Charity handed the jar of jalapeno slices to Rancor.

He spooned out a pile. "What could you know that I don't?"

"Many, many things. For instance, did you know that Finney's grandfather named his budding publishing firm after Hedda Hagen Ringling?"

Rancor took a swig of beer and smacked his lips. " 'Beer is proof that God loves us and wants us to be happy.' Benjamin Franklin."

"Yeah, I have the same T-shirt. So I take it you didn't know."

"Never really thought to ask about it. That's right, it's HHR Press, isn't it? Why on earth would he do that?"

"Scuttlebutt is she gave him the money to set himself up."

"But the company is in Seattle."

"Yes, but Finney moved there from Sarasota. He was the librarian for Cà d'Zan."

Rancor dropped his sandwich. "Really? How intriguing."

"Why intriguing?"

He got up and went into the living room, returning with a heavy volume. "Casting about for something to take my mind off your succulent attributes the other day, I picked up this biography of John Ringling. One of the dullest renditions of an exciting life I've ever come across. The author spent seven hundred pages detailing the contents of every room in the mansion and arguing with himself over the provenance of each stick of furniture."

"Rancor…"

"Well, in one slightly more stimulating passage, he noted that the librarian was a very close friend of John's. He devoted a paragraph or two to their relationship and also to that which developed between the librarian and Hedda after she married John. Seems he left rather suddenly. Don't recall his name." He started to page through the index.

"It was Finney. Edgar Finney. Did the author describe the relationship between him and Hedda? Warm? Chilly?"

Rancor flipped through the book. "Ah, here it is." He read silently. "It just says they spent time together doing research ahead of the Ringlings' trips."

"So why would Hedda give him the money to establish a business in Seattle?"

"Maybe she didn't. Maybe John was the secret benefactor."

"Then Edgar would have named the company JR."

"True. The only other explanation is that they were secret lovers."

Charity shook her head. "Remember Hedda's letter to Mistinguett? She was heartbroken that John wanted a divorce."

"She also mentioned hiding something from him."

"Perhaps it was the money she gave Finney?"

"You said yourself that was a rumor. I think the opinion of a board-certified biographer who has spent years studying the Ringling family—"

"Or at least their belongings."

"—should carry more weight than the fruit of some reporter's wild imagination."

The telephone rang. Charity picked it up. "Yes? Yes, it is. Yes, he's here. Just a moment." She handed the receiver to Rancor. "It's Bernard Guttersnipe. He sounds lugubrious."

"It is always with a heavy heart that he faces the world. Except on Tuesdays."

"What happens on Tuesdays?"

"He's merely depressed." He held up a finger. "Bernie? Rancor here. What's up?" He listened. "Oh, she did. Oh, you did. Oh, she did. Okay, thanks for letting me know." He hung up. "Do you have any more beer?"

"Rancor! What did he say?"

"That, as I requested, Isabella paid him a visit. However, instead of enlisting his help, she told him she'd located Finney in Seattle and asked him for money. Which he gave her."

"Why?"

"Why what?"

"Why did he give her money?"

"You've seen her. Everyone wants to give her money. Among other things. Guttersnipe is, after all, a man."

"But she must have given him a reason."

"I told you, she's broke. She promised him she could get Bernie's manuscript back from Finney, but she needed airfare. And several hundred dollars for the hotel and meals."

"And maybe a Michael Kors bag to match her Lamborghini."

"You sound skeptical."

"I'm beginning to be."

"You're sure it's not simply the ugly pustule of jealousy erupting?"

Charity closed her eyes in a fruitless attempt to obliterate the image. "What would I have to be jealous about?"

He touched her chin softly, then, when she opened her eyes, ran his hands up and down his sides. "I mean, look at this magnificent body. You'd have to be an idiot not to want this all to yourself."

She rose. "Mother must have raised a dummy then. I'm going to work."

He rose too. "Can you drop me off?"

"I was going to walk."

"Oh great, then I can borrow the car."

"What for?"

"I want to talk to the police."

"About the skeleton? I'm sure they've been waiting on pins and needles for you to spell it out for them."

"Charity, if you're ever to aspire to being a good writer, you must learn to avoid banal expressions such as 'pins and needles.' "

"I'll work on it. What are you going to tell the poor ignorant police?"

"That they shouldn't drop the case. I think there's more to it."

"Are you sure you don't want to prolong it just so you have more fodder for your ghost book?"

He hesitated. "Well, that would make a good

excuse for goosing them. Yes, I may use that. They'll want to help Rancor Bass put together the definitive ghost studbook—especially if they get to be in it."

"I'm not sure they'll want to be in it. Especially if you make them look like jerks."

"I would never do that. The police are our friends. As are fire fighters and first responders and…uh…scout masters."

"I recall in *Shades of Yellow* you made the entire Cincinnati police force out to be morons."

"One book."

"And in *Murder Cuts Both Ways*, the chief of police was the murderer, his crime covered up by a corrupt department."

"Two."

"Or there's—"

"All right, all right. So we've established that you've read all my books. It's no wonder you want to sleep with me."

"What?"

"I said—"

"Never mind. Take the car. Don't speed. And don't diss Captain Kelly. He has no sense of humor."

"Yes, ma'am." He picked up the car keys and went out whistling. Charity filled a travel mug with coffee and set out on foot.

She had finished the write-up on the Presbyterian church's annual bridge tournament when George stuck his head out. "Is it ready?"

"How's this?"

"Florence Kingsley won for the fifth straight year, prompting the usual accusations of folding mirrors and marked cards from Hermione Bladder of Neptune

Avenue. Reverend Sitter calmed the waters but kept rather a close eye on Mrs. Kingsley throughout the evening."

George skimmed the article. "Did they come to blows this time?"

"No. The tournament committee made sure they were at separate tables."

"Those two have been feuding for years."

Charity's head popped up. "But aren't they sisters?"

"Yes, and their husbands are best friends. It's been very entertaining."

"Unless you happen to be Reverend Sitter."

"True. Okay, don't forget to do the write-up on the Our Lady Queen of the Sea ball. I only need a paragraph, since Kevin got some good pictures of the attendees." He shook his head. "I sure wish Melanie Springsteen's husband had the guts to tell her not to wear sequins."

"Never gonna happen." Charity's phone buzzed, and she pulled it out of her pocket. She didn't recognize the number. "Hello?"

"Charity? It's me."

Heart sinking, she said, "What is it, Rancor?"

"I was…uh…wondering if you could bail me out."

She looked at George, who raised his eyebrows. She spoke resignedly. "Don't tell me. You've been arrested *again*?"

****

"In my defense, I was only doing what you told me to."

Charity handed the check to Frank. "Me! You can't blame this on me."

"You said I should give back the ring."

"I told you not to take it in the first place."

He turned to the policeman, his face pleading. "At least now you'll reopen the case, right, Sergeant Ingersoll?"

The big man shrugged. "That's up to the Sarasota County sheriff. As you have laid out so eloquently, the ring could belong to any number of folks."

"Well, not really." They all looked at Charity. "I mean, we did the research. Of the nine schools with initials *U* and *M*, only three had alumni who fit the description. You eliminated one of them, Frank."

"Randall Bartlesby? Yeah. Too bad his wife didn't catch up with him. What a bum."

Captain Kelly walked in. "It doesn't matter what information you've been keeping from the police...*illegally*. Rodney Biddlesworth is our man, no question. He had a wife named Gwen, and he disappeared after a rather shady character reneged on a rather shady deal."

"And the skeleton appeared to have been immersed in water. Yes. But Biddlesworth graduated in 1931."

"So?"

"He was married in 1933, just a short while before he went missing. So why would Gwen give him a ring in 1931, when they weren't married until two years later?"

Frank rubbed his chin. "It's not a wedding ring."

"No, but he didn't have a wedding ring. You would have found it."

Kelly snorted. "I would have found this one if you hadn't stolen it. Besides, 1931 could refer to his class year."

Rancor took a breath. "Yes, it could. But my point is, there's another person who fits the criteria. Robert Bass III."

"Bass? A relative?"

"My grandfather. He graduated from the University of Maine in 1932. However, unlike said Biddlesworth, he was married in 1931. To Gertrude." He gave the last word a triumphant flourish. No one paid him any attention.

The captain turned to Charity and said morosely, "I suppose you're going to tell me he disappeared in Florida."

"As a matter of fact, yes. In 1933."

"Same year as Biddlesworth? In Sarasota?"

Rancor nodded.

Frank jumped in. "What about his wisdom teeth, eh?"

"They were removed in 1930."

"*Hmmph.*"

Kelly heaved a sigh. "All right, we'll look into it. Meanwhile, please restrict your larcenous habits to late night forays to the refrigerator. Where are you staying?"

Rancor's face went blank, and Charity flushed an unbecoming mauve. The policeman looked from one to the other. "I...see. Charity, he's in your hands. Don't let him leave town."

"Um...yes, sir."

The two walked swiftly out of the station, keeping a good two feet of space between them. He tossed her the car keys. "By the way, how did you get here?"

"George dropped me off." They were on Gulf of Mexico Drive before Charity spoke again. "So, when's your court date?"

"Oh, geez, I forgot to ask." He drummed his fingers on the dashboard. "I hope I'm in town for it."

She veered to the curb and stopped. "Rancor Bass, you heard the captain. Don't you dare disobey him."

"Well, someone has to go to Seattle."

She started up again. "Why?"

"For Finney. Duh."

"What about him?"

"Honest to God, your memory's a virtual sieve. Remember? He's in Seattle. And Isabella went after him."

"Well, what's it to you?"

"I want my manuscript. And I told Atalanta I'd try to retrieve hers." He leaned over and kissed her. "I want to read it anyway—she says it's the juiciest one yet. Zombies with two penises. Or is it peni?"

"You can't."

"Can't what? Read her book? Look, I've read lots of porn. Hers are spicy, but it's more the freakish characters that draw me in. In fact, her last—"

"I won't let you go."

"Okay. You go."

"Me!"

"Look, it might work better with you. He's a sucker for a pretty face. Just ask Atalanta. Or Isabella."

"What about Jemimah?"

"God, woman, have you ever seen her?"

"The photo on the back of her books is very appealing."

"That's because it's of her granddaughter. Jemimah Heartsleeve is eighty-two. And even at twenty-five, she was a dog."

Mulling over this revelation, Charity pulled back into the lane and nearly hit an old man as he tried to cross. She swerved, coming within an inch of ramming an oncoming Cadillac. She swerved again, brakes squealing, only to barely miss the old man a second time. Rancor grabbed the wheel and straightened the car out, leaving several people staring after them. Somewhere, a dog barked madly. "On second thought, maybe I should strap you into a comfy armchair and hand-feed you. It may be the only way to keep you safe."

"Stop it, Rancor."

"I will if you promise to go to Seattle for me."

Charity refused the bait. "What am I supposed to do there?"

"I'll tell you over dinner. What are you cooking?"

"I'm not. I don't."

"You don't cook?"

"No. Other than the occasional rewarming of take-out and the odd boiled egg, I hate cooking."

He smiled wickedly. "All right, let's go to Publix."

"Can't we just stop at Olaf's deli and get sandwiches?"

"No." He gently lowered her raised fist. "I'll cook."

They spent an hour in the grocery store, Rancor popping all kinds of expensive items into Charity's cart. When they reached home, he disappeared into the kitchen. A few minutes later, he called, "Don't you have any cookware?"

She pulled a box out of the closet and brought it to him. "There may be some pots and pans and stuff in here."

He rummaged through it. "How about bowls? Skewers? Chopping board?"

Having no response she could reasonably expect him to accept, she said nothing.

He glared at her. "Okay, you'd better go up to Walmart." He tore the back off a cereal box and handed it to her with a pencil. "Take this down." He listed nearly every kitchen gadget Rachel Ray had ever recommended. "Hurry. I'll get things prepped while you're gone."

When Charity returned with her packages, she walked into a kitchen that smelled delightfully fragrant. "Smells like mint."

"That's for the *çaçık*."

"The what?"

"Ja-juk. It's a yogurt cucumber dip. Goes nicely with the kebabs. Hand me the skewers." He checked out the portable, single-use grill she'd bought. "Disgusting. Take it out to the balcony." He turned away from her and started chopping rapidly. She watched for a minute on the off chance he'd start juggling his knives like a Japanese *teppanyaki* chef. When it occurred to her that this could put her in harm's way, she beat a retreat to the living room.

She had her feet up and was nursing a gin and tonic when he announced dinner was served.

The small table in her dining nook was set and covered with dishes. He brought out two plates mounded with white rice topped by grilled chunks of meat. "Shish kebab over basmati rice."

She picked up what looked like a toasted Rice Krispies treat. "What's this?"

"That's the *tah-dig*. The traditional way to cook

rice in Iran is to let it simmer until all the moisture has gone, then a little more until the bottom of the rice is browned and crisp. Dip it in the *çaçik*."

Charity took a spoonful from every dish. "Wherever did you learn to cook like this?"

"Oh, here and there. I do lots of research for my books—sometimes field research."

"Research on everything except criminal procedure, huh?" She chewed a piece of lamb redolent of cumin and garlic. "Have you been to Iran?"

"Yes, as well as other parts of the Middle East. I think Turkish food is the best, rivaled only by Lebanese. All very fresh and simple. Try the *çoban salata*."

"Which one's that?"

He passed her a wooden bowl. "Turkish for 'shepherd's salad.' A little something a shepherd whips up for lunch when he's moving his flock."

She tasted the mix of juicy tomatoes, crunchy cucumbers, and thinly sliced red onion, flavored with lemon and Italian parsley and topped with crumbled feta. "Yum. Pass the wine."

"I'm waiting."

"For what?"

"Acknowledgement of my culinary skills. A genuflection—if not too abject—would be acceptable."

"Yeah, yeah. Is there any more rice?"

Later that evening, they cuddled on the couch and stared through the glass doors at the darkening sky. "I love the way the sky gets this rich navy color, so the black shapes of the palms stand out like silhouette portraits."

"*Mmm*." He began to nuzzle her neck.

"Oh look, there's Polaris. Or is it Venus?"

"*Mmm*." He turned her to him and kissed her throat. When his lips began to move down toward her breasts, she stood up and straddled him.

"What are you doing?"

"Taking over."

"I'm willing."

****

"So how soon can you get to Seattle?"

"I don't recall acceding to your request."

"You ate my food. You owe me."

"You ate me." She giggled. "You owe me."

Rancor leapt out of bed. "I promise to cook another memorable meal for you when you return. Do you like Thai?"

"I don't know—I've never had it."

"My God, woman, where were you raised—under a rock?"

"That would be physically impossible."

"Then in a cave." He hauled her up. "Go make the reservation. Bernie is counting on you. Not to mention Atalanta."

"Can't you people do anything yourselves?"

"Not really. The idea of dealing with the real world frightens us. We're like baby birds."

"No, you're just cheap."

"Ha ha. Now scoot."

Charity found that she had accepted the inevitable without much struggle, even though she had an awful feeling this was only the beginning. She made the reservations and informed George of her mission. The latter, though inclined to bluster, slowly came to agree that this whole affair might prove to be a real scoop for the paper. "I can see the headline: '*Planet* Reporter Tracks Down Fugitive Publisher'…or should it be 'Property Thief?' We could be instrumental in bringing him to justice."

"And you could receive a token of her gratitude from Atalanta L'Amour herself."

"Or from Jemimah Heartsleeve." He almost sighed. Charity didn't have the heart to tell him that he wouldn't exactly swoon at an embrace from the elderly romance writer.

Rancor drove her to the airport. "Okay, here's his last known address. I'm not sure if he's in hiding. I reserved a room for you at my family's hotel. Call Isabella when you get there." He kissed her and watched her go in through the automatic doors.

****

As she pulled her suitcase off the baggage carousel, she felt a tap on her shoulder. "Hello, Charity."

She spun around. "Isabella! How did you know I was coming?"

"Rancor called me. He said you're going to help me find Finney." She looked down her flawlessly chiseled nose. "Not that I need *your* help." Closing those huge cerulean eyes to half slits, she studied Charity. "Rancor didn't say why he couldn't come himself. I'm guessing you're here as a reporter. Am I right?"

Perfect. "You've found me out. Yes, George—my publisher—asked me to come. He sees a juicy story in it for the *Planet*." Her innocent look was almost genuine. "You don't mind, do you?"

Isabella seemed about to reply but instead turned on her heel. She said over her shoulder, "Can I drop you at your hotel?"

"Thanks, but I have a rental car."

"Oh?"

Charity could almost see the little cells clicking over. *She wants to keep tabs on me.*

"Well, let's meet for dinner once you're settled. I'll give you a ring at...?"

Charity saw no reason not to give her phone number, although she didn't trust the sly look in Isabella's eyes. She signed for the car and followed the agency's directions to the hotel. A discreet brass plaque next to the door said simply "Bass ~ Seattle." The unpretentious entrance belied the luxury within. The lobby—sleek and modern—put Charity off momentarily. That is, until the concierge ran around from behind the desk and shook her hand vigorously. "Miss Snow? I am Mr. Waters, the manager. Mr. Bass called to say you were coming. May I say what a privilege it is to welcome you to one of Seattle's finest boutique hotels. I do hope we can make your stay an agreeable one."

He rang a little silver bell. "Joseph will take you to your room." Joseph, a very tall, thin young man in a black and blue uniform, materialized and picked up her bag. As they headed toward the elevator, Mr. Waters called, "Please don't hesitate to ask for anything, anything at all. Any friend of Mr. Bass is a friend of ours." Charity reflected that, while brother Rothschild might hold Rancor in low regard, that opinion didn't extend to the staff.

Joseph opened the room door, and Charity stifled a gasp. Large picture windows filled two walls, affording a glorious view of the harbor. "That is Elliott Bay, miss.

And beyond it, Puget Sound."

"It's beautiful." Through a door, she glimpsed a bathroom with gleaming chrome fixtures and walls tiled in peach and cream. After placing her suitcase on a rack, the bell hop went through and turned on the taps.

"My heavens, the water's coming from the ceiling!"

"Isn't it neat?" Joseph didn't try to hide his enthusiasm. "For most of our guests, this is their favorite amenity."

"I'm going to take a shower immediately—maybe two."

She gave him a five-dollar bill, and when he'd gone, twirled around the room. On the desk, she found a bucket with a split of Moët & Chandon champagne. A rose lay across her pillow.

Once settled, she called Rancor. "I can see why your brother banned you from the Bass hotels. You'd only detract from the ambience."

"Yes, they are generally even more beautiful than I am."

Charity let that pass. "Guess who met me at the airport?"

"Isabella. I told her to fetch you."

"Well, you didn't tell *me*. I have a rental."

"Oh darn. I hope you didn't insult her. We need her to find Finney for us."

"I'm having dinner with her tonight. What do you want me to tell her?"

"She already knows everything I know. Why does she think you're there?"

"I insinuated that I wanted a scoop. I think she believes me—why else would I traipse across the country?"

"Because you adore me, and you want to have my babies."

"Guess again. George went along with this because he thinks there's a good story in it. I hope he's right."

"It'll work as the ostensible purpose." He paused. "By the way, Jemimah Heartsleeve gave me a ring. She says Atalanta called her, hoping to present a united front. She also received a letter from Holdridge—he hates the phone."

"Will she help?"

"No. She wants no part of this 'hounding of poor Michael,' as she calls it. She defended him fiercely, suggesting that authors have more reason to steal manuscripts than publishers. She made a cryptic comment about so-called serious writers lusting for more of the pie. I can't be sure—knowing Jemimah— whether she meant actual pie or profits. Did I mention she's a trifle overweight?" His tone turned sour. "She's so successful, I don't think she cares that much about one or two manuscripts."

"There is a lot of piracy—you can't stop it all."

"I know, and I'm used to it. But I draw the line at my own publisher taking me to the cleaners. What if he decides to put his own stamp on my story?" She could almost hear him shudder. "It could ruin my entire reputation! Oh my God...I need a stiff drink. Did you remember to get some more whiskey?"

Up until the last question, Charity had been inclined to sympathize. "I'm going to get ready for my date."

"Date? Oh, Isabella. Take her to Etta's. She likes oysters."

"Rancor? Hang up."

"But—"

She hung up. An hour later the room phone buzzed. A rather breathless voice chirped, "Miss Snow? Miss Isabella Voleuse awaits you in the lobby."

"I'll be right down."

Isabella—this evening in a ravishing black shift and three-carat diamond earrings—tapped her foot. "There you are. Do you have any preference as to food? I recall you like…hearty meals."

One. Two. Three. "How about Etta's? Mr. Waters says it has good oysters."

"Etta's? That's near Pike Place Market. Not far."

Isabella led her to a dark blue Lotus parked at a fire hydrant. A policeman stood near it, his ticket book out. When he turned and saw Isabella, he dropped the book and caught himself just before saluting. "This your car, miss?"

Isabella drifted over to him. Standing close, she cooed, "Yes, it is, Officer. Is there a problem?"

The poor man's chest collapsed. He burbled, "No…no…not at all. Beautiful…car. Beautiful car. Just admiring it." He took a deep breath and brought his voice down to a normal level. "You might want to consider moving it away from the hydrant. You never know when there might be a fire."

Isabella laughed gaily. "In Seattle? Nothing's dry enough to burn. But we'll take your advice, Officer. Thank you so much. Charity?"

Oh, so it's "we" all of a sudden? "Coming."

They drove the few blocks to the market and parked in a garage. As they walked down the street to the restaurant, a light rain began to fall. Umbrellas went up all around them like rabbits out of a chorus line of magicians' hats. They ran to the entrance. Isabella entered first, for which Charity was grateful. Various cries and ejaculations indicating feverish adoration came from within, and they were led to a table in the window by a serially bowing maître d'. "Is this adequate? Would you prefer another table, mademoiselle? Can I get you a cocktail?"

He didn't seem to notice Charity until she cleared her throat. "May I sit down?"

"Oh, yes, mademoiselle. You are...with the lady?" She could swear he almost asked if she were the "lady's" maid.

"Yes, I am. And I'd like a vodka gimlet, straight up."

He didn't write it down but gazed at Isabella. "And for you, mademoiselle?"

"I think...yes. A champagne cocktail. Thank you *so* much, Antoine."

Charity watched her. *She actually fluttered her eyelashes at him. Gross.*

When they'd been served the drinks, Isabella took a dainty sip and put her drink down. "Have you been to Seattle before?"

"No. It seems rather dark."

"Well, it *is* winter. The summers here are quite pleasant."

"So you are based here?"

"Yes. I worked for HHR Press as the editor-in-chief. I edited most of the top-name writers, including Rancor."

"I see. So if Michael Finney is on the lam, you're out of a job."

She shook her head with regret. "Indeed I am. But"—she bent toward Charity and whispered—"I'm thinking of going into business for myself." She sat back as the waiter opened her menu for her. "I'll have the oysters, please. A dozen. And perhaps a bowl of chowder. How about you, Charity?"

Charity had had a moment to absorb the prices and squeaked, "Just the soup, please."

"A bowl or a cup?"

"A c-cup."

Isabella smiled, a feline gleam in her blue eyes. "Shall we have wine?"

Charity gulped. "A glass of..." Her eye went rapidly down the list "...the house Pinot Grigio." *Between Rancor and Isabella, I'm going to have to take out a loan.*

After dinner, Isabella dropped Charity off at her hotel and waved gaily through the mist. "I'll call you tomorrow."

The message light blinked on the hotel phone in her room. She pressed it. She could barely make out Rancor's voice through the static. "Charity? I have a bead on Finney. Call me."

Instead, she took a second shower, letting the warm water cascade over her shoulders. Then she called room service. After a turkey sandwich and glass of wine, she went to bed.

Jet lag woke her at midnight. She pulled the phone over and dialed the number Rancor had left, not surprised to see it was the land line in her apartment. "What's up?"

"Charity? Why are you calling? It's..." She heard some rustling. "It's three in the morning! I knew you to be thoughtless. I didn't think you *cruel*."

"*You* called *me*, Rancor."

"I did? Oh. Well. Guttersnipe got a text from Finney. I want you two to try and catch him tomorrow. Or rather, today."

"Where?"

"There's a tugboat race down by the wharf this afternoon. The hero in Bernie's new book…well, if you could call him that. Bernie's heroes tend to be as lugubrious as he is and twice as aggrieved…Where was I?"

"Bernie's hero."

"Oh yes. He's a tugboat captain, and Finney said he'd take pictures for him."

"Why would Finney do a favor for one of the authors he's ripped off?"

"Ah, that's the sixty-four thousand dollar question, isn't it?"

Chapter Fourteen
Flying Fish and Wild Geese

"Charity? It's Isabella. I know where Michael will be today."

Let's see how good her sources are. "Where?"

"He promised Bernie Guttersnipe he'd take pictures of the tugboat races this afternoon. I'm sure we can catch him on the wharf."

Hmm. "Okay."

"I'll pick you up at noon."

At twelve o'clock sharp, the concierge buzzed her room. "Miss Voleuse is here."

This time Isabella wore a beautifully cut emerald green wool suit and matching bag. Charity was pretty sure the heels were Jimmy Choos. *Gee, I wonder what she wears when she* has *money.*

The woman waved gaily. "Hurry! The races start in forty-five minutes." She drove through the narrow streets of Seattle like a demon. Pedestrians and cars melted out of her way. They parked and walked down the hill to the entrance to Pike Place. Isabella checked her watch. "We have time. Let's walk through the market rather than the street. It'll be fun." She smiled happily.

They pushed through the crowds into a covered area. Before them, stacks of glistening silver trout and salmon, piles of gray shrimp, and crab legs as long as

Tina Turner's legs lay in ice-filled bins. As Charity approached, a fish about a foot long went sailing through the air right before her nose. She heard the yell a second too late. "*Opa!* Watch out." The fish came sailing back the other way, smacking the top of her head. A young man in a red-splotched vinyl apron ran to her. His black eyes snapped with laughter, but his tone was solicitous. "Are you all right, ma'am?"

She wiped at the brine running down her temple. "I guess so. What on earth are you doing?"

He backed away, seemingly perplexed by the question. Isabella waited until an audience had gathered before taking Charity's hand and confiding in a ringing mezzo-soprano, "That's right, this is your first time out of...where *do* you come from? Alabama? Appalachia? It's part of the tradition here at Pike Place. Seattle has such an abundance of seafood that the boys started tossing fish at each other. It's a test of skill."

"But aren't they slippery?"

Isabella rolled her eyes. "That's why it's a test. Sort of like catching a greased pig."

Charity thought it all seemed rather adolescent. *And not really good for business. I mean, who'd buy a fish that's been hurled around like a frisbee?*

Isabella nudged her a little too hard. "Come on."

They entered a second section—this one filled with vegetables. Charity recognized the tomatoes and lettuces, but the hundreds of types of mushrooms stumped her. Beyond them, stringy things, queerly shaped squashes, and hairy brown objects were piled high, little signs attached. She read, "Lotus Root, 45¢/lb," and "Fu Qua, 25¢ each."

They moved on to the fruit section, full of objects

equally exotic. People—mainly Asian—jostled her. Charity stopped at a fruit juice stand and bought a cup of honeydew melon juice. When she looked around, Isabella had disappeared. "Isabella?"

The press seemed to thicken around her. She stood uncertainly. An Indian man followed by two large Indian women in saris brushed past her, spinning her around. "Isabella?" No response.

Panic swept over her. She couldn't breathe. *I have to find an exit. I have to get out of here.* She fought her way toward a red neon sign that flashed "Western Avenue," finally emerging onto a cracked and broken sidewalk. She sucked air into her aching lungs and fought for composure. After a minute, she felt steady enough to look around her. Across the cobblestone lane a street performer juggled hoops. A man in chef's whites strode down the street carrying a tray of bread on his head. Charity peered back through the market entrance. No Isabella. Nothing looked familiar. *Should I start walking or stay in one place?* She decided to do a bit of each. She walked a block, hoping she was going in the right direction, then halted for a few minutes. At the end of the market lay a small park. People sat on the grass eating or gazing out at the bay. In the center rose two totem poles. She went to the iron fence and looked down. Far below lay the port. In the distance, tugboats tooted and chugged away from the pier.

How on earth do I get down there? A man directed her to a stair that took her three flights down, spitting her out on a busy highway. Five lanes lay between her and the port. The tugboats were gone, but a fireboat edged close to the pier and anchored. All at once, it turned on its hoses. Jets of water spurted up fifty feet, the streams crisscrossing each other in a beautiful display. It reminded her of a picture she'd seen once of the Fountain of Trevi. She scanned the area. Still no sign of Isabella. *If she's anywhere, it will be the docks.* She crossed at a light and made her way toward the water, fighting her way through a mob of people who surged toward her. *Finney was going to take pictures of the races.* She peered at the men who passed her, but every single one had a camera either swinging from his neck or in his hand. She tried to remember Rancor's description of his publisher. *Balding. Short? It's no use.* She couldn't find Finney without Isabella.

She turned back to the hill, wondering what to do. Her cell phone rang. "Charity? Where the hell are you? I've been looking for you everywhere!"

"I'm on the pier. Where did you go? I lost you in the fruit section."

"I'm still on Western Avenue. I'll wait for you up here."

"Don't you want to come down? Isn't Finney supposed to be here?"

"It's too late now. The races are over. He'll have gone."

Disappointment flooded Charity's brain. *I just want to find him and go home. Isabella is a really, really poor substitute for Rancor.* "All right, meet me at the top of the stairs."

"Will do."

Isabella greeted her with a kiss on both cheeks. "Next time, hold my hand. This is a big scary city."

Charity wasn't sure if she were joking or not.

"Do you want some lunch?"

Ulp. She swallowed hard. "Maybe a hot dog or

something."

"Oh, we can do better than that." Charity listened to the sound of bankruptcy bells tolling as Isabella led her to a little hole in the wall. They slipped in. Behind a high counter, sweaty, thick-armed women shouted orders. Isabella bought Tuscan chicken paninis while Charity got a couple of beers from the cooler, and they went to sit on a bench in the park.

Across the street, a line of people snaked down the block. "What's going on over there?"

Her companion gave the crowd a quick glance. "The line? It's for Starbucks. That one is supposed to be the original store. People come from all over the world to have their picture taken in front of it." She snickered, not a pleasant sound. "Poor saps don't know it's not actually the original. The first one opened in 1971 on Western Avenue in a building that was demolished five years later." She took a swig from her can, not a pleasant sight.

Charity tried the beer. "Why, it's good!"

Isabella wiped her mouth with a paper napkin, leaving the rose-colored lipstick annoyingly unsmudged. "It is, isn't it? Seattle has several micro-breweries. And some wonderful vineyards. You should visit them while you're here."

"Do you think we'll ever find Mr. Finney?"

Taking a tiny bite of her sandwich, Isabella said slowly, "We'll have to eventually. I'll spend this afternoon following up leads."

"Oh. In that case maybe I *will* do some sightseeing."

"I'll give you a call later today then. Finished?"

Better leave some for my supper. Charity put the

rest of her sandwich back in the bag. "Yes."

As she reached the hotel, a cold sun managed to peep through the fog. She shivered. Mr. Waters looked up. "Oh, Miss Snow. You look chilled. Why don't you go through to the library and sit by the fire. I'll have Joseph bring you a hot chocolate. Or would you prefer tea?"

"Tea would be nice." She found the room he indicated, decorated like an English study with an oriental rug, over-sized leather chairs, and a fireplace. *The Basses certainly do up a hotel rather well.* She pulled a quilt over her and curled up on the cushion.

She didn't know how long she'd slept. The sky outside was still overcast. *I wonder if they ever get an actual downpour here, or does the rain just dribble you to death?*

The concierge came in. "Miss Snow? You're wanted on the house phone."

Instead of the yearned-for Rancor, she heard George's gravelly voice. "How's it going?"

"Not too good. We missed Finney today. Although, on the bright side, I've had a close encounter with one of the odder customs of Seattle."

"Oh?"

She told him about the fish tossing.

"Charity, you're supposed to be working, not playing with your food. If you're hoping to get a discount on day-old fish, you don't need to. You have an expense account."

"I do?"

"I'm sorry." His voice was deceptively offhand. "Did I forget to mention it? A hundred-dollar-a-day allowance, thanks to Arlo's generosity. I'm not paying for the room because Bass said he had that covered. Evidently his family owns the hotel."

Thank God. I won't have to subsist on soup. "Yes, his family owns a string of specialty hotels in Maine, Florida, and elsewhere."

George sniffed. "Then why is he hitting me up for cash all the time?"

"It's just his way of showing affection."

"*Hmmph.* Back to Finney. Do you have a description of the man?"

"Only what Rancor told me. Short and balding."

"Could be me."

"Funny, that's not how I picture you."

"Suck-up. Well, keep me posted." He hung up.

Charity had left the desk and started toward the elevator when her cell phone dinged. The sultry tones of a seductress—no doubt the fruit of years of elocution lessons—came through the line. "It's me, Isabella."

"Any word?"

"Yes! We're in luck. I discovered that he's heading to Whidbey Island tomorrow for a concert and wine tasting."

"Whidbey Island?"

"North of Seattle. Puget Sound is loaded with islands. Whidbey's the largest. They have seven vineyards, a naval air station, and a decent theatre. They even have a distillery. You want to give it a whirl?"

"Sure."

"I'll pick you up at eleven. We catch the ferry for Langley in Everett, about an hour from here."

"Ferry?"

"Yes. It's the primary mode of transportation in Seattle. Only way to get to the mainland from most of the islands. Don't worry. You won't get seasick—it's a big ship. Holds maybe a hundred cars."

Despite Isabella's snide comment, Charity felt her excitement build. A ferry ride! The only ferry she'd ever taken crossed the St. Johns River south of Amelia Island. It consisted of a thirty-foot-long barge that transported one car at a time. "Doesn't worry me, I'm from Florida, remember? We live on the water." *So what if I've never been on anything bigger than a bass boat?*

Isabella responded with a dismissive, "Fine," and rang off.

A couple got off the elevator and passed her, heading to the exit. The woman, her heavy face bright red with anger, was berating her companion, an anorexic teenager. "I don't care, Jeremy. It's almost six o'clock, and I haven't eaten in two hours. We're going to McDonald's *now*."

It reminded her that the only thing she'd consumed all day was half a panini. *Might as well take advantage of the expense account.* Charity turned around and went to the concierge's desk. "Mr. Waters, can you recommend a restaurant?"

"Certainly." He pulled out a large folder. "There's the Metropolitan, or the Pink Door. They're near the market. Our own restaurant, Boka, received a three-star rating from Zagat. It's right around the corner, and very quiet."

"Sounds perfect."

She found the restaurant easily and entered just as the rain began in earnest. The room was a vision in pink lights and wave patterns, from the bamboo walls to the curved banquettes. A waiter in a crisp white shirt and pink tie handed her a menu. She looked at the appetizers, dropping a finger over the prices. *What George doesn't know won't hurt him.* "This Skagit River Ranch chicken liver pâté sounds enticing."

"Yes. The rhubarb adds a touch of sweet-tart citrus to it. You'll like it. May I suggest the grilled razor clams?"

Charity thought of the little pencil-sized clam shells she collected on Longboat Key. "Would it be enough?"

"Oh yes, here in Puget Sound, they grow quite large. They come with pickled ramps and cherries."

"All right."

"And the grilled Little Gem lettuce to follow?"

"After the entrée?" *I've never heard of that.*

"Yes, a salad after the meat dish makes for a nice *digestif.* It is served with fruit and a pink peppercorn vinaigrette."

"All right." *I suppose that means I'll have to forgo dessert.*

An hour and a half later, Charity waddled into the hotel. Mr. Waters pressed the elevator button for her. "I take it your dinner was satisfactory?"

She patted her stomach. "Indeed." *I could get used to this.*

****

Isabella picked her up in the morning, and they drove north along the coast. Most of the area was heavily built up with tracts of small houses and strip malls. Charity began to wonder where the wild Pacific Northwest lived. They reached Everett and got in line for the ferry. Once they'd parked, they climbed a gangway up to a large snack bar with booths and tables.

"Oh look. There are doors to the outside deck." When Charity started toward them, Isabella called, "I'll just stay here. I don't want to mess up my hair. The wind is pretty damp." She looked at her companion's thick, glossy braid. "I suppose you don't mind having your hair get all frizzy."

Charity was getting used to Isabella's little barbs and paid her no mind. She walked quickly to the doors and opened them, only to be thrown nearly prostrate by the wind. She struggled forward and made it to the railing where she hung on for dear life. The channel was quite narrow, and she could see the island in the near distance. Gulls soared overhead, and the smoky gray water churned under the ferry. The sky wasn't much lighter than the water. A pair of dolphins decided to accompany them, and Charity watched them skip over and under the waves in front of the ship. Beyond the island, white-capped mountains loomed.

They pulled into the pier, and people scrambled to return to their cars. Men in yellow vests herded them down a ramp to the tarmac. The Lotus was one of the last off. Isabella pointed at the terminal clock. "We don't have much time. The winery closes at one." She pulled out onto the road. "I think it's this way."

Something told Charity they were going to get lost.

Isabella roared down the one-lane country roads, taking first a left and then a right, then another right. Where the street curved, they came to a familiar intersection. Charity pointed at a grocery store. "Didn't we pass that already?"

Isabella followed her pointing finger. "Oh dear. I'm sorry. We seem to be going in circles. No matter. We can catch him at the theatre. "

"Do you know where it is?"

"It's right in the middle of Langley. We can ask directions."

Charity refrained from noting that they could have done that for the winery. "Why don't you have GPS?"

"Couldn't afford it."

"Oh." *I suppose you have to cut corners somewhere.*

A few minutes later, they entered a small village. A large brown building sat at the corner, a sign declaring it to be the Center for the Arts. "This is it."

They pulled into an empty parking lot. "Not a lot of interest in the show, I guess."

"Maybe not." Isabella got out. "Wait here." She went inside. Returning a minute later, she jumped in the car and slammed the door. "Damn. I got the date wrong. The show starts tomorrow." She gave Charity a roguish look. "You'll think I'm awfully incompetent."

I think you're deliberately screwing this up. "I guess we'd better head back."

"We can catch the three o'clock ferry if we hurry."

And don't get lost. Charity was quiet on the way home. *I want to talk to Rancor about this. I think our Miss Isabella may have a different agenda from the one agreed upon.*

Isabella let her off at her hotel. It was still fairly early, so she decided to take a walk. She wandered down First Avenue until she came to an area of old brownstones. She stopped at a historic marker and read aloud. "Pioneer Town, the original downtown Seattle, founded 1852." Underneath the marker lay a pile of brochures. She picked one up.

Pioneer Town flourished during the Klondike Gold

Rush of 1897. The buildings are some of the best examples of nineteenth-century Romanesque Revival urban architecture in the United States. Nearby is the hundred-year-old Smith Tower, once the tallest building on the West Coast. Also in Pioneer Square stands the city's first monument, a Tlingit totem pole stolen from Alaska. Be sure to take the Seattle underground tour. There you will see the sunken storefronts that literally melted below the level of the sidewalk in the Great Fire of 1889.

She wandered around the square a bit, then headed up Cherry Street. At number nineteen, a man was replacing a plaque by the door. She noticed the old plaque leaning against the wall. She peered at it, unable to read the letters upside down.

"Ma'am? Can I help you?"

"Oh, sorry. I was just wondering what the sign said."

"Hang on." He picked it up and showed it to her.

HHR Press

~

Established 1933

He squinted up at the building. "Been here for generations. Not many of the old firms left." He frowned.

"Has Seattle grown a lot?"

"Twice as big as it was a decade ago, yeah. My great-grandaddy came out here to pan for gold."

"And did he find any?"

"Nope. Found a wife though. And the time to have eleven children."

"Oh my."

"Nowadays, we're lucky to have enough time for

one." He pulled a dog-eared photo out of his wallet. "That's my boy, James."

She peered at the black and white school picture of a little boy sitting stiffly. "How old is he now?"

"Twenty-one, and lucky he ain't in jail."

Unable to think of anything encouraging to say, Charity asked, "So…who's taken over the building?"

He put a screw in the new plaque. "Called IV Enterprises. One of those shell companies I think. You ask me, it's the Chinese behind it. They've bought up a lot of real estate in Washington."

IV? Sounds like a medical company. "Have you seen the new owners? Did they hire you?"

"Nope, just their secretary—or maybe their front. Classy." The man fanned his face. "A real looker."

"Well, thanks." She turned around and realized she had no idea in which direction to go. "Can you tell me how to get to the Bass Hotel?"

"The one on First Avenue? Sure."

When Charity reached the hotel, she went straight up to her room and called Rancor. He answered on the first ring. "There you are. I've been waiting all day. Report!"

Was there an "I miss you" in all that? "We went to Whidbey Island and got lost looking for the winery. Then we discovered that the play Isabella said Finney was going to didn't start 'til tomorrow. So we came home."

"*Hmm.* Isabella seems to be off her game."

"Or on it."

"What do you mean?"

"I'm beginning to wonder if she's deliberately missing Finney."

253

"Protecting him?"

"Maybe. And guess what."

"I don't want to. Just tell me."

"I came across HHR Press. Only it's no longer HHR Press. It's IV Enterprises. The handyman thought it might be a shell company."

"Pretty impressive for a handyman. Are you sure he wasn't a cop or something?"

She thought of the dog-eared wallet and the little boy, James. "No, I don't think so."

"Then we're on our own."

"What do you mean?"

"Well, Isabella told me she would get in touch with the Seattle police—see if they could keep tabs on Finney."

"She didn't mention that to me."

"Maybe I misunderstood her."

"Taken in by her perfect smile?"

"Nah. Although it is brilliant, isn't it?"

Why does he do that? "I'll talk to you tomorrow."

"What? That's it? No air kiss?"

"Save it for Isabella."

****

The ringtone woke her at eight the next morning. The same deep-throated voice purred, "Ready for another stab at it?"

No. "What have you got?"

"Michael made a reservation for lunch in the restaurant in the Space Needle. I'm betting he's meeting with whoever he sells the manuscripts to. We can confront them both."

I'll give her one more chance. "Okay."

"I'll pick you up at one. Oh, it's pretty fancy. Do

you have a nice dress? If not, I can lend you one of mine. Of course, we'd probably have to let it out some."

Such a darling woman. "Thanks, but I packed something appropriate." *Make that,* should *have.* "I…uh…I've got some things to do this morning. Why don't I take a taxi and meet you there?" She called the lobby. "Mr. Waters, is there a clothing store nearby?"

Four hours later, she met Isabella at the entrance to the Seattle landmark, sporting a brand-new gray-and-red plaid dress that brought out both the silver in her eyes and the copper in her hair. They took the elevator up to the SkyCity Restaurant. The round room was awash in hazy light from the floor-to-ceiling windows. Charity felt slightly dizzy and wondered if the altitude was getting to her. Isabella said loudly, "You do realize the restaurant is turning, don't you?"

Sure enough, when she looked out and down, it was clear that the room was slowly moving. The maître d' greeted them. "Yes, indeed. SkyCity rotates three hundred sixty degrees every hour, affording our patrons a truly panoramic view of Seattle and Puget Sound. Now, may I have the name of your party?" He held a pen poised above the reservation book.

"We don't have a reservation. We've just arrived in the city. We're all alone and simply *famished.* Could you by any chance find us a table for two?" Isabella gazed soulfully into the man's eyes and then down to his chest. "Cecil?"

Cecil regretted very much, all the while bestowing admiring glances on Isabella, but there were no tables available. Perhaps the ladies would care to make a reservation? He opened the book. "We have an opening at two p.m. on…March 4. That's a Tuesday."

Oh, a Tuesday. *Why didn't you say so?*

"That's too bad. We're only in town for a few days. Actually"—she moved a little closer to him—"we'd just like to speak to a patron. A former colleague. His name is Michael Finney."

He looked the list over. "I see no Michael Finney here. Perhaps it is under another name?"

Isabella's lip quivered oh so slightly. "Oh dear, it must be. He is lunching with someone, but I don't have the other man's name. Could we perhaps stroll around a bit? Spy him out?"

"I'm afraid not. It is against our policy to allow people to hop tables. I am so sorry." He looked genuinely grief-stricken.

Charity leaned in. "Could we have a drink at the bar?"

The great Cecil appeared to have noticed her for the first time. "Well, that can be arranged. Right this way."

Charity started to follow him, but Isabella grabbed her arm and hissed urgently, "No, let's forget it. If we see him, they won't let us talk to him. I think we should go downstairs—catch him on the way out."

Charity let herself be piloted out to the elevator, but when they got to the bottom she shook her arm free. "Look, this is getting ridiculous. I'm—we're—wasting our time. My flight leaves tonight. Please, just take me back to my hotel."

"You sure? Okay."

Is it my imagination or did she just relax? "You can keep us up to date." *I won't sit by the phone though.*

Isabella didn't speak again until she dropped

Charity off at the hotel. "Have a good flight. I'll let Rancor know how we fared."

"It's all right—we've been in constant touch." *Take that.*

Isabella blinked, but her face remained bland. "Nonetheless." She waved gaily and roared off.

Charity called Rancor and told him about the latest washout. "I'm sure now she's doing it on purpose. She was pleased to hear I'm leaving tonight."

"What would she be playing at then? It doesn't make sense. We only lost a few manuscripts. She lost her job because of Finney. She should be even more desperate than we are to find him."

"Maybe she's known where he is all along."

"You think she's in on it with him?"

She hesitated only a moment. "I do."

"You're sure you're not just suspicious of a pretty face?"

"Rancor, stop it. You should have seen her expression when I said I'd had it. She positively glowed. Her plan has been to take me on all these wild goose chases—with Finney always out of reach or disappearing just before we get there." She thought of something. "She did it with you too."

"Me! Oh, you mean, the Amtrak and New York sightings? *Hmm.* Are you suggesting that he was never there at all?"

"No, but the question arises: how would she know where he was going to be if he didn't tell her?"

"It could have been the undercover police detective she's been working with."

"What! Why didn't you tell me?"

"I just found out. Remember Isabella said she was

going to contact them? Well, I asked her. A Detective Snyder has been trailing Finney."

"According to her. Did you call the police and confirm it?"

"Not yet. I just got off the phone with her. I'll call them next...I suppose you want me to pick you up at the airport."

"Yes, I do."

"Heavy sigh. Are you bringing me a present?"

"No, Rancor."

"Another heavy sigh, this time slightly more martyred." He hung up.

Charity felt at loose ends again. What to do? *I know. I'll go over to the IV building and see if anyone's about. Maybe they can tell me what happened to HHR Press.* She took her purse and walked to 19 Cherry Street. She rang the bell. No answer. A passerby said, "Who are you looking for?"

"The company that just bought this building."

"I don't think they've moved in yet." The drizzle chose that moment to turn into a full-fledged deluge. The man shook out his umbrella. "You'll have to come back tomorrow."

Even though Charity stood on the landing shivering in the downpour, it didn't seem to occur to the man to offer to share his umbrella. He pointed to the corner. "There's a bar over there. You might want to get out of the rain." He walked on.

Charity made a dash for the building. The bar—more a pub—was dry and snug. A fire blazed in the corner. She found a seat next to a mousy little man. The last few strands of hair had been carefully combed over his pate, and he sat hunched over, a tartan scarf wrapped tightly around his neck, a cup of cocoa between his palms. She ordered a Rusty Nail.

He glanced at her. "Interesting choice of drink."

"I thought it would warm me up."

He coughed. "February in Seattle not toasty enough for you?" His voice was hoarse, but Charity imagined it would still be a bit grating in better health.

"I got caught in the rain."

The bartender brought her her drink.

The customer seemed inclined to chat. "You live around here?"

"Just visiting."

He sipped his cocoa. "Not many natives around anymore. All newcomers."

"Really?"

"Me, I'm third generation. Granddad came here from the east coast. Set up a business. It prospered. That is, until I came along." His face drooped.

Charity felt sorry for him. "What kind of business?"

"Publishing. Established a little publishing firm right here on Cherry Street. Didn't do badly. Had some big-name authors. All gone now." He stared into his cup.

Oh my God. It's him. "Was it HHR Press by any chance?"

He turned surprised eyes on her. "How did you know?"

"I…uh…passed it on the way here."

He gave her a keen glance. "It doesn't say HHR Press anymore."

"The handyman was changing name plates when I passed, and the old one was still there. What happened?"

He signaled for more cocoa. "A while ago, I discovered a substantial chunk of funds missing from the firm's accounts. I suspected the accountant I'd brought in to do our taxes but had no real evidence." He put three lumps of sugar in his cup and stirred. "Anyway, I could have survived that, but then something much worse happened."

"What could be worse than losing all that money?"

"For a publisher? Piracy. You know it's rampant nowadays? Chinese, Indonesians, Indians—all stealing books. Lost five major manuscripts. Even if the authors don't sue me, they were my biggest moneymakers. Had no choice but to go out of business. Thank God for Isabella."

I'd better pretend I know nothing about this. "Isabella? Is she your wife?"

"No, Isabella Voleuse is my editor."

"What did she do?"

"Bought me out. Don't know where she got the money. We closed on it two weeks ago."

"Oh." *Wait a minute...IV...Isabella Voleuse. Ha.* Charity sipped her drink. "What will you do now?"

"Dunno. All I know is publishing. When I get her check, I'll figure something out."

"Her check?"

"The settlement check. She was supposed to mail it the day after closing, but it hasn't arrived yet."

Something tells me he shouldn't wait up for it. "So you have no idea who stole your manuscripts?"

"Uh uh. Could be anyone." His eyes turned shifty. "Say, you're asking a lot of questions. You're not a reporter, are you?"

Charity had a moment of panic. *Is it painted on my face?* "No, no."

He relaxed a bit. "I don't know why I told you all that. It's supposed to be a secret."

"Why?"

"Because of the will."

She waited. When he didn't go on, she prompted, "The will?"

"My grandfather's will. The Finneys are not supposed to ever change the name of the company—even if we sell it. My father put it in his will as well. If the family finds out, I stand to lose my trust fund."

"But why not make that a condition of the sale?"

"I did. We had the whole thing written up, but when we went to closing, that language had been deleted. Isabella said it was an oversight, and she would have it corrected on the final papers."

Let me guess. "She forgot?"

He nodded miserably. "If the family lawyer discovers it's now IV Enterprises, I'm in deep kimchee."

"Kimchee? What does that mean?"

"Oh, it's an expression my father always used—he picked it up when he was in the Navy in Vietnam. Kimchee is this fiery hot kind of sauerkraut. He used it instead of 'shit' for the sake of my mother."

Charity nursed her drink. "I'm Charity, by the way. Charity Snow."

"Michael Finney."

I know. "What did your lawyer have to say about the omission?"

"Oh, I didn't have a lawyer. Isabella said the buyer needed one but not the seller."

I'm not sure which is worse—a shyster like Isabella or a patsy like Michael. "I see. Well…" She rose and put a bill on the bar. "Good luck. If you want to keep the trust fund, I suggest you get yourself a lawyer."

"I suppose I'll have to. If only I didn't have to wait 'til I'm forty to access the money. Then I'd be in great shape." He finished his drink.

Charity's curiosity got the better of her. "Is it a lot?"

"Oh, yes. When Grandfather left Florida, his benefactor gave him fifty thousand dollars to set himself up. He established the press, but he also invested well. It's worth several million now."

"Whew." *Wait a minute. Maybe he can shed some light on at least one question.* "Your grandfather—why did he leave Florida?"

Finney's eyes grew shifty again. "Not…not sure. We think it had something to do with a woman. He had a good job in Sarasota. You know the Ringling Brothers circus? Well, John Ringling not only ran the circus but also owned a lot of real estate in Sarasota. He built a fabulous mansion and art gallery and established a significant library collection devoted to works on art and history. Edgar Finney was his librarian."

"Were they close? Ringling and your grandfather?"

"Oh, very close. Grandpa always said Ringling was one of his best friends."

"So it was perhaps John Ringling who gave him the money to get started."

"No, no. Something…something happened. Grandpa left very precipitously—I never found out why. But he definitely got the money from Ringling's wife."

"Mable?"

"No. Hedda. His second wife."

Chapter Fifteen
Cards and Letters

"What do you think?"

"I think," said Rancor, spinning the wheel to zip around a pickup truck, "I'd like to find out why Finney's grandfather ran off to Seattle with Hedda's money."

"Why?"

"Why not? I love mysteries." He honked his horn at a bicyclist, who teetered dangerously close to the lane. The rider reeled, and the bike fell over. Charity watched him shake his fist at Rancor as they zoomed away.

"But what does it have to do with the problem at hand?"

"You mean, who actually stole the manuscripts?"

Charity thought about pointing out that her quest involved the identity of the skeleton, not Rancor's thief, but after her encounters with Isabella, she had a stake in the mission too. *If only to nail her.*

He mused, "Hedda...Finney. Tommy...Ringling. *Hmm.* Look, Charity, I know you're focused on the skeleton for your story, but I can't help but think there's some kind of connection among all these loose threads. Wait!" He slammed on the brakes.

"Rancor!"

"What? Oh." He looked up to see a tractor trailer

behind him, frantically swerving to avoid hitting the Mini Cooper. He gave the driver a cheery wave and pulled off the road into Olaf's parking lot. He turned to Charity, taking her hand and gazing deeply into her eyes.

She had begun to pucker for the kiss when he put the car in gear and pulled out into traffic again. "That should give that trucker time to get farther down the road." He cut in front of a Lincoln. The nonagenarian driver gawked at him and screeched to a halt. As they sped up, they heard the tinkle of breaking glass behind them. "I've been thinking. Standish said the adult skeleton died in the 1930s. Did he say how old little Tommy was?"

"Wasn't he seven?"

"No. I mean, how old was his skeleton?"

"Captain Kelly confirmed his death date as 1926. Why?"

"Perhaps they were closer in time than we thought. Perhaps the two deaths are related."

She frowned. "Rancor, you missed the turn."

"Sorry." He made a quick U-turn, setting up yet another round of near-crashes. "Well?"

"I don't know. Right now, all I want to do is get out of these travel clothes and into a hot shower."

He sniffed with exaggerated distaste. "I was going to suggest that very thing." He followed her inside. "I'll wait for you in the bedroom."

"No, you won't. I need some rest. Don't you have *anywhere* else to stay?"

Rancor sulked. "I suppose I could crash with George, but then we'd have to tell him about my little predicament."

"He already knows."

"Really?"

"Why do you think he let me go to Seattle?"

"Oh, right." He picked up her car keys. "I'll see you later." And before she could grab the keys back, he skipped out the door.

Charity had had a long shower, a small sandwich, and a big glass of beer before Rancor showed up again. "George say no?"

He shrugged. "I think he was about to agree when he saw his wife leering at me. Being godlike has its drawbacks."

"You wouldn't know."

"I did manage to confirm that little Tommy died in 1926."

"We knew that."

"Yes, but what we don't know for sure is when the other victim died."

"It had to be at least five years later."

Rancor shook his head. "Not if the ring didn't belong to the man in the pit."

"Interesting idea." Charity embarked on this new train of thought. "It could have been dropped—"

"Or fallen—"

"Down the shaft separately—"

"By a broken-hearted lover."

"R—cut to the quick by G."

"*Hmm.*"

Rancor jumped up. "So the ring could still belong to my grandfather. Jilted by Trudy, he betook himself to Florida."

"Why not go to Nebraska as ordered then? And Trudy was pregnant with his second child, so their relationship couldn't have been all bad. Aunt Gertrude said her mother died of a broken heart. That wouldn't have happened if she had given him the old heave-ho."

"You've forgotten. Mother told me that in fact Trudy was on the verge of divorcing Robert but died before she could initiate proceedings." He began to pace. "My aunt obviously feels a philandering father is preferable to a disloyal mother when it comes to the family honor."

"Okay, then who the hell is the skeleton?"

"Biddlesworth!" Rancor did a little jig.

Charity began to giggle.

"What?"

"This sounds like the plot of one of your utterly implausible novels."

"It could be, couldn't it? I say, I'm going to write this down."

Charity went into the kitchen and poured another beer. "I just thought of something else. Biddlesworth didn't die in 1926."

Rancor slumped. "I'd forgotten. He went missing in 1933, didn't he? And we know he was alive until then because he had those dealings with Calvin Hagen. Damn." After a bit, he took heart. "Still, the ring could be Robert's."

"Don't you think that's a bit of a stretch?"

He scratched his neck. "You are no fun at all."

She smiled with satisfaction. "Good."

"Because you see, while you with such easy indifference relegate Tommy T to a mundane accident and the benighted Biddlesworth to a watery grave, you haven't answered the question of my grandfather's disappearance."

"Am I supposed to?"

He stopped. An uncertain look passed over his face, catching Charity off guard. "I…I thought we were in this together?"

A feeling she couldn't name rushed through her, one that filled every pore with a heavy sort of heat. It weighed her down, made her sluggish. Time slowed. She watched with vague interest as her knees buckled, and the floor rushed toward her. Just before she smacked into it, two strong arms caught her, lifted her up, and held her in a crushing grip. "Charity? Are you all right?"

"Yes. Yes. Oh, Rancor." After that she couldn't talk because her lips were smashed against his and her chest against his and she couldn't breathe at all but she didn't really need to because he was breathing for the both of them.

A while later, they sat down on the couch. Rancor traced her cheek with his finger, his eyes wondering. Charity felt at peace. She had recognized the hot, heavy feeling and accepted it. Now to explain it to Rancor.

"Rancor? I—"

The phone rang. He picked it up. "Who? Is that you? Where are you?" He listened for a minute, then said, "Wait there," and hung up.

With a sinking feeling, Charity asked, "Isabella?"

"No." He stood. "Can I borrow your car?"

Charity was so struck by the fact that he'd actually asked her that she didn't reply. As he opened the door, she finally yelped, "Who was it?"

"Michael Finney."

****

Charity woke with a start. The television was

muted, but all the lights were on in the apartment. The clock told her it was three, and the dark sky told her it was the middle of the night. *Where is Rancor?* The answering machine didn't blink. The cell phone seemed to have become a permanent accessory to Rancor's wardrobe. She rose from the couch and went to the window before she realized there was nothing to see. Sudden fear ripped through her. *He's hurt. A car accident. Finney murdered him.* She started to dial 9-1-1 but thought better of it. *What would I say?* Rancor had left without telling her where he was going or why. *Was Finney calling from Seattle?* No, Rancor told him to wait "there." *He must be in Sarasota.* But why didn't he bring him home? She thought about the mousy little man. He didn't seem the murderous type. He did seem the type to be fooled by a beautiful woman. *Actually, probably by any woman.* Or any man. *It's a wonder he lasted as long as he did in publishing.* She'd have to look into who actually signed the authors—maybe his father had been the one with the initiative, and the firm had merely coasted under Michael.

She still stood by the window. The sky had begun to lighten, and streaks of pink light shot over her head from the east, spraying the western sky with bits of sunrise. At last she went into the bedroom and lay down. *He'll call when he can.* And if he didn't, she would go to the police.

The telephone rang insistently. Still groggy, she groped around the bedside table for her phone and only realized it still lay on the couch when it stopped ringing. A distant voice said, "Charity, are you there? It's Rancor. Call me at your cell number when you get this message."

She decided to wait until both the throbbing of her heart and the tremor in her legs had subsided. When she called, he picked up immediately. "Charity, I know you were worried about me, but I'm fine."

Well, I guess you don't need me to hold up an end of the conversation. "No, I wasn't. Just curious."

There was a pause. "Oh. Well, Finney and I had quite a night."

"He didn't strike me as the party animal type."

"No, no—we were most civilized. In fact, we stayed at the airport bar all night talking, just the two of us. When I dropped him off at his hotel, he didn't seem eager to put me up, so you are free to indulge in my company indefinitely."

"Swell. Say, I've been wondering. How did Michael get my phone number?"

"Jemimah gave it to him. She's the only one who answered his calls."

"I see. Are you going to tell me what you two talked about?"

"I think that had better wait until he's with us. Suffice it to say, you were right about Isabella."

Aha. "That she's a shrew?"

"No, that she's the manuscript thief. Look, can I freshen up? We're meeting Michael for lunch."

She asked, with little hope, "His treat?"

"Charity, come on. He's in as dire financial straits as I am. You're currently the only one gainfully employed."

"What happened with Publix?"

"They…uh…had to let me go. Something about being 'untrainable.' "

"Rancor! We're not talking about brain surgery.

What did you do? Crash the grocery carts into cars?"

"How did you—? It was only two cars." His tone was defensive. "Fortunately, Mr. Gibbons, who happens to be the former CEO of Publix, didn't mind the small indentation—more of a dimple really—on his 1967 Corvette. Unfortunately, the Mercedes belonged to the mayor, and he was not quite so agreeable. They compromised by firing me." There was a pause. "Personally, I considered the mayor tearing my last paycheck into tiny pieces and blowing them in my face a trifle gratuitous."

"Oh, Rancor."

He began to wheedle. "Come on, Charity. It'll be worth your while. What he's got to say will make a helluva scoop."

Damn the man. "All right—where are you?"

"Right outside."

Sure enough, a rather disheveled Rancor stood at her door. Somewhere he'd picked up a tie, which was askew, and a black smudge, which stained his chinos. Also, his face was dirty. Charity surveyed the damage. "Take a header, did you?"

"As a matter of fact, yes. Tripped over an utterly superfluous curb. I intend to write an indignant letter to the airport authority—they make no accommodations for the disabled. However, since my reflexes are superb, I managed to land on the verge rather than the pavement."

"Face down I see. Good thing we had that rain last night."

He wiped his brow, carving a white streak through the brown gunk. "I can always count on you for sympathy. May I use your bathroom?"

"Take off those muddy shoes before you move another inch."

He did. When she stepped aside to let him past, he marched to the bathroom without looking back.

An hour later he emerged, drying his hair with a washcloth. "You're out of towels."

Charity trilled, "Oops, sorry."

"I had to use several washcloths—one for my penis alone."

"I'm not surprised. Are you hungry?"

"Starving. We're to meet Michael at one. Could I have some toast? Maybe an omelet? And sausage if you have it."

"I'm making toast." She poured him a cup of coffee to take the sting out of her two-star hospitality and popped two slices of bread in the toaster. They ate silently. She put the dishes in the sink and got her purse.

"Where are you going?"

"Um, to work?"

He checked the calendar magnet on the refrigerator. "What day is it, anyway?"

"Tuesday."

"Odd. I could have sworn it was only Monday." He shook his head. "I must have lost a day somewhere. Ah well"—he pecked her cheek—"I'd better come with you. There's work to be done on the ghost book!"

Charity didn't think that required an answer.

Rancor sat at the spare laptop in the office playing solitaire until it was time to meet Finney. They drove to Pattigeorge's. Lunch was in full swing, and they had to wait for a corner table. Finney arrived just as they were seated, looking much more chipper than Rancor did. In fact, his face shone pink with good humor, and he walked with a brisk step. "Hello, hello! I see you made it safely home, Bass." He bowed to Charity. "We meet again." The corners of his eyes creased in delight. "So you see, my instincts were right. You *are* a reporter."

Charity smiled at him. "Yet it was an entirely fortuitous meeting."

"Fortuitous, yes." He held her hand. "Also quite cheering."

There's more to this man than meets the eye.

Rancor interrupted, his tone abrupt, "Sit down, Finney." When Charity gave him a surprised look, he added, "I mean, won't you have a seat, Michael?"

Do I detect a touch of the green-eyed monster? Ha.

The waitress appeared and spoke solely to Rancor. "I'm Portia. I'll be your server today. Can I get you anything, sir?"

Rancor fixed the girl with a steady gaze and recited, " '*Sweet Portia,*

If you did know to whom I gave the ring,
If you did know for whom I gave the ring
And would conceive for what I gave the ring
And how unwillingly I left the ring,
When nought would be accepted but the ring,
You would abate the strength of your displeasure.'
We'll have iced tea."

She backed away slowly, her eyes darting right and left.

Rancor, faced with an astounded silence, said, "What? When is *The Merchant of Venice* not appropriate?"

Charity replied, "In many ways, you remind me of Bassanio."

"Ah, the hero. Dashing, suave, beauteous to behold?"

"Profligate. Mercurial. Empty-headed. So, are we going to order?"

They decided on pizza, arguing amiably about anchovies—Rancor won. "You can't have pizza without anchovies. It's un-American."

Finney laughed. "But is it constitutional?"

Portia brought the tea and took their order, studiously avoiding Rancor's side of the table. Rancor waited until the glass was at the publisher's lips before trumpeting, "Michael had a talk with his mother." Once the busboy had mopped the table and given everyone new napkins, he continued. "Do you want to tell it or shall I?"

The little man glanced furtively around the room.

"Your mother's not here."

"I know that. It's just...have you...have you seen Isabella around? I don't mean to sound paranoid, but I think she's been following me."

Charity turned to Rancor. "That reminds me. Did you ever find out if the police had a tail on Mr. Finney?"

Finney's eyes bugged out. "A tail? What for?"

Rancor poured sugar into his tea. "I...uh...forgot to call. Anyway," he added hastily, "It's moot now. Isabella's in Seattle, and Michael's here."

"Are you sure she's in Seattle?"

"Uh, no. Michael?"

The little man threw his hands up. "I don't know where she is. She keeps calling me—from London, Paris, Washington, DC. The last call came from Albuquerque." He stared dolefully at his plate. "When I ask about the check, she says it's in the mail."

Charity patted his hand but couldn't bring herself to fib. *You're never going to see a check, dear.* Then something else he said caught her attention. "Wait. She called you from London and Paris? You were never there?"

"Me? The first time I've left Seattle in five years is to come here."

Charity shot a triumphant look at Rancor, who said mildly, "We've established that you were right. No need to make a federal case out of it."

She turned to Michael. "Why *are* you here anyway?"

He glanced at Rancor. "It's a long story."

Rancor said, "Maybe we should begin with your mother."

"Okay." He took a swig of iced tea.

Charity watched him. "I take it you told your mother about the sale?"

"I had to. She's eighty-four, so she doesn't get out much, but when she does, she always visits the office. She would have seen the new sign."

"IV Enterprises?"

He nodded. "So I brought her some candy—she loves that horrible ribbon stuff you get at Christmas—and sat her down and told her I sold HHR Press."

"What did she do?"

"Well, she reacted as I anticipated, railing about how I'd let the family down and it was lucky my father—not to mention my grandfather—wasn't around to see this happen to his beloved company. She reminded me that Grandfather had founded it in 1933, and it represented the quintessential small, independent, publishing firm."

Here's my chance. "Mr. Finney—"

"Please, call me Michael."

"Michael, who actually contracted with the authors in your…is it called a stable?"

Rancor made a rude noise.

Michael hesitated, then, with a tiny grin, replied, "Yes, I believe it's called that. That was my father. You remember him, Rancor, don't you?"

"I suppose you're expecting me to whinny."

"Rancor!"

"All right, all right. Indeed, Andrew was a remarkable man. I had four books under my belt at Harper, and he stole me away with visions of top billing, huge promotional blitzes, my name in lights…or was it on Broadway? And then Michael took over and…" He didn't look at the other man. "Er…sorry, old chap." He lapsed into a troubled silence.

Charity hadn't finished. "And Isabella Voleuse. Who hired her?"

"I did. She came highly recommended. She is an excellent editor."

Rancor stirred. "Well…she had the advantage of working with five seasoned writers. Most of the time she merely soothed ruffled egos and sent the manuscript along without comment."

"Oh, my." The news seemed to distress Finney. "I didn't know that."

Charity said quietly, "Or maybe she didn't pass the manuscripts on at all."

"To be fair, we don't know when she started her racket. We only know about the five missing ones."

Rancor called the hostess over. "Velma, isn't it? What a lovely name. Velma, I'm afraid Portia has her hands full. Would you mind bringing me a Beck's? There's a good girl."

Velma, sixty if she was a day, reacted positively to being called a girl. Cheeks flushed, she peeped, "Right away, Mr. Bass."

When she had gone, he put his hands on the table. "Back to the subject. What else did your mother have to say?"

"That was the striking part. Once she'd calmed down, she insisted that I do whatever it took to have the name of HHR reinstated. Then she said something about a promise, an oath, and a deed."

"Deed to a house? To the firm?"

"I don't know. When I pressed her, all she said was, 'Go to Cà d'Zan. The answer is there.' So I packed my bag, and here I am."

Charity cried, "Cà d'Zan! That's John and Mable Ringling's house. You told me your grandfather was the Ringlings' librarian."

"Yes. He managed their collection of works on art and architecture. They even gave him a room in the house."

Rancor leaned forward, his eyes alight. "I believe he was quite close to them."

"To John, yes. He never knew Mable—she died in 1929, I believe. He came on in 1931."

The pizza arrived. Rancor slid a slice onto Charity's plate and handed the platter to Finney. "Was Ringling married to Hedda then?"

Charity answered. "If I remember correctly, they were married in 1930."

Rancor took the platter back and set it beside his plate. "Did he get along with Hedda?"

Michael nodded. "By all accounts."

"I read that Edgar Finney left Sarasota without warning. Any idea why? Could he and John have had a quarrel of some kind?"

"Or he and Hedda?" Charity didn't intend to be left out of the deliberations.

The other man shook his head. "Mother did mention her father-in-law tendered his resignation rather unexpectedly, but she never told me why. I just assumed he wanted to go into business for himself. No one ever mentioned a rift. If true, why would Hedda give him the money?"

Rancor finished off the pizza, to the distress of his companions, and signaled to the waitress. He pointed at Charity. "She'll take the check, thanks."

After she had paid, he and Michael walked her out to her car. She pulled out her keys. "Where to?"

"Cà d'Zan of course."

"I have to get back to the office."

"No, you don't. I told George you were on the track of something big."

"I am?"

"Yes. An enigma."

"Any particular one?"

"What is behind this irrevocable promise to retain the company name? Was the relationship between Edgar Finney and Hedda Ringling friendly or hostile? I don't think we can necessarily assume she financed him as a gesture of good will. Could it have been blackmail? A bribe?" He opened the driver's side door. "I'm convinced we'll find the answer at Cà d'Zan."

"Oh, you are. What was your first clue?"

"There's no call for sarcasm, Charity. I'm in charge whether you like it or not." He went around to the other side, leaving Michael to wedge himself into the rear seat.

Charity tried not to wail. "But what does any of this have to do with the skeleton? That's the story we're supposed to be following." *No point in even bringing up the ghost story anthology.*

"Who knows? Maybe the skeleton is the real Edgar Finney, and an imposter went to Seattle."

"After Finney quit? Then why did he quit?"

Michael piped up from behind them. "Excuse me, Rancor, but I should know my own grandfather, and I distinctly remember him bouncing me on his knee."

"Did he look like you?"

There was a pause. "Mother often remarked on the...striking family resemblance."

Rancor's lower lip trembled. "Ah." He turned to Charity. "We won't learn anything unless we go to Cà d'Zan. So step on it."

They drove down Gulf of Mexico Drive and around St. Armands Circle to the Ringling Bridge. Turning left on the Tamiami Trail, they entered the parking lot of the Ringling complex a few minutes later. Charity bought their tickets in the visitor's center. *Another hundred dollars I could have spent on rent.* "So where do we start?"

"The house, of course. That's the actual Cà d'Zan. It means House of John in some local Italian dialect. Bit pretentious if you ask me." Rancor went to the ticket counter. "We want to see the library in the house. Is it open to the public?"

The cashier, an old man with iron gray hair and a peppy attitude, chirruped, "Why, aren't you the lucky ones! It's only open on Tuesdays. The docent can give you a tour. You're in for a real treat."

"What about the rest of the house?"

His pep collapsed like an under-inflated football. "Oh gosh, I'm sorry. You can tour the ground level, but the upstairs is closed to visitors. We have a shortage of staff today—tomorrow is Valentine's Day, you know." He winked at Charity. "Sorry."

They took the tram. Along the way, they passed the Circus Museum and Mable Ringling's rose garden, ending at a circular drive before the entrance to the house. The façade, of pink stucco embellished with glazed tiles, rose two levels, topped by a large, ornate cupola. A marker informed them that the design was modeled after the Doge's palace in Venice, and finished in 1926 at a cost of one-and-a-half million dollars.

Rancor grunted. "Do you suppose 1926 was the watershed year of Ringling's fortunes?"

"You mean, maybe once he paid for Cà d'Zan he had nothing left for the Ritz-Carlton?" Charity stepped back and gazed upward. "Possibly."

They handed their tickets to a bored young woman who led them past the Gothic-arched wooden door to one painted in gold leaf. Cherubs blew kisses from the elaborate raised panels. Entering a wide foyer lined with statuary and paintings, Charity pointed. "Look at that, a full set of armor."

Michael smirked. "Every house should have one of those."

They passed through the magnificent dining room, set for twenty, and then a small bar lit by Tiffany stained-glass windows. A padded-leather door in one wall led them to a room lined with bookcases. Michael was headed to the desk when a short, busy woman of about thirty-five came forward. "Hello! I'm Deirdre Penney, curator of the collection. Welcome to the library of Cà d'Zan."

Michael and Charity assumed listening poses. Rancor ignored the docent and wandered over to a window. After a pause sizzling with reproach, Mrs. Penney plunged on.

"First, you should know that most of the collection is now housed in our Education Center. This little room was Mr. Ringling's study." She pointed out the stacks, filled with titles like *Seventeenth-Century Portraiture* and *Rules for Authentication of Works of the Dutch School*. "Please, sit down if you like." When they had settled into plush green wingchairs, Mrs. Penney began to talk about the house. "Mable was the principal overseer of the construction. She chose the building materials and the furnishings, even the paintings. The Ringlings often picked items up at auction. For example, the crystal chandelier in the living room originally hung in the Waldorf Astoria Hotel in New York." She sighed. "Such a tragedy that Mable died only three years after they moved in."

Charity said idly, "And then John married Hedda."

Mrs. Penney's face tightened. "Yes. By all accounts, the marriage was not a happy one."

Rancor asked, "Is this part of the collection catalogued?"

"More or less. The last official librarian began work in the 1930s, but he quit rather abruptly, and then, when Mr. Ringling died in 1936, it languished. I maintain the furnishings and the paintings, but the books are more or less as they were when he left."

Rancor went to one wall and pulled out a large tome. Mrs. Penney made a move toward him, but he waved her off with an imperious gesture. "It's all right, I'm a writer."

This seemed to flummox her, and she sat down with a plop. Rancor flipped through the pages. "This one's on Italian renaissance architecture. Look, here's a picture of the Palace of the Doge in Venice. Isn't Cà d'Zan modeled after it?"

Mrs. Penney rallied. "Yes, it is. The turrets and statuary niches—"

"Do you have anything on the history of the Ghost Hotel?"

"Ghost Hotel?"

"Ringling laid the cornerstone for a Ritz-Carlton on Longboat Key in 1926 and stopped work on it the same year. You don't know about it?" He gave her a disgusted look and dropped the book onto the desk.

The lady did not back down. "On the contrary, I know quite a bit about the magnificent hulk that sat empty on the southern tip of Longboat Key for almost forty years. Why—"

"Hey, here's a book about it." Michael picked up a volume from one of the tables.

Charity took it from him and, switching on the lamp, she began to read.

"*Ringling entered into a contract with Hegeman-Harris Company, Inc., of New York in February of 1926. Work began March 1926. The building's plan called for more than two hundred rooms, three golf courses, dock facilities, and a rail line that would bring passengers right to the hotel. Due to money troubles, Ringling ordered the work stopped in November, with barely one-third completed. Although Ringling and his successor John Ringling North maintained that eventually they would resume construction, the shell lay vacant until 1963."*

Finney remarked, "So Ringling never gave up on the hotel."

"Despite the fact that he was basically insolvent by 1929."

Rancor, who had been perusing the shelves, spoke up. "I wonder why he never tried to sell it?"

Mrs. Penney answered. "There is no evidence that John Ringling ever considered selling the property. I understand it was rather a bone of contention between him and the family. Mable agreed with him, but Hedda—his second wife—called it an albatross and pressed John to unload it."

"Could that be one reason he divorced her?"

"I…uh…don't know." Mrs. Penney seemed suddenly uncertain.

Rancor took the book from Charity. "I just thought of something. The letter."

The other three stared at him. "What letter?"

"From Hedda to Mistinguett. Remember, Charity? She said John had served her with divorce papers…"

"I do remember." Charity spoke slowly. "Didn't she also say something about an 'incident'?"

"You're thinking they had a fight over the hotel?" His brow creased in thought. "He didn't actually divorce her until 1936—ten years after construction was discontinued. It couldn't have had anything to do with that."

"Why not? The wreck still stood, and the Ringlings were scrambling for cash."

Rancor stuffed the book into an empty space on a shelf. After tapping her foot for a long minute, Mrs. Penney pulled it out and inserted it in its proper place.

Rancor looked as though he were tempted to move it again, so Charity raised her voice. "Let's get back to the problem at hand. We're looking for something to do with Edgar Finney."

Mrs. Penney's eyes opened wide. "The last librarian?"

"The very one." Rancor swept his arm out. "May I introduce you to his grandson, Michael Finney?"

"How do you do." She gave the publisher an appraising look, which softened when he smiled at her.

Rancor steamrolled on. "Michael owns—or rather, owned—HHR Press in Seattle, founded by his grandfather in 1933." He studied the woman. "You wouldn't happen to know why he named his company after Hedda Hagen Ringling, would you?"

She shook her head. "No idea, although they were friends. According to her letters, she spent a great deal of time in the library. She said Finney was very attentive and helped her in her research. She would always check sources before she and John left on their treasure-hunting trips to Europe." Her eyes grew misty. "I always thought there might be a bit of tender feeling there."

"You mean, you think the librarian had a crush on Mrs. Ringling?"

Michael huffed. "Or the other way around."

Rancor opened his mouth for what Charity assumed would be a derisive comment, but Deirdre cut in, her expression sentimental. "It's just the romantic in me. She and John were having problems. She had no one to turn to, since the servants were still loyal to Mable." She sighed. "Hedda must have been quite lonely."

Rancor looked at Charity. "HHR as a tribute to unrequited love?"

"Maybe."

Finney spoke up. "Then why did he quit on such short notice?"

Mrs. Penney said, "Because he knew he could never have her. He must have been a true gentleman." She gave Michael a speculative glance.

He started and blushed. "The men in my family have always been quite...er...old-fashioned."

"How nice." The two edged closer to each other.

Rancor remarked, "I read somewhere that Finney left Cà d'Zan because of a feud with Hedda. Something about a book." His eyes flickered.

Is he trying to smoke her out?

"Hogwash."

"So...you've come across nothing to suggest a breach?"

She hesitated. "Well, there were rumors at the time that they had had a disagreement over something. I believe John Ringling wrote about it in one of his journals." She looked at Michael. "Did I mention he and Edgar were good friends?"

Michael moved to a chair next to hers. Rancor took Charity's hand and pulled her toward the door. For once his whisper did not carry. "Let's give the two lovebirds a chance to get acquainted."

"Where are we going?"

"On a tour of the house."

"Good. I want my money's worth."

Under the watchful eye of the guard, they wandered around the great hall and the ballroom. Passing through a butler's pantry, they entered a cavernous kitchen, devoid of people. Rancor pointed to a narrow stairway. "This must be the servants' passage to the second floor. Come on."

He ducked under a velvet rope.

"Rancor! We'll get caught."

"Not if you're quick. Hurry." A small door at the top opened onto an interior gallery that ran around three sides of the house. He began opening drawers in the occasional tables scattered about.

"What are you looking for?"

"I don't know."

"Well, that's an exercise in futility."

"Not really. I'll know it when I see it. Remember, Michael's mother said he'd find the answer in Cà d'Zan. There must be something here, something obvious."

"What were the three things she mentioned? A promise, an oath, and a deed. Maybe we should be looking for a deed."

"Right. Okay, there's nothing here." Rancor opened a door. "This must be the maid's room." They checked the bureau and under the cot. "Nothing."

The next room clearly belonged to a lady. Satin pillows were piled high on a canopy bed. On the dresser lay a set of sterling silver brushes. "Hedda's?"

"You know," said Charity as she checked under the bed, "this house has been a museum for decades—I doubt if there's anything here that hasn't been examined a million times."

"No one was looking for a deed."

"Or a promise. Or an oath. What would such things look like?"

"A promise could be a ring."

"And an oath?"

"I don't know—a coat of arms? The Boy Scout pledge? Some kind of inscription?"

"Come on, let's try the next room." This turned out to be another small room with a simple cot, wash basin, and chest.

"There. On the chest. Initials."

Rancor bent down. "E. F. And over here—several books from the library with index cards stuck in them. This must have been Edgar Finney's room."

"That's right. Michael mentioned he'd been given a room in the mansion." Charity pulled up the mattress. "Hullo, what's this?" She drew a folded slip of lavender-colored paper out. "It was stuck in one of the springs." She opened it. "Looks like part of a note."

Rancor took it from her. "Female handwriting. First section is torn off. All I can make out is '...*can never be, not after last night. Remember your promise. H.*' Gotta be Hedda."

"Why? Why not a maid?"

He held up the scrap. "Look at the stationery— embossed vellum. And it's the same color as the letter we read at Beatrice's house. Unless the maid stole Hedda's writing paper, it's Hedda."

Charity reread the fragment. "This is so baffling. What did he promise? Is this a Dear John letter?"

"Could be. It sounds as though the affair had already happened, and she's ending it."

"Maybe, but it doesn't comport with her letter to Mistinguett. She sounded genuinely upset that Ringling was divorcing her."

"Maybe she'd gotten over Finney by then." Rancor put the note in his pocket. "Now for the master bedroom." They walked around the gallery, taking care to stay out of sight of the guard. A laminated card by a door indicated John Ringling's bedroom.

The room was large and faced west across Sarasota Bay. Below them, a vast terrace of variously colored marbles set in a zig-zag pattern spread out like a giant chessboard. Two carved beds in the Renaissance revival style of Napoleon III sat against one wall. Opposite them stood a rolltop desk. "Will you look at all the velvet in this place? It had to be sweltering in the summer."

"I believe they spent their summers in New York or traveling in Europe."

"That's right—they had their own train."

"Do you suppose the ghost is Mable?"

"You mean, the woman in the Pullman car? Maybe. Another story to pursue after this is over."

Charity was captivated by the view. "I read that Ringling moored his steam yacht *Zalophus* here." She watched as a gaggle of pelicans floated past. "There must be a regatta over at the sailing squadron. See all the boats milling around?"

"Yeah, yeah. Come on, we've got work to do." Rancor began methodically searching the bureau drawers. The massive walnut desk was locked. "Do you have a hairpin?"

"A *hairpin*? What year do you think this is anyway?"

"Sorry—getting into the spirit of the age." He gazed at her. "With that long red braid of yours, you could be the Irish cook."

"Thanks a lot!"

"Well, the lady of the house would have her hair bobbed…and I guess wouldn't have a hairpin either." He stood still. "Wait, they're called bobby pins, aren't they? I wonder…Who was Bobby and what was he doing in a girl's hair? Was he an early Don Juan? A hairdresser? And another thing—"

"Rancor."

He sighed. "So how do I pry this open?"

Charity rummaged through her purse. "I think…yes, I have one of those eyeglass repair kits." She pulled out a tiny screwdriver. "Will this do?"

"Perfect." He fiddled with the keyhole until they heard a click. Rolling it up, he had to catch the pile of letters that tumbled out. He handed a bunch to Charity. "Go through those."

"What am I looking for?"

"A deed, I guess. Anything to do with Edgar Finney."

She dutifully went through them. "Mostly letters from creditors demanding payment."

"Here are some more."

Meanwhile, Rancor pulled each drawer out and shook it.

"What are you doing?"

"There's always a secret compartment in these desks—a false bottom or something. Ah." He slid a flat piece of wood out. "Eureka." He set aside a heavy gold wedding ring and held up a business card. A small note had been clipped to it. "It says, '*Edgar, you know what to do.'* " Rancor slipped the note off and stopped, staring at the card. Silently, he handed it to Charity.

Of heavy white stock, it had a logo stamped on it—the letter *B* in raised green ink inside a blue circle. She turned it over. Someone had written in large block letters "ELEVEN P.M. AT RC."

Chapter Sixteen
The Frog Prince

"Wow."

"Wow."

Rancor put the papers and drawers back in the desk and rolled the top down. "Let's get out of here. I want to think this through with a glass in my hand."

Charity had a feeling he didn't mean a magnifying glass. "What about Michael?"

"We'll pick him up on the way out."

They snuck down the back stairs and strolled down the hall to the library, where they found Michael and Mrs. Penney in deep conversation.

"Hello, hello," Rancor shouted heartily. "Getting along famously, are we?"

The blush showed right through the sparse hairs on Michael's head, reminding Charity of a round, red balloon. "I…uh…Deirdre and I were talking books." He didn't seem to expect them to believe him.

"Deirdre, huh?" Rancor's mouth twitched. "We're heading out. Do you want to come or…?"

Finney cast a sideways glance at the docent. "The house will be closing in a few minutes. Deirdre…Mrs. Penney…has kindly accepted my offer of a ride home. She usually takes the bus."

Charity pressed her lips together to hide the smile. "Um, Michael, you came with us, remember?"

"Oh! Oh dear." He turned to Mrs. Penney. "I'm so sorry. I wasn't thinking."

"That's all right."

She turned away, but he hesitated. "Perhaps I could accompany you on the bus?"

She turned back, a lovely smile on her lips. "That would be very nice. You are most certainly a gentleman, just like your grandfather."

Rancor backed out. "Give us a call, and I'll come get you, Michael." He ran down the sidewalk to the parking lot. Half an hour later, they sat in Tommy Bahama's on St. Armands Circle. Once the waiter had brought their margaritas, he drew the card and the note from his pocket and smoothed them out on the table. "So…what have we got?"

"A fragment of a letter probably written by Hedda, a business card, and a note to Edgar."

"Let's set Hedda's missive aside for the time being. Give me the card." He pointed at the logo. "That's the Bass family crest. We know my grandfather was in Florida. This card has to be his."

Charity was less certain. "You said your great-grandfather had business interests in Florida already. It could have been any Bass employee."

Rancor bit his lip. "Perhaps. At any rate, it means we were involved with Ringling in some way. I say for the time being we work under the assumption that it was Robert."

"No."

"No?"

"I think we're getting ahead of ourselves. Let's stick with the facts we have. I propose we call the card owner Mr. X." Charity turned the card over.

" 'ELEVEN P.M. AT RC.' Two questions arise: what is RC? And who was Mr. X going to meet?"

"Well, the card was in John Ringling's possession."

"Then why the note to Edgar?" She pointed at the small square of paper. " 'You know what to do.' "

"Sounds ominous, like he's telling him to put a horse's head in X's bed. Cool."

Charity ignored Rancor's breathless hiccup. "*Or*...could he be telling Edgar to meet with Mr. X?"

"Then why not say that?" Rancor closed his eyes. "Maybe we're barking up the wrong tree. Maybe the note and card are totally unrelated."

"Weren't they clipped together?"

"So Ringling was a neatnik." Rancor sipped his drink thoughtfully. "Let's move on. So two people met at RC...RC...of course! The Ritz-Carlton. The Ghost Hotel."

"Makes sense." Charity finished her drink. "To recap. We have all these threads intersecting at an elevator shaft on a starless night some eighty years ago."

"Why starless?"

"Must have been."

"This isn't fiction you know, Charity. You can't just create the atmosphere you want."

To shut him up, Charity raised her eyes and her voice. "Who was there at the pit? Why were they meeting there?"

"And why in the middle of the night? I can't see a man like John Ringling sneaking around his own building site, especially considering his bulk."

"And why kill the person you're meeting?" Charity

rubbed her chin. "You know, it's possible it was an accident. It was probably pitch dark—"

"Starless?"

"Precisely. Mr. X doesn't see the pit and falls into it. Edgar—or Ringling—panics and runs back to Cà d'Zan."

"And then what? Why not just tell someone? If it was Finney, why bolt?"

"I would imagine because his employer would be none too happy with him for misplacing an associate." Charity stood up. "Too much speculation. I think we have to go back to the skeleton. Forget the Ringling circus for now."

"Ha ha. You think perhaps a call to Auntie G. is in order?"

"Yes." She paid the bill and they drove home. As they reached her door, Charity's cell phone rang. Rancor pulled it out of his pocket. Charity toyed with the idea of ripping it from his hand but decided to wait. He pressed Talk. "Oh, hello. Sure, give me the address." He hung up. "Our Romeo needs a ride home. He sounds reluctant."

"It's only a first date."

"Yes, but look what we did on ours."

Charity scoffed. "I can't see the timid Michael Finney—nor the decorous Deirdre Penney—in a passionate embrace."

"You'd be surprised what lurks in the heart of a jellyfish." He kissed her. "I'll be back later."

But he wasn't back later. About midnight Charity gave up and went to bed. The moon had gone down when she felt warm breath on her cheek.

"Hello, precious."

She opened her eyes. "Where have you been?"

"With Michael. We've been inspecting a crime scene."

"The pit?"

"The very same. It seemed appropriate to recreate the setting—see if it helped."

"And?"

"Not really. I mean, the mysterious Mr. X and Edgar—or John—wouldn't have met in an elevator."

"Of course not. There was no elevator. Remember? After Tommy T fell in, they boarded it over. No, it was an accident. In the dark Mr. X tripped, broke through the rotting boards, and fell into the pit."

"You're asserting he also fell on a knife multiple times?"

"Oops—I'd forgotten about that."

Rancor ran his fingers down her spine and around to her breast. Flicking at her nipple, he murmured, "*Hmm.* I wonder…passionate embrace…*hmm.* Look, I've got some things to do in the morning, so we'll have to cut our lovemaking short. Come here."

She thought fleetingly about playing coy. In the end, that seemed an unnecessary waste of time.

****

Rancor was gone when she woke up. She made herself breakfast, checked the news on her laptop, and headed to the office.

"Hello there, stranger." George seemed preoccupied.

"Sorry—we've been chasing after the murderer."

"Murderer! Oh, you mean of the skeleton? What've you got for me?"

"We're pretty sure the police are wrong."

"Oh, they'll love to hear that."

"I'm sure." She turned serious. "Rancor thinks it's someone from his family's company, possibly even his grandfather, Robert Bass III."

"The murderer?"

"No, no. The victim."

"Whoa. Tell me more."

She told him about Finney, of their search of Cà d'Zan, and finding the card and note.

"You seem to have an embarrassment of facts, none of which hang together." He rubbed his hands. "Let's get to work." He sat down at his desk, but his gaze went beyond Charity to the outer office and he paused. "Um, we have a visitor."

Charity swung around. *Isabella.*

The woman sashayed in. Today, her blonde hair was swept up in an elaborate French twist, held with a ruby-studded clip that matched her ruby-red dress. A long, thick gold chain swung fetchingly between her breasts. "Why, Mr. Fletcher, I thought I had an appointment?" Her long lashes flipped up and down. She did not look at Charity.

"Yes, yes, you did, Miss Voleuse. I'm at your service. Charity, would you excuse us?"

Charity opened her mouth to refuse but, at a look from George, left.

An hour later, Isabella came out, her expression one of smug satisfaction. She didn't say a word to Charity but sauntered out. Charity marched into George's office. "What was that all about?"

"Er...um...Miss Voleuse—Isabella—thinks Rancor is dragging his feet on the ghost story anthology. I must say I agree. I've yet to see a chapter."

"That's because we're still in the research phase."

"Well…" His eyes went vague. "She seems to think Rancor is spending too much time with you—that she would be better suited to work with him, having edited several of his other books."

"Really." She hoped her voice oozed with sufficient venom.

"Yes. She has offered her services to Kumquat House to nudge him along. I passed it along to Arlo, and he agreed."

"But George, she wants to steal the book!"

"What are you talking about?"

"I told you about how we kept missing Finney in Seattle. I think she deliberately led me on a wild goose chase. We've determined that she is actually the one stealing manuscripts. Not Michael."

"Michael…Finney?"

"Yes. I think she bought the press from him so she can publish the books under another name."

"Huh. She didn't tell me that."

"It's now IV Enterprises. And she has yet to pay for it."

"You mean, for the business?"

"Yes. Poor Michael—he's going to be cut out of the will now, and he won't even have her money."

George indicated a chair. "All right, spill."

She told him about the Finney will, the stipulation that the name HHR Press be retained in perpetuity, and Isabella's missing check.

"I see. And this fellow has proof that Miss Voleuse is the manuscript thief?"

Charity paused. "N…no. But he has no reason to lie. It makes sense—her pretending to look for him, her wanting to buy the firm…" She petered out.

George tapped a pencil. "Promise, oath, deed. Huh. It was Finney's mother who said the answer to the riddle is in Cà d'Zan?"

"Yes, but we didn't find anything there."

"Perhaps Finney should talk to his mother again."

"There's an idea. And Rancor's going to talk to his Aunt Gertrude again."

"Keep me in the loop, Charity." He picked up the receiver. "I'd better phone Arlo."

Charity left him, went back to her desk, and clicked on her schedule. "Oh my God, it's Valentine's Day." She felt again that bite of loneliness that always came on holidays. Rancor was hardly the type to acknowledge the occasion. She sighed. *Maybe I'll see what Jane is doing for lunch.*

Jane was amenable, and they met at the Crab and Fin. It was crowded with couples gazing adoringly into each other's eyes. Charity focused her attention on Jane. "So how's your boyfriend doing?"

"Darryl? I don't know. I haven't seen him for two weeks." Jane didn't seem particularly downhearted.

"You two haven't broken up again!"

"No—at least I don't think so. I never know." She sighed. "It's his usual MO. We have a wonderful night together…" She winked. "Very…er…stimulating, if you catch my drift."

Yes, yes, I do.

"But then *phhhttt*. Nada for up to a month. He claims it takes him that long to recover from our exertions, but I don't believe him."

"Do you think he has another girlfriend?"

"Not sure. He used to go on about how we weren't

really compatible—"

"But you two are perfect for each other!"

"You know that and I know that, but tell it to Darryl. He grudgingly agrees that we have the same tastes in music and food and movies and other stuff, but he's not convinced there isn't some Héloïse out there for his Abélard."

Charity patted her hand. "I'm sorry."

"What about you? Still having it on with the great writer?"

"I don't want to talk about him."

"I see." She sipped her drink. "Another fantastic Valentine's Day, huh?"

"I guess."

By mutual consent, they talked of less painful topics for the rest of the meal—politics, the culture wars, taxes, and the rise of a local Wiccan movement. Jane pointed at a tall, broad-shouldered woman in black, her bosom covered in strings of Mardi Gras beads. "It's this blue moon, I think. Witches and weirdos come out to play."

"Well, that's Florida for you." After dropping Jane off at her store, Charity put in a few hours at the office and went home.

As she trudged up the stairs, rain began to fall, sparking a chorus of cheeps from the tiny native treefrogs. It seemed to grow louder and louder. When she reached her door, she found out why. A huge green bullfrog sat in a small wooden cage on the mat. A tag attached to it said, "Kiss Me." When she picked up the cage, a guttural voice croaked, "If you don't kiss me, you won't get your present." She looked around but couldn't see anyone. The voice came again. "Down here."

The frog regarded her solemnly, its large eyes unblinking. She spoke to the air. "I am not going to kiss a frog."

"Ah, but I'm a special frog. A prince of a frog. Kiss me."

She had to admit she was tempted. "If I let you out, you'll hop away." *Why the hell am I talking to an amphibian?*

"Then you'd better kiss me quick."

She shrugged. The rain turned into a downpour, and she moved under the shelter of the overhang. With hesitant fingers, she opened the little door. The frog hopped out. Quick as a flash, she bent down and touched her lips to its back. Surprisingly, it was neither slimy nor wet. She resisted the urge to wipe her mouth. The frog croaked once but remained crouched on its haunches, gazing at her. She shook her head. "No sense in asking. I'm only doing it once."

"Wait."

"Wait for what?"

"Wait for it…" There was a flash of purple smoke. When it cleared, the frog was gone, and Rancor sat on the step. "Your prince. As ordered."

"How did you do that?"

"A magician never reveals his secrets." He opened his palms to reveal a bouquet of gardenias. "For you. Will you be my valentine?"

She held the flowers and inhaled deeply. "They're my favorite—how did you know?"

"I made inquiries. Jane is delightful by the way. Didn't care much for Darryl."

"Find out why he only sees her once a month, and

she'll be your slave for life."

"That would make a refreshing change."

"More than you deserve. Coming in?"

"Yes. I have to watch you change into something more suitable for Michael's on East."

"Rancor! I can't afford that."

"You don't have to—I have secured a source of funding."

"I don't want to know."

"No. You don't." He closed the door behind him. "Now, you haven't answered my question."

Busy with the flowers, Charity didn't reply. He took the vase from her and set it down. Then he took her in his arms. "Will you be my valentine?"

At that, something broke inside her, and the tears flowed.

He dried them. "Should I take that as a 'yes,' or a 'get out of my sight, you ogre'?"

She kissed him, unable to talk.

"Go then. Put on that pearly white dress you wore in Paris. And leave your hair down this once."

She obeyed, savoring the prospect of a Valentine's Day that just might turn out to be the best ever.

****

"Where did you get that frog anyway?"

"What frog?"

It's going to be like that, is it? "Did you call Aunt Gertrude yet?"

"No." He idly tickled her nipple. "I had more important things to do."

"It's noon. You'd better call her."

"I can't. I have to go to work."

"Wait—does this have anything to do with your

new revenue stream?"

"As a matter of fact, yes. I have managed to worm my way back into the good graces of the store manager at Publix. He has seen fit to give me a second chance, although I'm banned from collecting carts in the parking lot. I received my first paycheck on Friday. I am now gainfully employed—as opposed to writing for a living."

She patted his head. "I am so proud of you."

He gave her a wry grin. "I'm actually getting quite adept at stacking shelves. Mr. Twittle put a gold star next to my name. If I play my cards right, I could be employee of the month."

"You can do anything you put your mind to."

He gathered his clothes and went to the bathroom. "I must make my toilette—the customers expect box boys in clean boxers."

He left a few minutes later. Charity arranged her flowers one more time, smiling to herself.

Six hours later, Rancor skipped up the beach steps to her apartment.

"Well, there you are. You'd better call Auntie before it's time for her bingo."

"Mah-jongg."

"I thought she played canasta?"

"Isn't today Thursday? Thursdays, it's mah-jongg."

"Whatever."

He dialed a number. "Aunt Gertrude? Rancor here. I'm sorry to bother you again, but I thought you'd like to know that I may have found Grandfather...No, of course he's not still alive...Well, I suppose he could be, but in his current condition—if I'm right, that is—then I'd have to say no. Listen, Auntie, your father snuck off to Florida rather than go to Nebraska, right? Good…Oh, you did? What did it say?" He held his hand over the receiver. "She found a telegram Robert sent to his wife in a box of old photos." He turned back to the phone. "What's that? Really! That's *very* interesting. Thanks, thanks a lot…Who? She's pregnant *again*? Oh dear, how many does that make—thirteen? Only four? Well, tell her congratulations, and I'll be up to see it once it's college age…Sorry, I missed that last…What did I want to tell you about Grandfather? I just wanted to give you a heads-up…Yes, I'll call you back…All right, toodle-oo."

"What did the telegram say?"

"I can't believe my sister-in-law Alice is going to spew out yet another infant—I think the last one still has his umbilical cord attached."

Her voice dangerously low, Charity said, "The telegram?"

"Oh, evidently Robert sent one to his wife."

"That would be the long-suffering Trudy?"

"Yes, our long-suffering Trudy who had managed to get herself pregnant a second time." He turned pensive. "While Auntie would never divulge, methinks the Bass men must all enjoy singular endowments. They certainly reproduce at prolific levels."

Charity made a mental note to get that prescription refilled immediately.

"Anyway, he told her he was on the point of making a really fantastic real estate deal—one that would knock the proverbial socks off his father. He seemed very confident."

"Did he say what it was?"

"No. He said he would write as soon as it was

settled. He said he had a meeting to seal the deal that night."

"And?"

"And that was the last anyone heard from him."

"And they moved on. I remember. Did his wife at least believe his message? That he was working on a great deal?"

"I doubt it. Up to then, the best deal he'd ever closed was a hundred dollars for his cousin's bike."

"Something tells me his cousin wasn't planning to sell said bicycle."

"Your intuition serves you well."

Charity peered at him. "You're holding something back. Did Aunt Gertrude happen to tell you the date of the telegram?"

Rancor leveled a grave look at her. "February 10, 1933."

Chapter Seventeen
Conspiracy Theories

"February 10, 1933. That must be the day he died. Or that night."

Rancor drummed his fingers on the table. "So we have definite proof that Robert was the person who arranged the meeting and can dispense with the inscrutable Mr. X. Whoever he met must be the murderer."

"If it was murder."

"Don't be silly—a man couldn't stab himself that many times."

"I'm not being silly." Charity poured herself a glass of water. "Last night while you were busy keeping me awake long after my bedtime, I remembered something. The CSI guys found a bunch of short iron rods in the pit. Say Robert tripped and fell in. He might have landed on them."

Rancor rubbed his chin. "You're hypothesizing that the holes made by the rods would resemble stab wounds on a skeleton?"

She nodded. "In which case, it was an accident."

"Give me a minute." Rancor got up and paced the room. "Doesn't work. For one thing, the rods would still be stuck in his ribs. For another, the CSI man—was it Ken or Doug?—said they were buried in the corners. The skeleton lay in the center of the pit."

Damn. "All right, so it was murder. Could the killer have been John Ringling himself?"

"Because he had the card? No...I've been thinking about that. He must have meant for Edgar to go to the meeting."

"But why meet at the Ghost Hotel?"

"Why else? The deal they were negotiating was its sale. Robert Bass wanted to buy the hotel from Ringling for Bass, Inc."

"Of course! He was sure this would get him back in his father's good graces. What a feather in his cap."

"Yes, adding a five-star hotel to the Bass chain would be a great coup."

"Even if it was a dump."

"Dump..." Rancor stopped pacing. "That gives me an idea. Didn't you tell me Calvin Hagen was involved in unsavory real estate deals?"

"Yeess. Why?...Oh! You're thinking *he* was the one arranging the deal with Robert. For Ringling?"

"Makes sense, doesn't it?"

Charity put her glass down. "But Mrs. Penney told us Ringling didn't want to sell."

"True. All right, how about this? Ringling discovered Hagen's maneuvering and sent Edgar to tell Robert the deal was off."

"So this was all Hagen's idea?"

"Yes."

"But at some point, wouldn't he have to get Ringling's approval?"

"*Hmm.*" Rancor ambled out to the balcony but soon came rushing back. "Would that approval have to come from John himself? Didn't Deirdre also say that Hedda thought it was an albatross and wanted to get rid of it?"

"Yes. Oh!" She held a hand to her mouth. "Hedda was secretly arranging to sell the hotel behind John's back. Who else would she turn to but her own brother? No wonder Ringling wanted to divorce her."

"So where does Edgar Finney fit into all this?"

Charity spoke thoughtfully. "If John learned about the meeting and sent Edgar to stop the deal, why keep quiet about it? Why hide the card in the secret drawer?"

"To keep Hedda from knowing her little scheme had been exposed?"

"But then why did Edgar cut and run?"

Rancor picked up the keys. "We need to find out exactly when Edgar Finney left and what reason he gave."

"Where are you going?"

"To find Michael."

"At this hour?"

He checked the clock. "Oh, good grief. We've been yakking all evening. I didn't realize it was almost midnight." He leered at her. "We'll have to occupy ourselves until visiting hours are upon us."

Charity took his hand. "I have an idea."

****

"Open up, Michael, it's me."

Charity punched Rancor's arm. "Despite your irrational belief that your name is universally renowned, Finney doesn't necessarily know your *voice*."

"That doesn't make sense. I can still be considered renowned whether or not my mellifluous tenor is familiar to the masses." At a look from her, he raised his voice. "It's me…Rancor."

The door opened onto a rumpled man in striped

pajamas, bits of sleep stuck in the corners of his eyes. When he saw Charity, he bleated, "I'll be right with you," and slammed the door in their faces.

A minute later, he opened the door again. This time he wore a trench coat, belted but unbuttoned. Charity half expected him to throw it open, exposing his manhood to them. Instead, he ushered them in. "Sorry for the delay. What can I do for you?"

Charity searched for a place to sit down. Clothes and newspapers covered every flat surface. A suitcase stood open on a rack, objects apparently tossed into it at random. The bathroom floor was littered with wet towels. She finally sat gingerly on the edge of the bed. Michael drew the curtains aside, flooding the room with light.

Rancor stood in the middle of the squalor, hands on hips. "You've only been here a few nights, Michael. How could you manage to make such a mess?"

The other man hung his head. "I didn't expect company."

"*Hmmph.* Well, it's a good thing you didn't bring Deirdre back to your hotel."

Finney's eyes grew wild. "I'd never…never…" He gulped.

Charity took pity on him. "Of course not. Perhaps we'd better tell you why we're here. Rancor?"

"We think we've solved at least part of the mystery. The skeleton we found in the pit is that of my grandfather, Robert Bass III."

"And how do you know that?" Michael pushed some newspapers off the only chair and sat down.

"Because we found his card in John Ringling's desk."

"You searched his desk? In Cà d'Zan? Isn't that illegal?"

Rancor brushed that aside. "You were downstairs making whoopee with the docent—we had to keep ourselves busy. Now, do you want to hear our story?"

"Okay."

Rancor related their discoveries and conclusions. "So we still don't know what Edgar was doing there."

"If he was there. You only have the note from Ringling, and that could have meant something else entirely." He stared at the wall, his face meditative. "Do you think Hagen set up the meeting?"

"The thought had occurred."

"At Hedda's instigation." Michael leaned back, exposing the rumpled pajamas. Charity longed to button his coat but didn't dare frighten the poor man. "Or…Could my grandfather have been negotiating with your grandfather on her behalf?"

Charity spoke. "Unlikely, since it was John Ringling who sent him to the meeting—or wanted him do something about it."

"Wait a minute…" Rancor went to the window and gazed out at the passing traffic. "We may be jumping the gun. Edgar could have done both."

"Huh?"

"He could have been acting for Hedda but, when Ringling discovered the plot, turned on her."

Michael gasped. "My grandfather would never betray a trust!"

Charity put a hand up. "By helping Hedda go behind John's back, wouldn't he have been doing exactly that?"

Rancor apparently felt the need to quell the rising

tension and said quietly, "If not Edgar, then who did Robert arrange to meet?"

She clasped and unclasped her hands, thinking. "Hedda herself?"

Rancor scoffed, "This was the 1930s. Would a lady meet a man at midnight in a deserted hotel? I don't think so."

"Except in one of your books."

"I beg your pardon—my heroines are not imbeciles."

"But they're often floozies."

Michael cried, "Hedda Hagen Ringling was no floozy!"

Charity raised her voice. "Could I have a glass of water, Michael?" This had the effect of completely unraveling him. He flailed his arms and honked like a demented goose. Rancor went to the bathroom, filled a glass from the tap, and gave it to Charity. She sipped. "This is getting us nowhere. Someone met Robert Bass III in the Ghost Hotel on February 10, 1933, and killed him."

"Okay. So, let's review the remaining questions." Rancor went to the minibar and retrieved a candy bar. "One, we need to find out the reason Edgar gave for his hasty departure. And two, the date that Edgar left for Seattle."

"Why?"

"If it was before February 10, Edgar can be eliminated as a suspect."

"We know he founded the press in 1933. Deirdre"—Michael blushed at the name—"told me he left sometime in early 1933. She has yet to find a letter of resignation."

"Nothing in Ringling's papers?"

"No."

Charity took a bite of Rancor's candy bar. "Perhaps your mother knows more than she's saying."

Michael bristled. "My mother is a saintly woman. She would never, ever prevaricate."

Rancor filled the coffee machine and plugged it in. "Is that all she told you? To look in Cà d'Zan for the answer?"

"Yes, that and the comment about the deed, the oath, and the promise."

"You must call her back."

Finney looked alarmed. "I doubt whether she's calmed down from my *last* call. I don't want to talk to her again until I've resolved the issue of the firm's name."

"Damn it, Michael! No matter what Isabella's been up to, you did sell her HHR Press fair and square. She's entitled to name it whatever she wants."

The little man opened his mouth, but Charity interrupted. "She would be if she had actually paid him."

Michael nodded in agreement. "I still haven't received the check."

"Oh, really? That's different then. At least until you have it in hand, the company is still yours. Call your lawyer."

Michael cast a quick glance at Charity. "I…uh…don't have one."

Rancor gawked at him. "*What*?"

Charity nudged him. "Isabella told him he didn't need one." Rancor rounded on Finney. Before he could speak, Charity said loudly, "The firm must have a lawyer on retainer."

"We do...but he's hired by the company. He's not supposed to work on my private affairs."

"This isn't private. Call him."

"Why?"

"To see if it's too late to back out of the settlement."

"I don't know..." He accepted a mug from Rancor. "We did sign the papers."

"I'll bet they're not valid until the money exchanges hands."

Finney picked up the phone and went into the bathroom, closing the door behind him. "Lawyer confidentiality, don't you know."

"Huh?"

The two waited ten minutes. Finally, Finney came out, shuffling slowly, head down. "He says there is a window of opportunity, but very small. I'd have to take her to court to prove she had defaulted on the payment."

"That could take years."

"And if she came up with the funds during that time, I'd be up a creek."

Rancor poured himself some coffee. After a minute wasted darting nasty looks at him, Charity filled her own mug. "So...we have to get her on the stolen manuscripts."

"You think she's the culprit?"

"Well, we know it wasn't you. She led us on a merry chase, didn't she?"

Charity spoke into the silence. "She's here, you know. In Florida."

"Oh dear."

Rancor gazed at her. "How do you know?"

"She came to see George—tried to convince him to give your ghost book to her. She said you couldn't be counted on to finish it without her help."

Rancor rolled his eyes. "Is the woman mad?"

"Or stupid?"

Rancor shot her a look. "She's not stupid. She must feel invulnerable though."

"Ah yes." Charity let a drop of jealousy trickle out. "One cannot say no to the beautiful Isabella."

"That's probably it." Charity gave him a quick glance, but his expression remained stolid. "Look, it's getting late. How about if we grab some lunch?"

"Great idea." Finney showed them the door. "I'll be with you momentarily."

"Okay."

They piled into the Mini Cooper. As they drove down Tamiami Trail, Charity mentally went over her bank account. Rancor had informed her that he'd spent his first paycheck on the frog—"and the flowers," he had added with a rare touch of sensitivity. *Maybe I can extend that expense account a few more days. After all, I didn't take advantage of it for half my Seattle trip.* Engaged in happy daydreams of dollars from heaven, she almost missed the turn to the keys.

"Hey!"

She zipped in front of a minivan that had braked while its passengers gawked at the enormous statue of the sailor and the nurse embracing, and crossed the Ringling causeway to St. Armands Circle. They found a parking spot and walked over to the Columbia Restaurant. It was crowded, but the tall brunette who ran the desk with ruthless efficiency promised a table for three in ten minutes. As they waited, Charity scanned the customers. Her gaze halted at a far table. She pointed with a trembling finger. Rancor whispered, "Isabella."

"Who's that with her?"

"Why, wouldn't you know? It's the inimitable Holdridge K. Wheelock."

"He of the 'I cannot accompany you but will gladly write a strongly worded letter' fame?"

"The very one. I wonder what it took to get him to break away from his probing study of the holistic approach to ant farming?"

Charity noted Isabella's loose white gauze outfit, just barely opaque enough to hide the billowing mounds of her breasts. "I can't imagine."

Rancor frowned. "If he found Isabella, why didn't he contact us?"

"Why don't you go ask him?" *Did I really suggest that?*

"Maybe I will."

Michael cringed. "I don't want to talk to her. She makes me nervous."

"Fine." While the other two hung back, Rancor strode over to the table, stopping to say a word to the hostess. While his back was turned, Charity saw Wheelock hand a thick manila envelope to Isabella. She thrust it into her briefcase just as Rancor arrived at their table.

"Why, Rancor Bass. Fancy meeting you here." Even from a distance, Charity could make out the mellow tones of a carefully crafted baritone.

"Hello, Holdridge. I see you've come to help Isabella with her…problem."

The man—his shock of white hair and flowing beard falling just short of a bad impression of Ernest Hemingway—stood and held out his hand. Isabella fluttered her lashes at Rancor and gave him a dazzling smile.

"We were just finishing up, or I'd ask you to join us. Are you alone?"

Rancor turned and pointed at the little troop pretending to read the menu. "No, I'm with my coauthor Miss Snow…and Michael." He beckoned them to approach, but Michael hid behind Charity and refused to budge. Charity left him with the hostess and approached the table.

Wheelock jerked. "Finney? What's he doing here?"

"His mother sent him. And he wanted to find you, Isabella."

"Me?" She contrived to look both amused and eager. "If he wanted to turn himself in, he could have gotten hold of me at any time." She took a sip of her drink. Charity noticed her hand shook slightly. "However did you catch him?"

"Oh, he wasn't as hard to find as you thought." Rancor's tone bordered on threatening.

Isabella tossed her blonde locks. "I've been doing my best. Ask…" She glanced at Charity. "I'm sorry, I seem to have forgotten your name. Prudence? Patience? Some virtue." She didn't wait for an answer, but went on smoothly, "You know I'm happy to help in any way. I presume you're going to have Michael arrested."

"Why would I do that?"

"For stealing your manuscript of course. Poor Holdy here lost his only copy of *Customs and Rituals of the Caribbean Puritans*." She patted his arm fondly.

"You know he refuses to back up his manuscripts. Too...er..."

"Twenty-first century?"

"Yes, well..." She rose, picking up her purse and the briefcase and sidling around Rancor. "I have a meeting. Must be off."

He let her go. Charity had half expected him to lock handcuffs on her but realized there was nothing they could do until they had solid evidence. Once Isabella was out of sight, Rancor sat in the seat she had vacated. Michael edged nearer. Rancor fixed Wheelock with a hard stare. "What are you doing here, Holdridge?"

Charity couldn't resist. "And what did you give Isabella?"

"What? Oh...er...just an article I wrote. She wanted to look it over." His eyes wandered to the waiter. "I really must go."

Rancor put a hand on his forearm. "Not yet. Holdy, did you ask Isabella about the manuscripts?"

"Er...yes...yes, I did. She...she says she believes Michael is responsible..." Here he nodded at the little man. "I told her it was more likely those Chinese pirates again. They must have hacked into HHR's computers and ripped the submissions off."

"In that case"—Rancor was dangerously calm—"there's nothing we can do about it."

"That's right." The author stood up quickly and knocked his chair back. "Just chalk it up to bad luck." A vein in his neck pulsed rapidly. "So, I hear you're working on a ghost story anthology? A little out of your wheelhouse, no?"

Rancor threw a nonchalant arm over Charity's

shoulder. "You know I can write in any genre, Holdy. Besides, it gives me a chance to work with a real pro. I've found a great publisher too."

"Oh? You're not staying with HHR?"

"Didn't you hear? Michael sold it. To Isabella."

The man's eyes grew wide, and his face flushed. "No, I… No. She didn't tell me. I've…uh…I've got to go."

"Where are you staying?"

Wheelock looked as though he wanted to lie but couldn't think of a plausible one. "At the Ritz-Carlton in Sarasota."

"Great, we'll have to get together for a drink."

The man slunk out of the restaurant. At the entrance, he glanced back, then disappeared. Charity and Finney sat down at the table. "Now what?"

"Now we eat."

"What about Isabella?"

"She'll keep. Does she know George has canceled their agreement?"

Charity pulled out her cell phone and dialed. "George? Have you called Arlo yet to explain the deal's off with Isabella Voleuse? Yes? Did you tell her that she's out yet? Great—no, no. Whatever you do, don't tell her. Right. Yes, I will, when I get there."

After a meal in which conversation revolved around anything but Isabella, Charity felt better. They dropped Finney off at his hotel and headed back to Longboat Key. As she put the leftovers in the refrigerator, she said, "So, what do we do about Bo?"

"Bo? Oh, you mean Isabella. The only hold we have over her is her lack of payment. As long as she doesn't deliver, Michael has a chance to get HHR back."

"What about the thefts?"

He clucked his tongue. "I'm afraid Wheelock's right. Unless we catch her red-handed with our submissions, she can blame a hacker."

"This is so frustrating."

"Fear not—we'll get her somehow. I wonder what Wheelock is doing here? *Hmm.* I think I'll give Atalanta a call."

"Why her?"

"Well, Jemimah isn't the bright stick she used to be, and besides, she said she wanted no part of this. Come to think of it, she was right about poor Michael."

"What about Mr. Guttersnipe?"

"Bernie? He has no imagination. Besides, Isabella told me he and Holdridge haven't spoken in years."

"Atalanta is the erotic paranormal romance writer, right?"

"Yup. Although recently she's made noises about branching out into a different genre. She may be able to help. I want to see if she's heard from Isabella or Holdridge recently."

He dialed a number. "Atalanta L'Amour, please. Rancor Bass calling." He held a palm over the receiver. "She's gone and hired herself a social secretary. Thinks it makes her look more swank…Betty? It's me, Rancor. I've got news for you." He told her about Isabella and Finney. "And today we saw her lunching with Holdridge…Really? *Hmm.* You don't say. Let me know if you find it." He hung up.

"Betty?"

He answered absently. "Betty Jones—Atalanta's real name. "

"Ah. So what did she say?"

"That Wheelock had been to visit her last week. First he tried to convince her that the manuscript thefts were committed by a Chinese pirate. When she wasn't persuaded, he slyly suggested Michael might be the guilty one."

"How did she react?"

"She changed the subject. She told him she was on the last draft of a new book—a mystery set in Manhattan. He joked that she sure didn't want to submit it to Michael and she said, oh no, she was keeping the only copy under her mattress and planned to hand carry it to her agent." He poured himself a glass of water. "Yesterday, she discovered the manuscript was missing."

"Wheelock?"

"She doubts it. Several people have been in the apartment since his visit, including the maid."

"Did she ever leave him alone in the room?"

"Good question. I'll give her another call." He stood. "But first I think I'll pay a visit to the new Ritz-Carlton. I understand it's a bit more commodious than the old one."

"Ha ha. Drop me at the paper, would you? George wants to know why he can't tell Isabella yet."

As she waved him off from the *Planet* parking lot, it occurred to her that she no longer resented his treating her car—not to mention her apartment—as his own. *Oh dear, I may be getting used to having him around.* She walked up the steps.

The last person she expected to see sat—still in her white gauze outfit—in George's office. *Isabella.* She gestured wildly at George through the glass. He came out, closing the door behind him.

"You didn't tell her anything, did you?"

"No. But it hasn't been easy putting her off. She wants to see Rancor's manuscript."

"No problem. He doesn't have one."

"Ah, well, that will help." He peered at her. "You'll enlighten me once I've gotten rid of her?"

"Of course."

Charity waited, pretending to work at her desk, until Isabella stood up, whereupon she strolled to the door and stood with her back to it, blocking the exit. When Isabella came out, she chirped, "Oh, hi. How did you like the Columbia?"

Isabella didn't seem happy. "On the touristy side."

"Did you try the white sangria?"

"I believe so," she said absently.

"It's sooo good, isn't it?"

"Yes, yes, it was."

"And where are you off to?"

Isabella gave her a piercing look. "I have some errands to do. Why?"

"Oh…" Charity managed an artificial titter. "We don't have many public restrooms on the island. You might want to use our facilities before you go." She walked to her laptop and sat down. "As my grandmother always used to say, 'Try to keep empty.' "

Isabella hesitated, then shrugged. "Thanks." She left her briefcase and purse on the chair and went through the door marked Women. Quick as a pickpocket, Charity opened Isabella's briefcase and took out the envelope Holdridge had given her. She popped it into her desk drawer and began typing furiously. Isabella came out, retrieved her bag, and left without a word to Charity.

She listened for the roar of the Lamborghini to diminish and drew the envelope from her drawer. It was sealed. She went to the break room, set the kettle on, and steamed it open. George walked in as she slid a sheaf of papers out of the envelope.

She looked at the title page, then silently handed it to George. He read it aloud. "*The Sexpot Shifter and the Burning Cave*, by Atalanta L'Amour. Final Draft." The author's name had been crossed out with blue ink, and "Sebastian Frye" inserted in its place.

Chapter Eighteen
The Lady Packs Heat

Rancor put the manuscript down and sipped his coffee. "Are we looking at the smoking gun?"

"Gotta be."

"Atalanta says the maid saw Holdridge go into the bedroom. When she asked him what he was doing, he claimed he was looking for the bathroom."

"Holdridge must have nicked it then. That means he's in on it with Isabella." She buttered a piece of toast. "So what's next?"

"We'd better get this to the police."

Charity paused. "Do they have jurisdiction?"

"We'll find out. It's always best to start at the first rung."

"Okay."

They found Captain Kelly in his office. "Hey, Charity, haven't seen much of you lately. What are you working on?"

"Oh...er...lots of stuff. Right now we want you to bring a case of intellectual property theft."

"Whoa. We're talking felony here. It's probably something that should go to the district attorney. What have you got?"

Rancor gave him a quick rundown.

"Let me guess—it's Chinese or Indians. Piracy's rampant nowadays."

"Nope, although the perpetrators will try to claim that. We only got proof of their identities yesterday." He slapped the envelope on the desk.

Kelly pulled the papers out. "Who's Atalanta L'Amour? Sounds pretty spicy."

"She's a famous writer. This manuscript was removed from her apartment by one Holdridge K. Wheelock who turned it over to Isabella Voleuse to publish under a false name."

"Holdridge Wheelock? Isn't he the author of that hilarious book on Christopher Robin? Why would he steal anybody's work? Guy's probably a millionaire."

Rancor snorted. "Average annual income for a writer—unless he's a superstar like me—is nine thousand dollars. Holdy lives off his pension."

Charity felt a sudden twinge of doubt. "To tell the truth, we don't know why he's doing it."

"Isabella's probably promised him a cut of the profits."

"Huh." The policeman tapped the book. "What does all this have to do with you, anyway?"

"Rancor's also had a submission stolen."

Kelly shot a look at Rancor. "Isn't it copyrighted?"

"Technically, but it disappeared before it was actually under contract, so I have no way to prove it's mine."

"I see." Kelly stood up. "This is way out of my zone of expertise. I suggest you get a lawyer. Then, if he thinks you have a case, we can get a search warrant."

"What good would that do?"

"I'm assuming Wheelock or his accomplice has the books hidden somewhere. If we found more like this one—with the name altered—we could go to the assistant DA. I believe here in Florida intellectual property theft is considered grand larceny."

"What happens if we don't find any more manuscripts?"

"Then I don't think you have a case. You can always try civil court."

"Thanks." Rancor's tone was dry.

They drove home, Rancor muttering to himself. He slammed upstairs, got the whiskey from the cabinet, and poured himself a stiff one.

"Sun isn't over the yardarm yet, my good man."

"And your point?" He knocked it back but, after a slight hesitation, set the bottle down on the table.

Charity took a can of peanuts from the refrigerator and began to munch. "What are you so upset about?"

"There's no way we can bring a criminal case against Isabella or Holdridge."

"Why not? We should at least consult a lawyer."

"Doesn't matter. Jemimah isn't interested, and Bernie has made so many enemies in the legal profession, no one would lift a finger for him."

"What about Atalanta?"

"Since her manuscript is the only evidence we have, she would have to bring the case herself, and I'm not sure I can talk her into that."

"If Wheelock stole that manuscript, he likely took the others. What happened when you went to see him?"

Rancor reached a hand out for the bottle but let it drop. "He's skipped."

"Gone?"

"Kit and kaboodle. Or lock, stock, and barrel. Take your pick."

"Well, we know where he lives."

"You don't think he's already cleaned out any evidence that points to his collusion with Isabella?"

Charity tapped a finger. "That probably means Isabella discovered the book is missing from her briefcase."

"And told Wheelock."

"So they'll both be long gone."

"Not necessarily." They turned at the lilting voice. Isabella stood in the open door, a black Beretta in her hand. She stepped forward. "Give me the manuscript, Charity."

She thought fast. "I don't have it."

"You took it. I know you did."

"Yes, I did, but we gave it to the police." *So he gave it back to us. So what?* "It's evidence." She stared at Isabella and spoke deliberately. "Intellectual property theft is a felony."

Isabella's mouth shut tight. Her gaze moved to Rancor.

He wore his most impenetrable expression. "That's right. Why don't you put the gun down, Isabella? It's only going to get you in more trouble."

She hesitated, then backed up a step. As she twirled to run, Rancor lunged at her, catching an ankle. She tumbled forward and let out a most unladylike squawk. The gun skittered across the floor, coming to rest at Charity's feet. She picked it up.

From the open door came a surprised grunt. "What the—?" There on the landing, grasping Isabella with both arms, stood Michael, his mouth hanging open.

Charity put down the gun and called 9-1-1.

A few minutes later, Isabella was gone, accompanied by two police officers and a plainclothes man. Michael, Charity, and Rancor sat at the kitchen table pouring shots of whiskey for each other. Michael finished his in one gulp and said, "You're going to need more whiskey, Charity."

Where have I heard that before?

He poured another tot. "What's going to happen to Isabella?"

Rancor said, "Not sure. I suppose holding a gun on us is assault—"

"She didn't touch us." She glanced at Michael. "At least not on purpose."

"I don't think you have to touch anyone."

"But that doesn't make any sense."

"The law doesn't always make sense. Why—"

Michael broke in. "What happened with the manuscripts?"

Charity answered. "Captain Kelly suggested we get a lawyer's advice, although he didn't think there was enough evidence to charge her."

"But she swindled us!"

"As a publisher, you should know how difficult these cases are."

Finney put his head in his hands. "What else can we do?"

"I don't know." Charity stood and took the glasses to the sink. "By the way, what were you doing on my doorstep?"

"Oh, yeah." Michael almost smiled, then took it back. "My accountant left a message that funds had been deposited in the HHR account."

"Isabella's check?"

"He didn't say." His eyes filled with tears. "I hope not."

Rancor spoke up. "So HHR still has a bank account?"

"Yes—for the time being. Although...come to think of it"—he scratched his chin—"Isabella was supposed to make it out to me, not to HHR Press."

"Just another way to delay the payment while you sort it out with the bank."

He blew his nose. "I suppose."

Charity patted his arm. "Perhaps we can use Isabella's arrest as leverage."

Michael perked up. "Say, that gives me an idea. Could we offer to drop the charges in return for giving me back HHR Press?"

Rancor swung around on Michael, a light in his eyes. "It's worth a try."

****

"We're supposed to meet Michael at the station at nine."

"I think we have time for one more roll in the hay." Rancor reached for her.

"My, you have really lapsed into the well of trite phrases lately. 'Roll in the hay,' 'kit and kaboodle,' and...what was the other one?"

"Never mind the words. You will be amazed and awed by the originality of my actions."

A short time later, she grudgingly admitted that actions spoke louder than words.

"See, even you're prone to it."

"Is that a homonym I hear?"

"A mere pun."

"As a serious writer, you are supposed to hate puns."

"Really? Why?"

"I don't know. I read a book once that divided the literary world between those who loved and those who despised puns. All the respectable writers shunned them, or pretended to."

"Well, I love them." Rancor threw back the covers and rose. "It's time we got going. Upsy daisy."

They reached the police station just as Michael pulled up in a cab. Sergeant Ingersoll said, "Oh hi, Charity. What's going on?"

"We're here about Isabella Voleuse, Frank. This is Michael Finney, and you know Rancor Bass."

Frank acknowledged Rancor with a curled lip. "Yes, we here in the precinct are well acquainted with Mr. Bass."

Rancor managed to look chagrined. "I've learned my lesson, Sarge. Really I have. I intend to go straight from now on."

"Good to hear. Now folks, we need you to sign the paperwork charging Ms. Voleuse"—he pronounced the name with some reverence—"with assault. And in your case, Mr. Finney, with battery."

Rancor shot a patronizing look at Charity. "See? I told you, assault isn't the same as battery. It's—"

Michael cleared his throat. "*Erm*, is it possible to drop the charges? I...er...don't think she meant to hurt anyone."

The sergeant goggled at him. "She held a gun on you."

"She has a permit for it. She may have felt threatened. Don't you have one of those 'stand your ground' laws here in Florida?" His watery eyes pleaded with the policeman.

Frank turned to the other two. "How about you

guys?"

Rancor and Charity exchanged glances. "We have a proposition for her."

"We don't do deals."

"Well, could we have five minutes alone with her? Just to gauge her frame of mind?"

"I'll have to ask Captain Kelly. One minute." He went into the office. When he came out, he was shaking his head. "He says all right, but there has to be a cop in the room."

"That's all right—it's not like we're invoking lawyer-client privilege or anything. Speaking of, did she call a lawyer?"

"She made her one call. Name sure sounded like a lawyer, but he hasn't shown up yet."

Charity made a guess. "Could it have been to Holdridge K. Wheelock?"

He rubbed his jaw. "Something like that. Miss Voleuse didn't get through to him though. Had to leave a message. She seemed very upset." His face fell at the memory.

Rancor cackled. "I'll bet she was. Looks like old Holdy skipped out on her too."

Frank held an arm out. "This way." They entered a windowless room about eight feet square.

Another policeman brought Isabella in from her cell. Apparently, she had been allowed to refresh her toilette, for her hair shone and her teeth sparkled. Her makeup was perfect—even to the orange lipstick that matched her immaculate orange jumpsuit. Charity looked closer. *Oh my God, she's even got a tiny orange bow in her hair.* The policeman trotted behind her, his face worshipful.

"Miss Voleuse? Will you sit here?" He held the chair out for her.

"Thank you, Bobby." She gave him a gentle smile, adding just a dab of pathos. Bobby teared up.

Michael gestured at the other chair, but Charity said, "No, you sit. You have to make the offer." She and Rancor leaned against the wall.

Michael gazed at Isabella, his face inscrutable.

She cringed a tiny bit, then stiffened. "What do you want, Michael?"

Somehow the little Finney found his footing. His voice firm, his eyes unblinking, he said, "We have a proposal for you, Isabella. We will drop the felony charges in exchange for the abrogation of the sale transferring HHR Press to you."

Her eyes opened wide. "Absolutely not. The firm is mine."

He spoke quietly. "You haven't sent me the check yet. Until I have the money, the transaction is not final."

Charity watched Isabella carefully. If she had in fact deposited the funds, she would protest, but she said nothing.

Michael waved his hand about the room. "I suggest that if you don't agree, you will not be in a position, one, to get your hands on the money, or two, to send it."

Isabella may have been drop-dead gorgeous, but she was also very smart. It took her all of two minutes to decide. "Okay. How do we do it?"

Michael let out a breath. "We'll drop the charges. Then you can send me the paperwork from Seattle and—"

Rancor stepped forward. "Er, Michael? Perhaps we

should complete the transfer first."

Isabella pressed her lips together. "You're going to leave me in jail?"

Bobby's face brightened. "We'll take good care of you, Miss Voleuse."

Frank shook his head. "We can't keep her here, Bobby, not if they're not going to pursue the case."

Almost everyone in the room seemed disappointed. Michael spoke. "Rancor is right. I don't think we're quite ready to drop the charges, Sergeant. Perhaps you will allow Miss Voleuse to make another call." He stared at Isabella, waiting her out.

When she didn't answer, Rancor jumped in. "Yes, Isabella, have your lawyer draw up the nullification of sale papers and fax them to Michael."

Charity added, "Now you won't have to worry about the check—or anything." She smiled sweetly at the woman.

Isabella said lightly, although Charity noted a steely glint in her eye, "I'll just be going then—Bobby? Would you escort me to my cell? I need my briefcase and my cell phone. Thank you *so* much." She shot a bitter look at Rancor and let herself be led out.

Rancor slapped Michael on the back. "Well done!"

Michael looked quite pleased with himself. "I must say, I stood up to her, didn't I? Rather!"

Charity hated to sprinkle gloom on the festivities. *A killjoy's work is never done.* "Um…boys? Today is Sunday—she may not get hold of her lawyers until tomorrow."

Michael fell back on the chair. "If she's let out before that, we're screwed."

The sergeant began to say something, but Rancor

interrupted. "Perhaps she could have the papers sent here? That way, even if she's flown the coop we'll have them."

Charity touched the officer's sleeve. "Frank, can you have her ask her lawyer to fax them here?"

"Sure. But if you're going to drop the charges, you have to do it first thing Monday. Captain'll have my head otherwise."

"It's a promise. Call us when the papers come in."

The three left, springs in all their steps. Rancor opened the car door with a flourish. "What say we get a spot of lunch? I'm paying."

"I thought you'd blown your wad on the frog?"

Finney blinked. "Frog?"

"Never mind. No, that was last week's pay. I got paid *again* this week. Is this a great country or what?" He helped Charity in. "Olaf's all right?"

Charity remembered her last meal there without fondness. "How about Dry Dock? Milton's? Tide Tables?"

Rancor gave her an affectionate pat. "You have to get right back on the horse. Or is it a bicycle?" Both men appeared absorbed by the question.

Olaf's was pretty empty at that early hour, and they were led to a booth in the garden room. A blast of sun called their attention to the luxuriant bromeliads blooming among the spiky orange terrestrial orchids. Behind them, a bright crimson bougainvillea climbed a trellis. "Bloody Marys for everyone?"

"Sounds good."

Elsa appeared. Summoning her inner strength, Charity ordered the captain's platter. The waitress paused. "You know that's a lot of food. Do you want to share it?"

"No, but thanks for asking."

Michael chose the seafood Cobb salad and Rancor the potato-crusted grouper. No one spoke while they ate, Charity dwelling on the felicitous image of Isabella eating her lunch on a prison tray. *I hope it's a double bacon cheeseburger and fries with extra gluten on the side.*

Rancor lay down his fork. "So, where are we?"

"We're about to get my company back," crowed Michael. "I'll be able to tell Mother all is well."

"And hopefully she will convey what she means by a deed, a promise, and an oath."

Charity added, "Not to mention what we're looking for in Cà d'Zan."

"You don't think she meant the business card?"

"I can't see how. It was in Ringling's locked desk. I doubt if she expected us to break into it."

Michael sniffed. "That's for sure. You certainly shocked me."

Rancor wasn't listening. His eyes closed, he muttered to himself, "So how do we get her to spill the beans?"

Charity coughed. "Rancor, dear, you did it again."

"What did I do again?"

She tapped a finger on the back of his hand. " 'Spill the beans?' Is that the best you can do?"

He slapped his forehead. "I *am* out of practice. The sooner we solve this murder thingy the sooner I can get back in the groove...Damn!"

Charity bestowed a forgiving smile upon him. "Perhaps if you simply shut up?"

Michael sucked the last bit of drink from his glass,

leaving the ice cubes to clank and shuffle. "I shall call her tonight."

"Your mother."

"Yes." He accepted a second Bloody Mary from Elsa.

Charity mused. "Do you think she knows who killed Robert Three?"

"I don't see how, but she should know when and why Edgar left Sarasota."

"You're assuming his departure had something to do with the murder, but he could have left for an entirely different reason."

"Mrs. Penney's notion about his 'tender feeling'?" Rancor directed a shrewd look at Michael.

She nodded. "Hedda was happily married. He knew he had no chance with her. He had to leave Cà d'Zan."

Michael put his glass down. "But what about the card? Ringling told Edgar to go to the Ghost Hotel."

Rancor shook his head. "That's not a given. We don't really know what Ringling meant by his note. But if Edgar did go, he had to have witnessed what happened before or after Robert's death. He didn't want to be forced to testify because—"

"Because Hedda killed him. Has to be."

"Why?"

Charity, busy with her thoughts, didn't answer right away. After Elsa replaced her drink, she steepled her fingers. "Okay, here's the story. Edgar followed Hedda on John's instructions. He saw her murder Robert. Struck with the horror of it, he ran home, packed, and left."

"Wouldn't he have told John?"

"No—that would have implicated Ringling. He had to keep his name out of it. All of Ringling's business dealings depended on it—and his finances were already on the skids."

"What about the note and Robert's card then? No one but Ringling could have hidden it in his desk."

"True, but that was only to keep Hedda from finding it and realizing that he knew about her deceit. He must have assumed Edgar had taken care of the problem and didn't ask further."

"But this doesn't make any sense. Why would Hedda kill the man she wanted to do business with?"

Michael ventured. "Perhaps he was also her lover?"

"No. Hedda loved Ringling. We know that from a letter she wrote."

Rancor put down his glass. "Wait. Biddlesworth."

"What about him? Honestly, Rancor, do you have to keep strewing red herrings in the path? Biddlesworth was thrown from the boat and drowned. Period."

"Biddlesworth is immaterial, but he is relevant. I'm talking about Hedda's brother, Calvin Hagen. We're pretty sure he killed Biddlesworth. Maybe he killed Robert as well."

"Oh, for heaven's sake, why don't you make him responsible for the 1919 White Sox cheating scandal as well?"

"It's not that wild a theory. He was a crook. He's the most likely person to have helped Hedda arrange the deal. He could have been there that night."

"Even so, the same question applies to him. Why would he knock off a potential client?"

"He knocked off Biddlesworth."

"Who was his partner, not his client."

Rancor waved at the waitress. "I need another drink."

Charity sipped hers. "Maybe we should look at Standish's report again. I only skimmed the summary. There might be something else in it. Did they check Biddlesworth's dental records?"

"Yes, remember? He had his wisdom teeth out. So did Robert."

"Ah, but I was chatting with Dr. O'Brien, my dentist, the other day."

"A cordial relationship with a man who makes his living torturing people? I'm jealous."

Charity said dreamily, "He's really the sweetest thing. He says if I come to him regularly, I'll be able to keep my teeth longer than I live."

"Well, that will be helpful if some forensic dentist in the twenty-fifth century wants to probe the jaw of an ancient sex kitten."

She ignored him. "I mentioned the skeleton and how its teeth had been knocked out. He confirmed that, if a professional had extracted a tooth *prior* to the blunt trauma, he would have removed the root, but that that section of bone would show a different state of decay. He said that a forensic dentist—they're called odontologists, by the way—"

"Great—now I can finally finish last Sunday's crossword puzzle."

"—could tell if the victim had had moderate to severe periodontal disease from the amount of bone loss."

Rancor threw down his fork. "Wait a minute! The Standish report should show whether the victim had periodontal disease or not, shouldn't it?"

Charity was dubious. "I don't know...Would a physical anthropologist even recognize it, much less put it in his report? Dr. O'Brien says—"

"Enough with your new flame."

To stem the tide of hostilities, Michael interjected mildly, "Standish is an expert. He must have a working knowledge of jaws. If it *is* in the report, we can check both men's records—that is, if the police haven't already done that."

"I doubt it. Remember, they settled on Biddlesworth and would have none of Bass."

Charity cried, "But you showed them the ring!"

"Which worked for Biddlesworth just as well as it did for my grandfather."

"Wait a minute. What about ring size? Did they measure that?" Michael held his hand up and wiggled his fingers, knocking over his glass.

Elsa materialized with a sponge and a scowl. "Did you want another drink, *sir?*"

"I'm so sorry, no, I'm fine." He tried to help her but only succeeded in spreading the puddle far enough to drip into Charity's lap.

"Michael!"

"Oh dear, oh dear."

While everyone else scrambled to blot the spill, Rancor took the opportunity to roar with laughter. Olaf walked over, looked at the mess, and joined him.

He was still laughing as they walked across the street to the *Planet* offices and Charity's car. "I'm going down to see our good police chief."

"What for?"

"I want to see a man about a—"

"Dog?"

"No. A finger."

Charity pulled him out of the driver's seat and got in. "We're coming with you. In case the papers have arrived."

"Oh yes," Rancor said with a malicious grin. "We do want to free the radiant Isabella as soon as possible."

"Before those salivating policemen take advantage of her." Michael grinned back at him.

Rancor knit his brow in a display of manly concern. "Perhaps I should keep an eye on her after she's released. She may be a flight risk."

Charity took his arm. "No, you'll be busy this evening. Besides, if she does run, she'll run to Holdridge."

"Gawd, what does she see in him? The man's a prat."

"A useful tool?"

Michael added, "Or the other way around?"

"Nah. He's not that bright."

"Maybe you're right. She offered him a share—"

"And," said Rancor with a superior air, "he would jump at it, since his books sell almost as well as an epithalamium published the day after the annulment."

"Run that by us again?"

"What? Annulment?" When the other two leaned toward him with undisguised menace, he said quickly, "Epithalamium. Poem written for the bride and groom. One of fifty types of poems. I can list them all." He took a deep breath. "Limericks, haiku, idylls, rondeaux—"

"That will do, Bass. Can we get back to the problem at hand?"

"Yes. The problem being, how do we keep the little tykes from stealing any more manuscripts?"

"Good question. Michael?"

"Once I get HHR Press back, I'll publish an article detailing their activities. No respectable firm will deal with either one. And we'll get Atalanta to blab about it to all her friends in the Manhattan literary circles."

Rancor sighed happily. "Who knows? Maybe they'll be reduced to pilfering the memoirs of suburban housewives from vanity presses."

When they reached the police station, Captain Kelly was gone for the day. Frank greeted them. "Hey, you're just in time. The Seattle real estate lawyers faxed the settlement papers."

"Wow, this must be why those guys get the big bucks. I wonder if HHR pays their retainer too?"

Michael nodded miserably. "Isabella said it was only fair. How ironic that I have to pay *them* to get my company back." Frank gave the papers to Michael, who took them gingerly, as though they burned his fingers. He looked at Rancor. "Should I tear them up?"

"No! Keep them. Knowing Isabella, she'll have a second copy. This has the cover letter stating that the sale is null and void. You can whip it out if she tries any funny business."

"Okay. Is it all right to drop the charges against Isabella then?"

"Sure."

They signed the forms and waited in the lobby for Isabella. It took half an hour for her to appear. Somehow, she'd managed to change into an ivory linen jacket dress, the Chanel pearls looping in carefree ropes down her back. Rancor nudged Charity and whispered,

"Do you suppose she got Bobby to retrieve a fresh ensemble from the hotel?"

"*Shh.*"

Isabella said nothing to them but took Bobby's arm and walked, head high, out to the street. A taxi pulled up, and the young policeman handed her in. She waved languidly at Rancor, then spoke to the driver, who sped off.

The phone at the desk rang. Frank picked it up. "Sergeant Ingersoll, Longboat Key Police Department. Yes? Miss Voleuse? She's just been released…No…you don't have to send it…Sure, no problem."

Rancor cocked his head. "Was that Holdridge Wheelock? Did he finally return her call?"

"Uh uh. Some other guy." He checked his log. "A Mr. Guttersnipe." He guffawed. "What a moniker!"

"It's not his real name. So what did he want?"

"Said he'd secured bail money for her, but since the charges have been dropped, there's no need for it." He glanced at the phone. "Funny. He sounded awful gloomy—kinda like that donkey in Winnie the Pooh."

Michael piped up. "Eeyore."

"Yeah."

"Despondent? Despairing? World-weary?" Rancor smiled. "That's our Bernie. *Hmm.* When Holdy didn't come through, Isabella must have decided to cadge the money from him."

Charity shrugged. "He's given her money before." She took Frank aside. "Will the chief be in tomorrow?"

"No, ma'am, he always takes Monday off to go fishing with his father. He'll be in on Tuesday."

"We'd like to see him."

"No problem. What's it about?"
"Teeth and fingers."

Chapter Nineteen
Teeth and Fingers

"The case is closed, Charity."

Rancor pushed in front of her. "Correction, Kelly, the case is *cold.* Not closed."

"Funny, here I thought only the police could decide whether to reopen an investigation."

"But, Chief," Charity pleaded, "I need to tidy up a few loose ends for my article. I only want to have another look at Standish's report."

The police captain relented but refused to look at Rancor. "All right. For *you*, Charity. Frank! Get me the Standish report on the Chart House skeletons please."

"And…er…could we have the autopsy report as well? From the medical examiner?"

"Yes, yes. Now get out of my office."

They took their spoils to the interrogation room. Rancor chose Edwards' report, and Charity picked up Standish's.

Rancor finished first. "Looks like Edwards measured all the long bones—tibia, femur, etc., but not the fingers. So we can't use ring size to identify him."

Charity said glumly, "And Standish found no evidence of any other bone fractures prior to death, except for his finger."

"Looks like the only things left to check are the teeth."

"I'm afraid so." She read on. "The teeth were knocked out by blunt force—"

"Say, I just thought of something." He riffled through Edwards' report. "Yes, I thought I read this. They found some teeth fragments with the victim." He read further, his frown deepening. "Damn. Not large enough to help in identification."

"Must have been a real haymaker to do that much damage."

"With a pretty heavy object. A baseball bat maybe." Rancor put his chin in his hand. "That eliminates Hedda as a suspect, you know."

"How so?"

"It'd take a powerful person to do it. A man."

"Or a woman if she used some kind of leverage."

"Yes, of course. I'm sure Hedda always carried her trusty crowbar around in her purse."

"You're still fixed on Calvin Hagen then?"

He nodded. "The idea has a certain rhythmic charm."

"Okay." Charity closed the folder. "We're going to have to talk the captain into calling in a forensic dentist."

"Can't we just hire one?"

"With whose money?"

"Oh."

"I'll do that while you call Aunt Gertrude."

"Oh dear, she's going to think I'm trying to elbow my way into her will." He checked. "Unless I'm already in it, in which case she'll cut me out. She's a crusty old bird."

"Nonetheless, we need your grandfather's dental records."

"You really believe she can lay her hands on them?"

"I haven't even met the lady, and yet I'm positive she can."

Rancor pulled out a cell phone. Charity immediately felt around in her bag for hers. "Ah, there it is." She eyed Rancor with suspicion. "Since when did you acquire a smartphone?"

"This? Oh, I…uh…borrowed it…from Michael."

"What happened to that disposable one you had in Paris?"

"Used up all the minutes. And anyway it only accepted euros."

Charity's cell buzzed. "Hi, Michael…You think you left it where? Sure, I'll call the restaurant." She put her phone in an inside pocket of her purse and zipped it shut. "That's it. We're stopping at CVS for a prepaid phone."

His eyes lit up. "How generous of you." He kissed her cheek. "I'll just go outside and make that call, shall I? You tackle Kelly."

When they met again in the parking lot, Charity was smiling. "He's such a dear. He ranted a while, then got on the horn. A Dr. Nash will meet us this afternoon at the morgue to take a look at Exhibit A."

"And dental records for Robert Bass the Third—together with his schedule of vaccinations and school grades—will arrive by post in two days."

"Post?"

"Gertrude despairs of the return of the pony express and has resigned herself to trusting the post office with her precious correspondence. Unfortunately, she always springs for heavy insurance and insists the recipient sign for the envelope." He patted her shoulder. "We've done well. Perhaps we should repair to a local tavern to partake of some light refreshment while we wait for the dentist."

"What about Michael?"

"Michael hinted that he would like some time off from our exertions to get to know Mrs. Penney better. They are taking a scenic cruise of Sarasota Harbor on *Marina Jack* today."

"How romantic!"

"They are sweet together. Not like us."

A pang hit Charity right under her left center rib. "What...what do you mean?"

He took her in his arms and kissed her hard. "We, my dear, are brazen, bawdy, and hot."

"Th-that's...okay, then." She felt a little shaky.

After a filling lunch of spaghetti and meatballs at Ciao d'Italia, they drove to the morgue. Kelly arrived at the same time, accompanied by a pudgy man with sandy hair. The police chief greeted them. "Charity. Mr. Bass. This is Boynton Nash, from the LECOM School of Dental Medicine. He's a forensic odontologist."

Rancor took the opportunity to nod sagely.

Kelly turned to his companion. "Boynton, this is Charity Snow, reporter for the *Longboat Key Planet*, and Rancor Bass."

Nash held out a hand to Charity, his eyes round with admiration. "Ms. Snow, it is a *real* pleasure."

A woman in a lab coat opened the door. "The subject is in Room Five. Would you come this way?"

Nash gestured to Charity to precede them. "After you, Ms. Snow." She walked ahead, fully cognizant of Nash's appreciation and Rancor's displeasure, and enjoying every minute of it. She swished her braid.

They entered a frigid room lined with steel cabinets. The skeleton lay on a table in a large basin. Charity surveyed the remains, feeling slightly sick. "Why is he in a tub?"

"Only way to hold him together."

Mr. Nash accepted a pair of gloves from the assistant and began to examine the bones. "Male adult, fairly young—no sign of osteoporosis. *Hmm.* Someone knocked out all his teeth." He looked up. "Boxer?"

"No, we think it was deliberate, to make identification impossible."

"Ah, so he was murdered?"

"Stabbed to death. The physical anthropologist who examined him—"

"Standish?"

"Yes."

"Prick."

Rancor agreed. "Right on the money."

"*Nevertheless.*" Kelly cut off the banter before it could take a turn toward the tasteless. "Standish set the year of death between 1930 and 1935."

"*Mm hmm.*" Nash probed the jaw. "Wisdom teeth removed much earlier. Signs of moderate periodontal disease."

"You can tell that?"

"Look here at the upper left section of the maxillary. No soft tissue left of course, but where the gum receded you can see the topography is asymmetrical, indicating bone loss. Patient probably had some deep pockets—tens and elevens."

"Tens and elevens?"

"A measurement of the distance between the

original gum line and how much it has receded." He stood up. "That's about all I can tell you. Do you have any dental records to match?"

Kelly handed him a file. "These belong to Rodney Biddlesworth. He's the most likely prospect."

Nash looked at them. "Sorry, you've got the wrong guy then. Biddlesworth had no periodontal problems at all."

"But everything else fits." The police chief's voice rose half an octave. "Wisdom teeth gone—"

Charity said mildly, "A lot of people have their wisdom teeth taken out."

Kelly faced Nash. "Right age, placed in Sarasota in the correct time frame, disappeared without a trace, water in his lungs, ring found that matches his graduation year and college—"

Rancor interrupted. "Unless the date of the inscription—1931—refers not to the class year but to the date of his marriage. Robert Bass III eloped in 1931."

Nash looked from one to the other. "What are you talking about?"

"There's one other possible identity for the skeleton."

"Well, did your second man have periodontal disease?"

"We'll find out in a couple of days. I'm having his records mailed here."

Nash took off the lab coat and hung it on a peg. "If that's all you've got for me, I'm going to head back to school. I have classes all this week."

"Oh, dear. Can we bring the records up to you when we get them?" Charity tried to keep the frustration out of her voice, without much success.

He smiled at her. "Sure." He took a card from his wallet and gave it to her. "Call and leave a message when you have the records."

"Thank you so much, Dr. Nash."

He hesitated. "Um, Ms. Snow, if you're…uh…free Saturday night, we're having a…um…faculty party and—"

A heavy hand landed on his shoulder. "Sorry, Dr. Nash. The lady has another commitment." From the anguished expression on the dentist's face, Rancor was probably squeezing rather hard.

****

Rancor waited by the mailbox for a day and a half. When the mailman came up the walk with letters in his hand on Thursday afternoon, he stopped just short of tackling him. "What've you got for me, Murray?"

The old man wiped the sweat off his brow. "And who might you be?"

"What difference does that make?"

Murray, a postman of the old school, straightened and pulled in his considerable gut. "It makes a difference to the United States Postal Service—and by extension, Homeland Security. *Sir*. I can't give you mail to which you are not entitled."

"Do you have a letter addressed to Rancor Bass, care of Charity Snow?"

His adversary slowly and deliberately leafed through the pile, lifting each envelope up and peering at it. "Don't see it here. Say, are you the Rancor Bass that writes those books my wife devours?"

"At your service."

"Well, that's real friendly of you. Maybe you'd

sign a copy of one of them for her—she'd be awful pleased."

"Yes, of course, bring it along, happy to, now, if you'll excuse me…"

Murray blocked his way. "You know, if you were to have one on hand right now, that would be swell."

Rancor peered suspiciously at the mailman, who, with his deadpan face, could have been Buster Keaton's stand-in. "Let me guess, if I give you a book—"

"And autograph it."

"And sign it, you'll conveniently find my letter in your truck?"

"I'd be happy to take another look."

"Done." Rancor went back to Charity's apartment, retrieved the least dog-eared volume from the bookcase, and took the steps two at a time. Meanwhile, Murray had miraculously located a fat envelope postmarked Bangor, Maine. They solemnly made the exchange. When Rancor returned, Charity said, "What were you doing with Murray? It looked like some sort of handoff."

"Your precious mailman, aka Bernie Madoff, held up Aunt Gertrude's letter for ransom. I had to give him one of my books." He stopped and gazed upward. "Hey, I just remembered something. An ancestor of mine was a notorious train robber—a Sam Bass. *Hmm.* I'll have to ask Auntie G. about him. Maybe I could slip him into a story…"

"You gave him one of your books? I didn't know you had any here."

"I don't—why would I have any here? I barely have a change of clothes here. I took your copy of *Shades of Yellow*. Oh, and thanks."

"*What*? Rancor, you really take the cake."

"Another trite phrase. What am I going to do with you?"

For answer, Charity marched into the bedroom and started throwing Rancor's things in a garbage bag. He followed her. "What are you doing?"

"I'm taking your stuff to Goodwill. I'm sure there are lots of men far more deserving of these jeans than you."

He took her hand. "All right, I'm sorry. I'll get another copy from Michael—and sign it with a very *personal* note. How's that?"

She wasn't quite ready to forgive him, but she dropped the bag. He kissed her hand. "Now, let's go see what Gertie has to say."

Back in the living room, he opened the envelope. Under a handwritten note lay several pages of dates and squiggles. Rancor read the note.

Dear Rancor,

Dr. Allenby—he's the dentist who took over from old Dr. Wright, and I must say, although young, he's quite thorough and very respectful. At any rate, he was so kind as to go into his archives to find these papers. I can't imagine what you want with your grandfather's records. Seems rather queer to me. At any rate, Dr. Allenby (he's really quite good, though very young) says he may even have an impression. I think he means a mold of Robert's teeth, not one of those comedic spectacles. Let me know if this helps—is it for one of your books?

Love, Aunt Gertrude

P.S. Alice sends her thanks for the baby blanket. I presume she will write you herself, but one never knows with your generation.

"Okay, let's see." He pored over the papers. After about five minutes, he looked up. "I have absolutely no idea what any of this means."

"Here, let me." Charity contemplated the squiggles and numbers. "It's no use. I'm going to call Dr. Nash."

Rancor scowled. "If you must."

The odontologist answered on the first ring. "Oh hello, Ms. Snow! It's good to hear from you. I mean…er…this case is quite fascinating, isn't it?" He paused, perhaps remembering the pain of Rancor's grip. "I have a class this morning, but if you'd like to come up after two o'clock, I'll take a look." He gave her directions.

Three hours later, they drove across the Cortez Bridge and headed east into Bradenton. "There it is, on the right."

They turned into the parking lot of a long, pink-stucco building crouched among the palmettos. A young man in scrubs took them down a corridor to a door marked "Boynton Nash, DDS, PhD." The doctor came around his desk and held a chair out for Charity. She handed him the envelope. "Okay, let's see what you've got."

He skimmed the pages. "Yes, sir, these teeth belong—or rather, could have belonged—to our skeleton. See there"—he pointed—"there's a ten, and there's an eleven-millimeter pocket. And some on the right side as well." He looked wistful. "Too bad the actual teeth are gone. I wonder what the killer did with them? It would confirm the identification."

"Are you willing to sign a document that says these are the dental records of the victim?"

"I can say they are most likely those of the skeleton. You'd need a DNA match to be certain. Who do you think it is, by the way?"

"Robert Bass III."

"Bass? He's a relative?"

"My grandfather."

"Oh my. I gather you are only now discovering what happened to him?"

To Charity's amazement, Rancor's face crumpled. In a broken voice, he whispered, "Yes."

Rancor was subdued the entire ride home. When Charity parked at the police station, he stayed in the car. "You go tell him."

Charity nodded and went in. "Captain, may I speak to you?"

"Sure. What's going on?"

"We've just come back from seeing Dr. Nash. We showed him Robert Bass's dental records, and he confirmed that they were probably identical to the skeleton's."

"Probably? He wasn't a hundred percent certain?"

Damn. "He said something about DNA."

"Charity, you know we don't have the resources to get DNA from corpses that old."

"Why not? They did it for Richard III. And I think a forty-thousand-year-old Neanderthal. Surely we could find some DNA on an eighty-year-old skeleton. Can't we at least ask the Sarasota CSI lab?"

"And who would we match it to?"

"To Rancor Bass."

He raised his eyebrows. "I see. Is Mr. Bass willing?"

"I...uh...haven't talked to him about it yet."

"He has to be willing."

"I'll make sure he is."

"But what about Biddlesworth? Standish's report showed he'd been immersed in water for some length of time. If Bass didn't drown, how would his skeleton show signs of water damage?"

"I don't know." Charity's high spirits began to sink. "Everything else works though. There must be some explanation."

Kelly closed his eyes. "There is one other possibility."

"Yes?" She hoped her eagerness wouldn't put him off.

"The elevator shaft."

"What?"

"I'm going to make a call. Hang on." He dialed a number. "Leo? Nick Kelly here. Can you do me a favor?...Yes. I want you to meet me at the Chart House...What? No, not for happy hour. This'll just take a minute...Okay, okay, beer's on me. See you in ten." He hung up.

"Leo?"

Kelly picked up his hat. "A friend. He works for the Corps of Engineers. Let's just say I have a hunch."

"I'm coming too."

"I didn't expect you not to."

She jumped in her car and followed the captain out onto Gulf of Mexico Drive. Rancor didn't ask where they were going, which—she reflected—was good, since she couldn't enlighten him. When they reached the Chart House parking lot, a tall man in khakis and thick glasses stood by the pit. "What do you want, Nick? I'm dying of thirst."

The policeman pointed down. "Could you check the soil layers in the pit? I want to see if there's any evidence of water seepage."

"Sure thing." The man jumped down and took a flashlight and a large magnifying glass from his backpack. He examined the walls of the pit for several long minutes. Finally, he stuck out a hand, and Kelly hauled him up.

"Well?"

"Indications of standing water for at least a month in the bottom three feet. I'd say when the shaft was abandoned—"

"Closed. A small boy fell in it and died."

"Ah. Well, at some point after that, groundwater must have seeped into the pit." He pointed at the Chart House. "Hope that's what you wanted to hear, because by my watch, it's Miller time."

The police chief looked at Charity. "The last hurdle?"

She took of skip of happiness before realizing the implications of Leo's findings. "No, not yet. Nash said we need DNA proof that it's Robert Bass."

"All right. I'll give CSI a call. Then I have to go treat Leo to his pound of flesh."

He dialed a number. "Get me Jefferson...Bill? Can you swab someone for DNA this afternoon? Good, I'll send him down...No, he's not a person of interest. We're looking for a match for a John Doe. Yeah. Thanks." He hung up. "He's waiting."

"Where is he?"

"Same building as the morgue. Second floor. But Charity"—he held up his hand—"no matter what happens, I'm shutting down the investigation."

She almost panicked. "Why? If it is in fact Robert Bass III, we have to find out who killed him."

He studied her. "Why the sudden interest?"

Charity put a supplicating hand on his. "Don't you see? It's all connected somehow. Isabella and Finney, and the Bass family and the Ringlings—there's a thread there. We just have to find it."

Kelly leaned on his car. "You want to tell me about it?"

The implications of what she'd been saying suddenly struck Charity. "I...uh...no, not right now. I will though...as soon as we get the DNA results. Yes. I will." She backed away. *Or maybe later.*

She ran back to the Mini. Rancor still slumped in the passenger seat. "Rancor, wake up!"

"I am awake." His voice sounded raspy and clogged.

Has he been crying? "You have to go give your DNA."

"Why?"

"So we can confirm that the skeleton belongs to your grandfather."

"What difference does it make?" He sounded uncharacteristically withdrawn.

"Don't you want to find out who killed him?"

"We know who killed him. Calvin Hagen."

"Okay, then, don't you want to find out *why*?"

"Charity, give it up. We'll never know."

She got in the car and started the engine. "You're pathetic, you know? You brag about how clever you are, you lord it over people—treating them like...like serfs, but inside you're just a coward. You're one of those writers who'd rather sit in his cave and imagine the world the way he wants it. You can't deal with it as it is."

"Are you finished?"

No. "I don't know."

"Charity, it just hit me. I mean, if we're right, my grandfather was murdered. He never saw his children grow up. Never saw my father hit his first baseball. Never saw Aunt Gertrude in her beautiful yellow gown, all set for her senior prom. Never saw them graduate. Never held me in his arms. If he *wasn't* a reprobate after all, do I really want to know?"

Having no good answer for him, she gripped the steering wheel and focused on the road.

Rancor kept his head down. In a low voice, he continued. "You're not wrong about writers—we do relish the ability to make characters act and plots twist the way we want them to. It's hard to accept that that power doesn't extend to the real world."

She glanced quickly at him. "Is that really why you write? For the power?"

"No. We write to ease the need, the desire, the *lust* if you will, to have people moved by those characters and plots—to be affected by our words, to have them color the way our readers look at their lives. We literally ache to share our vision with others." He paused. "Charity, my father never gave me his blessing. Perhaps my grandfather would have. If we know for sure what happened to him—that it wasn't his choice to leave us—it makes the loss even more painful."

She pulled into the parking lot of the lab and turned off the engine. Drawing his face to hers, she kissed him gently on the forehead. "I don't agree. His children and grandchildren should have the opportunity to be proud of him. You should try all the harder to redeem his memory."

He was silent, then whispered, "Okay."

Charity reflected that this was the first time Rancor had allowed a vulnerable side to show. The rush of affection almost crushed her chest. "Let's go."

The lab assistant swiped the inside of Rancor's cheek and put the swab in an envelope. "We'll compare this to a sample from Skeleton 59-A's bones. It'll be a couple of hours. Can you wait?"

"N—"

"Yes."

They sat on a hard bench in the waiting room. Rancor kept his head in his hands. Charity twiddled her thumbs. When that grew tedious, she went to finger games. "Here is the church, here is the steeple, open the doors, and—"

"Charity, please."

The young woman came out. "Dr. Jefferson will see you."

They were ushered into a tiny cubicle. A man in the requisite white coat sat at a desk reading a file. He looked at them over his half glasses. "Interesting."

Rancor revived some of his old swagger. "Us? Yes, we are."

"No, the specimen. His body is a textbook example of a sedentary life and a diet of too much meat and too little fiber."

"You can tell that from the DNA?"

"No, from the bones." He marked something on the form with a pen. "This is the first time I've had a chance to study DNA from old bones. I had a blast."

"And?"

The man took his time, perhaps appreciating the unaccustomed attention. "Um...well. The DNA told us he was a Caucasian of English ancestry, with black hair and brown eyes, tending to plumpness. No diseases at the time of death. What did he die of, by the way?"

"Murder."

"Ah."

"Um, Dr. Jefferson, did you...do you have the results of my DNA test?"

He pulled another sheet of paper closer and read it. "Well, I hope this is what you wanted to hear. It's a match to the dead man." He gave Rancor a quizzical look.

Rancor sat down on a straight chair, his eyes on the floor. Dr. Jefferson stood up and said firmly, "I'll have the results sent to Captain Kelly." He indicated the door, and the two went out ahead of him.

Skirting the marina, Charity took a quick left off Marina Drive. "What are you doing?"

"I'm taking you for a drink at Marina Jack's."

"Good." He laid his head back.

The waitress had just delivered mojitos when Michael passed by the table, Mrs. Penney on his arm. They were laughing. Michael saw Charity and Rancor and stopped. "Hi there. What have you two been up to?"

"We found out who the dead man is."

"The one in the elevator shaft?"

"Yes."

Deirdre leaned in. "What are you talking about?"

Michael patted her hand. "I'll explain later. Who is it?"

"My grandfather."

He whistled. "Well, I hope it's a relief to know what happened to him."

"That's just it. We don't."

"You know he was stabbed to death."

"That's right, but by whom?"

Michael took a step back and held his hand up. "Don't look at me—I haven't a clue."

"Oh, but your mother may."

Chapter Twenty
A Deed, an Oath, and a Promise

"I am not going to bother Mother again. I've got HHR Press back, and we have money in the bank. It would really upset her to trot out past family troubles again. She's too old for it. *I'm* too old for it."

"Michael, you promised us you would!"

Finney shut his mouth tight, an expression of mulish obstinacy hardening his flabby features.

Rancor stood up and stalked away. Charity looked from Deirdre to Michael. "But if you don't help us, Rancor will never have closure. Besides, don't you want to know what part—if any—your grandfather played in it?"

"Not really."

Charity realized that her first impression of Michael Finney had been right on the mark. Here he stood before her in all his mediocrity, without courage, without will, without mettle or purpose. She feared that there would be no resolution for her lover.

Mrs. Penney let go of Michael's arm. "Miss Snow, does this have anything to do with Hedda Ringling and Edgar Finney?"

"We think so."

"Well, then, Michael, if your mother has any information on Edgar Finney, you should ask her. It's important that we have a complete history of the

Ringlings."

"But Deirdre—"

"Michael."

"Um. Okay. I'll call her tomorrow."

She beamed at him. "That's wonderful! I'm so proud of you."

So this is how you handle a spineless wimp. "Why don't you two come over for dinner tomorrow night? You can call her from my place."

Michael started to refuse, but Deirdre said, "How delightful. We accept. Say, seven?"

"Perfect. Michael knows the address."

Deirdre gently turned her man in the direction of the door. When they'd gone, Rancor stalked back. "I'm sorry, I just couldn't stand to look at him. What a sheep."

"Luckily, he's latched onto a lioness."

"What do you mean?"

"Deirdre wants Edgar Finney's story. So Michael is going to call his mother."

"Good for her, but how do we find out what Mrs. Finney says?"

"Taken care of. They're coming for dinner. We can coach him on the questions and listen in on the answers."

Rancor kissed her. "Since the estimable Mrs. P. is not within range, you'll have to do."

"Thank you."

****

The next morning dawned bright and clear. Charity found Rancor on the balcony tossing crumbs of bread down to the beach. A flock of gulls screamed and fought over the tidbits.

"You're not supposed to feed the birds."

"Why not?"

"They poop all over my beach."

"It's not your beach."

"It's as much mine as theirs. Now stop it, and come eat some breakfast."

They had finished their coffee when Charity picked up her purse. "Shall I drop you at Publix?"

He checked his watch. "I'll be early for my shift."

"Well, you can do some shopping for dinner tonight."

"I suppose you expect me to cook." He emitted a heavy sigh. "The drudge work never ceases."

"Trust me, you don't want me to cook."

"Other than the odd boiled egg. I remember. Well, it's a good thing you're perfect in every other way."

"Yes, it is," she remarked serenely.

She left him at the delivery entrance of the grocery store and spent a quiet day writing up her article on the fish fry at Pirate's Landing.

At least seventy people consumed sixty pounds of fresh-caught mullet and all of Mrs. Connally's famous coleslaw. As a token of appreciation for the hard work of the fishermen—Joe Moroni and Bill Bacon—a brand new fish-cleaning station was unveiled. Unfortunately, this had the effect of reigniting the only recently buried feud between the two, and fists flew. Distracted by the melee, no one noticed the flock of pelicans landing on the station until it was too late.

When she reached home, Rancor was busy in the kitchen. "They'll be here any minute, Rancor. Hurry up."

"Yes, dear. Right away, dear. I'll just finish

harvesting the lower forty before I paint the barn, okay?"

"As long as you get the stuffed galantine of turkey roasted and the eight-layer torte baked."

"Be done in a jiff."

The doorbell rang. "Welcome, Deirdre. Michael."

Michael had a worried look on his face. "Charity, did you by any chance…"

"Why, yes, I did." She handed him his cell phone.

"Thanks, I—"

"No need."

Rancor came out. "Shall we eat first, then call your mother?"

Michael's chin wobbled. Deirdre said, "Why don't we relax and have a drink?" She held up a bottle of wine. "Then, after Michael's talked to Mrs. Finney, we can discuss it over dinner."

Charity reflected that Mrs. Penney seemed to have a knack for taking command. *Fine. Whatever works.*

Rancor poured wine for Deirdre and whiskey for himself and the other two, then they all sat down in the living room, faces turned expectantly toward Michael. He fidgeted. "Perhaps I should call her from the bedroom?"

"No, dear. Now, what are you going to ask her?"

"Well, I guess I should start by telling her I have HHR Press back."

"Excellent."

"Then I'll ask her about Grandfather."

"Good," said Rancor. "Get her to spell out what she meant by the deed, the oath, and the promise."

"She wouldn't before—why would she now?"

"Because you will tell her we went to Cà d'Zan as

she directed and found the note and the card. See what she says about that."

"All right." He gulped down his drink and picked up his phone. It jiggled in his hand. The group waited tensely. "Hello, Mummy? It's me, Mikey. Did I wake you?" He checked his watch. "Oh, of course, it *is* much earlier there. Really? How much rain? I see. What? Oh…oh…I'm sorry to hear that….What did the vet say?…Well, if he feels you should put Snookums down, then…No, of course not, he's a sweet dog. It was only four stitches. I forgave him ages ago." He looked up to see three pairs of eyes shooting daggers at him. "Listen, Mummy, I have some good news. I got HHR Press back. Yes, she…the lady who wanted to buy it…yes…she decided not to, so I have the purchase agreement back. Yes, I thought you'd be happy to hear it." He listened to what seemed to be a long tirade, holding the receiver an inch or so away from his ear. After a while, the strident voice slowed. Deirdre touched his hand.

"Oh! Oh, er, Mummy? Speaking of 'deed,' remember when we talked last week? Uh huh. And I asked about Edgar Finney and why he went to Seattle, and you said something about a deed, an oath, and a promise?…Yes, well, we did as you advised. We went to Cà d'Zan. By the way, I met a nice lady there." He squeezed Deirdre's hand. "What? Well, sometime, yes, but I…no, I'm not ashamed of you…yes, I'll ask her, but Mummy, I'm trying to ask *you* something."

Rancor started to reach for the phone, but Charity stopped him. Michael spoke quickly. "At Cà d'Zan, we found part of a letter in Grandfather's room. We think it was written by Hedda Ringling. It mentioned a promise.

Would that be the promise you meant? Yes?" He seemed to be listening. "Yes, but Mother—what was the promise?"

Deirdre whispered, "Was it to leave Sarasota and not come back?"

He nodded mutely. "We also found a business card in John Ringling's room. Ringling had written a note on it to Edgar. Do you know anything about that? No? Oh. Really? That's not what you sent me there for?" He shot an inquiring glance at Charity.

She mouthed, "Ask her when Edgar left Cà d'Zan."

"Mummy? Do you know exactly when Grandpapa left Cà d'Zan? You do? Let me write it down." He scribbled on a pad. "And why did he leave?...No, I'm sorry. I didn't mean to upset you. What's that? Deed? A horrible deed? Who did it?"

Rancor looked at Charity. "Not a property deed, a deed deed."

She tapped Michael's shoulder. "Was it a murder?"

Michael waved her off and listened intently. "I see. And after that, he made the promise... And she took an oath? What was it? Okay." He put a hand over the receiver. "She says she took an oath to underwrite HHR Press in perpetuity."

Deirdre gasped. "Who is *she*?"

"Hedda Ringling."

Rancor's voice trailed up to a shriek. "And the deed? *What about the deed?*"

Michael returned to the receiver. "Mummy? What was the deed? All right then, who did it?...Why not? We need to know, Mummy. Not me...someone else. Yes. Okay...Cà d'Zan again? All right. And look for...what did you say? The blood? Anything else? No, you don't have to walk Snookums now. Mother…" His shoulders sagged. "Yes, Mother. No, Mother. Good night, Mother." He hung up. "That's it."

Wisps of steam were rising from the top of Rancor's head, so Charity took over. "Let's eat."

They filed into the dining room, and Charity brought out a large tureen. She ladled stew into soup plates and passed them down the table. Deirdre sniffed. "This smells wonderful. What is it?"

Rancor growled, "*Navarin d'agneau.*"

"Pardon me?"

Charity, who had read the recipe over Rancor's shoulder, translated. "It's a lamb stew with green peas and new potatoes. We'll have salad after." *At least I learned something on my trip to Seattle.*

Rancor grimaced. "Charity insisted a homey meal would go down better than my famous vindaloo curry."

They fell to and gradually, under the attentive ministrations of Mrs. Penney, Rancor came back to himself. "Yes, I got the recipe from Jacques Pépin. Did you know he was invited to the United States to invent recipes for Howard Johnson's frozen dinners?"

"I never! Did you hear that, Michael? You'd think he'd be ashamed to admit it."

"Not at all—he was proud of his work. Anyway, I was in New York at a book festival, and he stood in line for an hour to get my autograph. To thank me, he offered to give me a cooking lesson. I didn't have the heart to tell him I have a degree (among several others) from the Culinary Institute of America." He waited for the oohs and aahs and went on. "He did teach me one thing—to deglaze with dry sherry rather than wine. It does add a certain subtle smokiness, don't you think?"

It went on like that until Charity had had enough. "We need to hear from Michael. Now tell us everything your mother said."

Rancor interrupted. "We already know what she said. Snookums will have to be put down."

"And *also* that she knew about the letter but not about the card."

"And she wants us to go back to Cà d'Zan. Does she think this is a game?"

Charity stuck a bowl of rum pudding napped with whipped cream and dried currants under his nose. "Dessert?"

The others ate theirs. When Charity thought things had calmed down, she asked Michael, "Now, when did Edgar Finney leave Cà d'Zan?"

"February 11, 1933."

"*Hmm.*"

"*Hmm* what?"

"The last time Trudy heard from her husband—"

"The telegram?"

"Yes." Charity laid down her spoon. "It was dated February 10, 1933."

****

They decided to meet at Cà d'Zan the next morning. Deirdre said, "I'm working tomorrow, so I can take you in as my guests before the museum opens."

This cheered Charity no end. "Thank you! It means I'll have enough change to put gas in the car."

Rancor waved her aside. "More important, we'll have the place to ourselves to search."

Michael, Rancor, and Charity arrived at the employee entrance of the complex at seven, and

367

Deirdre let them in. "We'll have to walk down to the house."

It being a beautiful day, only Rancor complained. They reached the house as the sun struck the cupola. Deirdre unlocked a side door, and they passed through into the dimly lit foyer. Their voices echoed under the high ceiling of the great hall. "Where do we start?"

"Not a clue. All she said was 'look for the blood.' "

"It must be a stain on something. Or a painting?"

"Michael and Deirdre, why don't you take the downstairs, and we'll split the upstairs." Rancor went to John Ringling's room and sent Charity to Hedda's. She checked the inside of the bureau drawers, the floor, even the bedspread. They met in the hall. "Nothing."

"Let's try the other rooms."

A few minutes later, Rancor came up behind Charity, who was sitting on an upholstered chair overlooking the living room. "Anything?"

She shook her head. "We should probably try to bring the police in on it—CSI could find old blood better than we can."

"Let's see how the others fared." They found them in the great hall. Michael lounged on a delicate settee while Deirdre idly but superbly played a nocturne on the grand piano. "Any luck?"

Michael shrugged. "I even checked inside the piano."

"The kitchen is spotless. I suppose we could start going through the volumes in the library…" Not even Deirdre seemed happy at the prospect.

Rancor idly swung the velvet rope that surrounded the suit of armor. One of the stanchions began to tip, and Charity leapt to right it. Rancor paid her no mind and began to pace. "Blood…blood. Maybe she didn't mean real blood. Maybe 'bloodlines'? A genealogy?"

"Another reason to check the books."

As all four desperately tried to think of some other avenue of approach, they heard a key turn in the front door lock. A young woman came in. She stared at them curiously. "Deirdre? What's going on?"

"Oh, hi, Sally. These are my friends." She glanced at the others. Rancor nodded. "They're on a…a scavenger hunt. For the…uh…the Humane Society. You know, animals."

"Scavenger hunt? You mean, like, to raise funds?"

Deirdre nodded vigorously. "Yes, yes. For the pandas…I mean, er, puppies. We…they…must find items on a list and…and people contribute to the cause."

Charity said brightly, "We had to get a photograph of Hedda Ringling—"

"Yes! And a newspaper clipping about the Ringling yacht—"

"And," Michael chimed in, "a menu from the Ghost Hotel!"

Rancor shot him a look and added quickly, "Of course we've already collected those." He gave the girl an imploring look. "Now all we have to find is a blood stain."

Sally considered, lips pursed. "Blood stain, huh? I don't think I've seen one on any of the furnishings. Maybe the carpet…" She looked past Rancor. "How about the knife? Would that work?"

"Knife?"

She gestured at the suit of armor. The handle of a silver knife shone dully from a mesh belt at the figure's waist. "Steve Gardner—the curator—says the knife in the scabbard doesn't belong to the same period as the armor. It's all rusty, which he says means it's made of inferior metal. The brown stains might look enough like blood for your purposes."

Michael read the little card attached to the armor. "Why doesn't he think the knife came with the armor?"

"Mr. Gardner says"—she wrinkled her nose—"that it was likely one of those purchases by Hedda Ringling, who—he says—didn't know her...um...behind from her elbow when it came to Renaissance art."

Charity murmured, "Robert Bass was stabbed to death."

Rancor kept his face very still. "Thanks so much, Sally. Do you mind if we check it out?"

The girl looked around warily. "Steve's not in yet. I'm pretty sure he wouldn't want you to touch it."

Deirdre patted her hand. "My dear, I take full responsibility. I'll speak to Steve about it later. It is for *such* a good cause, you know."

Rancor said airily, "We'll return it by close of business. The curator will never know it's gone."

Sally hesitated, then nodded. "All right, but I'm splitting. You never saw me, okay?"

"Not a problem." They watched her disappear into the kitchen. Rancor stepped up to the armor, wrapped a tissue around his hand, and yanked the knife out of its sheath. He gave it to Charity, who slipped it into her purse. They walked to the exit.

"I have to stay here, but call me later if you have news," said Deirdre.

When they reached the parking lot, Rancor held out his hand. "Let me see it."

Charity drew it out, still keeping the tissue wrapped around it. Russet stains covered the blade. "It has to be the murder weapon."

"How do we find out for sure?"

"Jefferson at Sarasota CSI. He'll help us."

Dr. Jefferson was very busy but promised to test the knife that evening. "I'll let you know."

"You already have Robert Bass III's DNA. Can you compare it?"

"Sure, but I won't get back to you until Monday. Lab's closed tomorrow."

Charity spent Sunday pacing, Rancor spent it drinking, and Michael played endless games of solitaire. He finally went back to his hotel after Charity grabbed the cards and threw them away.

The phone rang at eleven Monday morning. Charity picked it up. "Hi, Doctor." She listened. "Oh, that's great. What? Another person? Any idea whose it is?...Yes, I'm sorry, of course you wouldn't." She banged the receiver down. "He found DNA from two different people on the knife. One is Robert Bass's."

"And the other?"

"He doesn't know."

"Calvin's." Rancor whipped out his cell phone and dialed a number. "Michael? Meet us at the forensics lab *now*. Address?" He twirled a finger at Charity. She wrote the address down and held it up before his face. "Two thousand one Siesta Drive. Second floor." He hung up. "We'll have to figure out a way to get Hagen's DNA."

"Wait! Hedda would have the same DNA as her brother, wouldn't she?"

He stopped. "Or close enough. I wonder if she was

cremated?"

"At any rate, there must be something of hers at Cà d'Zan that would still have her DNA on it."

"Deirdre doesn't work on Mondays. We can't just barge in there on our own."

"I'll call her on the way. Maybe she can figure something out."

Charity let Rancor drive, knowing that, despite the risks, they would get there faster. Michael waited for them in the lab parking lot. "Why are we here?"

"Lab found DNA of two people on the knife."

"Oh? Do they know who it belongs to?"

Rancor started to talk, but Charity put a hand on his arm. "Wait..." She nodded at Michael. "Why couldn't the blood be Edgar's? If he in fact was there that night?"

He gaped at her. "That would mean..."

"It could mean any number of things. He could have grabbed the knife away from Hagen. He could have been the one who hid the knife in the armor. He—"

Michael's mouth dropped open. "Are you accusing my grandfather of conspiring to cover up a murder?"

Rancor patted his shoulder. "No, of course not. But, just to be sure, would you let them take a DNA sample?"

"No!"

Charity said soothingly, "As soon as we eliminate Edgar, we can go to Cà d'Zan and find something with Hedda's DNA."

Michael looked puzzled. "Why would you want that?"

"Because Rancor thinks Calvin Hagen, Hedda's

brother, was the murderer. If the blood is a close match to Hedda's DNA, it's likely Calvin's."

Rancor declared, "And we have our villain. And we can all go home."

The little man hesitated. Charity quickly took his hand and led him into the building.

The same young woman swabbed Michael's cheek and took it to the lab. "It's been very quiet, so we should have results fairly quickly."

Four hours later, they waited impatiently in the reception area. Dr. Jefferson appeared, wreathed in smiles. "Well, I must say today is a banner day for our new rapid DNA-testing equipment. Used to take up to six days, but with this new automated system we've brought it down to a few hours."

"Fantastic." Rancor was increasingly agitated. "But what's the verdict?"

"It's a match. Whose DNA did we use?"

They all turned to face a trembling, red-faced Michael. Before anyone could speak, the young woman came bustling out. "Dr. Jefferson? Could you come back to the lab? Ernie wants to talk to you."

Jefferson excused himself and followed her. A few minutes later he rushed back out. "The plot thickens, folks. Ernie—he's our forensic serologist—says he found the DNA of a third person on the knife. Did you only find the one skeleton? Could it have been a double murder? Murder suicide? Murder, murder, suicide?" He flapped his arms excitedly, then sat down at his desk and picked up his phone. "I've got to call Fred—he'll want in on this."

Before he could dial, Rancor held up a hand. "Wait! A third person's DNA? You mean blood?"

"No, not blood. Skin cells. On the handle. Probably from a finger. Just a smidgen, so he didn't notice it until now."

Rancor turned to Charity. "Must be Calvin's."

"I...guess." She pressed her lips together.

"What's the problem?"

"I still don't understand why he would kill his...what's that called? His mark?"

Rancor paced. "I've got it. Hedda. She wanted to stop Calvin...Or—"

"No. She wanted to sell the hotel, remember? Maybe Calvin was horning in on it, and she killed him."

Michael squeaked, "Killed her own brother?"

Rancor slammed a fist into his palm. "That doesn't work."

"Why not?"

"Wrong body."

"*Hmm.*"

"And anyway, then there would be DNA from four different people."

Charity looked at Jefferson. "Can you tell if it's a man or woman's DNA?"

"Sure. I'll only be a minute."

Before they'd even settled on the lobby's hard plastic chairs he came back. "Woman's."

Rancor halted. "Dr. Jefferson, can you do us one more favor?"

The technician looked at his watch. "Depends."

"If we brought a sample of something that belonged to Hedda Ringling, could you compare it to the DNA on the knife?"

"Hedda Ringling? As in, John Ringling's wife?"

"The very one."

"Wow. Okay, get it here by eight a.m. tomorrow, and I'll see what I can do."

Deirdre had come through and met them at the Ringling entrance with a handkerchief tied in a neat bundle inside a plastic bag. "No one will miss it. It's one of twelve from her dresser. I wrapped some of the hair from her hairbrush in it. One or the other should do the trick."

The following day, they once again sat or paced in the lab's lobby. Jefferson opened the glass door and beckoned to them. "Want to see it?"

Michael held back, but Charity and Rancor followed him. "What are we looking at?"

"On one side, you'll see the DNA from the strand of hair on Hedda Ringling's hairbrush that you brought me. The other came from the cells on the knife handle."

Charity didn't want to admit she was completely at sea, but Rancor, naturally, had no such scruples. "A match, right?"

Jefferson nodded.

For some reason, the news left Charity unsettled. *Have we solved the case? Or just made it murkier?* "Okay. Thanks, Dr. Jefferson."

As they reached her car, the doctor came outside. "Don't you want the evidence back?"

"Oh, yes, of course." Rancor took the envelope from him and popped it in the trunk. "Michael, I propose you pick up Deirdre, and we'll go to lunch. We need to see where we are."

They met at the Dry Dock. The hostess led them to a table in the corner overlooking the bay. They ordered beer. "I do *not* want pizza again," announced Charity with little hope.

"Aw, come on."

"Me neither," said Michael firmly.

"Okay, fine. I'm getting lobster then."

Deirdre spoke up. "Who's paying?"

Charity batted her lashes at Rancor. "It's Dutch treat. He can have whatever he wants."

He changed his order to soup and a half sandwich, and the rest of them chose seafood salads. When the waitress had gone, Rancor put his hands on the table. "I think we have all the answers now. I propose we take it to Kelly."

"Oh, really? Do you care to confide in us?" Charity couldn't keep the sarcasm out of her voice.

"Sure." He gave her a look that said, "It's not rocket science after all." "All right, it's the spring of 1933. Work has been on hold at the Ghost Hotel since November of 1926."

"So the place is derelict."

"Yes, but John Ringling hasn't given up on resuming construction. He refuses to listen to any suggestions that he sell the place or knock it down."

Charity put in, "However, Ringling needs money desperately. He's remarried after his beloved Mable's death, to a socialite who expects to live in the style to which she's accustomed. She has a brother who—"

"As in almost every family, gets himself in regular trouble. According to Deirdre, Hedda wanted to sell the hotel but couldn't convince Ringling. Deirdre says—"

"I'm sitting right here, Rancor."

He ignored her. "Deirdre says, the couple had several major arguments on the subject. So—"

"I said no such thing."

"At any rate, I'm guessing Hedda's brother Calvin

took his sister aside and offered to find a buyer. She agreed on the condition that he keep his inquiries confidential. Okay, now we bring in my grandfather, Robert Bass III."

"Another one of those brothers whose activities are a constant thorn in his family's buttocks."

He gave Charity a dismissive wave. "On the contrary, he tries as best he can to succeed, to prove his worth to his demanding, inflexible, unsupportive father. He secretly goes to Florida—"

"Why?"

"Because that's where the land deals are. Do you honestly think his father intended to build a hotel in Nebraska? No, he sent Robert there to molder, but our enterprising lad was too smart for that. He turned his fine Roman nose—a family trait—to the land of sunshine and soon-to-be millionaires. As the brochures—mostly written by John Ringling—all proclaimed in large capital letters, Sarasota would be a booming metropolis within a decade, home to a majority of Americans—at least the ones with wads of cash. A place where a guy could make a fast buck—"

"Or spend it. Remember, they learned he was in Florida because he had the gall to send his expense invoices home."

"All right, all right. Perhaps my rhetoric is getting away from me. Spend it indeed, but in pursuit of a good cause. Robert went looking for property on which to build a luxury Bass hotel and make his name a household word—at least in the Bass household."

Deirdre put her glass down. "So he arrives in Sarasota. How does he find out about the Ghost Hotel?"

"Doesn't matter. Hedda approaches him—"

"You mean Calvin."

"Yes, of course. Hedda ran in circles much too ethereal to make the acquaintance of a young real estate guru." He broke off to finish his beer. "For his part, Robert would naturally be too modest to broadcast his identity as a scion of the noble house of Bass."

"Naturally."

He raised his eyes to the ceiling. "I can just see Hagen, the cunning salesman, his oily, purring voice reeling my grandfather in. Oh yes, he'd say, he was a big player in the Sarasota land scene, his eyes flitting hither and yon. In fact, he would whisper, clutching at Robert's sleeve, he knew of a hotel that would only need some minor work to finish, one he could get for him at a bargain basement price. Can I have another beer?"

The waitress set a tray down and passed around their meals. Charity batted back Rancor's attempt to move a hefty portion of her salad onto his plate.

"Go on."

"So Hagen arranges to meet Bass at the hotel."

"Wait a minute. What about Hedda? We know she was there from the DNA on the knife."

"To be precise, we only know she touched the knife. She could have found it, or the killer gave it to her."

"But that means Calvin didn't."

"Didn't what?"

"Touch the knife. Only three people were in contact with the knife. We've identified the other two."

"Hagen could have wiped his prints off."

Michael said firmly, "In that case, the other prints would have been obliterated as well."

This stumped Rancor, but only for an instant. "We know what a chiseler Hagen was. He probably set Hedda up to take the fall."

"So where does Finney come in? His blood was on the knife as well."

"Um." Rancor took a quick bite of sandwich.

Deirdre spoke up. "None of this tells us *why* Mr. Bass was killed. It doesn't sound like it was in anyone's interest for him to die."

Dead silence greeted this remark.

Finally, Charity said, "Maybe we'll never know."

"That's not fair."

"Well, at least we know what happened to your grandfather, Rancor."

Manifestly dissatisfied, Rancor finished his sandwich. "I guess it'll have to do."

The waitress brought their check. Rancor patted Charity's cheek. "You've got this, right?"

Sigh.

Deirdre said comfortably, "Perhaps you've forgotten that we agreed to split it. Mr. Bass, your share is fifteen dollars." She held her hand out. Slowly, he drew out his wallet.

Charity noticed it had several credit cards and a bulging wad of bills. "You rat!"

"What? It's payday. I was saving this to buy a trinket for you." He blew her a kiss.

"Right. Admit it, you're the biggest tightwad on the planet. You've had me believing you're two steps from the poorhouse door and—"

"I have been. If it weren't for timely infusions from Aunt Gertrude, I'd have had to survive on your paltry largesse for the occasional morsel of food tossed under the table."

"And your travel bills."

"Those? They were courtesy of Arlo."

Deirdre broke in. "Before you two come to blows, why don't we adjourn to your place, Charity, and continue the discussion?"

The other three were amenable.

As they walked into the apartment, Rancor's phone rang. "Oh, hello, Aunt Gertrude."

The old lady's voice skirled through the wire like a banshee's. The others could hear her easily. "Is that you, Rancor, dear?"

"Yes, Auntie. What is it?"

"Well, a letter addressed to you came in the mail. Very peculiar. I thought your mailing address was that one in New York, although I can't imagine why you keep a flat in that horrible city. You did promise to come back to Camden."

"Someday soon, Auntie. What about the letter?"

But Gertrude had gone off on a tangent. "Did you give this address to someone? You really shouldn't do that—who knows what kind of riffraff will turn up at my door. And with Orville still working such long hours and Rebecca so far away now—you know they bought that house up near Penhallow? Oh, by the way, it's an international letter. Postmarked London."

Rancor's eyes widened. "London? Who's it from?"

"A B. Abernethy. I didn't know you knew anyone in London. We do still have British cousins, though. There's Amelia Bass, and her sister, Theoline. They never married, you know. Very sad. Why—"

"Auntie? Could you hang on a minute?"

"What? Not too long. This is long distance, dear.

I'm not made of money."

Charity reflected that some quirks definitely ran in the family. Rancor held his hand over the receiver. "It's a letter from Beatrice. I wonder if she discovered another ghost?"

Charity whispered urgently, "Ask her to read it."

"Auntie? Could you read it to me?"

"Oh dear, no. That would not only be wrong, but I'm sure it's illegal."

"I think it's all right if I ask you to do it."

"Well, I *could* send it first class mail if you're in such a hurry."

"Auntie, letters *always* go first class mail."

"Well, then what's the point in calling it first class? I mean, that's just silly. There's first class and cabin class—no, that's on a ship. Did I tell you I made the crossing on the Queen Mary when I was ten? I'm sure I did. Your mother is beginning to cut me off halfway through almost every reminiscence I attempt. She has the temerity to tell me I've told it before. Well, I say, if it's a good story once, it's a good story a thousand times. But no, Clara has to…" The rest of her rant gradually petered out into low grumbles.

"Auntie, I think your stories are marvelous. I never tire of hearing them. In fact"—he winked at Charity— "I've used some of them in my books. No, I didn't tell you before in case you didn't approve."

"But Rancor, isn't that plagiarism?"

"Er…I changed them just enough…I assure you, no one would recognize you."

"Well, that's all right then."

"So, would you mind reading us—I mean me—the letter? It could be important."

"I suppose so." The screechy voice rose another decibel. "It says, '*My dear Mr. Bass.*' Oh my stars, maybe this is to my brother. I'd better check…"

"Auntie, I am acquainted with the person who wrote the letter. It is definitely addressed to me."

"If you're sure. You know how your father gets when his privacy is violated. Why, the other day I said something completely innocuous related to his secretary, and he went off on me like some Mr. Hyde. It was quite upsetting. Now, where was I?"

"Reading the letter to me."

"Right. '*My dear Mr. Bass, I am so glad you gave me your address, as I have come across something in which I'm sure you're interested. I ventured up to the attic once more (in the company of Irma and Frederick to be safe) and found—in addition to another bullet hole—a second letter from Hedda Ringling to Mistinguett. It had somehow fallen into a crack in the floorboards. It seems to be earlier than the other one we looked at.*' My, this sounds enthralling, Rancor. Bullet holes!"

"It's for a new book, Aunt Gertrude."

"Ah, I see. I shall continue." A paper rustled. " '*Here is her letter in full. "My dearest Jeanne…"* ' "

"Jeanne! Who the hell is Jeanne?"

"Rancor! Your language!"

"Yes, but didn't the cover note say the letter was to Mistinguett?"

"I declare, young man, your manners do not reflect well on your upbringing. I've a good mind to write a stinging note to Clara on this subject. I—"

Charity whispered to Rancor, "Remember? Mistinguett's real name was Jeanne Bourgeois."

"What? Oh." He spoke into the receiver. "I apologize, Auntie. I forgot myself. Do go on."

"Well…I will. But I'm greatly disappointed in you." After a pause heavy with censure, she went on. " '*It has been absolutely horrible since we returned from Paris. John has been in a foul mood what with all the money problems. I did as you advised and refused to lend him any more. Do you know, he actually raised a fist and shook it at me! I was terrified. The servants (except for Lucy, my maid, of course) all seem to take his side. I think they're still loyal to Mable's memory*—' "

Rancor raised his eyebrows at Deirdre who nodded with satisfaction.

" '—*all except for E. He has been my champion, my knight in shining armor*'—my, what flowery language. I…just a minute…"

The listeners waited. Rancor finally said, "Auntie?"

"I'm here. I confess I felt rather warm all of a sudden. Now I've dabbed my forehead with a touch of lavender water I'm all right. Let's see, where was I? Yes. '…*my knight in shining armor throughout this marriage. But, Jeanne, the most awful thing has happened. Yesterday, I asked him to come to my room. I wanted to consult with him on my intentions for the hotel*—*remember, I told you Calvin had found a potential buyer? Before I could speak he…oh, it's so hard to write, but if I don't get it off my chest, I'll go mad. Thank God I can write to you, my dear. He professed his undying love and asked me to run away with him! I admit I was flattered, but still, it was a shocking imposition. Needless to say, I ordered him out of the room.'* " They heard an outraged squeak from Gertrude. "Very properly so. My heavens, the impudence of this man—"

"Auntie? Is that the end of the letter?"

"What? No. There's another paragraph. If you'll be quiet, I'll finish reading."

"Yes, Auntie. Thank you, Auntie."

"She goes on. *'Missy, what do I do? He was my only friend. What with this new hitch in our plans, I had been about to ask him to accompany me tomorrow night, but now I must try to avoid him. Fortunately, John trusts him implicitly, so I'm not worried that he will suspect E's attachment. We shall be sailing to Europe this spring, and you and I will be able to have a cozy chat or two. Your friend, Hedda.'* " Gertrude raised her voice another decibel. "There's a third page. Do you want me to read that as well?"

"Yes, please."

"All right, but I expect a dollar in the mail to cover such an egregious amount of time on the telephone. I believe this is from the sender, Mr. Abernethy."

"Mrs. Abernethy."

"What? Oh, it's from a lady? Well, I never…"

"Auntie?"

"All right, but I disapprove of these long-distance romances. Most inappropriate." She began to read. " *'My dear Mr. Bass—I do hope you keep us informed as you unravel this mystery. We shall be partners in sleuthing! Yours, Beatrice Abernethy.'* She has written a postscript. *'P.S. Lindsay and Sylvester have been models of decorum since their foray into my attic. They bring me flowers once a week (neatly cut from my garden and wrapped in wet newsprint like fish and chips) and even mowed the patch of grass in my back yard. Do visit when you can. And bring your delightful friend Miss Snow. We had such an amusing tea.'* That's it."

Rancor and Charity exchanged a knowing smile. "She's a sweetheart, isn't she?"

Deirdre broke the spell. "Rancor, could you ask your Aunt if the letter from Hedda is dated?"

"Good idea. Auntie, is there a date on the letter?"

"Just a minute...Why, it's just a few days ago. My, the international mail has really become quite efficient. In my day, it would take weeks to receive a letter, and if it were a package, well..."

"I meant on the letter Beatrice quotes."

"Oh, let me see...Yes, I didn't notice it before. February 9, 1933."

"Aunt Gertrude, you are a peach. Thank you, thank you, thank you!"

"Well, aren't you sweet. Maybe I shall reconsider complaining to Clara about your manners. Despite some youthful transgressions, you've become quite a courteous child. Why—"

"I'm so sorry, I must go, Auntie. Give my love to Mother and Uncle Orville." Before she could start in again, he hung up and whooped. "Who, what, where, and now why."

"What are you talking about?" said Charity crossly. "All we know is that Deirdre was right—Edgar had a crush on Hedda."

"Don't you see? He pledged his troth the *night before* she went to meet Robert at the Ghost Hotel."

Deirdre said slowly, "And she rebuffed him."

"He was angry, hurt."

"He wanted to lash out."

Michael spoke for the first time. "Then why didn't he kill Hedda?"

Chapter Twenty-One
Confessions and Proposals

No one seemed to have an answer to the question. Finally Deirdre said, "I don't know about you people, but I'm dog tired. I'm going home."

Charity gave a relieved sigh. "A fresh start would be good."

The two men looked at the women, amazed. "How can you stop now? We're so close."

"Are we? We have the means and opportunity, but still no motive for Bass's killing. We need more information." Deirdre marched out the door. "Michael, are you coming?"

The little man sprinted after her. Rancor watched them leave, his face puckered like a toddler about to have a tantrum. Charity patted his head. "Don't make me call Aunt Gertrude."

He blew out his cheeks. "All right. I suppose one more night won't matter. Grandfather has been waiting more than eighty years for his exoneration. Shall we?"

The clock said two a.m. when Charity sat bolt upright in bed. She threw her arms out, whapping Rancor's temple.

"Wha—? Ow!"

"I've got it! Hedda killed Robert, and Edgar— because he was in love with her—helped her hush it up. That's got to be it. That's why she promised to keep him financially afloat—it was a form of voluntary blackmail."

Rancor rubbed his head. "We still have no motive. Hedda was trying to sell the hotel to Robert—what could he have done to make her want to kill him?"

"Come on to her?"

"Nonsense—she must have been twenty years his senior. On the other hand…" He stopped. "Maybe…*hmm*."

"You have an idea?"

"I have to sleep on it. Good night."

"Rancor!"

"What? You were the one who wanted a fresh start in the morning."

"*Hmmph*."

Rancor apparently took that as acquiescence and turned over. Within a minute, she heard a loud snore.

He refused to talk at breakfast, saying merely, "I have to run over to the newspaper office to check something. I'll meet the three of you for lunch at one."

"What are you going to check?"

"I just want to tie up a loose end."

"*Hmmph*."

"Your vocabulary used to be richer."

"*Hmmph*."

"See you later."

Michael, Deirdre, and Charity waited at the Blue Dolphin as the minutes ticked by. Finally, Rancor ambled in. "Hey, folks. Did you order me a beer?"

Charity spoke for them all. "No. Where have you been?"

"I told you—the *Planet* office. Studying the archives. George was very helpful. Apparently, you have not been keeping him updated on our adventures, and he's planning to transfer that raise he was going to give you to me. As a bonus. Also, you're supposed to cover the Longboat Ladies Beer and Marching Society dance next week. You'll have to rent a tux."

Charity waded through the verbiage to the far bank. "What were you looking up? Oh, thanks, Tilda." She accepted the beer and took a long pull.

Rancor gazed longingly at the bottle. "That looks awfully good. Will you share?"

"No." At his bearish expression, she relented. "Tilda, could you get Mr. Bass a beer too? Bud Light."

Tilda uncapped the bottle and set it down reverently before Rancor, but Michael grabbed it, holding it just out of reach. "All right, we've waited long enough."

"Well, you know I've maintained all along that Calvin Hagen was the murderer."

"Except there's no DNA evidence for that."

"I know, but being the thorough researcher that I am, I wanted to eliminate that angle before I presented my new theory. We knew from Hedda's letter to Mistinguett that Calvin had arranged the meeting, but she also said something about a hitch in their plans. I thought to myself, *hmm*. Perhaps Hagen had bowed out. Could that explain why she wanted Finney to accompany her—because otherwise she'd have to go alone? Hoping to erase the stain of impropriety you've been so quick to ascribe to her—"

"Me!" Charity dropped her fork.

"Well, someone did. Anyway, I examined past issues for any news articles that mentioned Hagen. I found the series reporting on the disappearance of our friend Biddlesworth, which speculated on Hagen's involvement. He was never charged, so the rumors eventually died down, and the *Planet* went back to its normal hyperbolic coverage of bridge tournaments and bingo parties."

"Ahem. Do you mind?"

"Oh, sorry, Charity, forgot you worked there. So did George. Maybe because you haven't shown up for a while. Now...where was I?"

"Hagen."

"Well, I had about given up when George asked if I wanted to go through the police blotters. The paper uses them to write up the weekly column on petty crimes. Did you know that Longboat Key isn't even *included* in the map of the Manatee County incident reports? The worst infraction committed here in the last ten years was when old Mrs. Hinckley took a frying pan to her neighbor's head because she refused to give her her recipe for gumbo. Anyhoo," he added hastily as the others rose like angry villagers, "I checked the Sarasota files and guess what? A Calvin Hagen had been arrested for public drunkenness in the wee hours of February 9, 1933. He was not bailed out—by his brother-in-law John Ringling—until the afternoon of February 11. He was therefore incarcerated during the events in question."

The other three nursed their drinks. Tilda brought sandwiches for everyone but Rancor. "You didn't order lunch for me either?"

Tilda gave him an adoring smile. "I'll get you something right away, Mr. Bass. What would you like?"

"Why thank you, Tilda. I'll have that scrumptious

sandwich—the one with turkey."

"The Rachael?"

"That's the one. Oh wait!" He signed his name on a napkin with a great number of flourishes. "Perhaps your sister would like my autograph."

"Oh, Mr. Bass, thank you! I'll...uh...make sure she gets it." She ran off to the kitchen clutching the napkin. Rancor watched her go, his eyes on her shapely rear.

Charity stepped hard on his foot, bringing his attention back to the conversation. "So, Calvin Hagen is off the hook. Are we then working on the assumption that Hedda offed Mr. Bass?"

"Not at all."

Tilda appeared with a plate piled high with French fries and a sandwich six inches thick. She dropped it in front of Rancor and said breathlessly, "Another beer, Mr. Bass? It's on me...I mean, my sister."

"Sure, thanks." He gave her a brilliant smile, dwelling for a minute too long on her ample bosom, before continuing. "Okay, here's the thing. Deirdre gave me the idea—"

This prompted a quizzical stare from that lady. "What idea?"

"*Shh.* That Edgar had a crush on Hedda. The letter Beatrice sent confirmed it."

"Doesn't that point to his wanting to protect her?"

"Or to a ferocious possessiveness." At this, everyone looked at Michael. He went pale—or rather, paler.

"I can't see it," said Charity.

"It doesn't have to run in the family. Are you going to let me finish?" He took a large bite of sandwich and chewed slowly.

"Rancor…"

"Okay, Hedda went to meet Robert Bass the night of February 10. Evidently, the hussy had no compunction after all about wandering the streets in the dead of night."

"*Now* you condemn her." Charity's tone was growing increasingly restive.

Rancor ignored her. "On the other hand, it *was* the Roaring Twenties…Oh wait, we'd moved on to the muffled thirties. Anyway, Hedda appears to have flouted the conventions and set up a rendezvous on her own."

Deirdre interrupted. "Perhaps she was forced to because her brother was *hors de combat.*"

"Good point. I'm glad to see you women are coming around. I always say, give the filly the benefit of the doubt. She—"

At this, Charity made a sound deep in her throat which terrified not only her companions but the couple in the next booth, who grabbed their boxes of leftovers and made for the exit.

"Moving on…" Rancor picked up the pace. "So, John Ringling gets wind of her plan somehow and sends Edgar to stop her. Whether he knew of the deal or thought Hedda was having an affair, we'll never know." He took a swig of beer. "Now, Edgar is still smarting from Hedda's rejection. He goes to the hotel. It's dark—there would have been no street lights in that area then." He shot a glance at the smoldering Charity. "Plus it may have been overcast."

She cheered up. "So…starless?"

"Possibly. He sees Hedda huddling with a stranger

and immediately assumes the worst. Maddened by jealousy, he stabs Robert to death."

"That would explain the number and severity of the wounds."

"Yes. Hedda is horrified. She grabs the knife from Edgar and puts it in her purse."

"Aha. That's why Hedda's DNA was only on the knife handle."

"Yes."

Michael put his mug down. "So who knocked Robert's teeth out? It couldn't have been Hedda."

"No, but it was probably her idea. Remember, CSI found some shards of oak with the skeleton. Edgar must have picked up a stake—"

"Or retrieved it from the pit—remember, Tommy was killed by a falling beam."

Rancor nodded approvingly at Charity. "He used it, then threw it back down on the body."

Deirdre leaned forward, her sandwich untouched. "Then what happened?"

"They go back to Cà d'Zan. Hedda is about to call the police, but then she realizes that her secret negotiations will have to come to light, and Ringling will be furious. He's already served her with divorce papers once. She knows he'll do it again if he finds out. So she makes a deal with Edgar."

"But what about Robert? How did they know no one would come looking for him?"

"She must have told my grandfather that she wanted to keep the deal under wraps, and he went along with it. He was probably thrilled at the prospect of springing the completed transaction on his father."

"Thereby mitigating the well-deserved reprisals for

flouting his father's orders to go to Nebraska." Charity clapped her hands.

"So, you see? It all makes sense."

Michael pushed the food around on his plate. "So, to sum up. Edgar kills Robert. He and Hedda drop the body down the elevator shaft. They return to Cà d'Zan and hide the knife in the suit of armor. That's the deed."

"Here comes the oath and the promise," said Deirdre eagerly.

"Yes. Edgar swears he'll leave town and never return. Hedda promises to set him up in business and keep him financially secure."

"That's what Michael's mother said."

"Yes, and I think if you confront her with my description of the events, she'll have to confirm it."

"I don't know…" Michael stared at his plate. "She gets so upset. Do we really have to bring it up again?"

Deirdre lifted his chin. "My dear, we need to settle this. I know it's hard to accept that your grandfather was capable of murder, but think of it more as a crime of passion. And contrary to what some people think"— she looked pointedly at Rancor—"passion is in the Finney blood. Look at how you fought to regain HHR Press." She blushed ever so slightly. "Not to mention your…er…enthusiasm in other pursuits."

Rancor stared at her, and Charity held a hand over her mouth to stop the giggle. Michael didn't seem to notice them. He straightened and slapped a determined expression on his wishy-washy face. "I'll do it. Then we can get on with our lives."

They returned to Charity's apartment. After a few hems and haws, Michael dialed his mother's number. "Mummy? It's Mikey again….Oh you were?" He put a hand over the receiver and whispered, "She says she's been expecting my call."

Rancor waved at him. "Go ahead."

"Mummy, we found the knife." He listened intently for a full five minutes, his face alternately shocked and frightened. He finally said, "Thank you for telling me…No, of course not. It was a long time ago. All right, I love you too. I'll be home soon."

No one said a word. Michael sat quietly, hands in his lap, his eyes closed. Not until Deirdre coughed softly did he speak. "My grandfather, Edgar Finney, murdered Robert Bass III and threw his body down an elevator shaft at the Ghost Hotel on February 10, 1933. He confessed it to his son on his deathbed. It was supposed to end there, but my mother listened at the door and heard his confession. Father died without telling anyone, and my mother intended to do the same, until I lost HHR Press. She decided she had to explain, so I would understand why I had to get it back."

Deirdre sat down next to him and took his hand. "And you did, my dear. You righted the wrong."

A tear coursed down Michael's cheek. "But my grandfather…a murderer!"

She spoke decisively but gently. "Not a murderer. A lover. I'm sure he thought he was protecting Hedda. Remember, she said he was her knight in shining armor."

Rancor muttered so low only Charity could hear. "More like Bad Sir Brian Botany."

Deirdre raised Michael to his feet and led him out to the balcony. When they were out of earshot, Charity turned to Rancor. "Bad Sir Brian Botany?"

He grinned. "A. A. Milne.

'*Sir Brian had a battleaxe with great big knobs on;*
He went among the villagers and blipped them on
the head.' "

He mimicked someone whapping another with a
stick. "Take that and that and that!"

Charity decided that to respond would only
encourage the man. After a minute, she said slowly,
"So...all the threads were connected after all. The
skeleton, the publishing firm, the Ghost Hotel. Even
Tommy T. It's funny..."

"Funny ha-ha or funny weird?"

"Both. If it weren't for Isabella—"

"I knew you two would eventually hit it off."

"Er, sorry to disappoint." She smiled at Finney as
he and Deirdre came in. "I'm very much looking
forward to reading Michael's exposé." She tapped her
lips with a finger. "I wonder if Frank has a mug shot of
her. I could frame it and put it on my bureau."

Rancor pinched her. "So? What about Isabella?"

"I mean the manuscripts. If she hadn't stolen them,
we wouldn't know about Edgar or Hedda or Calvin..."
She looked at Rancor. "You wouldn't have been broke
and accepted Arlo Mickenbacker's offer. You wouldn't
have come to Longboat Key..."

"And we never would have met." They gazed at
each other, dismay intermingled with a tentative joy on
both faces.

Behind them, Deirdre cleared her throat. "There's
one more question to be answered." She turned to
Michael. "Did your mother say *why* Edgar killed Mr.
Bass?"

Michael made a sound halfway between a chuckle
and a groan. "It wasn't out of a jealousy after all. Edgar

didn't know it was Bass. He believed it was Calvin Hagen."

"But…Robert's card?"

"Edgar didn't know about the card."

"He didn't see Ringling's note?"

"Mother says he didn't know about either one."

Charity threw up her hands. "So why did he go to the Ghost Hotel that night?"

Rancor jumped up. "I've got it. Ringling found the card with the rendezvous details on it, figured out what Hedda was planning and wanted Edgar to stop it. He was going to give the note to his friend, but instead just told him to go to the hotel that night. Then he hid the papers in his desk."

"Right. So my grandfather knew that Hedda would be at the Ritz at eleven that night, but he didn't know why." He paused. "I should perhaps explain that Hagen had been blackmailing his sister, which she had confessed to Edgar."

Rancor whistled. Deirdre put a hand on his arm. "Go on, Michael."

"She had something in her past that couldn't come out—Mother isn't sure what it was but thought perhaps she was still married to someone else. When Edgar arrived at the hotel, he spied Hedda, but before he could approach her, he saw a second figure. In the dark, he could only make out his silhouette and took it into his head that she was meeting her brother to deliver a payment. He flew into a rage and stabbed the man—to protect her, his darling. When he learned the truth, he realized that—for all the reasons you gave, Rancor— they had to keep it quiet."

Charity stirred. "What about John Ringling? Did he

know about the murder?"

"No. Neither Hedda nor Edgar told him. Naturally, he wouldn't ask Hedda directly about the affair, preferring to let the matter rest. Edgar packed his stuff and left the next day."

Deirdre said, "It was fairly soon after that that Ringling served Hedda with the final set of divorce papers. She said on several occasions—"

"Including in her letter to Mistinguett."

"That she was shocked and surprised to be served. She thought she'd gotten away with it."

"She did keep her oath to support HHR Press."

"That's why he named it that—to enshrine his love for her."

Michael said, "Mother told me one more thing. Mrs. Ringling set up a trust from which funds are disbursed on a regular basis to HHR Press. That's where the latest check came from."

"And why it was deposited to HHR Press and not to you."

"Yes."

****

"Oh look, Isabella's landed on her feet." Rancor shook open the paper. "Come in off the balcony, Charity. I don't want to have to shout."

She appeared, mug in hand. "*Shh*. Do you have to yell? Mr. Flibbet in 1G is giving me the fish eye again." Her cheeks reddened. "You don't think he can hear…hear…"

"Our boisterous lovemaking? I always make sure to leave the windows open. Old man, alone, bored. He deserves a little diversion, even if it's only vicarious."

Charity knew it was useless to remonstrate, so she

asked, "What did you want?"

"Here on page six. Isabella was seen at Per Se—for you gals from Alabama, that's the 'in' restaurant in New York City...Where was I?" He ran a finger down the text. "Ah, here it is. She was seen with—I'm quoting here—'the prominent writer Bernard Guttersnipe.' " He closed his eyes. "Funny, I don't remember Bernie being part of the Manhattan party scene."

Charity looked over his shoulder. "He seems to be the center of attention now."

"Who wouldn't, with Miss Arm Candy fawning over you?" He read on. "Oh my God. You know what they're celebrating?"

"What?"

"The release of Bernie's new book, *Love Among the Hominids: a Prehistoric Romance*."

"So?"

"Doesn't sound like 'modern progressive' fiction, does it?"

"What are you getting at?"

He threw the paper down. "It's not the drivel Bernie usually writes because it isn't. It's a clever, complex murder mystery set in the Pleistocene Era. It was originally entitled *Dead before Her Time*."

"How do you know all this?"

"Because it's *my book. Love Among the Hominids* was my subtitle."

Charity dropped into the other chair. "*Bernard Guttersnipe's* the thief?"

"Not his real name," Rancor said absently. "Yes, it looks that way." He brooded. "Makes sense when you think about it. We know Holdy's incapable of strategic thinking, and Isabella—well, she's smart, but her beauty's really her greatest weapon. They couldn't have pulled it off without someone wielding a Machiavellian-grade intellect."

"Guttersnipe?"

"Guttersnipe."

"But he and Wheelock weren't on speaking terms."

"Or so Isabella would have us believe. Now I think of it, neither Bernie nor Holdy ever mentioned a quarrel."

Charity put down her coffee and reached for the pitcher of juice. She halted, pitcher in hand. "Wait. Sangria. Remember when you talked to Wheelock at the Columbia? He was clearly surprised to learn about IV Enterprises."

Rancor took the pitcher from her and poured himself a glass. "True. So I was right—Holdy was a mere pawn in a ruthless game played by Isabella and Bernie."

"Bernie as the puppet master?"

"Yes. Remember, he called just after we sprang Isabella from the pokey. He—not Holdridge—was the one she begged to bail her out. The boss."

"He was also the only one who didn't respond to your request for help. Atalanta and even Wheelock pitched in—"

"Or else, in the case of Ms. Heartsleeve, exhibited a hitherto undemonstrated mental acuity by tipping us off to the real culprit."

"Huh? Oh, right, I'd forgotten—didn't she tell you to consider authors rather than publishers?"

Rancor snapped his fingers. "That's what meant by 'lusting after the pie.' I do believe she was trying to hint at Bernie's complicity."

Charity picked up her phone. "What are we going to do?"

"Do? Nothing."

"*Nothing*?"

"For now. Trust me, my love, I have the matter well in hand. We'll just cast a wider net."

****

"I'm going to miss Michael." Rancor poured the pink concoction from the blender into a highball glass and handed it to Charity. "But probably Deirdre more. Your Singapore Sling, my lady."

She took it and they walked out to the balcony. Sunset was in full swing, and a throng of onlookers stood on the beach below them gazing toward the western horizon, where carmine missiles pierced the hyacinth clouds and streaked across the sapphire sky. "It was so sweet, the way he proposed right there in the library at Cà d'Zan."

"It would have been more romantic if she hadn't been giving a lecture to forty-five Girl Scouts at the time."

"I disagree. The way he stood up in the back and asked her to marry him." She sighed. "It was like those proposals on the Jumbotron."

"If you ever do that to me, I'll turn you down."

"Not to worry," she said comfortably. "You've already proposed."

"I did? Did you accept?"

"Not yet."

"Any plans to do so in the near future?"

She paused. "I'm thinking about it."

He pulled her onto his lap. "How can you refuse to

marry the great Rancor Bass, slayer of dragons? I'm a catch."

"What do you mean, dragons?"

"Didn't I tell you? Atalanta is suing Bernie, Isabella, and Holdridge for ten million dollars. Considering she hired the best lawyer in Manhattan and has the backing of twenty other authors who were treated shabbily by the trio, we think she has a good chance to win."

"Are you involved?"

"I'm the star witness."

"Well, we'd better get married before you testify. I don't want to have to grapple with any more rabid packs of admiring fans than you have already."

"If you mean Jane, she's invited me to speak at her book club."

"See?" Charity sipped her drink. "It's begun already."

"I'm planning to talk about my work in progress."

"You mean the ghost story anthology?"

"Oh, that? I...er...sent it off last week. George was so astounded he forgot to ask what, if any, contribution you'd made."

"You didn't." Charity's mouth fell open. "Tell me you didn't take full credit."

"I beg your pardon. As far as I can tell, you have been in the bath since the denouement of our little tale. Someone had to put pen to paper. Or stylus to tablet...Gosh, I just realized civilization has come full circle and reverted to Sumerian technology...Where was I?"

"Selling me out."

He had the effrontery to be smug. "Arlo loved it.

He says it will be released next month and wants us to come up to New York for a grand gala to celebrate its launch." He looked her up and down, a skeptical frown on his handsome face. "Do you even *have* a dress that isn't a hand-me-down from Eloise or Pippi Longstocking?"

"I have a ball gown from the Longboat Ladies' Sewing Circle production of *La Traviata*. Would that do?"

"I'm guessing that's what they're wearing in Tara this year." He leaned away from her fist. "But it will have to do."

****

Later that evening, Rancor slid from the bed and began picking up the clothes scattered willy-nilly across the floor. As he laid a neatly folded shirt on the quilt, she reached out and traced the thin white line that ran from his nipple to his stomach. "You never told me how you got this scar."

"That's because I don't want to."

"Come on, Rancor. I've told you all my secrets."

"So what? There's nothing embarrassing in them—unless you count that blunder with the ducklings."

"We don't have to revisit that right now. Come on, give."

"All right, but if I see a lip twitch or an eye twinkle, I'll spank you."

"Oh, sure. If you're trying to bribe me, it can wait until after your confession."

Rancor paused.

"What is it?"

"I'm thinking there are hidden depths in you. I *like* them. Okay, here's the story. You wouldn't know from my present calm, mature, manly demeanor that I was a bit of a daredevil in my youth." He ignored the snicker. "As you know, I grew up in Maine. Winters being what they are there, I learned to ice skate at a young age. I was—naturally—exceedingly good. So one snowy December afternoon, my sister and a cousin and I decided to go skating. It had been unseasonably warm for the prior two weeks, but the night before we'd had a hard freeze, so Geoffrey and Rose and I went to check on the ice in the local pond. Rose thought it was a little thin, but, being the youngest and the most intrepid—"

"You mean foolish."

"You choose your adjective, and I'll choose mine. At any rate, I insisted we try it. I pushed Geoffrey out to the middle and proceeded to skate rings around him. Which apparently softened the ice enough that he broke through. I rushed to his aid...and fell in as well." Here he turned away from Charity, but she could tell from the deep purple color of his ears that he was blushing furiously. He mumbled something.

"What was that?"

"Rose saved us."

"Your sister pulled you out."

"She pulled both of us out. At the same time. And carried us to the bank." He turned, an agonized look on his face. "I never, ever lived it down."

Charity somehow managed not to laugh but only by dint of kissing Rancor passionately. Once she was sure he had been pacified and her hysterical giggle smothered, she asked, "So, what's this work in progress you're going to talk to Jane's group about?"

He beamed. "A new romantic suspense. It will have a fast-paced plot complete with a glamorous villainess, corpses, and a brilliant hero who cracks the case."

"You're going to write up our Ghost Hotel story."

"With a different title and new, more flamboyant names."

"A work of fiction, then?"

"What can I say? I'm a genius. And soon to be rich again." He took her in his arms and waltzed her about the room. When she was out of breath, he sat her down on the bed and checked his watch. "Midnight at last. All right, go ahead."

"Go ahead and what?"

"Go ahead and propose."

"Me? Why should I?"

"Because, my dear, it is Leap Year Day. You are required to do the honors."

"It is?" She got up and checked the calendar. "Oh my God, you're right."

"So…down you go."

She stared at him. "What…here? Now?"

"On your knees, woman."

Charity waited as long as she dared, then put a pillow on the floor and kneeled on it. "Rancor Bass, you wretch, will you marry me?"

He stared at her, his mouth open. "You're proposing? Really?"

"Isn't that what you demanded?"

"Yes, but…but…" He put his head in his hands. A muffled voice, full of question marks, siffilated between his fingers. "What could you possibly see in me?" He raised his face to look at her.

She checked for a curled lip, a cynically raised eyebrow, a sneer, but found only damp eyes. "I see a man who hides his warmth behind quips, and who shutters his true feelings with arrogance and flippant remarks."

"Can you see a man who's terrified? Who is so used to being deified that he can't come down from the clouds lest an exquisite soul such as yourself wipes away the misty drops and finds only a man?"

"I saw him."

"And?"

"I figured he needed a lift. And possibly a meal."

His eyes danced. "How about a place to stay?"

"Nope. He has to live with his Aunt Gertrude."

"*Forever?*"

"Only until the wedding." When he attempted to negotiate, she said firmly, "No, sir. I promised. Now pack your bags and come back in a week."

A week later—the promise fulfilled—they proceeded to the oath and, later that evening, the deed.

A word about the author...

Although she has lived or traveled in every continent except Antarctica and Australia, M. S. Spencer spent the last thirty years mostly in Washington, DC, as a librarian, Congressional staff assistant, speechwriter, editor, birdwatcher, kayaker, policy wonk, nonprofit director, and parent.

She has two fabulous grown children, a perfect granddaughter, and currently divides her time between the Gulf coast of Florida and a tiny village in Maine.

Ms. Spencer has published ten romantic suspense/mystery novels.

http://msspencertalespinner.blogspot.com